THE LOCKER ROOM

USA TODAY BESTSELLING AUTHOR

MEGHAN
QUINN

Published by Hot-Lanta Publishing, LLC

Copyright 2019

Cover Design By: RBA Designs

Photo Credit: Rafa Catala

www.authormeghanquinn.com

PROLOGUE

EMORY

R ule number one in college: don't lose your friends at a house party . . . especially when you're drunk.

Technically this is a loft party though, so . . . am I really breaking the rule?

My head falls back against the wall, my empty red cup rests in my hand and is clutched to my chest as I scan the giant loft space on the third floor of a renovated warehouse. I climbed up a fire escape in heels to get here, risked the safety of my ankles to be a part of something special, because apparently this is the place to be on the weekends.

The Baseball Loft.

As I've been told by my best friends, this is where you earn a golden ticket invitation to the exclusive but highly sought-after locker room—where dreams come true.

Supposedly.

Don't take my word for it.

But rumor on the street is: the best orgasms take place in the

Brentwood Baseball locker room. Legends say one girl had a five-minute orgasm on the tile floors of the shower.

Five-minute orgasm in exchange for a week's worth of ringworm. Not sure I'm interested.

But alas, I'm here, drunk off my ass, boobs practically spilling out of my shirt, and my mascara slowly melting off my eyelashes and onto my face, morphing me from new-in-town college girl, to trash panda from the racoon clan.

"Dottie, Lindsay," I say weakly, moving my head from side to side. "Where art thou?"

"You need help?" a deep voice slurs next to me.

I look to my right through very blurry vision and make out what I'm going to assume is an incredibly attractive man. But then again, I'm drunk—the whole *mascara melting off my eyes* in full swing —and I've been fooled once before.

But hey, I think those are blue eyes. Can't go wrong with that . . . reasoning that will be thought better of in the morning.

"Have you seen Dottie or Lindsay?"

"Can't say that I have," he answers, resting against the wall with me.

"Damn it. I think they're making out with some baseball players. Have you seen any of those around?"

"Baseball players?"

"Mm-hmm." I nod, shutting my eyes for a second but then shooting them back open when I feel myself wobble to the side. The guy catches me by the hand before I topple over, but thanks to his alcohol intake, he's not steady enough to hold us up and . . . *timber* . . . we fall to the couch next to me.

"Whoa, great placement of furniture," I say, as the guy topples on top of me.

"Damn near saved our lives."

I rub my face against the scratchy and worn-out fabric. "How many people do you think have had sex on this thing?"

"Probably less than what you're thinking."

The couch is deep, giving me enough room to lie on my side

with the guy in front of me, so we're both facing each other. He smells nice, like vodka and cupcakes.

"So, have you seen any baseball players around? I'm looking for my friends."

"Nah, but if you see any, let me know. I can't find my room."

"You live here?" I ask, eyes wide.

"Yup," he answers, enunciating the P. "For two years now."

"And you don't remember where your room is?"

"It has a yellow door. If the damn room would stop spinning I'd be able to find it."

"Well . . . maybe if we find your room, we'll find my friends," I say, my drunk mind making complete sense.

"That's a great idea." He rolls off the couch and then stands to his feet, wobbling from side to side as he holds out his hand to me.

Without even blinking, I take it in mine and let him help me to my feet. "Yellow door, let's go," I say, raising my crumpled cup to the air.

"We're on the move." He keeps my hand clasped in his and we stumble together past beer pong, people making out against walls, the kitchen, to an open space full of doors. "Yellow door, do you see one?"

I blink a few times and then see a flash of sunshine. "There." I point with force. "Yellow, right there."

His head snaps to where I'm pointing. A beam of light illuminates the color of the door, making it seem like we're about to walk right into the sun. I'm a little chilly, so I welcome the heat.

"Fuck, there it is. You're good." Together, we make our way to the door, pushing past a few laughing people and into the quiet den of his room.

Black walls, white trim, one window looking out over the water; the guy has a nice place. I scan the space, looking for any sign of my friends but come up short, only finding a large bed with a black comforter, a metal-looking desk, and a large white dresser with a giant TV mounted on top.

Not a friend in sight but what a cozy spot to take a little rest.

3

"I don't see my friends."

He looks around. "I don't either, but fuck, my bed." He throws his arms out to the side and bellyflops on the mattress, bouncing a few times before settling his head on his pillow.

I stare at him a few moments. Tight jeans shaping his ass and thighs, white shirt that shows off every muscle in his back, handsome face. Not a bad view. But that's not what's enticing me to move forward. It's the warm and fluffy-looking pillow right next to the guy.

Like a cloud calling my name . . . *Emory, come here, Emory, rest your head on me.* I make one of the best decisions of my life.

Don't mind if I do.

I propel my body forward like a dolphin slicing through the water and flop down on the mattress, resting my head right on top of pure heaven.

Oh, that's nice.

Real nice.

Smells like fresh soap and feels like my head is being hugged by cotton.

See, best decision I ever made.

The mattress shifts next to me, and I peep my eyes open to see the guy with the nice ass hovering over me. He glances down with heavy lids and then back up at me.

I smile lazily up at him, a little nervous that I'm puckering my lips, but honestly, I can't be in control of anything my body is doing right now.

He's about to tell me I'm the most luscious and beautifully smelling girl he's ever met—like a field of flowers on an epic spring day—

"Uh, your boob popped out of your shirt." He points at my chest. *What now?* Spring flower—

That's no spring flower compliment.

I must be completely and utterly exhausted, because instead of reaching up to stuff the wayward boob back in my shirt, I cry out, "Oh, no," but make no attempt to fix the problem.

"Does it usually do that?" he asks, looking very concerned for me. "Try to run away?"

I shake my head, the softness of the pillow making my eyes heavy. "No, this is the first time the little lady tried to escape." Barely able to lift my hand, I tap his forearm and say, "Be a dear and lecture the poor thing and stuff it back into place."

"I've never lectured a boob before."

"You got this. You're a strong, confident man with a commanding voice. Give that breast a berating." When he just continues to stare at me, I shift my head to the side and rub my cheek against the smooth fabric of the pillowcase. "Don't be shy," I encourage him. "Just lift it up and shove it back in."

He rests his head next to mine, the mattress shifting and bouncing with his movements. Still staring at my boob, he reaches up and cups it in his hand. "Heavy," he says quietly.

How sweet.

And utterly romantic.

I've never been told I have a heavy boob, but by God, it makes me smile. Good job growing, Emory.

His abnormal but delightful compliment is the last thing I remember before I drift off and fall into a deep slumber.

It's the last thing I remember before I wake up in the middle of the night in a stranger's room, passed out with my boob in said stranger's hand. *So much for tucking her back in.*

Welcome to Brentwood U.

CHAPTER ONE

EMORY

This map is useless.

Easy to read, my ass. I need a magnifying glass to make out any of the color-coded buildings on this thing and unfortunately, I left my magnifying glass in my other skirt. That was sarcasm, if you didn't catch it.

Standing next to a wonky-looking tree, I try to act as casual as possible—hip popped out, interested glances, the usual—as I hide a school map beneath the pages of *Pride and Prejudice*, while offhandedly looking for the MacMillan building. But the wind—though subtle—isn't making things easy.

Recently transferred from Cal State, Fullerton, I'm attempting to avoid making a fool of myself on the first day of fall classes at my new school, Brentwood University.

Unfortunately, I'm way out of my element.

For one, I know nothing about this school other than they have the best library sciences program in the country. Making the transfer a no-brainer for me the minute I realized I wanted to be a librarian. I dabbled in business at Cal State, but who was I kidding? I had no right trying to figure out micro- and macro-economics.

A California girl through and through, Illinois is nothing like the palm trees and beaches I've grown up with. Don't get me wrong, there are trees here, huge, plush, green trees everywhere, the kind of trees Bob Ross made dance on his canvas. But the smog . . . I have no idea where that is. Breathing fresh air almost feels wrong. And apparently pizza is a big deal here. I've heard at least three separate arguments since I've moved about which pizza in town is best. Let's all be friends and be grateful there is good pizza here.

And even though this is a "small" school town outside Chicago, it's larger than life with boisterous personalities and ivy-covered buildings that cause me to believe I'm walking on the hallowed grounds where the prosperous were educated.

Plus, I had to buy leggings for all my skirts, because the temperature doesn't call for bare legs out here.

The wind picks up again, lifting my skirt and map at the same time. Not wanting to be known as the resident flasher on campus, I save the skirt—because even though I have leggings, I chose not to wear them today—and tamp it back down on my legs as the map lifts from my book, floats into the air, twirling and swirling only to smack a passing guy right in the face.

Whap.

"What the—?" He startles and I jump into action.

"I'm so sorry," I say, scrambling to hold my skirt down while clutching my parted book at my chest.

The map is slowly peeled away and a pair of beautiful light blue eyes peek past the paper first, followed by the sharpest jawline I've ever seen, defined and tense. Light scruff matches his dirty-blond hair that is swept to the left and cut short on the sides. Dressed in a green Brentwood baseball sweatshirt and wearing a jaw-dropping smile, he chuckles and hands me the map while eyeing me up and down.

Why is he so familiar?

Those eyes.

"Not a problem, but you could have asked for help if you were lost. Slapping me with a map is an aggressive tactic, effective, but aggressive."

That voice, that smirk. I know it from somewhere.

Feeling a light blush creep up my cheeks, I say, "Not used to the wind."

He nods and thumbs behind him. "Lake Michigan. It's a bitch in the winter." He studies me for a second and then nods at my map. "Where you headed? I can help." There is the smallest southern drawl in his voice, nothing strong, but enough to tell me he's not from Illinois.

I know that voice. I remember specifically thinking it was hot.

Tamping down my map and folding it in my book that I snap shut quickly, I say, "I promised I'd figure this all out on my own, but looks like I might need a little help after all."

"Don't blame yourself; this campus is a maze with no rhyme or reason. I was lost my entire first semester. Can't tell you how many times I was late to class."

"That's reassuring."

He tilts his head to the side and gives me a small once-over. "I know you." I don't say anything and just as his eyes land on my chest, a smile creeps over his face, a light bulb lighting in his head. "You're the girl who helped me find my room on Saturday."

Oh.

Shit.

It's the yellow-door baseball guy.

He leans forward, hands stuffed in his pockets and says, "I never forget a good pair of tits."

As if I wasn't blushing enough already.

"It's a shame I passed out with my hand holding one. I'm usually smoother than that. If anything, I think I owe you a nipple tweak."

If I opened my book back up, would I be able to sink into the pages, allowing the literature to swallow me whole?

"I didn't even remember passing out with a tit in hand until my buddy told me he walked in to make sure I was okay, saw me cupping you while we were both passed out." He scratches the side of his jaw. "Still getting shit for that."

I . . . what does someone even say to that?

"Don't worry," he adds. "I won't reveal your identity. Clutching a tit is between said man and a lady. No gossiping here. How's your boob, by the way? Still trying to run away?" He chuckles. I'm mortified.

I push my hair behind my ear and stare at my Mary Janes. "Uh . . . everything's intact. Thank you."

"Good, you calmed the old girl down." He takes in a deep breath, acting so casually. "Where you off to?"

Why are guys like this? So easygoing, as if they weren't humiliated enough to warrant crawling back into your mother's womb? I'm pretty chill, but reliving a moment like Saturday night isn't a top priority of mine. More like "let's forget it ever happened" because passing out with my boob in a strange man's hand isn't one of my finest of moments. Nothing to scrapbook.

Wanting to move on from reminiscing, I say, "I'm looking for the MacMillan building. I have class in ten minutes, and I have no idea if I'm in the right area or not." I need to get some distance from him. "I can figure it out though. Uh, good to see you again." I start walking away, showing confidence in my shoulders even if I have no idea where I'm going.

"Hold up." He grabs my shoulder before I can slink away and turns me in the opposite direction. "Going the wrong way." Oh hell. "I'm headed there as well, so you can walk with me." Of course he is. He grips the straps of his backpack as he nods in front of us, casually directing me where to go.

"Oh, that would be great. Thanks." Not really, but doesn't seem like I have a choice at this moment. I fall in line next to him and immediately feel awkward, unsure of what to say to this guy whose hand became my boob's overnight cushion as we drooled on his ultra-comfy pillows.

Do I compliment his pillows?

Ask him if he still thinks my boob was heavy?

Tell him I don't normally let my breasts fall out of my shirt?

Lucky for me, his easygoing personality reflects in conversation. "Are you a freshman?"

"No. Junior transfer. What about you?" Might as well fill in the awkward silence.

"Junior as well, but I've been here since I was a freshman." He holds his hand out to the side. "Knox Gentry."

I take it and give it an uncoordinated shake as we keep walking forward. "Emory Ealson."

"Well, Em, what class are you headed to?"

Em. Not even my parents call me that, but I'm not about to make a stink about it, not when he's my personal tour guide.

"Developmentally Effective Learning Environments."

"Huh." He smiles at me, sticking his hands back in his pockets. "Me too." That's unfortunately convenient. "What are you majoring in?"

"Early education. I plan on getting my master's in library sciences."

"Is that why you're hiding a map of the school in your copy of *Pride and Prejudice?*"

Busted.

"Was it that obvious?"

"No one is *that* into the insufferable Mr. Darcy." He tacks on a dramatic eye-roll, and, even though he's insulting one of the greatest heroes ever written, I can't help but get a little excited because it seems like he's read it.

I mean . . . he called Mr. Darcy insufferable. My little literature heart beats wildly because an attractive man has clearly read my favorite book of all time.

"You've read *Pride and Prejudice?*"

"Fuck, no. Watched the BBC special. Colin Firth was the shit, a real dick to Lizzie."

Poof, there goes my excitement. Only a man could think that being *a dick to Lizzie* made Colin Firth *the shit*. This man is completely classless.

"And don't get me started on the exhausting mother. Stop pawning your daughters off on people. Show a little self-respect, lady."

We reach a grey stone building with the smallest plaque I've ever seen tacked onto the side. MacMillan Building. I would have never found this place.

"It was her duty as a mother to marry her daughters off," I reply, following him closely as a stampede of students make their way through the narrow halls.

"Maybe if she chilled out and wasn't so shrillingly annoying, there would have been a longer line of suitors waiting to scoop up the harlots."

"Harlots? Elizabeth and Jane were anything but harlots. Lydia, on the other hand . . ."

He stops at a door and rests his hand on the handle. "Jane, as a single woman, goes to Bingley's *Netherfield Park* at his request and happens to spend the night? Harlot." He opens the door for me and waits for me to step in, but I don't budge.

"She was sick. She didn't spend the night to have relations." I'm nearly spluttering my responses to this dweeb. But, *relations,* Emory?

"Sick because the crazy-as-shit mother sent her on horseback during a storm. Fucking insane asylum, that's where she belonged." He ushers me into the classroom with his hand to my back. "Maybe if the mom sat back with some brandy, things would have been different. Their love could have matured organically."

"Without her meddling, Elizabeth and Jane would probably have ended up as old maids or with intolerable suitors like Mr. Collins."

"He was good enough for Charlotte Lucas." He shrugs as if the statement doesn't peel the nails off every Janeite in the country.

"He was a travesty," I shoot back, literary passion taking over. *Now, he was insufferable.*

Ignoring me, Knox walks down a few steps into the lecture hall and turns down a row toward two other guys wearing the same sweatshirt as him. Both tall in their seats, the one wearing a backward hat is broader than the other, but they both seem just as commanding as Knox. Just as confident . . . just as cocky.

I stand in the stairway, unsure what to do. Do I follow him? Sit next to him? Or find my own seat? After all, he did consider Mr. Collins a good enough suitor. The horror!

When he notices my hesitation, he rolls his eyes dramatically with a sigh, walks back to where I'm standing, grabs my hand and ushers me down the row until we both join the other two guys.

"What's up, Gent?" the one with the backwards hat asks and then eyes me over Knox's shoulder. "Who's your friend?" Oh, please God, don't say the girl whose boob made me pass out the other night. I'd rather die.

"Em," he answers simply while leaning back in his chair and adjusting his hood. "Junior transfer, she slapped me with her campus map." He glances at me and gives me a sly wink before turning back to his friends.

And right there, in that moment, despite our fresh disagreement, I know he's a nice guy.

He could have been an obnoxious dick and pointed me out to his teammates, but instead, he kept it simple.

Cool.

I respect him for that.

"He's been slapped by worse," the guy with the backward hat says before holding out his hand. "I'm Carson, and the guy sitting next to me with his face glued to his phone, that's Holt."

"Nice to meet you," I say, shaking his calloused hand.

Holt barely glances up from his phone and says, "Hey," and then tunes us out returning to the digital world.

"Where did you transfer from?" Carson asks, leaning on the small desk attached to his chair, fist to his cheek, peering over at me as if he has a schoolgirl crush.

I push a piece of my long brown hair behind my ear and say, "Cal State, Fullerton."

"She's a librarian," Knox adds for me, screwing up the facts.

"Hope to be a librarian. I want to master in library sciences."

"No shit," Carson says, giving my bare legs a quick glance. "Never saw a librarian in such a short skirt before. It's hot. Makes me want to check out some books."

Oh Jesus.

"Dude, that was lame." Knox chuckles to himself while shaking his head. "And don't get all heart eyes on her, she has some fantasized opinions about *Pride and Prejudice.*"

"Ah, hell," Carson groans and leans back, as if he's done with me. "Let me guess, she doesn't believe the Bennet sisters were whores."

"Correct." Knox stares forward with a smirk playing at his lips.

"That is an awfully harsh word for a pair of women who didn't even show ankle," I counter, crossing my arms over my cropped sweater vest. I might have taken the sexy-school-girl look a little too far today with my plaid skirt, button-up white blouse, and navy sweater vest. At least I'm not wearing knee-highs. Just simple Mary Janes.

"As far as you know," Knox replies, with a wiggle of his eyebrow. "They did enjoy showing off their dirty hemlines."

I'm about to counter with a serious tongue-lashing when the professor walks in and drops his suitcase on his desk, sounding off a loud pop in the small lecture hall.

"Developmentally effective learning environments, that's the class. Get out if you're in the wrong place. I'll give you ten seconds." He holds out his wrist and stares down at it.

Yikes.

"This should be a fun class," Knox grumbles under his breath while shifting in his seat.

At least we can agree on that.

～

"He was a fucking whack job," Knox says as we step into the fresh air.

"Yeah, the fact that he was sneering at us the whole time doesn't bode well for us," Carson says before taking a sip from his water bottle. "I'm heading to the gym. What about you two?"

"Gym," Holt answers, still plugged into his phone.

"I'm grabbing something to eat," Knox says and turns toward me. "Want to come?"

"To get something to eat?"

"Yeah. Food. Are you hungry?"

Am I hungry? Yes, it's lunchtime, and if I don't eat my meals I grow fangs and get real nasty, but do I really want to eat with Knox? It's bad enough he was writing notes to me on his computer, continually pointing at the screen during class, so I don't know if I should spend more time with this guy.

His notes to me were simple: *see that kid in the red, third row up? He's a Rubik's cube genius,* and, *girl two seats in front of you keeps giving you the stink eye.*

And *this professor has the sweatiest armpits I've ever seen.*

I might have laughed at that one.

"Look at her trying to decide," Carson says, calling me out. "She's unsure, man, so you need to convince her."

"Yeah, show her why your company is worth her time," Holt says, pocketing his phone and looking at me for the first time.

Squaring his shoulders, Knox gives me a once-over and says, "What do you need to know? Name it."

Uh, I wasn't expecting an inquisition for a ticket to lunch, nor was I expecting an invitation at all.

"He's the cleanest in the loft," Carson says, sticking up for his friend.

"Cooks the best steak on the team," Holt adds.

15

"He also can dance like a two-year-old."

Knox's face scrunches. "Fuck you. I dance like a goddamn king."

Holt points at Knox's hips. "Great pelvic action."

"Knows how to work his hands."

"Can't sing worth a damn, but loves to sing anyway."

"Sleeps in matching pajama sets."

"No, I fucking don't," Knox says quickly and then shakes his head at me. "I sleep in boxer briefs."

"Give him a chance, and he'll pay for your lunch. He has an unlimited dining card," Carson says, really trying to show up his friend.

"And he knows people, so he always ends up getting free dessert."

"It's true," Knox says, with a shy smile.

They drive a hard bargain, but there is no way I can eat lunch with this man. Not when I can barely look him in the eye after what happened on Saturday. It's bad enough I have a class with him. It almost sounds as though his friends are trying to sell him to me, as if they think I'm deciding whether to date him or not. And *that* would be a big no, given I just got out of a relationship and am not looking for another.

I shift my bag on my shoulder and pull out *Pride and Prejudice*. I clutch the classic to my chest and say, "Sorry, I have a date with Mr. Darcy. I'll catch you later."

I spin around and start walking away just as Carson and Holt make a raucous sound due to my dismissal.

From behind me, Knox calls out, "Hey."

When I turn around, I find him standing there proudly, hands clipped to the straps of his backpack, a lift to his chin, and a devastating smile on his face. He's not affected one bit from my brushoff. "Darcy is a tool. Want a real hero? You know where to find me." *Cocky ass.*

I can't help the lift of the corner of my mouth as I turn around and continue walking away, unsure where I'm going, just trying to get as far away from Knox Gentry as possible. He's obnoxious, opinionated, and very much the typical jock. He called Jane and Lizzie *harlots*. There will be no friendship between Mr. Gentry and me. Mark my words.

CHAPTER TWO

EMORY

"Are you almost done in there?" Dottie calls out from the common area. "The food is here."

"One second," I say as I finish reading the last paragraph of my early childhood and development chapters.

Lying on my stomach on my bed, I move my finger along the last few words in my book and then snap it shut. I'm starving but swore to myself I wouldn't leave the bed until I finished my reading, even if my stomach was growling out the lyrics to the alma mater.

Dressed in my matching silk shorts and top—it's the only bedwear I enjoy—I pin my long brown hair to the top of my head and make my way to where Dottie and Lindsay are waiting, Thai food spread across the coffee table.

We've been best friends since the age of five, growing up together and battling our way through social awkwardness and our love for books. We spent our days in Temecula—the town we grew up in—walking to the nearest Alberto's, ordering the California burrito and splitting it in threes, rotating with who had to deal with the middle. We took it back to Dottie's house where we would chow down and hold book club meetings.

Nothing was better than that.

And then we entered high school and Neil Langston came into my life. Fresh from Napa, his parents moved to Temecula to start a wine label. He was handsome, kind, and thought I was the most beautiful thing that ever walked the planet. We dated for six years and in those six years, I started to drift away from Dottie and Lindsay and became wrapped up in my boyfriend. They went to Brentwood after we graduated, and I stayed close to home to be with Neil, who was gearing up to be a part of the family business.

It wasn't until a few months ago that I realized he wasn't only interested in the family business, but his dad's assistant as well. I'll spare you the details of the compromising position I found them in, but I will tell you this . . . I lost my mind in that moment.

Yup, I snapped.

Everything turned black, and before I knew what I was doing, I walked right up to bare-ass Neil, who was balls deep in said assistant, doggy style—okay, so I guess I am giving you the details —and I smacked his nuts.

Exactly, you read that right.

I bitch-slapped his nuts so hard—twice—*thwack, thwack*. I made him yelp like a chihuahua who just had his tail stepped on.

And when I stepped back to watch them dangle and sway in pain, I snapped one last time, stepped back up and plowed my fist into them—*kapow!*

Knuckles to balls.

Fist to family jewels.

It was a snappy jab with a forceful blinding rage behind the drive, giving me enough momentum to almost shove them into his intestines.

I can still hear the strangled sound that came from his mouth right before he fell to the side, erect penis pointing to the ceiling, hands gripping his precious junk. The assistant—don't know her name, don't care—scrambled to the headboard, sheets pulled up to her chest as she screeched bloody murder, most likely afraid I was coming for her knockers next.

She, who most definitely knew about Neil and me—*why do women do that to another woman?*—didn't deserve my attention, but man, would I have deflated those puppies real quick.

Thwack. Thwack.

Instead, I hovered over Neil, pointed at him, and said, "Your penis has always been borderline too small, but I dealt with it because I loved you. Now, I'm happy to say I no longer have to wonder if you're in me or not." I saluted the assistant and said, "I'm sure you know this, but when he comes, he has to beat his leg up and down like an excited puppy. It's revolting."

After that, I packed everything up, gave my parents a kiss on the cheek, and made my way to the Midwest, just outside Chicago, where I reunited with my best friends, and now share a three-person dorm room. I'm getting my life back together.

Well, for the most part.

Passing out with my boob in a stranger's hand might have been a mild setback.

"Are we watching *Big Brother?*" Dottie asks when I take a seat on the stiff couch the dorm room provided.

"Is that even a question?" I ask while grabbing some peanut chicken and putting it on a plastic plate that's seen better days. I'm not going to complain though, because Dottie and Lindsay welcomed me back into their lives without blinking an eye, so whatever they have for household items, I'm good with. "Juno is such an asshole."

"No one likes Juno," Lindsay says, around a mouthful of veggies. "But . . . I kind of love him."

"What?" Dottie and I yell together.

"What is wrong with you?" I ask. "You can't love him."

"I love to hate him, is that better?"

"Much," I say, taking a big bite from my plate.

"So . . ." Dottie says, with a huge smile on her face. "Saw you on campus today."

"Yeah?" I ask. "Why didn't you say hi?"

"You seemed quite busy." Dottie and Lindsay exchange smiles. *Oh crap.*

"Just say it." I sigh while tucking my legs under my butt. I know the look that was just exchanged between my two friends. I'm about to be put through the wringer.

"You were talking with Knox Gentry." She squeals. "Do you even know who he is? Did you meet him at the baseball loft? Did you give him your phone number?"

See . . . wringer.

"I didn't know who he was, but I know who he is now. I sort of met him at the baseball loft, but he actually caught my campus map . . . in the face, and handed it back to me. He recognized me from the party." I'm not going into detail how he recognized me—*I never forget a good pair of tits*—because it's not necessary to let people know about my boob being a self-soothing sleep contributor to drunk men. "And no, I didn't give him my number. We are in a class together, and he might have asked me to lunch, but I told him I had to read."

"What?" Dottie nearly explodes out of her seat. "Why on earth would you do that?"

I casually shrug, keeping my eyes trained on the peanut chicken in front of me. "I just got out of a serious relationship where my boyfriend of six years was cheating on me. Not quite ready to jump back into the dating game."

Dottie's face softens with understanding. "That's totally understandable, but you are allowed to have fun, you know. Lunch wouldn't have killed you."

"Oh, don't worry, I plan on having fun." I smirk.

"You want to go to the locker room then?"

"What?" I asked confused, fork poised at my mouth. "Is that a club?"

"Uh, no," both Lindsay and Dottie say at the same time.

Taking the lead, Dottie says, "The locker room is the actual men's locker room."

"Ew, why would I want to go there?" I vaguely remember Dottie and Lindsay talking about the magic of the locker room the other night but can't quite place the details due to the amount of alcohol I consumed.

After blinking a few times, as if I'm the one who's crazy, Dottie says, "Emory, the locker room is the most exclusive place on campus. It's the holy grail, the mecca of all orgasms."

"In a locker room," I deadpan. "Where guys are sweaty and smelly? That's the place to be?"

Lindsay rolls her eyes and sits forward, as if she's explaining the simplest thing to me. "It's not like other locker rooms in movies where the guys are gross and disgusting. It's completely different. It has leather couches, brand new carpet every year—because they can afford that—wood lockers with nameplates, and mini fridges scattered throughout stocked full of electrolyte drinks." She raises her fist to the air. "Electrolytes, damn it. That means you'll never cramp up."

Dottie steps in when Lindsay loses her mind over sports drinks. "They have these amazing showers where steam billows and billows to the point that you're in this cloudy, sweaty, sex-filled wet room. It's erotic, in high demand, and rarely offered, but when you do get a golden ticket to the locker room, it's where dreams come true."

Lindsay leans in even closer, her eyes crazy, her mouth twitching. "I heard once a girl orgasmed for five minutes straight up against the shower tiles while water was pouring down on her."

"I heard that too," Dottie confirms. "You could hear her moans from the basketball court."

"Yes." Lindsay gets excited. "The band heard it while practicing. They thought a stray cat was caught in the bleachers or something."

"Okay, hold on." I hold my hands up. "Are you telling me, girls beg and plead to be taken to the men's locker room to have sex?"

"Not just any locker room, the baseball locker room. There's a big difference."

"How so?" I ask Dottie.

She holds up her hand and ticks off her finger. "Basketball is the third most successful sport on campus. They are driven and do well, but their locker room is scum compared to the baseball team." She holds up two fingers. "Football is the second-best sport on campus and even though we do very well, that locker room is disgusting. Good guys, but their football pads will shrivel your nipples quicker than you can take off your bra." She holds up her third finger. "Baseball is number one. Recruits come from all over the country to play for Coach Disik, because it's almost guaranteed you'll become a major leaguer if you train under him. We win the college world series almost every year. Brentwood is the breeding ground for baseball players, and it's why they have the nicest locker room. It's why it's the sexiest place to be, because if you're lucky enough to get an invite, that means the guy who takes you there is serious about you."

I scoff. "Oh please. I highly doubt any girl who goes to the locker room to have sex is marriage material."

Dottie and Lindsay exchange glances. And almost on a whisper, Dottie says, "Every girl who's gone into the locker room has been married to that player within five years."

"Please." That can't honestly be true.

"It's true," Lindsay says, backing up Dottie. "It's like an unspoken rule to all players. You don't take in one-night stands; you take someone into the locker room that you plan on keeping forever. It's almost as if it's a blessing to your relationship."

"Like holy water," Dottie adds, dipping her fingers in her water and flicking it around. "But instead of water blessed by God, it's electrolytes provided by The Coca-Cola Company."

Lindsay looks wistfully toward the ceiling. "I can only imagine what it's like to be taken in there."

"Probably full of fungus and farts."

Lindsay points her finger at me sternly. "Don't you dare ruin

23

this for me. I'm going to get a ticket to that locker room, I just know it."

"Don't you need a guy to invite you? Someone you're serious with?"

Smiling, Lindsay says, "Sure do, which leads me to ask, you wouldn't mind going to the baseball loft this weekend, would you?"

Dottie rolls her eyes. "She has a thing for one of the freshmen. He has no idea what he's getting himself into. Poor guy."

"A freshman, really?" I couldn't imagine dating a freshman. Straight out of the high school womb, fumbling and confused. It's rare to find a guy who's talented in the bedroom. Not that I'd really know that from firsthand experience. Neil had been my first, and I haven't bothered with anyone since. Still on the scarred side. It would be nice to go into a fling, knowing there is some experience behind those greedy hands. *And especially if they have a dick I can actually feel when it's erect and inside me.*

"He's really cute. Has that whole hair-flip thing going on and amazing blue eyes. I don't mind being his Mrs. Robinson."

"Jesus," Dottie mutters.

"But you two will go with me? It's jungle theme this weekend."

"What does that even mean?" I ask, frankly a little terrified there's a party at their loft every weekend, with themes nonetheless.

"It means we get to dress up as slutty animals. Isn't that exciting?"

"Positively thrilling," I answer sarcastically before shoving another forkful of chicken in my mouth.

I will admit this, the classes at Brentwood are a lot more challenging than back home. I'm in the library more often than not, sneaking in snacks whenever I get the chance.

I found a study room in the back with a door that no one seems to use, so whenever I'm here, I snag the space, roll out my snacks and water—even though they're technically not allowed—and spend the rest of my night after my classes studying. I love Dottie and Lindsay, but I'm a little jealous because studying comes easier to them. They just get it. I have a little trouble retaining knowledge, so when we're in the dorm together, they're always chatting it up, not giving me a chance to crack open a book. I learned that from the first two nights after school started. Now I hang out in the library, joining them for dinner when I'm done.

It's a good routine, a solid one. I still feel a little behind, but it's only the first week, so I'll catch up.

And that's the reason I'm in the library right now, on a Saturday, writing notes into my notebook when Lindsay and Dottie come barging into my sanctuary.

"Good God." I let out a deep sigh. "You scared the crap out of me."

Both of them have their hands on their hips as they stare me down. "What are you still doing in the library?"

Their makeup's done, hair's curled, and even though they're wearing sweats, I know there's another outfit under their clothes from the jungle-looking makeup they have on.

"Studying." I gesture to my books. "What does it look like I'm doing?"

"You need to be getting ready for the party tonight."

"You know, I was thinking about that." I lean back in my chair and bite on the tip of my pen. "I think I'm going to skip it tonight, maybe curl up with a book and get lost for a while."

"No way," Dottie says, slamming my book shut while Lindsay starts to pack up my things for me. "You're not getting out of this party. We lost a lot of years together thanks to Neil the Nimrod, so we have some time to make up. You're going to that party with us."

"But—"

"Nope." Lindsay shakes her head. "No excuses. You are going, you're going to like it, you're going to drink, you're going to flirt, and then we're going to Kennedy Fried Chicken after to eat a bucket of chicken. Do you hear me?" Lindsay is practically lifting me out of my chair as she speaks.

Bag in hand, both corralling me out of the room, I have no choice but to follow them. "You have two more years with us and then all of this is going to be over and we're going to have to act like adults," Dottie continues. "After we graduate, you can turn down the party invites, but until then, your Friday and Saturday nights belong to us with the occasional Sunday Funday and Taco Tuesday."

"That's four out of the seven nights in the week. At that rate, I'll never graduate. Remember, unlike you two geniuses, I have to study."

"Don't worry." Lindsay pats my arm. "We won't let you fail. We might have fun but we also are on the Dean's List for a reason. It's the first week, Emory. We have plenty of time to make a dent in the books, and we will, but let's enjoy being together again."

Okay, when she says it like *that* . . . I guess she's right.

We make our way back to the dorms. Since we're juniors, we still had great choices available for what dorm we wanted to be in so of course we took a brand-new three-person suite. When Dottie and Lindsay were freshmen, they had to live in a two-person bedroom with a shared floor bathroom, so even though our place is small, they've reassured me we're living in the lap of luxury.

Lindsay flings the door open and flops my stuff on the couch before she turns toward me and points to my room. "Your outfit awaits you."

Oh boy, this can't be good.

"What do you mean?"

"We can't let our girl show up to the party without looking properly decked out," Dottie says and slaps my ass. "Now hurry up. We need to pre-game at The Point first, eat some nachos, then head to the party."

"The Point?" I ask, making my way into my room.

"The bar below the loft. Keep up."

Another little shove into my room and my eyes focus on the

scraps of fabric laid out on my bed. "You can't be serious," I call out.

"You have half an hour. Make it work," Dottie calls out and shuts my door.

Great. Thirty minutes. How on earth will I make sure *every* part of my body is covered up?

CHAPTER THREE

KNOX

"Does the jungle juice need to be refilled?" I ask, eyeing the Gatorade cooler propped up on the counter where people stand in line for a cup.

"Orson just refilled it," Holt says over the booming music.

I take a sip of my beer because jungle juice is not for me—I get shitfaced every time I drink it and end up flashing my ass. *Every time.*

Being one of the designated party houses on campus has its pluses and minuses. We never have to go anywhere when it comes to partying, but we always host, which means making sure our rooms aren't used for fuck closets and our shit isn't stolen, because believe it or not, people are assholes.

Jason Orson is our designated party planner. A sophomore with a knack for stupid ideas, he's in charge of every party at the loft. And the reason I'm shirtless, looking like Rambo, is because Jason had the brilliant idea of throwing a jungle party. Whatever the hell that means.

I will admit though, seeing everyone's interpretation on the jungle theme is rather entertaining. There are some random trees, vine ladies, animals, and then the baseball team who went the Rambo route with cut-up shirts tied around our biceps and heads, Army pants, and war paint brushed all over our bodies. It's not the worst getup, but we turned the heat off—since people will be in and out—and my nipples are lined up to cut glass.

"Is your girl coming tonight?" I ask Holt, who keeps scanning the crowd.

"She said she was going to be here, not sure when."

"Is she finally giving in to your annoying texts?"

He lifts his beer to his lips. "I think she's humoring me, but I plan on changing that tonight."

"Hey," Carson says, stepping up next to us. "Did you hear that Kavinsky was called up to pitch tomorrow?"

"No shit," I say. Frank Kavinsky was our number-one pitcher when I was a freshman. A workhorse obsessed with tea—he swears by it—he's made his way quickly through the minors with his wicked cutter and solid work ethic. I only had one year with him, but I learned a lot, and I've tried to follow in his footsteps, following his work ethic and positive attitude.

"Looks like all that tea helped." Carson chuckles. "We still have some of that crap in one of the cupboards if you guys ever need some of his special tea."

"I'm good," I answer, looking to the side to find a familiar face walk through the door.

Long brown hair, straight and flowing past her shoulders, with the sweetest pink lips I've ever seen, Emory Ealson makes her way into the loft wearing a black crop top, black skirt, and whiskers across her blushed cheeks. Is she a cat? In the jungle?

Doesn't matter what she is, all that matters is her tits look amazing in that top, and her legs look damn good under that extremely short skirt.

Carson knocks me in the arm. "Isn't that the girl from our class?" I nod, licking my lips. "Damn, she's hot."

"Don't even fucking think about it." I turn to him, laying my claim.

He chuckles and shakes his head. "Settle down, man. You practically pissed all around her the other day. I get it. Just don't make things awkward for us in class."

"That happened once." I roll my eyes. "You think you would have forgotten about that by now."

He taps the side of his head. "I never forget that shit, especially when she poured my morning smoothie all over us."

"At least we smelled like fruit." I shrug my shoulders, even though I made a mental note never to get involved with a crazy person again. When she wouldn't stop licking her lips while talking to me—as if I was a juicy steak ready for the taking—I should have known she'd go psycho on me.

Lesson learned.

Carson nudges my shoulder. "Are you going to go talk to her?"

"Got to be patient, man. Can't look desperate." I casually sip my beer.

"If you don't talk to her soon, Romeo will swoop in." Carson points to Brock "Romeo" Romero who has his eyes fixed on Emory as she makes her way through the crowd to the kitchen.

"Shit," I groan, causing Carson to laugh as I move toward the kitchen, making a beeline for Emory.

I bypass a few people trying to get my attention, but instead of stopping to chat like I normally do, I give them a quick smile and hustle to Emory, stepping right in front of Romeo as he's about to step up, giving him an old-fashioned cockblock before he can make a move.

"Didn't know I'd see you here," I say as a greeting, making a quick glance toward Carson, who's laughing with Holt, both aware of how I boxed out Romeo.

Whatever. Romeo is a sophomore, so he can suck my taint for all I care. I have seniority.

Not even looking up at me, Emory reaches for a cup and says, "My friends dragged me here." When she goes for the jungle juice, I stop her, pulling her gaze in my direction.

"Plan on stripping down for everyone to see you naked tonight?"

"Huh?" she asks, a cute crinkle to her nose.

"I suggest you stay away from this stuff unless you want to get seriously drunk."

"Is that so?" She eyes me suspiciously. "Well, I have to study tomorrow, so I prefer not to be hungover."

Her voice is so sweet, with a touch of sass to it. I like it a lot.

"You can have one of my beers." I reach behind me to the fridge that one of the freshmen is protecting—you always have someone standing guard—and I grab a beer for her. I pop the top and hand it over.

"Bud Light?" she asks in a distasteful tone.

"Did you think you would be getting a microbrew? It's a college house."

"Still"—she takes a sip and cringes—"I thought you'd have a little more class."

"You're giving me too much credit." I nod my head toward the corner of the loft where there are less people. When she doesn't initially follow me, I turn back around, grab her hand like I had to in class, and pull her across the loft until we're settled in the corner. I lean against the wall and prop one leg behind me.

She eyes me, giving me a full once-over.

I do the same.

She's damn hot, and I'm regretting my actions last Saturday, passing out mid grope.

Finally she says, "You seem to have lost your shirt." She motions with her finger over my bare chest.

I look down at her legs and reply, "Must be where the other half of your skirt is."

"Think they're making out in a laundromat somewhere?" She takes a sip of her beer and cringes again. A few more sips and she'll get used to it; always happens for me.

"If they are, I hope they use the gentle cycle."

Her brow pulls together. "Not sure if that makes sense."

"Oh, because half of a skirt and a shirt making out in a laundromat does?"

"In children's books, sure."

"What kind of perverted children's books did you read growing up?" I counter.

"You know, the classics," she answers causally. "One Fish, Two Fish, Red Fish, Blue Fish and Skirt and Shirt, Lovers for Life."

"Ah, yes, I forgot about that passionate yet eye-opening youth literature that took the New York Times by storm."

"I have five signed first-edition copies in a box in my parents' attic. Banking on them to clear out my student loans." She sips her beer, flips her hair behind her shoulder, glances at my chest again.

"Five?" I answer sarcastically. "Damn, forget college loans, you're set for life."

"You think?" She glances around. "What the hell am I doing here then?"

"To see me of course," I answer with a smile.

She rolls her eyes. "More like dragged to this party because my roommate has a crush on one of your freshmen."

"Yeah, which one?" I look over her head, eyeing all the partygoers.

"No idea, but apparently he has amazing blue eyes."

"Amazing, huh? Has to be Gunner. I was even stunned by his eyes when he was recruited." No joke, the dude won the lottery for irises. I'm even jealous with how . . . aqua they are.

"Not ashamed to admit that?" she asks, shifting on her heels.

"Not even a little." I give her another once-over, taking in her long, toned legs, her smooth stomach, thankfully visible due to her why-bother-wearing-me top. Her body is drop-dead gorgeous, but when you reach her eyes, they speak nothing of vixen, rather more like pure innocence. A total contradiction that has my mind reeling. "So, what are you supposed to be? A cat?"

She glances at her outfit and sighs, taking another sip of her beer. She almost seems bored to be at the party. "I'm pretty sure

I'm supposed to be a panther but my roommates fell short in the costume department."

"Yeah, really short," I add, eyeing her barely-there skirt. "Please tell me you're wearing something under that."

"Nope," she answers, sipping her beer and then smacking her lips. "I like to feel the wind in my undercarriage when I'm walking."

I wince. "Undercarriage? Fuck, I don't want you to call it that."

She laughs and shakes her head. "I'm not a lady of the night, Knox. Of course I have something under this skirt." She lifts up the side, flashing tiny black boy shorts. "Honestly, I'm going to be a librarian. I need to be sensible."

Sensible? More like hot as fuck. I saw partial ass cheek.

I grip my beer close to my mouth and take a deep breath. "A sensible librarian wouldn't flash a horny college guy her underwear."

"Well, maybe I'm more of a modern-day librarian then." She winks and starts to walk away.

"Hey, where are you going?"

She looks over her shoulder. "I have more people to flash. Don't think you're the only lucky one."

Damn, that doesn't sit well with me.

Not one fucking bit.

CHAPTER FOUR

EMORY

"The first week was great, so you have nothing to worry about, Mom."

I try to keep my voice down as I walk through campus, not wanting to look like one of those students with a homesick mother —I've heard the phone calls in passing before.

No, Mom, I'm not drinking.

Yes, Mom, I'm staying out of trouble.

Of course I'm taking my vitamins.

I haven't even touched the condoms you gave me.

"And Dottie and Lindsay, they're showing you around?"

"Yes," I say in exasperation. "They're my best friends, who changed dorms to make room for me, do you really think they were going to throw me in a frat party and say good luck?"

"Maybe," my mom answers.

"We worked through everything with Neil. They're happy I'm here, trust me; if anything, they're helping me have more fun."

Like going to baseball parties where there are hot baseball players I should stay away from, one "horny" one in particular.

"Oh? What kind of fun?"

"You know, getting me to crawl out of my shell. Experience life."

I don't need to mention the whole boob in the hand, passing out with a stranger kind of fun. Nor do I mention the party we went to this past weekend, because there are things parents need to know and things parents don't need to know. Partying with a bunch of jocks with healthy libidos is not something a mother needs to know about her daughter.

Even if nothing happened.

I don't need the pregnancy lectures, or the packages sent from home full of contraceptives and pamphlets on being a young, single mother.

Or a letter stating my mom is not ready to be a grandmother yet.

Yup, all things I've received in the mail before, even when I was living at home. I love my mom, but she likes to make a point with a flair for dramatics.

"As long as you're being safe then, have fun."

"Of course I'm being safe," I sigh just as I spot a familiar sweatshirt out of the corner of my eye. I glance to the right and make eye contact with Knox Gentry. A smile graces his handsome face, his hands are stuffed in his pockets, and he's making a beeline for me. Oh hell. "Hey Mom, I have to go. I'm heading into class."

"Okay, sweetie. Give me a call later this week so we can catch up some more."

"Sure. Love you."

"Love you too."

I hang up just as Knox reaches me and slings his arm around my shoulder for a brief side hug. "How's my favorite panther?"

What's that heavenly scent?

Man . . . that's what it is, just pure man.

Or Ralph Lauren.

Because I'm not an ice queen, I return the hug and then pull away while subtly taking in a long whiff of his fresh scent. "Favorite panther? Really? I thought that was the girl you were making out with on Saturday."

Yup, after he was all buddy-buddy with me, I saw his lips doing work elsewhere. Not that it matters, we are by no means dating, but it's nice to know that although he put himself front and center as my welcoming party, he's not actually caught up in me. I can see now that I lost sight of who I was when I dated Neil. Our worlds revolved around each other a lot. But here, I'm me. I'm not part of *Neil and Emory*, and I like that freedom. I refuse to believe I caused Neil's cheating. Sex with him was mediocre at best, and I've been released from pretending now. Kind of liberating. So, Mr. Gentry can lip lock with whoever he chooses.

Not even showing an ounce of shame, he says, "She was a jaguar, huge difference, and we weren't making out. She kissed me once and I returned it because, why not?" He tugs on my jacket. "Why? Jealous?"

"Not even in the slightest," I answer, turning around so I can talk to him while walking backward. "Was interesting seeing your type."

"Yeah, and what do you think my type is?" he asks, chin lifted.

"Really short skirts."

He chuckles and then eyes the plaid skirt I have on today—with stockings. "They don't have to be really short necessarily. I'm good with mid-thigh."

Without even thinking about it, I tug on my skirt that lands perfectly at mid-thigh. "Don't you think you should get to know a girl before you start mentioning skirt length?" I ask, just before I trip over someone behind me.

Knox reaches out and grabs my hand, steadying me before I take a tumble. He waves to the person I ran into, points at me and says, "Still hungover from Sunday Funday."

The guy I ran into doesn't say anything but instead makes a snotty face and takes off in the other direction.

"Man, he's rude," Knox says before draping his arm over my

shoulder again as we continue to walk to the class we share. "When are you going to give me a chance to get to know you, Em?"

His addicting cologne entices me to stay under his embrace, instead of shrugging him off like I should. But, God, it's like bathing in a bag of pheromones over here. "You have now."

"We are five minutes from class."

"Well then, you better start asking questions."

"Brutal." He chuckles but then doesn't waste any time in getting down to business. "Where did you transfer from?"

"California."

"Cali girl? Explains the skirts. It gets cold here, so I hope you're ready to pull on some pants."

"I gathered that." Our steps fall in line with each other, and it seems so easy to be walking side by side with him. Strangely, it doesn't feel as weird as I'd expect. For the last six years, there's only been one man's arm that's hung over my shoulder, and it certainly wasn't as muscular and solid as Knox's arm. Neil was barely two inches taller than I am, so I never felt so . . . cradled, for want of a different term. And it's nice. Freeing somehow. Whereas Neil wasn't openly warm and tactile, Knox is, and we're barely friends.

"Why did you transfer?"

"Wanted a new beginning."

"Someone wrong you?" he asks casually.

"Ex-boyfriend, but that's not anything we need to get into right now."

Instead of answering right away, Knox pauses and then says, "He's an idiot for ever letting you go."

It should sound like a line, an automatic response a guy would have to get inside a girl's pants, but it doesn't come off that way when Knox says it.

It's genuine and to be honest, it makes me want to lean in a little closer to this guy.

"He is an idiot," I confirm.

"So, you're here, starting a new chapter in your life. How's it going so far?" He opens the door to the lecture hall and ushers me in, sticking close by my side as we make our way through the crowd to our classroom.

"Well, there's this guy who I seem to keep running into—pretty sure he wants to be the hero in the story—the secondary characters are the best friends a girl can ask for, even though they make her dress like a 'panther,' and the story arc seems to be in my favor so far."

We reach the classroom, and he opens that door for me as well. Chivalry isn't dead in this one. "Think the guy you keep running into will become the hero of your story? Solidify it?" he asks, wiggling his eyebrows.

"Doubtful, probably just a funny side character."

He grips his heart. "Ouch, Ealson, that hurts."

I pat his shoulder. "You'll survive."

When I go to sit up front, he snags my backpack, halting me in place. "Where do you think you're going?" He thumbs toward his friends who are sitting in the back. "We have seats already."

"You might, but I prefer to sit in the front."

He shakes his head. "Not going to happen. Who else am I going to write notes to?"

"I bet Carson would enjoy a love letter."

Knox turns to look at Carson, who's waving enthusiastically at us. "Look at that goon, he'll be heartbroken if you don't sit with us."

"He'll be heartbroken, or you will be?" I raise a brow in his direction.

"A man never reveals his true feelings after the fourth encounter. Don't you know anything about love arcs?"

"Third," I correct him smoothly, even though his literary knowledge can easily bring me to my knees.

He steps down to my level and holds his hand out, ticking off the times we've seen each other. "Today, the jungle party, last week's class . . . and the night your boob tried to run away."

I grip his hand and push all his fingers down. "We don't mention that night."

"I might if you don't sit next to us."

"Blackmail? Really, Knox?"

"It's not beneath me," he answers with a charming smile.

Rolling my eyes and letting out a long sigh, I walk back up the stairs and scoot down the baseball row—that's what I'm calling it.

"Ealsonnnn," Carson says, holding out his hand for a high five. How barbaric a greeting, but I give it a quick snap and sit down. Holt nods in my direction but is still stuck in his phone, texting away. I should get used to seeing the top of his head, because I've seen more of his unruly hair, than his actual face.

Leaning over, Knox whispers, "See, aren't you happy you're sitting with us? We're a good time."

"You're annoying."

"Annoyingly fun."

Shaking my head, I take out my computer and get ready for class. Looks like I'm adding more secondary characters to my new story . . . just not a hero.

Knox nudges my arm and grants me his devastatingly good-looking smile.

Most definitely not a hero.

∾

I hate him.

I hate him with every fiber in my being.

Knox Gentry is dead to me.

"Em, wait up." He chases after me but I keep up my pace, trying to get as far away from him as possible.

But my short strides can't get past his long and powerful ones and before I can get more than ten feet away, he has his arm around me again, laughing quietly to himself.

"Come on, you can't be mad at me."

"You made me snort in the middle of class when everyone was quiet."

He laughs some more. "It's not my fault that I'm funny."

I stop and face him, arms folded across my chest. "Professor Culpepper now knows who I am and not in a good way."

"He's a douche. You don't need to worry about him."

"He asked me what was so funny."

"And you gave him an amazing answer."

I shift my lips from side to side. "Saying *crackling pubescent voices* was not an amazing answer." It was the only thing I could think of on the spot without revealing what Knox wrote on his computer for me to read.

"It made the entire class laugh."

"Yeah, and now he thinks I'm the class clown." I wave my hand out to the side in anger.

"Nah, don't give yourself that much credit. Maybe a witty student, but not the class clown. You have to do way more to earn that title."

"Ugh," I groan and start marching away but don't get very far once again.

"Come on, Em, admit it was fun back there."

"It was not fun. I'm not sitting by you anymore."

"You wound me, Emory Ealson," Knox calls out. "Where are you going? Come have lunch with me."

"Never," I call out, turning toward him for a brief second, hiding the smile that wants to pass over my lips. He must catch it because before I can turn away, he returns the smile in full force.

Damn him.

Damn his smile.

And damn his notes.

And thanks to Knox Gentry, I'll never be able to look at Professor Culpepper the same way. Because when I was least expecting it, while the professor was mid-sentence, Knox so eloquently pointed out a cluster of freckles on Professor Culpepper's face that had a striking resemblance to the middle finger.

Look at his face, Ealson. His freckles are telling us to fuck off.

So, whenever I see him, all I'll see now is him flipping off anyone who looks him in the face.

Just absolutely perfect.

CHAPTER FIVE

KNOX

"Gentry, my office, now."

"Yikes, that doesn't sound good," Carson says as he sits next to me, tying his shoes before we head into the weight room.

"He always sounds like that, like he has clamps on his nipples and doesn't know how to take them off."

"Maybe you can assist him while you're in the office." Carson laughs.

"Little nipple play with Coach Disik? Don't mind if I do." I rub my hands together and then stand. "Meet you in the weight room. Don't get started on the bench until I get there."

"Be gentle on the old-man nipples, you don't want them falling off."

I cringe, thinking of dusty, old nipples falling to the floor and curse my friend under my breath for bringing that image into my head right before walking into our coach's office.

Brentwood University, well known for their athletic department, was the top school I wanted to attend when being recruited. I knew fresh out of high school I wasn't ready to be drafted, so it's why I chose to be recruited by colleges. When Brentwood offered me a full ride, I knew exactly where I was going. The biggest reason? Coach Disik.

A legend for putting ball players straight from Brentwood into the major league, I wanted to be another notch on his belt of players who came from his "farm system." Even though these last two years have been hell on earth with the commitment I've made to bettering my game, the difference in my play is astronomical, and I can only thank Coach Disik, even if he's a crotchety bastard with . . . dusty, old-man nipples.

I knock on his office and wait for his gruff voice to yell out, "Come in."

I pull the door open and take a seat in one of the black leather chairs across from his desk. No need for an invitation; I've been in his office enough to know the drill. The door clicks behind me and Coach Disik looks up from his computer and folds his hands over his stomach.

The white goatee that frames his mouth stands out against the deep tan of his skin from being outside for most of his profession. And under the brim of his hat are the scariest pair of light blue eyes you'll ever see, especially when there's an error on the field.

He can make your balls shrivel up to your belly button real fucking quick.

He lifts his hat and adjusts it back on his head before saying, "What are your plans for your senior year?"

"Uh . . ." I try to hold back my laugh. "Coach, I'm a junior this year."

"I'm not a fucking idiot, Gentry." Did I mention Coach Disik has no qualms about swearing at his players? You probably gathered that from the goatee and life-threatening eyes though. "I'm wondering if you plan on entering the draft after this year or not."

"Oh, well, my mom always said earning a degree should be a priority."

"And what do you want?"

"I want to be as prepared as possible."

"And do you think another two years under my coaching will prepare you?"

I shrug, wondering why we're talking about this. "I want to gain as much knowledge as possible."

He nods and leans back in his chair, his eyes never leaving mine. "I think you're a damn fool if you don't turn your name in for the draft after this year."

I wasn't expecting that, but *tell me like it is, Coach*.

He leans forward. "You can earn your degree over time while still playing, so that shouldn't hold you back. Scouts from all over are looking at you, wondering if you're going to put in for this coming draft. Your stats are among the best in the country, and you're more than ready to take the next step in your baseball career. There isn't much more I can teach you here. You need the experience, the challenge, and you're not going to get that playing college ball. Because you took the college route, you're eligible for next year's draft. What I'd like to see you do is take this year to build your strength and agility, perfect your technique, and then after the year is over, jump into the draft. You'll be picked up in the first round, if not a top pick."

"You think so?" My pulse is racing. Playing professionally has been my goal ever since I can remember, and now Coach says it's a possibility next year . . . hell, my nipples just got hard.

"Yes. I've spoken with scouts. They have their eyes on you."

"Who?" I ask, a little too excited.

"The Bobcats for one."

"The Bobcats?" I ask, nearly falling out of my chair. Fuck. "You serious? That's my fucking dream team." Growing up just outside of Dallas, I had no right being a Bobcats fan, but my mom was born and raised in Chicago, a huge baseball fan, so I've been a diehard Bobcats fan since I can remember. Whenever I played baseball in my backyard, I always pretended I was the starting shortstop for the Bobcats, and to even think that could be a possibility gives me goddamn chills.

Feel my nipples, seriously, so fucking hard.

"Keep it in your pants, Gentry," Coach says, making me chuckle. "It's a possibility, but you have to continue to work hard, don't let up, and don't settle."

"I won't, Coach, you know I won't. I'm the first one to show up for practice and the last one to leave. I spend more hours in the batting cages than anyone, I practically have a marriage with one of the batting tees."

"I do recall you proposed to it last year."

"She's been so loyal, I had to do something."

He shakes his head and then pushes a few papers around on his desk. "Enough with the bullshit. Stay focused, set a good example, and show the underclassmen what it takes to make it to the majors."

"I can do that."

"I wouldn't expect anything less, that's why I'm naming you captain this year."

"Seriously?" I ask, my brows raising in surprise. I had an inkling I'd be named captain, but it still surprises me.

Seriously, when Coach called me into his office, I had the brief thought that maybe he heard about the stupid jungle party and wanted to lecture me about it. Not this.

"Yes, you've earned the title, just don't fuck it up now."

"I won't." I grab the back of my neck. "Wow, Coach, I'm honored."

"You know the title comes with responsibility, right? Not only showing up on the field, but off it too. You're in charge of Thursday study hall, making sure all the underclassmen are paired up with an upperclassman so our team is succeeding in the classroom as well as on the field."

"Yes, just like Justin last year."

"Exactly. Keep the boys in line, which means tamping down the . . . jungle parties."

My face blanches as Coach rolls his eyes.

"You guys think I'm an idiot, but everything you do in that loft is reported back to me, so don't be fucking morons, you understand?"

"Yeah, sure. I mean . . . we can party still, right?"

"As long as it's not under the twenty-four-hour rule when the season starts and you do it responsibly. If I hear any stories about shit going wrong at one of your parties, I will break up that loft quicker than you can saddle your dick in your jockstrap. Understood?"

"Understood."

"Good." He leans back in his chair again and for the first time since I've known him, he smirks. "You're going places, Gentry. Just make sure to send me tickets to your first big league game."

"You're one of the firsts on my list."

He nods then says, "Get out of here and go lift. Time to step it up to another level."

"You don't have to worry about that, Coach; I'm already bringing it this year."

I take off and head toward the weight room with extra pep in my step.

Captain. The Big Leagues. Hell, that conversation couldn't have gone any better.

Pictures of previous student athletes flank the hallways, reminding me of the rich athletic history within these walls. *My photo might be up here one day.* My mom would love that. It's rare when Coach Disik has any seniors on his team, because his players are usually drafted after their junior year. I knew I had the potential to be drafted after my junior year, but to know it's closer to reality is fucking incredible.

This changes everything. My entire outlook over the next year. *Me.*

I was going to grind anyway, but now that I have a chance of accomplishing my biggest goal, I know where my head will be all year: on the field, in the weight room, and putting time in the cages.

"Oh shit, what happened?" Carson asks, taking in my concentrated brow when I walk into the weight room.

Still in shock, I hop onto the exercise bike next to him and start warming up my limbs. "He named me captain."

"Seriously? Holy shit, that's huge."

"He also said I need to enter the draft after this season."

"Could have told you that," Carson says, laughter in his voice. "You're going places, man, just don't try to take my kneecaps out when we're playing against each other and you're sliding into second in the big leagues."

I smile at my friend, who has exactly the same potential as me. "I can't make any promises."

CHAPTER SIX

EMORY

I pat my skirt down and sit tall in my chair, hoping I don't mess this up.

Mrs. Flower scans my résumé and questionnaire, her lips pursed, showing off her lipstick that's in desperate need of a touch-up. The color has fallen in the cracks of her lips, drying out and making her look a little impish.

Her lipstick is pretty much the only thing I can read on this woman. Talk about a poker face. If it wasn't for the abundance of wrinkles marring the corners of her eyes, I would think she was injected full of Botox from how expressionless she is.

I'm dying to know what she thinks. The silence is slowly eating away at me. Is she impressed? Annoyed? I don't have much experience working in a library, only a year, but that should be good enough for an internship, right?

I heard all the desired internships are within the athletic department, so working in the library should be a piece of cake, but then again, judging by the way Mrs. Flower has a perpetual crease between her eyes while reading my résumé, I'm going to assume it's not as easy as I initially thought.

Dottie is interning with her dad's multi-billion-dollar corporation whereas Lindsay, studying to be a teacher, is applying for internships at local schools. She was tempted to apply for an intern position in the equipment room at the sports events center, but we talked her out of that pretty quickly.

It's been a few weeks since we started school and even though Lindsay might be slightly obsessed with going to the baseball loft every weekend, we've been able to curb her craving by taking the train into Chicago on the weekends and exploring the city, doing touristy things like taking pictures in front of "The Bean" and catching some pretty amazing off-Broadway shows—courtesy of Dottie's dad. If it wasn't for her very wealthy father, we would be spending the weekends kicking a tossed-up piece of paper around on the floor. But he's always treated us as his daughters and spoils us. I'm not mad about it, nor do I forget how grateful I am to have such great friends in my life.

Slowly, Mrs. Flower sets the résumé down and stares me in the eyes through her red thick-framed glasses. I try not to wither under her gaze but hold strong instead.

"How are you with authority?"

"Handling authority or being authoritative myself?"

"Being authoritative," she says, eyes narrowing in. There's no question, Mrs. Flower—despite the fluffy last name—has no problem holding a firm upper hand. I'm pretty sure she patrols the library, occasionally bending over to pull the ruler out of her ass only to slap students across the tops of their hands with it.

"I don't have a problem with it, especially with peers. I don't like rule breakers." Solid answer.

She slams her hand on the desk, nearly causing me to piddle myself. By God, I think I just tooted from sheer surprise. *Hold it together, Emory.*

"Situation," she yells. *What's happening?* "You are returning books in the history section, and you hear giggling. You turn down the aisle of local history and see two hooligans fondling each other. Pants at ankles, bra on the floor, what do you do?"

Oh Jesus, okay, I see what she's doing. Better ways to interview, but I'm not going to point that out. Being that Mrs. Flower has her dress shirt buttoned all the way up her neck, I *shouldn't* be surprised by her question. Thankfully when going over interview tactics with Dottie, she told me to take a few seconds before answering so I don't say something stupid. For instance, my initial answer to Mrs. Flower's question was oddly, "Slap the guy on the bare ass with an encyclopedia and reprimand him for being indecently exposed in public." I'm going to guess that's not the answer she's looking for.

Think . . .

Naked. Penis.

Naked penis.

A picture of a hot dog comes to mind and I hold back a snort while curbing my lips down into a frown to avoid any type of smile.

Clearly I'm still far too immature to be doing grown-up things.

Okay, she wants authority; here is my version of being authoritative . . .

"I would, uh"—shit, don't pause, it shows weakness—"I would take a picture on my cell phone"—ha! Good one—"then tell them to get dressed and follow me to your office or else I will take the picture to the Dean."

She leans back in her chair, observing me.

Lips purse.

Hands fold over her desk.

Brows sharpen.

Okay, not the best answer. Threatening to expose someone's bare butt isn't kosher, nor allowed I'm sure, but then again, I wasn't really expecting that question. How do you apprehend fornicators in the library? They'll just bolt. Hell, I've shamefully done it before with Neil. You get caught, but you run for your life, your belts jingling as you trot in shame.

"You would take a picture?"

Nervously, I laugh. "I know it's not the best solution, but it's the only way I could think of that would hold them accountable for their actions rather than running away."

Mrs. Flower drums her fingers on the desk. "I'm not in the market to expose nudes, Miss Ealson."

Shit.

I saw that coming.

She probably thinks I'm a pervert, cruising around college libraries, collecting nudies from unsuspecting students. Granted, what an amazing coffee table book idea, but catching new adults with their pants around their ankles is not a hobby of mine.

Although, after tanking this interview, I might very well make it one.

"I know, I'm not sure why—"

"But I want justice." She slams her fist on her desk, startling me once more—all toots held in this time. At least there's a minor win I can mark in the pro column. "Which means if my new intern carries her phone around with her to snap pictures of these horny hooligans that run rampant in my library, then so be it." She pushes a piece of paper across the desk and says, "You're hired. You start tomorrow. Bring your phone, fully charged. I expect good things from you, Miss Ealson."

What?

I blink a few times.

Did I just hear her right?

Hired?

Holy. Shit.

"Seriously? I got the internship?"

"Yes, now stop wasting my time, I have things to do." When she glances at me, she picks up her number two pencil and points it directly at me as she speaks. "Don't let me down, Miss Ealson. I want you to bring the hammer down on these college students. My library is not for sex."

"Understood." I stand. "Trust me, when I'm on watch, there will be no fondling of penises in these sacred walls."

From the disgusted look on her face, I immediately know we're not at that stage of our working relationship. No mention of penis. Got it.

I apologize. "I'm sorry I said fondling penises. I won't say that again."

She points to the door behind me. "Just leave before I change my mind."

"Sure, yup. Thank you." I bow for some stupid reason. At this point, I barely have a hold on what my body does. "Have a good day, see you tomorrow. Yippee."

Hell, Emory, don't say yippee.

She glares at me one more time before I shut the door behind me. I lean against it a few seconds, clutching my folders to my chest. That almost seemed too easy. And maybe I was one of very few candidates for the internship, but I will take whatever I can get. It's one more step closer to achieving my goal. This experience will grant me so many more opportunities when I graduate.

Time to charge up that cell phone.

~

"Hey, Ealson, wait up."

That voice. I would know it anywhere by now. Knox is jogging up to me wearing athletic pants, a tight Under Armour shirt that clings to every part of his chest, and a backward hat. He's sweaty with rosy cheeks, and a giant smile lights up his face. I will say this about the man, he wears casual well . . . really well.

Iced coffee in hand, I pause and let him quickly bring me into a hug.

"Ew, gross." I push at his chest. "You're all wet."

"It's called hard work." He laughs and pulls away, glancing at my outfit. "Hot skirt, Em, how many of those do you have?"

"More than you need to know about." Resuming my walk to the dorms, he follows closely next to me. For a college campus so big, it's surprising how many times I run into him. If I didn't know any better, I'd think he implanted a personal tracker on me somewhere.

Note to self: scan body for personal trackers when I get back to my dorm.

"Are you coming this weekend?" he asks.

"Coming where?"

"We're having a party at the loft."

I bring my drink to my mouth but it's quickly snagged from my hand. In shock, I watch Knox take a long pull from the straw.

"Hey, that's mine."

"I know, but didn't you learn it's nice to share?" He takes another sip before I steal it back. With the underside of my shirt, I wipe the straw, giving it a good cleaning.

"I don't have fucking cooties, Ealson."

"I don't know that," I reply with a lift to my chin. "Who knows where your mouth has been?"

"I'll tell you one place it hasn't been, that it desperately wants to go." He wiggles his brows at me and glances down at my crotch.

Men.

I pick up my pace, trying to gather some distance, but it's useless. The guy has the longest legs ever and pulls me into his chest, arm draped over my shoulders. It's a position I'm starting to become accustomed to when it comes to Knox Gentry.

"Are you coming to the loft this weekend?"

"Eh, I don't think so."

"Why not?"

"I have plans," I answer curtly. Plans that include watching videos of jumping goats on YouTube. That shit is hysterical.

"What kind of plans?"

"Just plans."

He steps in front of me, becoming a human roadblock. With a lift of my chin, he forces me to look him in his devastatingly handsome face. "Tell me what your plans are because I don't believe you."

Shit.

How convincing is an addiction to goat videos?

Hell, I don't have any plans. None at all. I'm actually pretty sure the girls wanted to go to the loft this weekend since we haven't partied in a few weekends, but I don't want Knox to know that. He's utterly too cocky and confident and already got his way when it comes to sitting next to me in class. And I truly have no idea why he's bothering with that. I've told him I'm not interested, and there are *many* other girls who would be. Odd man.

I've tried sitting in the front, but he joins me. And when I purposefully didn't show up until one minute before class and sat as far away from him as possible, he switched seats. He's relentless. And maybe we haven't "talked" in class, but he keeps writing me notes, and for the life of me I can't seem to turn away from his computer to see them. It's really annoying.

"Uh, you know . . ." Why am I not good at thinking on my feet? "Washing my hair."

He snorts.

In my face.

And then tilts his head back and laughs.

I can't even be mad about it. If I wasn't trying to pass off my idiotic answer as the truth, I'd be laughing too.

"Ealson, nice try. You're coming to the party. I expect you there."

I prop a hand on my hip. "Oh, so because you expect me there, that means I have to be there?"

"No, but as a friend, it would be nice if you were there."

"I'm your friend now? When did that happen?"

He sighs and grips my shoulders. "Why are you so difficult?"

"Why are you so sure of yourself? You don't always get what you want, Knox."

"Clearly." He pushes his hand through his hair, his forearm rippling from frustration. "How about this, we grab something to eat before the party and if you decide you want to come after that, then you can."

"Soo . . . now you're doubling down on the time you want me to spend with you?"

He smirks. "Is that so much of a hardship?"

"Yes," I answer sharply and make my way around him. It's not actually hard to spend time with him, but I'm *really* not interested in his pursuit of me. I refuse to put a man like him on my radar. Nada. Nope. *Although, he is fun to tease.*

"Come on, Ealson. Say you'll come."

I turn around and smile. "And here I thought you were the type of guy who'd *tell me* when I can come." I shrug as his jaw drops to the pavement. "Oh well. Catch you later, Gentry."

CHAPTER SEVEN

EMORY

W*hap. Whap.*
Lindsay's fist pounds against my door. "Four hours and counting. Finish up that studying, because you're going with us whether you like it or not." She's been relentless all day.

I rub my hand across my forehead and lean back in my chair, my eyes going blurry from all the words I've read and highlighted and then rewritten in my notebook . . . because that's the kind of studier I am. I can't simply read it and highlight. I have to rewrite it, sometimes twice, for it to become engrained in my head. I go through notebooks like crazy from all the rewriting, but it's the only way I know how to learn.

And typing doesn't work. I have to physically write it in order for it to absorb.

It's why my hand has a cramp right now.

I've been studying since nine this morning. After we stumbled out of the dining hall fresh from breakfast, I locked myself in my room and cracked open my books. I took a small break when Dottie—the good friend she is—brought me some cheddar broccoli soup for lunch. Now that it's five, my stomach is grumbling, and I'm ready to take another break.

Since I haven't showered yet—yeah, it's been one of those days —I've allotted my study time to stop sharply at seven, but now I might be rethinking that. My mind is mush.

I need a mindless second.

Cue goat videos . . .

I pop open my computer and log in to the school chat system. Too lazy to grab my phone from my bed, I send Dottie a quick message before I open YouTube.

Emory: *Dinner, what's on the menu?*

Because she's always glued to her computer when studying, she answers right away.

Dottie: *Pizza is coming. Daddy dearest called earlier. Spent an hour on the phone with him. He told me all about this pizza he wants us to try so he's having it delivered.*

Emory: *Remind me to send him a thank-you card.*

Dottie: *You know he already knows you're thankful.*

Emory: *Still. It's nice to say thank you. Let me know when it arrives. I'll study some more until then. P.S. Please tell me he ordered grape soda to go with it.*

Dottie: *He isn't the best father in the world for no reason. Of course he got grape soda. Don't doubt the man.*

Emory: *Never will again. Knock on my door when it's here.*

I go to shut my chat box, pizza and grape soda waiting for me just around the corner, when a new chat screen pops up.

I catch the name right before I am about to exit out and pause.

Knox Gentry.

What is he doing messaging me?

Because the school wants students to experience what it's like to live and breathe in a community atmosphere, they allow any student to contact another through the chat system, but the chat has to be accepted first.

Since I've never messaged with Knox before, I only have the

choice to accept his chat or not. No preview to what he's said. Damn it.

I chew on my bottom lip, contemplating what I should do. More studying, or finding out what he wants.

Hell, I already know what he wants: me to show up at his party for some odd reason. I'm curious to see what other tactics he has to get me to come.

Not that he needs to, as I'm already going, thanks to Lindsay and Dottie, but he doesn't need to know that. I've watched a lot of goat videos recently, so maybe I should take a small break and have a little fun.

I earned it.

I click to accept his message as I place one of my feet on my chair. Time to get comfortable. I push my blue-light blocking glasses back on my nose and read what poetic diatribe I've received. From our past interactions and arguments, I'm sure it will be good.

Knox: *Yo.*

Oh wow . . . how prolific.

I chuckle, wondering what I was thinking, as if he was going to open with recited poetry or something. He is a "horny college student" after all—his words, not mine.

Shaking my head, I type back.

Emory: *You have one chance to make a good first impression in student chat and you open with yo? I expected more from you.*

Knox: *I wasn't going to waste a good opening on the possibility of you not accepting my chat.*

Emory: *Does that mean you have a secondary opening?*

Knox: *Obviously.*

Emory: *Do I get to read it?*

Knox: *I don't know. I'm trying to decide if you're worthy or not.*

Emory: *You're the one who messaged me. I can sign out anytime I want.*

Knox: *You're fucking brutal. Fine . . . *ahem*, here it goes; What's up?*

I laugh out loud, hating that he so easily entertains me. What a doofus.

Emory: *Wow, I think you just blew my socks off.*

Knox: *See why I saved it? Can't waste that shit on just anyone.*

Emory: *I hope you keep that opening a secret. Can you imagine the number of socks that would be flying off feet all over campus? It's dangerous.*

Knox: *Lethal.*

Emory: *I'm glad you saved it for me. I'm indebted to you.*

Knox: *Really? ((Rubs hands together)) Should I cash in now?*

Emory: *I'm clearly kidding.*

Knox: *Nope, I have it in writing ^^^ right up there. You're indebted to me. So I'm cashing in.*

Emory: *"Cash in" all you want, still doesn't mean I'm going to do whatever you ask.*

Knox: *Stubborn woman.*

Emory: *^^That's winning you friends.*

Knox: *Come to the party tonight.*

Emory: *Just jumping right into it, are you?*

Knox: *There is no theme. It's just to have fun. We have beer and some mixed drinks, and I can even offer you some pretzels.*

Emory: *Wow, you paint a beautiful evening. The pretzels are a real winning attribute.*

Knox: *I was going to save this as a last-ditch effort but since I think I might have you hooked with the pretzels, I'm going to bring my offer home and let you in on a little secret; just bought a fresh packet of Oreos. So if you play your cards right, you could be separating Oreos with me tonight.*

Emory: *Seriously? Oreos, how RARE! Well, then I must go because . . . Oreos.*

Knox: *Really? You're coming?*

Emory: *No. Have a good night, Knox.*

I shut the computer before he can respond and smile to myself as I look over to my closet, debating what I should wear tonight.

Oddly, I kind of want to blow him away, which means, I'll put more thought into what I wear. And maybe, I'll spend the rest of my time filling my stomach so I don't get stupid drunk. I did study all day. I deserve this.

And how could I really turn down Oreos?

CHAPTER EIGHT

KNOX

"Why does she have to be so goddamn difficult?" I ask Carson as I lean against the window next to the fire escape, surveying the party that I have zero interest in being at. "I mean, I've seen the way she looks at me, there's interest there."

"Didn't you say she had an ex-boyfriend that did her wrong?"

"Something like that." I lift my hat then settle it on my head, backward. I just got my hair cut so it falls smoothly over my head. I would have done my hair if I knew she was coming tonight, but I put zero effort into what I look like, not interested in being near anyone besides Carson. He's only sticking around because he hasn't found a girl he's interested in yet, but the minute he does, I'll make my way back to my room and lock the door.

Fucking pathetic.

I'm not feeling social right now. Emory has a great way of cutting down a guy's ego, and for the life of me, I can't figure out why I like it so damn much.

"Maybe she's super cautious. Maybe she dated another baseball player and he was a dick. You know how women will associate their feelings like that."

"Maybe." I sigh and take a sip from my beer bottle. "Jesus, you would think I was a sick fool in love with the way I'm acting."

"I was going to say that but didn't want to sound like an ass."

I push off the wall and shake my shoulders out, giving myself a little slap to the cheek. "Okay, I'm not going to waste this night just because some girl I hardly know turned me down for the tenth time."

"Tenth, really?"

"No, well, I'm not really sure, but it feels like that. I'm just going to find someone else."

"Pretty sure there is a line of college girls waiting to have their chance with you. Just call out a number, see who shows up."

"Not a bad idea." I give him a pat on the back. "See any brunettes wearing a skirt?"

Carson rolls his eyes. "If you're going to try to move on from another girl, don't go for the exact replica, dude."

I shrug. "It's my type right now."

He chuckles and then points. "Well, there's a brunette with a skirt, but not sure you can land her."

"Where?"

"By the beer pong table, near Holt's room."

I scan the crowd and when my eyes land on a laughing Emory, my stomach does a tiny little flip.

See? Fucking pathetic. Might as well put a dog tag around my neck that says: Return to owner, Emory Ealson.

Shit, she looks good. Wearing an off-the-shoulder white crop top that gives me a good glimpse of her cleavage, she paired it with a floral skirt that flares at her hips. She looks classy but sexy at the same time, a lethal weapon for my southern heart.

"Shit, she's here."

Carson pats me on the back. "Looks like you should go change because damn, she looks good."

"Nah, I don't want her leaving my sight. I'm going in."

"Good luck," Carson says with less confidence than I appreciate.

I would normally say I don't need luck, but with Emory, I might. She's different than other girls, sexy and intelligent with a hint of resistance that turns me on. I enjoy her banter and her ability to call me out on my shit. She's fucking fun, and I want to be around her more.

Beer in hand, wearing a simple black T-shirt and jeans, I shift through the crowd and walk straight toward Emory, who's talking to two other girls. I don't even bother to wait until they're done talking. Instead, I walk up next to Emory, put my arm over her shoulder, and bring her close into my chest for a hug. To my surprise, she laughs and presses her hand against my chest as she returns the hug.

That feels good, her tits pressed against me. Fucking amazing.

"Thought you weren't coming."

She looks up at me, those green eyes connecting beautifully with mine. "You can thank my roommates for making sure I showed up."

I glance at the girls in front of us who have huge smiles on their faces. I'm thinking I have the same look on mine as well. "Are these your roommates?" I point with the hand that's holding my beer bottle.

"Yup. This is Dottie and Lindsay."

I give them a quick wave. "Dottie and Lindsay, I owe you one. I didn't think this girl was going to show."

"She can be a beast at times, but whenever you need something, just let us know, we can convince her," Dottie says.

"I'll keep that in mind. Do you care if I steal your girl?"

"Have at it." Dottie ushers us away.

"Thanks, ladies, enjoy yourselves." Before Emory can protest, I take her hand in mine and lead her to the kitchen, where I ask one of the freshmen to grab me two beers and the Oreos I stuffed away. The dutiful teammate he is, he fetches them in an instant, and I take Emory to the window that leads to the fire escape.

"Uh, where do you think you're taking me?"

"It's either this or my bedroom. Take your pick, because I want you alone."

She pulls her hand away from me and folds her arms over her chest, her bare shoulders enticing me more than they should. "Who's to say I want to be alone with you?"

"Me. That's who. Now stop being stubborn and follow me. I promise a good time."

"As long as you keep your hands to yourself."

I scoff. "I'm a southern gentleman if anything, Em."

When I link her hand in mine and she allows it, I assume earning some private time with her is a go.

I help her out of the window and up the fire escape a few stairs away from the window so we can actually hear each other. Thankfully, I put a blanket out here just in case she decided to show up and I lay it on the metal stairs before we take a seat. We sit side by side, not shoved too close together thanks to the spacious fire escape—rare, I know—but close enough where our knees knock together. I set the beers behind us and hold out the Oreos. She eyes them for a second with a sly smile before popping open the resealable top. Her delicate fingers pull one out and instead of eating it right away, she holds it out.

Looking up at me, head slightly tilted, she says, "Grab the other side and twist. Whoever gets the most cream, gets to ask the other a question."

That's my kind of game. What do I want to know about this girl? I start conjuring up all the questions I have about her.

Tell me more about this douche ex-boyfriend.

What's your favorite sexual position?

Are you in favor of me sucking on your tits tonight?

Hmm . . . might be too presumptuous.

"What kind of questions? Anything we want to ask? Does the other person have to answer?"

"Sure." She shrugs. "I don't have much to hide."

"Much, huh? So, there are some things you care to hide?"

"Stuff you'll never guess, so we're safe." She nods at the cookie. "You in?"

"Hell yeah." I grip the other side and count, "One, two, three, twist."

We both twist and pull apart. I look down at my empty black cookie and then at the sly smile crossing Emory's face, who's wiggling her cookie at me. Damn, she's cute.

She pops the whole thing in her mouth and chews while she leans back on the stairs, giving me the perfect view of her smooth stomach and perfectly proportioned breasts.

Full B-cup, easily.

"How many girls have you brought out on the fire escape, Knox?"

Her question comes out low, seductive, and instead of answering right away, I'm staring. Staring at her perfectly glossed lips, so full, bigger than I remember. She can do some wicked things with those lips, things I want to experience.

"How many? Hmm, let me see." I chew on my half of the cookie and start counting on my fingers. "There was Victoria, Kristi, Tiffany, Sarah, Franci, Heather . . . Logan, but that was a short questioning phase my freshman year. Then Lynn, Gina, Marina—oof." Emory playfully whacks me in the stomach and then starts to get up. I pull her back down, laughing. "Stop. I've never brought anyone out here before. Believe it or not, I'm not the huge player you think I am."

"I don't think that."

"Please, I can see it all over your face. You think I sleep around, don't you?"

She looks down at her nails and says, "Well, you did kiss another girl the same night you tried to hit on me."

"Like I said, she kissed me, and I wasn't about to go dead lips on her. I have a reputation to uphold."

"Heaven forbid." She rolls her eyes.

"Rumors spread, Ealson. Last thing I need is for the student body to know me as the shortstop with dead-fish lips."

"That really sounds unappealing."

"See." I reach for another Oreo. "Now twist with me, I have some burning questions for you."

She eyes it for a second, her lips twisting to the side, questioning if she should break apart another cookie, but her curiosity wins out and she grabs the other side. "Okay, one, two, three, twist," she says, and we break the cookie apart.

I glance down at my plain chocolate cookie and curse under my breath as she plops the cookie in her mouth with another smarmy smile.

"Okay, what the hell are you doing? Are you aware of some twisting trickery that I'm not?"

"Just luck." She winks.

Why don't I believe her?

As she chews on her cookie, she mulls over her question for me. "When did you lose your virginity?"

I choke on my beer while trying to wash down my cookie. Shit, I wasn't expecting that.

She pats my back and then casually leans on the stair behind us, smiling at me. She's so cool and calm, unlike any girl I've ever met. She's not trying to fluff her hair or make sure her lipstick is perfect. Yeah, she dressed up tonight and looks fucking good, but she isn't high-maintenance. I like that. I like her.

A lot.

Once I gather myself, I wipe my mouth with the back of my hand and say, "Wasn't ready for that question."

She brushes her hand over her skirt and casually says, "You said we could ask anything."

"I guess so." I lean against the handrail and turn slightly on the stairs so I'm facing her. "Seventeen. My date and I had sex for the first time after prom."

"Seriously?"

I chuckle. "Yup, totally cliché and I'll tell you this, it was good for me, but given I lasted like thirty seconds, let's just say it wasn't the best for her."

Emory covers her mouth, eyes wide, and laughs.

"If any guy tells you he's good at sex right off the bat, he's a liar."

"How would you say you fare now?"

I lift a thick brow. "Interviewing for a position in my bed?"

"You wish. Just wanting to know if limp dick should be paired with your dead-fish lips."

My eyes narrow as I point at her. "Don't even fucking joke about limp dick. Jesus. Shit spreads quickly here on campus."

"So you've informed me." She smirks.

Goddamn, she's so . . . cool.

"So . . ." she continues, "are you limp or not?"

"Not," I answer quickly. "I'm actually really good in bed. Want me to show you?"

She holds up her hand. "I'm good. After having you pass out while holding my boob, I'm pretty sure I know the extent of your bedroom abilities."

I sit up taller. "That's not an accurate portrayal of my talents in the bedroom. I barely made it to my room that night, let alone kept my eyes open long enough to help your wayward boob back in place."

She just shrugs and picks up another Oreo.

I don't take it though, instead, I motion to the loft. "Come on, we're going to my room. I'll show you right now what I can do. Fucking question my abilities to pleasure a woman, I'll show you what pleasure is."

She attempts to tamp me down with her hand. "It's really okay. I believe you. You're the ultimate lover. Got it."

"I don't believe you mean that. You're being sarcastic." I point to her lower half. "Fine, if you won't go back in the loft, lift up your skit, I'll eat you out right here, right now."

For the first time this night, her cheeks flush and her cool façade finally shows a crack. Huh, would you look at that. And I thought her confidence was sexy, I think her embarrassment might just be even sexier.

"Not necessary." She holds out the cookie and I have an inkling about something. I hope to fuck I'm wrong, because this girl is hot and sexual.

No one gets that red over someone mentioning oral unless . . .

I twist the cookie and when I see that I finally have the most cream, I don't even take the time to celebrate, instead, my burning question falls straight from my lips. "Has anyone ever gone down on you?"

She looks away.

Fuck, I knew it.

Cheeks blushed, ears red, body language completely turning off. I hit a nerve.

"Answer the question, Ealson. I answered yours."

She pushes her thick hair behind her ear and stares at her cookie while answering. "No."

Jesus Christ, *how is that possible?*

"Are you fucking serious? How long were you with your boyfriend?"

"Doesn't matter."

"It sure as hell does. Tell me, how long?"

She pops the cookie in her mouth, dusts off her hands, and stands. She gives me a quick smile, a pat on the shoulder and says, "Thanks for the snacks. I'm going to go mingle."

I stand too. "Em, don't leave. We don't have to talk about him."

"Or we don't have to talk at all. I'll see you around, Knox."

Before I can stop her, she walks back into the party, leaving me on the fire escape with two beers and Oreos. Well fuck, that was short-lived. Real smooth, Gentry.

Real fucking smooth. I finally bridge the gap she keeps between us, and ask about the obvious no-go topic: her boyfriend. But, what the fuck? Emory is passionate, funny, resourceful, sexy, and a damn good time—yes, out of the bedroom too. What boyfriend denies his girlfriend something that should be synonymous with fucking? What sort of ass did she date? That's so fucked up, and I hate that I may have lost an opportunity to find out more about this girl. Because she deserves more. And I'm going to show her just that.

CHAPTER NINE

EMORY

"Why is this chicken so good?" Lindsay asks, shoving a fried leg into her mouth and gnawing on it like it's her last supper.

"Because you're drunk and will eat pretty much anything," I answer, looking out the window of the very popular Kennedy Fried Chicken. It's a drunk staple in Brentwood and not far from the baseball loft. It's why it's overly crowded with students who barely have their wits about them.

"Aren't you going to have any?" Lindsay asks, holding a piece of fried chicken out to me. Reluctantly, I take it and set it on the napkin in front of me, slowly picking away at the piece of meat. I'm not even close to being drunk, which is a shame because the feelings roaring through me could use a little alcohol to subdue them.

I was doing so well, actually having fun with Knox. I love teasing him, and I can tell he likes it too by the small smirks he passes my way, but when he asked about Neil going down on me, it resurrected so many hateful and hurtful feelings all at once. I knew if I didn't leave, I would have made a fool of myself, and I didn't want to do that, not in front of Knox.

In a rage-filled text conversation I had with Neil, after I gave him the old one-two blow to the nuts, he did more damage to my heart than he'd done to my eyes. He'd always said he wasn't really into oral sex, and I'd simply shrugged my shoulders and figured it wasn't that great anyway. He had, however, been all over me giving him blow jobs. He didn't apologize for cheating on me. He didn't even try to convince me it was the first time either. But then his final message came in, and that was the one that destroyed my heart.

Neil: *You were never enough for my needs. My tastes. She tastes fucking incredible. She makes me glad I never put my tongue in your cunt.*

There were no other text messages after that. I blocked his number wondering how I'd stayed with someone so cruel for as long as I did. I still can't comprehend it, and it's something I try not to think about because I don't want to go down that deep hole of depression again. Therefore, I tell myself to push it to the back of my mind like every other healthy individual.

"So, are you going to tell us?" Dottie asks, pulling me from my thoughts.

I plaster on a smile for my friends and say, "Tell you what?"

They exchange an annoyed look with each other and Lindsay says, "Uh, what happened with Knox on the fire escape? Did you kiss?"

Such Nosey Nellies, but I can't be mad, because there was a time in our lives where we told each other every last thing about our lives. I have to remember that.

"Kiss? No." I shake my head and then pull a piece of meat off my chicken. "We talked, played a little game of questions with Oreos, nothing too exciting."

"You didn't kiss? How on earth is that possible?" Lindsay, the boy-crazy friend, says. "He's so hot."

Ah, yes, the classic reason to kiss a guy, because he's hot. Not because of his personality or anything.

"Yes, you've mentioned that before. But I'm not ready to jump into another relationship. I just got out of a six-year one."

"Months ago," Dottie adds with a friendly smile. "It was months ago when you ended things. You're allowed to move on, Emory."

"I know. I'm just keeping things easy, that's all. I want to focus on school. Focus on me. I've been part of a couple for so long that it's nice to simply breathe, you know, not have to worry about another human for a change."

"I can understand that," Dottie says while taking a sip of her soda. "But does Knox know that? I saw the look in his eyes when he spotted you, and it's obvious he really likes you."

"He'll get over it. There are plenty of girls on campus he can dabble in. Trust me, I'm just a small blip on his radar."

"Not true," Lindsay says. "I've been going to the baseball loft ever since I was a freshman, and I've never seen Knox make a beeline for a girl like he did for you tonight." *And I've been with one guy so long I've probably lost my ability to see interest as genuine.* But my girls won't understand that. In some ways, I feel so much older from being in a long-term relationship. In other ways, naïve. Nevertheless, Knox Gentry is not on my radar.

"Must have been my perfume, I heard it has pheromones or something like that in it."

Dottie rolls her eyes. "Keep telling yourself that, Emory."

How does one choose what donut to get when there are at least twenty different flavors?

I'm in black leggings, an oversized sweatshirt that continues to hang off my shoulder, and my hair is piled in a mess on top of my head. It's my Sunday garb, and I have no shame in it. I have one mission today and that's to get a world-famous Frankie Donut, some coffee, and then walk back to my dorm, which is a mile away, making it a two-mile journey altogether and a guilt-free day of taking down a donut.

When I asked Lindsay and Dottie if they wanted to go with me, they rudely threw their pillows at their doors, pushing me away. I took that as a no.

I've learned very quickly they're not morning people. That's fine. I plugged my earbuds in, turned on my Spotify walking playlist, and took the journey down the Brentwood Boardwalk that borders Lake Michigan. The morning breeze coming off the lake and the bright sun shining down on me was exactly what my soul needed.

Now if only I could choose a donut.

I've let at least three people pass me in line, not wanting to make a rushed decision. This is my first Frankie Donut, after all. It has to be perfect.

I've narrowed it down to four. The blueberry streusel, the cherry lemonade, the old-fashioned with spice, and the cosmic chocolate cake donut. I refuse to buy all four, because two miles will only knock off so many calories.

Ugh, decisions, decisions.

My turn again, but I'm not ready, so I turn to the person behind me. "You can go in front of me."

But when I look up to find a very sweaty-looking Knox wearing a baseball cap and running gear, I'm a little stunned. He smiles at me, those white teeth gleaming against his tan face. "I'd rather watch you continue to be indecisive."

"Good Lord, how long have you been there?"

"Long enough." He nods at the case of donuts. "What are you thinking?"

"It's between four." I bite my bottom lip in embarrassment.

He takes a step toward the counter and says, "A water and four donuts please." He nods for me to join him. "Which ones? We can taste test them together."

I'm about to tell him I'm good, but when he smirks and pleads with those sinfully charming eyes of his, I can't help but give in.

It's a devilish smirk and a gleam in his eyes, born straight from Satan himself. Knox Gentry is a man who gets what he wants very often.

I order the four donuts I was debating between, as well as a coffee, and pull out my money from my sports bra. When I go to pay, Knox pushes my money to the side and says, "I got it, Em."

I consider fighting him paying for my breakfast, but with the long line behind us, I decide to not cause a scene. I watch as the girl at the register passes glances over Knox, appreciating his physical form, taking in his broad chest and winning smile.

Can't even be mad at her, because I'm doing the same exact thing.

Sweaty Knox is a sexy Knox.

He hands me my coffee, and I fill it with sugar and cream and meet him by the door. He holds it open for me and nods toward a little bench that overlooks the picturesque lake. I follow him and take a seat, soaking in the fresh morning air. There is nothing better in my opinion than waking up early enough to still taste the brand-new morning.

"Were you out running?" I ask, even though it's kind of obvious.

"Yeah, I try to get some miles in on the weekends, keep up my stamina. What about you?" Of course he does. Get some miles in . . . I get my miles in for donuts.

"I'd like to say I was working out," I say while dangling my feet off the bench seat, "but I basically walked to the donut shop and convinced myself that walking to and from my dorm would give me the go-ahead to take down some fried dough."

He chuckles. "I think that's fair. You really live in the dorms?"

He hands me a napkin and then pops open the donut box between us. An impromptu meetup. I can't say it doesn't put a smile on my face.

"Yes, what's wrong with that?"

"Nothing, I just don't know many juniors who still live in the dorms, that's all."

"Oh, well, Lindsay and Dottie didn't want to live in some skeezy place off campus, and since these were brand-new dorms, with all the amenities and a dining hall, seemed like a win-win. Don't have to make food, we have maid service every Tuesday, and we don't have to buy things like toilet paper."

"Damn." He leans back on the bench and splits the first donut in half—cherry lemonade—and hands it to me. "I've gone about this living situation all wrong. I have my own roll of toilet paper in my room that I keep hidden and take in and out of the bathroom with me, because no one ever refills the roll. Toilet paper is sacred in the loft."

"You're a smart man, Knox Gentry."

His brows lift in surprise. "Yeah, you think so?"

"Don't get too excited, you're just smart enough in my eyes to carry around your own toilet paper."

He winks at me. "It's the basic survival skills that are the most impressive."

He's so ridiculous. Fun, and easygoing, the kind of guy I could see myself becoming great friends with because he's super easy to talk to. I don't feel nervous or like I'm stumbling over my words around him, as he makes it easy with his gorgeous smile and kind eyes.

"What do you think of the donut? Good?"

"I think it has the potential to be one of the best donuts I've ever had."

"Big statement, are you sure you want to put that out there in the universe?" he asks, licking his finger. I carefully watch as his tongue peeks out and cleans the icing off his finger. Okay, that's oddly nice to watch.

Peeling my eyes away, I study the cherry lemonade donut. "I'm pretty confident about it."

He lifts up the blueberry streusel and says, "Then allow me to blow your mind." He breaks the donut in half just like the other one but instead of handing it over, he carefully raises it to the sky, letting the sun pay it homage, and then hands it over using both hands. "The holy grail of donuts. Enjoy."

"Don't be so dramatic." I snag the donut from him and take a bite.

Oh.

Damn.

Blueberry yumminess, streusel perfection, fried doughy-ness. This is pure heaven.

I try to hide the look on my face but he catches it and points, knowing all too well that he was right and there's no use hiding it.

Dropping my guard, I say, "Holy hell, this is so freaking good."

He smacks his thigh like a doof and then fist-pumps the air. "Yes. Told you, Em. Stick with me, babe, and I'll show you all the good things about Brentwood."

I smile, liking the way *babe* so easily rolled off his tongue. The only thing Neil ever called me was Emory. Yes, that's my name, but after six years of being together, you'd think he would have some sort of pet name for me.

Nope.

Knox is different though.

Do I find Knox Gentry attractive? Of course, there is no way any woman on this planet would consider him anything but good-looking, and his outgoing personality just adds to the appeal. But can I see myself with this man? Not really, at least not right now. He seems too good to be true—perfect actually—especially for a girl who was burned by her last relationship. There has to be a flaw somewhere when it comes to him, and I'm simply not seeing it yet.

"According to my roommates, you play shortstop, right?"

"Yup." He shoves the rest of his donut in his mouth and reaches for another but doesn't hand me the other half. Instead he rests it in the box, noticing that I already have my hands full with my partially eaten halves.

"Is it hard?"

"Is what hard? Playing shortstop?"

"Yeah. I mean, I haven't watched many baseball games but the ones I've seen, the shortstop always seems to be running all over the place. How do you know where to go all the time?"

"Second nature by now. I've been playing the position ever since I was seven. Over time, your body just reacts and knows where to go and when."

"Do you like it?"

"Love it," he answers, his eyes lighting up. "I love being in control of the infield and outfield, letting everyone know where the ball needs to go in every situation. I love giving signs to my teammates, trying to fake out the other team. I love the unpredictability of the game, unsure if we're going to turn a double play or if the pitcher is going to let a homerun fly. It's a back-and-forth battle every game, and the only thing you can do in the battle is refer to your basic instincts and the training you've put your body through, hoping it's been enough."

"Has it been enough?"

"Most of the time, but we have our off days."

"When does your season start?" I ask, taking another bite of my donut and then sipping on my coffee. I admit, this is a pretty perfect morning with the fresh donuts, beautiful scenery—including the man next to me. I'm glad I took the walk.

"We have some fall ball to test our freshmen and see where we have holes in our roster, but we won't start our real season until February where we have pre-season games, and then we go balls to the wall after that until June. We'll practice every day along with agility and weights and then individual practices with coaches."

"On top of your school schedule?"

He nods and brushes his hands off on a napkin. "It's intense, but you get used to it. We still have plenty of off time too, well, not plenty, but enough so we don't go crazy."

"And here I thought my new internship was going to take up a lot of my studying time."

"New internship?" He gets excited and rests his arm on the back of the bench as he turns toward me. "What kind of internship?"

"Just working in the library. I was excited about getting it, though. It will be great experience when I start applying for jobs."

"That's awesome." He leans over and tips my chin up with his finger. "Congrats, Em."

"Thank you," I answer, feeling my cheeks heat up. "It's not that big of a deal, but still exciting."

"Don't downplay your accomplishment. It's amazing, and you should be proud."

"Well . . . thank you." God, he makes me feel so . . . free inside, it's insane. Just being around him for twenty minutes I feel rejuvenated. I glance at the box of donuts and then at my watch. "I should start walking back, and I'm sure I've taken enough time from your run. Thank you for the donuts."

His face falls for a second, but he stands with me and picks up the box, handing it over to me. "Here, you take them. Running with donuts will be clumsy."

"Are you sure? You bought them."

"Yeah, for you."

I take the box in my hand and smile sheepishly at him. "Thank you. It was nice running into you."

"Yeah, remember that when I'm trying to sit next to you in class tomorrow. You can stop fighting it."

I take a few steps back. "Never."

He readjusts his hat and pulls earbuds from his shorts pocket. Before he puts them in, he says, "I wouldn't expect anything else. Have a good day, Em."

"You too." I give him a small wave that causes his smile to grow even wider.

So handsome.

With a quick wink, he sticks his earbuds in his ears and takes off running down the boardwalk, in the opposite direction I'm going. I take a moment to watch him, his strong backside, his muscly legs taking him down the boardwalk quickly, his broad shoulders shifting back and forth.

Yup, he's all kinds of perfect. Way too good to be true.

On a sigh, I tuck my donuts into my side and start making my way back to the dorms. I'd like to say I'll share these with Dottie and Lindsay, but Knox did say he bought them for me, so . . . I'll be sure to break into them when I'm studying later. And in class tomorrow, I'll report which ones I enjoyed from best to worst. It's my duty, after all.

CHAPTER TEN

KNOX

"Study hall, six sharp, don't be late," I call out to the team as they're taking their practice gear off and heading to the showers. "Freshmen and sophomores are required, upperclassmen, you know who you are, make sure you're there."

"Do we really have to meet in the library?" Gardner, a lousy and extremely lazy sophomore asks. I can't stand the prick, and he's probably the only guy on the team that grates on my nerves.

"Yes."

"But Venice allowed us to have study hall in the loft last year."

"And we had the worst grade point average as a team last year. Not while I'm captain. It's in the library, and there will be no fucking around. Got it?"

Gardner grumbles and walks off toward the showers as I take a seat next to Carson, who's eyeing me suspiciously. "We didn't have the worst grade point average last year."

"Shhhhhut up," I hiss while looking around. I lean in close and say, "Do you really want these fools hanging out at the loft all the time? We have enough teammates to deal with, and we don't need the young ones dicking around in our place too. Library is where we should be studying."

"Those chairs hurt my back."

"Then bring a goddamn pillow," I shoot back to Carson. He doesn't need study hall, as he's one of the most intelligent mother-fuckers I know. He's majoring in architecture while keeping his starting position at second base. My workload isn't half as much as his and I struggle, so I have no idea how he does it. Because he doesn't struggle with school, he's not required to go to study hall, but being the good friend he is, he attends.

I also think it's because he found his groove in study hall, and he's one of few guys who actually gets a lot of work done.

"Are we allowed to have snacks in the library?"

"No, and no drinks apparently," I answer.

"And you expect us to go there after practice when we're starving?"

"It's called eating and walking. Grab something from the cafeteria upstairs; you know they'll make you anything, and eat it while walking to the library. You're smart, dude, figure it out."

I roll my eyes and lift from my seat where I start peeling off my clothes. They don't need to know I might have a small ulterior motive for going to the library for study hall. It might have to do with a little brunette I can't seem to stop thinking about. I catch her once during the week in our class, but even at that, our interaction is brief. I've set a notification on my computer to let me know when she's on student chat, and it's rare. And it's even a crapshoot when it comes to parties.

Running into her at the donut shop was a miracle, and I tried to soak up as much of her as possible, but she cut our chance meeting short. Hell, I could have sat there all morning talking to her.

And do I have her phone number? Nope.

I've been too much of a pussy to even ask. Given our track record, I guarantee she'll say no if I ask. This is going to be a slow burn with this girl. And if I didn't see an ounce of interest in her eyes, I would forget about it, but when she looks at me, I can see it deep in her eyes. She's interested.

I take a quick shower, dry off, and get dressed. Unlike my typical athletic gear, I put on a pair of jeans and a long-sleeved Brentwood baseball shirt. I consider skipping the hat and doing my hair, but knowing the boys, they're already going to give me shit for wearing jeans, so I put a black BU hat on and start packing my backpack.

"What's with the jeans?" Carson asks, as he sits next to me by his locker, towel wrapped tightly around his waist.

"Got some shit on my sweats." It's a lie, but whatever. If I run into Emory, I don't want to look like a homeless man in sweats like I do every Monday in class. The least I can do is put some jeans on and a tight-fitting long-sleeved T-shirt. Give her a small show.

"Hendrix and his girl just got engaged," Holt says, pulling his gaze from his phone and holding it out to Carson and me. A picture of our first baseman from two years ago is on the screen, holding his long-time girlfriend and showing off a ring.

"No shit," Carson says, grabbing the phone for a better look. "Didn't he bring her back to the locker room his junior year?"

Holt nods. "Yup, he knew she was the one."

What a weird fucking tradition. I don't even know how it started. Well, that's not true, it started with this guy named Gary Bernard, a catcher back in the day. He brought a girl back to the locker room and she wound up saying yes to his proposal at the end of his senior year. He claimed the locker room had magical powers in convincing her. Ever since then, any player in a serious relationship has done the same and basically fucked anywhere of their choosing.

It's fucking weird.

But whatever, as baseball players we're superstitious, so I get it.

"Do you think I'll ever find a girl good enough to bring back here?" Carson asks with hope in his eyes.

"Keep going after the locker room hunters and no, no, I don't,"

I answer while zipping up my backpack and throwing it over my shoulder.

Locker room hunters are the thirsty college girls, looking for an invitation to the locker room where they've heard the best orgasms are created. *That* is another far-fetched tale because there's no way in hell, Felix O'Hare was able to deliver any kind of mind-blowing orgasm to his girl. The man fumbled with his hands more than any person I've seen before. He was a walking disaster.

"They're just so tempting and willing," Carson complains.

"Which means they're not long-term. If you want a girl worthy of what you have to offer, she's going to make you work for it. Keep that in mind."

"He could not be more right," Holt agrees, pulling our attention. "You have to work for it."

Interesting. Gripping the straps to my backpack, I ask, "Is there someone who's making you work hard?"

"Is that why you've been MIA at the parties?"

He pushes his towel through his hair. "Yeah, there is. And I like her a lot."

"Whaaaaat?" Carson asks in an exaggerated tone. "When the hell did this happen?"

"Over the summer."

Carson clutches his chest and practically spews heart eyes across the locker room. "Fuck, summer love. How presh."

"Don't fucking say presh," I say to Carson, who chuckles to himself. "I'm headed out. Don't be late tonight, and don't forget to grab something to eat."

"Are you going there right now?"

"Yeah, scoping out some space. Grabbing a panini on the way up. See you guys there."

I take off with two things on my mind: a chicken BBQ panini with bacon and finding Emory so I can "accidentally" bump into her.

~

There she is, looking so fucking good in a navy wool-looking skirt, white long-sleeved top that clings to every single curve of her body, and little ankle boots. Her hair is straight and pulled back into a ponytail and hell . . . she's wearing tortoiseshell-rimmed glasses to round out the whole hot librarian look.

Emory Ealson, you're driving me damn crazy.

I have twenty minutes before the boys are supposed to show up, so just enough time to get a conversation in with her before I have to act like a captain again.

I walk up behind her casually and lean over her shoulder. "Know where I can find a book on the best donuts in the Chicago area?"

Startled, she leans back and looks up at me.

"Oh my God, why did you use a creepy voice when asking that?"

I shrug. "Seemed like a good idea at the time."

"It scared the crap out of me." She sets a book down on the counter and turns around so she's facing me, arms crossed over her chest.

"I know you want me to say sorry, but I'm not going to."

"How honest of you."

"If you can count on anything with me, it's honesty."

"I guess a noble trait." She props her hands behind her now and scans me up and down. "You smell fresh."

I chuckle. "Took a shower after practice. It's the kind thing to do."

"Are you a smelly sweater?"

My brow creases. "No . . . do you want me to be? Would it make me less irresistible?"

"Mmm . . . you're pretty resistible as is."

"Is that why you keep glancing at my pecs? Go ahead, I give you permission, you can touch them."

"I'm not," she says louder than intended and then lowers her voice. "I am not touching your pecs."

I look around and then nod. "Ah, gotcha, I get it. You don't want to make everyone jealous." I grab her hand and take her behind a stack of books, out of sight from prying eyes. "Okay, coast is clear, you can fondle the goods."

Before she can protest, I place her hand on one and let her feel how hard I work out in the gym. I expect her to remove her hand right away, but when she doesn't and instead gives it a squeeze, I can't help but laugh out loud through the quiet library, drawing a few heads in our direction. Caught red-handed.

Like I just burned her with my nips, she whips her hand away and scolds me. "What are you doing here? Besides forcing me to grope you."

"Hey, I wasn't the one who squeezed, you were."

"Involuntary reaction."

"Sure." I smirk and stick my hands in my pockets, closing in on her. "How's the internship?"

She backs up against the bookcase—non-fiction in case you were wondering—hands behind her back, eyes slightly wider than normal. "Uh, it's fine."

"Is everyone being nice to you? If not, give me names, and I'll have the boys take care of them."

"I . . . I believe so," she answers in a slight stutter, possibly from my proximity as I close in on her.

"If they weren't, you would tell me, right?"

"I don't see how any of that would be your business."

"Ooo, you wound me, Em." I fake being hurt, clutching my chest briefly. "Don't you see, I consider you my business."

"No need," she says, growing a little taller, her confidence coming back in spades. She pats my chest. "I can handle myself, thank you very much."

She starts to walk by me, but I stop her with my hand to her hip and speak close to her ear. "Why are you being difficult?"

"I didn't think I was."

"You barely talk to me in class, you sure as hell won't go out to lunch with me. Can't you see I'm interested?"

She takes that moment to look at me, her thick eyelashes blinking a few times. "If you were interested, then manhandling me in the library is not going to get you anywhere."

"What does it take then?"

"To what?"

I lower my voice. "To get you to pay some attention to me." Christ, I sound like a whiney asshole, but damn it . . . *look at me, Emory.*

Her face softens as she moves her hand to my cheek. "Oh, Knox, are you not getting enough attention?" Her voice is sarcastic, borderline patronizing and for some fucking reason, I like it.

"No."

She chuckles. "Sorry to disappoint you."

She goes to walk away again when I catch her by the wrist. "Let me take you out, on a date."

"I'm good but thank you for asking." *Thank you for asking. I'm begging, Em.* I take a deep breath as I look into her eyes. I honestly don't think she's trying to be a tease, but there has to be some way to reach her. For her to realize I'm serious. *The truth.* If I could get her to stop the sarcasm to just find the truth . . .

Still holding on to her wrist, I pull her farther back into the books where I press her against the wall and peer over my shoulder to make sure no one is looking. I bend so we are eye to eye, forcing her to not look away.

"Tell me you don't have any sort of attraction to me. Tell me that right now and I'll leave you alone."

"Knox." Her voice shakes as she glances over my shoulder. "If Mrs. Flower catches me back here with you she's going to flip her shit."

"Then answer the question . . . quickly. Tell me you're not attracted to me."

"That's stupid."

"Why, because you can't?"

"You know I can't," she sighs in frustration. "Of course, I find you attractive, I would be blind and a liar to say I didn't."

"Then go out with me."

"Doesn't work like that. Just because I think a donut looks delicious, doesn't mean I'm going to eat the whole thing."

"What?" My brow furrows.

She rolls her eyes. "Just because I find you attractive does not mean I should go out with you."

"Why the hell not? That seems like a perfectly good reason to go out with me."

"Because, we're on different playing fields, Knox. You like to party, and you have an extreme schedule, and you like to write notes during class—"

"That you like."

"That's beside the point. I'm here to learn, to get my degree, and then move on to my master's. Studying is important to me, and because school doesn't come easy, I really have to work twice as hard as the average student, and I'm not ashamed to say that. I think you're hot, yes, and you're funny and I could easily see myself getting wrapped up in your world, but I can't, because that would pull me away from my goals. I was deterred once by a guy, and I don't want it to happen again."

"It won't."

Her lips thin. "It will. I know me and I know you well enough to understand how addicting your personality is."

"And that's a bad thing?"

"For a girl who can't afford distractions, yeah."

"Who's to say I'll distract you? I have a busy schedule like you pointed out."

"Exactly." She flings her arms out but keeps her voice low. "You're going to be so busy I'll spend my much-needed studying time wondering when I'm going to see you again, when you're going to text me, if you're going to call me that night."

"I'd make you a priority."

She scoffs and lowers her head. "No one has ever made me a priority, and not to sound like a bitch, but I don't really believe you could actually do that. Not for me."

I can see it in her body language, the defeat. No matter what I say right now, she's going to counter it with a reason why things wouldn't work out with her. That fucker must have really damaged her to make her believe no one would make her a priority. I might have a busy schedule and obligations, but there's one thing I know with absolute certainty: when I'm invested in something, I don't ever drop the ball.

And I'm invested in Emory Ealson. From the moment her map slapped me in the face, I knew this girl was something special, and I plan on showing her that.

I take a step back and resign to our conversation's end, making a promise to show her how serious I am. "Believe what you want, Em, but I'm different."

She lifts her eyes up, curiosity lacing her gaze. "I know you are, Knox."

"Good, so remember that, because I'm going to show you how much I mean every word I say."

With a parting smile, I take off toward the tables where I find a few teammates already congregating. It's going to be tough as shit studying, knowing Emory is only a few feet away, but I need to make sure she doesn't know that. She needs to see I'm serious about my studies too, and not here for a free ride. Maybe, if she sees I can put effort and time into friends, my role as captain, my studies, and my sport, she'll see I am not singularly focused. She'll see that I want her in my life too, and there is an important place for her. Because that's what my heart is telling me. Winning Emory Ealson is a necessity, not a challenge. *She's worth it.*

CHAPTER ELEVEN

EMORY

My computer dings, lifting my eyes from the torturous textbook my eyes have been glazing over during the past hour. Why is Language and Literacy Methods so boring? I should care about this, and yet, I can't seem to focus to save my life.

I keep thinking about the conversation I had with Knox the other day in the library. And this is proof, right here in the flesh, why I need to stay away from this guy, because I can't focus. He's on my brain and that's not helpful.

When I focus on the chat box that opened on my computer, I can't help but sigh. Speak of the devil.

Knox: *What are you up to right now?*

Should I answer him?

I really shouldn't. I've written the same sentence over and over in my notebook for the past five minutes, unable to retain it. I need to study.

Then again, maybe if I feed the unfocused monster in my head a little of Knox, it will settle down and return to getting the job done.

I chew on my pen, thinking of my choices.

This boy is dangerous. I feel it whenever I'm around him or whenever I see his name pop up on my screen. He could easily insinuate himself into my life—be all-consuming, despite what he said—and that's *not* what I want.

But maybe he doesn't want that.

Maybe he wants things to be light and fun.

I mean . . . I could do light and fun, right?

Chew, gnaw, chew.

I'm not sure if I'm a casual dater, BUT . . . it wouldn't necessarily kill me to see what he wants right now. *I think.*

I set my pen on my desk and reach for my keyboard. A little harmless break, that's all this is.

Emory: *Studying. At least attempting to. You?*

He types back immediately and if Dottie and Lindsay were in my room right now, I would have to hide my cheesy smile from them.

Knox: *About to leave the library. Just finished a paper. Are you in your dorm?*

Emory: *Yeah.*

Knox: *Meet me in the dining hall for some ice cream? I won't take up much of your time. I just need something sweet.*

I scan my outfit of holey sweats and tight-fitting long-sleeved T-shirt. No makeup, hair in a side braid hanging over my shoulder. Not my best day, not my worst. But it's not like I have to impress him. It's ice cream.

Emory: *As long as you don't mind hanging out with a girl who wears old, holey sweatpants.*

Knox: *It's my preferred attire. I'm headed there now, once I shut my computer. Meet me in five.*

Before I can stop myself, I type back.

Emory: *See you there.*

I exit out of the chat box and squeeze my eyes shut for a second, taking a deep breath. This will be fine, everything is fine. Casual, that's all this is. Super casual.

I can do casual.

I stand from my chair and look in the mirror, taking in my red holey sweats that hang off my narrow hips.

I was born to do casual.

I lean toward the mirror and smile; nothing in my teeth, that's a good thing.

I can be the master at casual.

I can teach a class in casual, that's how freaking casual I am.

I grab my keycard and head out my door past Lindsay and Dottie, who are playing MarioKart in the common area.

"Done studying?" Dottie asks, eyes trained on the TV just as she blows up Lindsay with a bomb.

"You rotten bitch," Lindsay seethes. "You just can't stand it when I'm first, can you?"

"Heading out," I call to them, not wanting to stick around for the trash talk. "I'll be back in a little."

"Heads-up, Dad's sending over Greek tonight," Dottie calls out before I shut the door to our dorm.

Greek sounds amazing, so I'll be sure to get a small ice cream. As I make my way down the dorm stairs—we have an elevator but I'm on the third floor so it's not a big deal to take the stairs—I think about how grateful I am to have Lindsay and Dottie back in my life. Yes, they may push me at times, but it's out of love. As I look back and consider how isolated I became because of Neil, I'm horrified. It was as though he had . . . emotionally imprisoned me. Thank God my girls never gave up on me.

In my sandals, sweats pushed up to just below my knees, I look like every other college student making their way to the dining hall straight from their dorms. It's why I don't feel too out of place meeting Knox in this garb, then again, I've seen him almost every Monday in sweats, so I don't think he's going to care.

Below the dining hall, there's a small convenience store that also doubles as an ice cream and smoothie place. I'm assuming this is where Knox meant when he said ice cream, and I guessed right because when I walk through the doors, he's standing there in a pair of black form-fitting sweatpants, an Under Armour long-sleeved T-shirt that clings to his impressive chest, and his baseball hat on backward. He wears athletic apparel well . . . very well.

When his gaze pulls away from his phone and meets mine, a bright smile stretches across his face. "Hey, Em." He walks up and pulls me into a hug. Caught a little off guard, I don't return it right away, but when he squeezes me tighter, I wrap my arms around him, letting my hand land on his muscular back.

Oh my. There's a whole bunch of hard back there. Neil's back NEVER felt like that.

"Thanks for meeting up with me." He pulls away and drags a hand over his face. "I spent the last four hours in the library trying to get this paper done and I'm toasted. Ice cream is the only cure."

"Are you a big sweets person?" I ask as we walk up to the counter.

"Guilty." He winks and then looks over the counter and into the cooler. "Can I get cookies and cream in a waffle cone?"

"Sure thing," the employee says.

"What do you want?" Knox asks, eyeing me.

"I'll take the strawberry cheesecake in a cake cone."

"Good choice," Knox says, reaching for his key card to pay.

Before he can scan it, I block him and say, "I can pay for this one."

"Nah, my idea, I'm paying." He scans his card, takes the ice cream for both of us, and heads over to a small table off to the side. When we take a seat, he hands me my cone, but not before taking a bite out of it.

When my mouth falls open in shock, he chuckles and says, "Just a friendly tax."

I point at his cone. "I want a bite."

"What? No way." He shields his cone away from me.

"Knox Gentry, it's only fair."

"You're going to take a giant bite. I need this ice cream more than you."

I wiggle my finger at him. "Bring it over here. It's only fair."

He studies me. "How about this, a bite for your phone number."

"Ha, nice try." I shake my head and lean back. "I'm not that desperate for a taste, which can I say, it didn't slip past me that you got cookies and cream. Are you obsessed with everything Oreos?"

"If you didn't order the donuts from Frankie's, I would have gotten the Oreo-encrusted donut." He takes a lick of his ice cream. "I'm an Oreo lover and will eat them with pretty much everything. You know how some people are obsessed with peanut butter and will even eat it on their burgers? That's my loyalty with Oreos."

"That's kind of . . ."

"Freaky?"

I chuckle and shake my head. "No, I was going to say cute."

His brows raise. "Yeah, well then, should I tell you I made an Oreo-encrusted steak the other night?"

I motion my hand to tamp him down. "Baby steps, Knox, don't show me all your freak tendencies just yet."

He holds his arms out wide. "I'm an open book to you, Em, and what you see is what you get."

"Should I be scared?"

He leans forward. "Maybe a little." His smile pretty much destroys any defenses I tried to wear on the way down here. He's entirely too charming and sweet, then again, so was Neil. It's the charismatic personalities I need to be cautious around. "I like your sweats by the way, super sexy."

"It's the holes, right? Sexy in a way you never thought possible."

"They're tempting for sure."

I cross my legs and say, "I've had them since middle school. I can't seem to ditch them no matter how many holes they have in them. It seems after each laundry cycle, they become more and more comfortable. They're like a safety blanket at this point."

"Don't ever get rid of them." He takes a bite out of his ice cream and leans back in his chair, observing me. "I like this side of you."

"What side is that?"

"Casual, not all dressed up. Don't get me wrong, your skirts have a good hold on my balls, but I like the comfy side of you. Makes me want to take you up to your dorm and cuddle you."

"Is that supposed to be a pickup line?"

"No." He pauses. "But if it was, did it work?" He wiggles his eyebrows.

"No," I lie because the thought of taking Knox back to my dorm to cuddle sounds incredibly appealing.

He's a large guy, broad shoulders with thick muscles wrapped around them, tall, must be at least six two, which is a good height for his sport, and his arms look like cannons, ripped and carved unlike anything I've ever seen. I can't imagine he looked like this in high school, but a few years under Coach Disik's tutelage and the once boy is a lean and powerful machine.

The way he shifts and the tightness of his shirt, I catch glimpses of the six-pack that's beneath the neoprene fabric of his shirt. And I shouldn't forget to mention the slight bulge I always see when he's wearing sweatpants. He's big. His hands, his legs, his shoulders, wide and broad, and if he wasn't so nice, I'd be intimidated by his sharp features and mesmerizing eyes that always hide under the bill of a hat.

"Have you always been a ball-buster, Em?"

"Not always," I answer honestly. "Took me a while to find enough courage to show my true self around guys."

"Really? Were you demure and quiet?"

"Pretty much." I take a big lick of my ice cream. "I was shy growing up, but it wasn't until college I actually let my true colors show. I think it was one of the things my ex started to really dislike about me. Probably what drove him away. He hated my jokes, my teasing, my outspokenness around his friends." I twist my lips to the side. "Now that I think about it, he would always reprimand me after, telling me not to talk to his friends like that."

"Sounds like your ex was a real dick."

"He wasn't at first. He kind of swept me off my feet in high school. Very charming, friends with everyone, took me under his wing and challenged me to break out of my shell." I glance up. "Kind of like you."

His brows draw together, and I can tell he didn't like that comment at all, but I think it's fair for him to know where my apprehension is.

"I'm not like him, Em."

"You don't know him."

He sits taller in his chair. "And you don't know me well enough to make that assumption."

"I don't." I hang my head, feeling a little guilty.

"Then get to know me." He leans over and lifts my chin. "Like I said, I'm an open book, Em."

Instead of anger, all I see is kindness, understanding, and if that's not my undoing, it's the smile that trails after.

Whispering, he continues, "Ask me anything."

I bite my bottom lip, trying to figure out what I should ask. What do I want to know?

"Don't be shy," he adds, casually draping his arm over the back of his chair. "I'll answer anything."

Honesty. If there is one trait I see in Knox, it's honesty. He knows how attractive he is, that eyes follow him when he enters any room. Yet he doesn't look for that attention. He's not exactly humble, but he is . . . unassuming. When Neil walked into a room, it was with attention-seeking noise. As if everyone in the room was much better because of his presence. *Asshole.* As much as I hate comparing the two, Neil had been the man in my life for too long not to. *Until he wasn't.*

And now there's Knox, a naturally charismatic, driven male, who's made more effort for *me* to notice *him*. So perhaps . . .

"Okay," I say. "Why are you so interested in me?"

"Because anyone who slaps me with a campus map in the face is someone I want to get to know."

"And here I thought you would say anyone who has a boob that can make me pass out is someone I want to get to know."

He chuckles. "The heaviness of said tit was just too over-whelming, and I had no choice but to take a nap mid lift."

"They're not that heavy."

"I can't remember. Here, let me reacquaint myself." He reaches his hand out, but I playfully slap it away.

"You're ridiculous."

"In a good way." He pops the rest of his ice cream in his mouth and wipes his hands with a napkin while I finish my ice cream as well.

"Be serious, why are you interested in me?"

He shifts in his seat, striking a very relaxed pose. "Fishing for compliments, Ealson?"

"No, just wondering why you're after me when you could have any girl on campus."

"Is it too far-fetched to say that you interest me? Do I need a specific reason drummed up in a romantic fashion, written on cream paper in calligraphy and in the form of poetry?"

"No, smart-ass." I laugh. "But I don't consider myself particu-larly special."

"And that's where you're wrong. You're all kinds of special, and I intend on showing you that."

"You really think you can win me over?"

He drums his knuckles on the metal table between us. "I *know* I can win you over. It's just a matter of time."

I cross my arms over my chest. "We'll see about that."

"Is that a challenge, Ealson?"

"It very well might be," I counter.

He reaches across the table, extending his hand out for me to take. "Then challenge accepted."

Because I like to give in to his antics, I take his hand in mine and shake on it, knowing his satisfied, gorgeous smile is what I'll remember as I fall asleep tonight.

CHAPTER TWELVE

EMORY

I challenged Knox on Thursday night, or did he challenge me? I don't know, but there was a challenge set and now it's Monday. I haven't heard a word from him.

Not even a peep.

There was no party at the loft, which meant the girls and I took a trip north, stayed at a bed and breakfast, courtesy of Dottie's dad, and studied in the sanctuary of the woods. It was wonderfully refreshing and energizing, but when I returned late Sunday night and still didn't hear anything from Knox, I shrugged my shoulders, attempting to ignore my sense of disappointment. Another man who is all talk. I was surprised, especially as I considered his sincerity in his words. *"I'm not like him, Em . . . you don't know me well enough to make that assumption."*

Oh well, it's nothing I should be wasting time thinking about.

Morning coffee in hand, I make my way to class, keeping a watchful eye out for Knox, but I don't run into him before class, nor do I see him or the boys when I enter our lecture room.

And just like that, worry sets in. Did they go out of town and I didn't know? Should I check their fall schedule?

Did the loft burn down? Is that why there wasn't a party? I mean if there was a fire, I feel like that would have been in the news.

Am I overreacting?

Feeling a little uneasy, I take a seat in the row we usually all sit in and nervously remove my laptop and set my backpack by my feet. Now I kind of wish I'd asked Knox for his number. A friendly text of *do you want me to save you a seat?* would have been nice right about now.

Even though I don't need to use it since I type notes, I take out a pen from my backpack and start tapping the desk with it. *Stop fidgeting, Ealson.*

Five minutes until class starts, they never push it this close, especially since Knox likes to have little chats before class starts, and then he continues those chats on his computer next to me.

I glance around the room, and that's when I notice everyone is sitting at the very front of the class, the first two rows. I sit up in my seat. Am I missing something?

No one is talking, and you could hear a pin drop it's so quiet, and everyone is facing the front of the room, heads straight forward, motionless.

What the hell is—

My Girl starts playing through a phone speaker out of nowhere right before the door to the lecture room bursts open at the top, startling the crap out of me. I glance to the side to find Holt and Carson smoothly dancing down the stairs wearing their matching sweatshirts and holding coffee and boxes of donuts.

What in the world?

Trailing behind them, Knox, decked out in jeans, a button-up and tie, with his signature backward hat follows closely behind, holding a bouquet of . . . are those campus maps cut into flowers?

Oh.

My.

God.

Holt walks to the row below mine as Carson walks down the row behind me, singing loudly while the class turns around and unfolds a banner, just as Knox makes his way toward me a huge smile on his face as he belts out the song. When the chorus rings through the room, the class breaks out in song and flips up a huge banner that says, "Say yes."

Say yes to what?

Oh good Lord.

I think he's taken this challenge a little too seriously.

Knox slides to his knees in front of me and the music dies out as he holds up the makeshift bouquet to me, that handsome smile caressing his face. I push my hand over my eyes briefly, my cheeks flaming, and my nerves causing my body to shake.

Everyone is quiet as Knox speaks up. "Emory Edith Ealson." I cringe, that is not my middle name. "Will you do me the great honor"—he pretends to wipe a tear from under his eye—"of being my seat mate for the rest of the semester?"

The class collectively "awws" and awaits my answer.

One girl shouts, "Say yes."

While a guy bellows, "You're the man, Gentry."

Of course, he got the whole class involved, this is Knox Gentry.

This is so ridiculous and unnecessary, but I get caught up in the whirlwind and nod like an idiot.

Standing, chest proudly puffed, Knox raises his fist to the air and screams, "She said yes."

The class cheers. Holt and Carson start handing out coffee and donuts in celebration just as our professor walks through the door, caught off guard by the raucous behavior of the class.

"Settle down," he shouts, causing everyone to take their seats, including Knox, who sits right next to me and drapes his arm over the back of my chair.

He casually reaches up and starts twirling a strand of my hair around his finger. It's intimate, something Neil never did, and I like it. Maybe a little too much.

Class gets underway and Holt hands Knox his computer. He opens it with one hand and starts typing out a note for me.

Thank you for saying yes. That would have been embarrassing as shit if you said no.

I snort and cover my mouth, imagining Knox's face if I had said no. I never could have done that. I like to joke around with him, but that would have been mean, especially since he went through a lot this morning to put on a show.

I type him back a response.

That was a little extravagant, don't you think?

From the corner of my eye, I catch a smile pulling at his lips. He types back.

Nothing is too extravagant for you, babe. This is only the beginning.

Oh God, why does that worry and excite me all at the same time?

~

"Can you put all those books away?" Mrs. Flower asks. "I'm going to my office so if you need anything, figure it out because I don't want to be bothered."

"Sure." I smile even though the lady I'm interning with seems to have a giant embedded, spikey stick up her ass. I don't think she knows what the term "being pleasant" means.

Her frail, praying mantis-like body travels down a dark hallway to her office where she shuts the door, closing her off from the rest of the library, and that's when I relax. I like it best when she's in her office, not hovering over me, watching everything I'm doing, and honestly, all she does is make me fumble my job responsibilities rather than help me learn.

I stack the returned books onto a cart and start to push toward the autobiographies when the library doors burst open and a group of men file into the library, jogging, looking sweaty and spent.

The baseball team.

At the front of the pact, Knox comes into view. They're all wearing their practice uniforms, their baseball hats, and running shoes.

"Emory Ealson," Knox whisper-shouts. "Front and center, Emory Ealson." His voice gets louder, sending a shrill chill up my spine.

My legs move faster than my brain can communicate, and I'm standing in front of him, shushing him before he can make a scene, if that's possible. The baseball team came flooding through the doors of the library, like a stampede with one thing on their minds, finding me. Pretty sure no one has their heads buried in their books right now. Instead, they're taking in the show that is Knox Gentry.

"Knox, what the hell are you doing?"

Hands on his hips, catching his breath, he says, "We're conditioning. We have five minutes to get back to the baseball field or we have to do the entire loop all over again." He takes another breath and Holt grips his shoulder, encouraging him. "I told the boys I was feeling weak, incapable of finishing our lap around campus unless I got a hug from you."

He's got to be kidding me right now.

"Knox," I scold. "This is not the time nor—"

"Shit, guys, hold me up," he says as he dramatically falls to the side, Holt and Carson falling under his arms, give him support. Dramatically. "I'm so weak." His voice rises again.

"Just hug him, Ealson," one of his players shouts from behind. "We have four minutes and forty-five seconds."

"I can't move. I'm immobile. Just leave me here," Knox says. Dramatically. Again. *Good God.*

"Never leave a man behind," Carson says, holding on to his friend.

A larger guy who's jogging in place, pleas with me. "I'll never make it back if we get under four minutes. Please just hug the man."

"Hug him, hug him, hug him," his team starts to whisper-chant, the library joining in, and that's when I fling my arms around Knox. The minute my arms wrap around him, he stands tall and reciprocates the hug, telling his team to fall out and sprint back to the field.

He stays a few seconds longer, keeping a strong hold around my body, and then he bends down to my ear where he whispers, "You look so fucking good in that yellow skirt by the way." He pulls away, tips his hat and winks before taking off, out of the library where his long strides quickly catch him up with his retreating team.

I am going to kill him . . . after I stop swooning for one second.

~

Knock, knock.

K nock, knock.
I lift my head from my book and turn to see Dottie standing at the threshold of my open door. We're all hovering over our books right now, at least I thought we were until Dottie showed up. We sprint study every night, setting a timer, and then we go out to dinner.

The timer hasn't gone off, so what the hell is Dottie doing?

"Did I not hear the timer?"

She wrings her hands in front of her, looking almost nervous.

"So, I might have broken our sprint studying protocol."

I remove my glasses and sit up straighter. "Were you on your computer?"

"Maybe."

"Dottie, you know the rules."

"I know, I know," she sighs. "But a student chat popped up and I couldn't help it."

"Okay, well thank you for confessing, but let's get back to work." I turn to my book.

"It was Knox."

Okay, maybe I need to take a step away from my book for a second.

"Knox messaged you? What did he say?"

"Well, at first he wanted to make sure this was the Dottie that rooms with Emory and he even quizzed me, making sure it was me."

"Really?" I can't hide my smile. "What did he ask you?"

"What you dressed up as for the jungle-themed party. What skirt you wore on Thursday, which I had no freaking clue. Apparently it was yellow." My smile grows. "He also asked what kind of ice cream you like, where you transferred from, and who our third roommate was. It's fascinating how much he knows about you."

"He's asked a few questions since I've known him."

"Yeah, well the boy has it bad."

"Why do you say that?"

"Because, he's on his way up here with food."

"What?" I jump from my chair, glancing at myself in the mirror just as there is a knock at the door. "Dottie!"

She cringes. "I'm sorry."

What I failed to mention is during these sprint sessions, we also do self-care. Currently, I'm wearing a green mask that's as hard as stone on my face, my hair is propped up in large rollers, toes separated and drying with a pretty purple nail polish, and I'm wearing a red terrycloth romper that does nothing special for my body but shape my rear end into the perfect mom butt.

From down the hall, we hear the door click open.

Shit.

Both of our eyes connect.

Lindsay.

I want to shout NOOO in slow motion, hurl my body down the hall and lock the door, but it's too late, as Lindsay's voice travels down the hallway along with a very familiar masculine one.

"What a surprise, Knox. Was Emory expecting you?"

No, no, she wasn't.

Eyes wide, I run to my door, slam it right in front of Dottie, and run around my room, trying to figure out what to do. He can't see me like this. Holey sweatpants are one thing, but avocado face and roller head is an entirely different image that should only be shared after marriage, when there is no escaping. From the back of my door, I snag my towel and start scraping my face with the dry fabric while simultaneously pulling out my rollers and dancing around my room to remove the toe separators.

"She's in here." I pause, eyes locked on the door, body still.

Holy shit.

I scrub even faster as my fingers get tangled in my hair. I step on my foot wrong while trying to remove the toe separators and lose my balance. I skid across the floor, one leg flying up just in time for Lindsay to open my door to Knox, who catches me flying, and then I fall straight on my ass.

There I am, lying on the floor, legs spread as an open invitation for God knows what reason—clearly not a graceful faller—hand tangled in the rat's nest that is now my hair, and half my face scraped off from the lack of water used while trying to get rid of my mask.

In a word. Disaster.

I've had my fair share of embarrassing moments before, but I would have to say, this is a low point for me.

The only thing that would make this worse was if I farted as I fell.

Thank God for small miracles.

From the doorway, three heads stare down at me, two of which I'm going to murder once the third leaves. Unlike me, Lindsay and Dottie don't have curlers in their hair or masks on their faces. Instead, they look like perfectly normal college girls, completely opposite to the beast they're staring at.

"Hey, Em," Knox says, so casually, as if I'm not a rabid gargoyle snarling on the floor. He walks into my room, gives it a courtesy perusal, and then lends his hand to help me up.

I'm tempted to army crawl away from the scene and slither under my bed with my towel tucked close to my side as my only remaining friend, but I think otherwise and take Knox's hand in mine, the one that isn't stuck in my hair.

He sets a box to the side and reaches up to my hair where he carefully frees my hand. He then bends down and picks up my towel and smiles when he brings it to my face. I stand there, perplexed and embarrassed that he's seeing me like this.

"You have something on your face." He wraps the towel around his index finger and then lightly makes one small swipe across my nose. "There, perfect."

I glance in the mirror and come face to face with a patchy green monster.

Oh my God.

Attempting to take a step back, he grips me by the waist and studies me, both Lindsay and Dottie still hanging out by my door. "You look mortified," he says, observation and surprise in his voice.

That would be correct. He's a smart one.

"That's because I am. Don't look at me. Close your eyes." I try to cover his face with my hand but he's too quick and too strong.

"No way in hell." He looks down my bodice and then back up. "I like this little number. I think my grandma wore something like it back in her day."

"Oh my God, things not to say to a girl."

He chuckles. "And the hair, it's different but it's doing all kind of things for me."

"Stahp," I groan, trying to push him away. His grip on me only grows tighter. "You realize this is the last time you're ever going to see me, right? There is no coming back from this."

"The hell it is." He glances down at his watch and grimaces. "I'd happily stay here and enjoy this visual feast, but I have to get to late-night weights." Letting go of me, he grabs the box he carried in and hands it to me. "Cookies . . . for my cookie."

Dottie and Lindsay both snort as my face flushes once again.

"I am not your . . . cookie," I say, the word so vile coming off my tongue.

He laughs some more and pats the top of the box. "These are the best in Brentwood. I'm sure your girls can vouch for me. Fresh from the oven, just for you. Go ahead, lift the lid, you know you want to."

I really do, they smell so good.

Giving in, I lift the lid and find one dozen of the thickest, most delicious-smelling cookies I've ever seen in my life.

Holy crap.

Cookies for his cookie indeed.

"Are those from Mr. Tom's?"

"The only place to get cookies in town," Knox answers Dottie, whose nose is sniffing the air. "And if Em's a good friend, she'll share with you two."

"I'm not." I slam the lid and place the box on my desk, eyeing my friends at the door with daggers. They could have avoided this entire embarrassment by remembering what I look like during power hour. But noooo, they had to let Knox in without even giving me a second to at least change out of my apparent grandma garb.

"I'll leave you guys to settle this." He takes a step forward and reaches for me, pulling me into a hug before I can retreat to the other side of the room. "I'll talk to you later, okay?" He kisses the top of my head and then once again lowers his mouth to my ear where he whispers, "Remember this, Em. I'll take you any way I can have you."

With those parting words, he gives Lindsay and Dottie a curt wave and then takes off. I stand there, slightly breathless, and tingly from head to toe.

He'll take me anyway he can have me. Well, boy oh boy, did he get a special part of me today.

"That seemed like it went well." Dottie smiles.

I point my finger and yell, "Out, both of you."

"But he liked your outfit." Lindsay chuckles, scooting backward as I reach for the door to slam it.

"You're both dead to me."

"But . . . don't you want to share those cookies with us?" Dottie asks.

"No." I slam the door and flop on my bed where I can no longer hold back the smile that cracks the corner of my lips.

~

K *nox: Party tomorrow night, are you coming?*

I pause my movie on my computer and open the preview message from Knox's student chat. Over the past two weeks, Knox has made it known how much he's interested in me. It hasn't been every day, or even every other day, but he keeps surprising me with gestures here and there. It's sweet, and he's slowly breaking down my wall, but not completely. Even though he knows the answer, every Monday after our class, he asks me to go to lunch, and I always tell him I can't.

But with every no, his smile gets bigger. I know he can see right through me and can see the yes on my lips. He's smart enough to know what he's doing to me. He's smart enough to feel the way I linger a little longer with each hug he gives me, or the way I lean into him more when he throws his arm around my shoulder. He sees the smiles I try to hide, the small touches I try to hold back, the way I dress up for him on Mondays, making sure I look my absolute best. He's observant, and even though I'm still trying to keep him at an arm's length, he is so close to breaking down the rickety barrier I've erected between the two of us.

I type him back.

Emory: *I don't think so.*

Knox: *Why not? Scared of the theme?*

Emory: *What's the theme?*

Knox: *Topless.*

Emory: *Are you serious?*

Knox: *No. LOL. There's no theme, just a beer pong tournament. I could use a partner.*

Emory: *Then you're going to want to ask someone with skill. I can barely toss straight.*

Knox: *I'll carry you on my back, Em. I'm a champion.*

Emory: I think I'll pass.

Knox: Then just come over to hang out. We can watch a movie in my room.

Emory: While a raging party is happening just outside the door? Won't that be weird?

Knox: Nah, I've hung out in my room during a party before, and it's not as loud as you think.

Emory: No, you have fun. I'm going to hang out here, get some work done.

Knox: Please.

Emory: Are you batting your eyelashes while typing that?

Knox: Yes, did it work?

Emory: I don't know.

Knox: Envision this, you, me, on my bed—clothed of course, I'm a gentleman, after all—the latest trending movie on Netflix and a calzone to split from The Hot Spot. My arm draped around you, you curled into my chest, sodas, a sleeve of Oreos . . . how can you resist that?

Emory: It's very tempting.

Knox: Then say yes.

Emory: How about an "I'll think about it?"

Knox: I'm going to take that as a yes. Shit, got to go. Text me when you get to the loft (512-555-3452) and I'll get you in the back way, avoiding all the partiers. I'll see you tomorrow.

He signs out, the little green online dot goes grey. Wow, that was quick.

Calzones?

Oreos?

Snuggling with Knox Gentry? It does sound like a dream.

One I don't think I can avoid much longer.

CHAPTER THIRTEEN

KNOX

I pound the inside of my glove, step up into position just as Coach knocks a ball in my general direction. I cut to the right, backhand the ball, jump into the air, and throw the ball across my body to the first basemen.

Executed perfectly.

I get behind the line and give Carson a high five as we continue to run through drills.

A freshman is up next, Ned Farkle—his parents didn't expect him to become a major league baseball player with that name, that's for sure. He's damn good though, and Coach hits him a screaming grounder that he fields with no problem, but then takes at least five steps toward first before throwing across the diamond.

Quick release; it's what Coach Disik lives by. Traveling across the field takes up too much time and it's not the fundamental baseball Disik teaches. I know this because it was a habit he beat out of me. Dropping the bat, Disik jogs out to Farkle and gets in his face, talking about needing a quick release. I take that moment to fade in the back with Carson who quietly turns to me and says, "Everything set for tonight?"

"For the party?" I mutter quietly from the side of my mouth.

"Yeah."

"No idea, Holt was in charge. Emory is coming over and we're going to do our own thing."

"Really?" Carson looks surprised. If I wasn't so damn confused over this girl, I would be insulted, but I'm just as surprised as he is.

"Yeah. She didn't seem up to party so I offered to hang out in my room."

"Hell, that's better anyway since you barely get any time with her."

Tell me about it. With my schedule, I haven't really had a chance to get to know Emory like I want or give her as much time as I promised, but I'm making it work; little glimpses here and there are better than nothing.

We're on the tail end of fall ball, which means we're going to be getting heavily into strength and conditioning as well as technical and individual training. We have a pretty good squad of newcomers who need fine tweaking—hence Farkle and his prancing across the diamond—which is something we always take care of in the late months of the semester. What does this all mean? I'll have more time to make Emory mine.

"Tell me about it. I pop in and out of her life, but I don't think I've been able to do anything long-lasting yet."

"Get low and then pop up," Disik yells, showing just how agile the old fart is by showcasing what he's talking about.

"She likes you though," Carson says, nudging my leg with his glove. "You can see it in class. She does not stop smiling around you."

"Yeah, I know the attraction is there, just need to seal the deal."

"And you like her, right? This isn't a conquest for you?"

"Yes, like that," Disik cheers. "Again, but this time with a ball." He jogs back toward the bat and hits another screaming grounder to Farkle, who scoops it up and takes two steps rather than five.

Better, but not what was asked of him. Not happy, Disik yells, "Again. Do it right or the whole team does pushups."

"Focus, Farkle," one teammate mutters.

"You know I'm not a douche," I say to Carson, just as another grounder is hit to Farkle. "I like her, and by no means is she a conquest."

Farkle scoops the ball up and sweeps across the field. One, two, three steps.

Jesus Christ.

Looks like I'm going to be taking this guy to the side and working on his release.

"Thirty pushups, everyone," Disik yells while flipping the bat and walking up to Farkle, hovering over him as he counts out every single pushup.

A few "Fuck you, Farkles" are said while grunting out pushups.

Once we're done, we pick up our gloves, and Coach lets out another warning to the freshman to do it right or we're spending the rest of practice conditioning.

"She's a good girl, Gent," Carson says while we intently watch Farkle get into position. "I wouldn't want to see her get hurt."

"When have I ever hurt a girl?" I ask. *What the hell?*

"When have you ever been this willing to be with someone, rather than just fucking around? I've never seen you serious about a girl."

"Which means I won't fuck this up."

Farkle scoops the ball up, takes one step, then shoots the ball across the field.

Thank God.

"Was that too much to ask?" Disik yells. "Jesus Christ, get in the back of the line."

"Or, you care too much that you will fuck it up."

"What the hell is your problem?" I ask Carson.

"Nothing, just be careful, man." He steps up into position and just as the ball is hit, he dives to the left, catches the ball, hops to his feet, and throws the ball over to first in one smooth motion.

He's the best second baseman in the country. He has the stats to prove it and mechanics to make any coach drool, even Disik, who nods his head in approval.

Even though I'm good at blocking out unnecessary shit when on the field, it's hard not to think about what Carson said as I'm getting into position.

I'm not going to screw this up. I might not have ever really cared this much, but that means I'm going to work harder when it comes to Emory. *Because she's worth that.*

Disik grounds a ball out to me and it bounces high, hitting me in the chest. Not even flinching, I grab the ball with my right hand and throw it to first. It wasn't clean, but it was effective.

"Good recovery," Diski yells, but I drown it out when I walk up next to Carson.

Muttering under my breath, I say, "I'm not going to fuck it up."

"I sure hope not, because she's perfect for you."

I couldn't agree more.

I check my phone for the hundredth time of the night and when it reads blank, I subtly pound the back of my head against the wall.

What the fuck?

I left a message on student chat for Emory, letting her know to get here around eight, and it's now nine thirty and there's no sign of her. Trust me, I've been scanning the party every five minutes, making circles like I'm herding cattle, looking for one girl and one girl alone.

Is she really not going to fucking show?

I know she said she would think about it, but hell, we've been playing this little cat and mouse game for a while now, so I thought that was her coy way of saying she'd spend the night with me rather than actually saying it.

Boy, was I fucking wrong.

I drag my hand through my styled hair—yeah, I fucking styled it—and scan the room once more as Carson comes up to my side and holds a beer out to me. I have yet to take a drink of anything tonight in the hopes I would be spending my evening with Emory.

"Dude, I hate to say it but I don't think she's coming."

I take the beer from him but hold the bottle at my side, not in the mood to drink. Give me five minutes when the bitterness of the night starts to kick in.

"I think I might punch someone," I say, clenching my fist at my side, my anger starting to boil over. "Fuck, I don't understand. I've done everything right. I get that her boyfriend was a dick and I sort of remind her of him, but fuck, I'm a goddamn different person. She should at least give me a chance to show that."

"Yeah, I don't know what to say, man," Carson replies while pulling a sip from his bottle. "Hey, aren't those her friends?"

"What?" My head snaps to where Carson is pointing. Sure enough, Lindsay and Dottie are gathered by the beer pong table, laughing and having a jolly fucking time.

Does that mean Emory's here?

I whip my phone out again, but there's nothing.

"Is she here? Did I miss her?"

"Nah, Brock would have told me. He's manning the door. I told him to text me when she got here so I could let you know. He said he hasn't seen her."

"Motherfucker." I grind down on my teeth. "What the hell. So her friends came but she didn't? Hell . . . now I'm pissed." I start to walk toward my room to give Emory a piece of my mind when Carson grabs my shoulder, stopping me in place.

"This was what I was talking about at practice. Take a deep breath and try to think about this rationally. Maybe there's a reason she's not here."

"Other than her stringing me along? I'm a fucking moron."

"Dude, seriously, calm down."

"Don't tell me to calm down." I shrug my shoulder away. "She should have at least said she wasn't coming." I pull on my hair and look over at her friends. "I'm going to get answers."

"Don't do it, Knox."

But it's too late. I'm already headed in their direction, anger simmering at the base of my skull, tensing my shoulders and clenching my jaw.

"Ladies," I say in greeting. They both turn around and when they make eye contact with me, both of their mouths fall open and they cringe at the same time. That's a weird reaction.

I go to ask where Emory is when Dottie presses her hand against my forearm. "Holy shit, we completely forgot to tell you. Oh my God, Emory is going to kill us, you can't tell her."

"Tell her what?" I ask, my emotions rocketing from pure anger to concerned curiosity.

"She wanted us to send you a message when we got here. She has a migraine and couldn't make it."

And concern turns to anger again.

Lame fucking excuse.

"That's the best she could do? A migraine? She could have at least faked breaking her leg or something. Given me an excuse a little more memorable."

They exchange glances and then Lindsay says, "No, she really has a migraine. She gets chronic migraines. They take her out. Ever since middle school. She can't move and or open her eyes. She lies in darkness, waiting for it to subside."

"Sure." I roll my eyes. "Tell her I hope she gets better."

I go to walk away when a hand pulls on me. I turn to find Dottie pleading with me. "We're not lying, Knox." She holds a keycard out to me. "Go see for yourself. She's in complete darkness right now."

I eye the keycard. "How do I know you won't text her the minute I leave?"

They both reach into their pockets and hand me their phones. "Knox, please don't give up on her. Her stupid-ass boyfriend was an absolute bastard, and he hurt her, so yeah, she's guarded. We lost her for a few years, and would tell you to fuck off if we didn't think you were good for her," Lindsay says. "Take our phones, give them to one of your teammates, and when you see we're not lying, you can text him to give them back. She's really sick right now."

"Threw up twice already," Dottie adds. "Something I'm sure she doesn't want you to know. It was so bad she couldn't have any lights on, so she asked us to tell you she couldn't make it. We got a little distracted and that's on us, we're so sorry, but please don't be mad at her. She wanted to be here. She even picked out a cute skirt to wear. She was coming, Knox, she really was."

Shit.

I think they're telling the truth.

I drag my hand through my hair again and check the time on my watch. "How long has she been alone?"

"An hour at least. We got here a little late."

"Shit. Okay." I take the keycard and pocket it. "Suite three ten, right?"

"Yes." When I go to walk away, Dottie says, "Don't you want our phones?"

I shake my head. "No, I trust you."

I take off toward my room, stuff a bunch of shit in my backpack, zip it up, and pocket my car keys. Looks like I'm spending my night in the dorms, something I haven't done since I was a freshman, but the choice to be next to Emory, especially when she needs someone in her corner? No-brainer.

CHAPTER FOURTEEN

EMORY

Deep breaths.

Just like that.

With a face mask over my eyes, I roll to the side and let out a long breath, trying not to get nauseous from the movement. But my hip is hurting from being on my left for so long that I need to rotate, slowly.

Every month, like clockwork, I get migraines that seem to cut me off at the knees. I was getting ready to see Knox when the nausea hit. A few minutes later, the pain behind my eyes struck, followed quickly by severe sinus pain. *Shit.* I knew at that moment I wasn't going anywhere but horizontal. Once a migraine hits, there's nothing I can do but let my body rest. I tried drinking water, threw some Ibuprofen at it, even some Icy Hot on my neck and shoulders, although nothing made a dent. The migraine hit me head-on—no pun intended—and I was out. Completely immobilized.

After throwing up twice, I was able to make it to my bed and turn off the lights with the help of Lindsay and Dottie. They set me up with a dark room, a trash bin next to my bed in case I was sick again, and a big cup of water.

I asked them to let Knox know, feeling terrible, but there is no way I would have been able to make it out of my room, my bed, let alone to a party. Noise. Movement. Light. All too much.

No, this is where I'm staying tonight.

I finally get into my new position, my head pounding relentlessly. I hear the door to our suite open, but I have no recollection of time at this point, so I'm assuming it's Lindsay and Dottie. When the door to my room partly opens, bringing in a little bit of light, I'm grateful for my eye mask.

"How was the party?" I croak. "Were you able to tell Knox I couldn't make it?"

"They did," a deep voice comes from the other side of the room, startling me.

"Knox?" I push my eye mask up and blink a few times, letting my pupils adjust to the sliver of light in the room.

"No, don't move." He's quickly at my side, setting a backpack down and sitting on the mattress. His hand goes to my head where he lightly strokes my hair. "Hey you. Are you okay?"

I squeeze my eyes shut and take a deep breath as my head continues to pound. "Nope," I squeak out.

"Shit, okay. What can I do?"

"Shut the door."

"Sure." He gets up and shuts the door. He returns to my side and strokes my forehead with his thumb. "What else? Can I get you anything to eat, drink? Any medicine? Heating pads?"

"No. Can't think about eating anything right now."

"Understandable. Have you thrown up again?"

"Oh God, they told you that?"

"Yeah, and I'm glad they did. My mom had headaches like this, and do you know what would help her?"

"What?" I ask, draping my hand over my head.

"My dad. He always helped." I hear Knox kick off his shoes and then he climbs over me so he's behind me. He scoots under the covers carefully, obviously trying not to rock the mattress too much, and slides his body against mine. "Is it okay if I hold you?"

"When have you ever cared about asking?" I chuckle.

"I don't want to hurt you."

He'd never hurt me. I know that at this point. Abandoning a party to make sure I was okay? That's coming from a man who doesn't have a hurtful bone in his body.

And honestly, at this point, there's no fight left in me. It seems inevitable. No matter how hard I try to keep my distance, he's going to be in my life.

"I'm not going to break," I tell him, and then I take a leap of faith. "Hold me, Knox. I want you to hold me."

His hand slides around my stomach and instead of pulling me into his chest, he moves his body closer to mine carefully. How he knows not to rattle me too much is astounding. Never once did Neil care for me in this compassionate, thoughtful, and selfless way. Knox's touch is gentle, soothing, and when he finally fits himself along my body, I can feel my muscles start to relax, and I melt into him.

"Is that okay?" he whispers, his voice like a velvety caress over my bare shoulder.

"Perfect," I sigh. "Thank you."

He kisses my shoulder and says, "Get some sleep, Em. I'm not going anywhere."

And he doesn't.

The first thing that wakes me up the next morning isn't the sun beaming through my dorm window, nor is it Lindsay's morning jams subtly coming through the wall. It's the large hand that's splayed across my stomach, a gentle thumb moving up and down the silk fabric of my camisole.

My migraine is gone, but my muscles are still tense in my neck, which always happens, but I'll take it over the incessant pounding in my head.

"Are you awake?" Knox's voice whispers, his breath minty fresh, his body lying on top of the covers.

I peek an eye open to find him hovering over me, a concerned look on his face.

I bring my sheet up to my mouth and say, "Hey."

He smiles. "Good morning. How are you feeling?"

"Much better, thank you." I take him in and notice his hair is wet. "Did you take a shower?"

He nods. "Didn't think you'd want to hang out with me after my morning conditioning."

"You worked out?" My eyes pop open even more. "It's a Sunday, you have conditioning on a Sunday?"

"Just a quick morning run, not the entire team, just me."

"What is quick in your book?"

"Two miles."

"Oh." I twist so I'm lying on my back. "That is quick."

"Felt stiff, wanted to loosen up a bit." He shakes his shoulders. "I like your shampoo, smells all fruity and shit."

"You used my soap?"

"And towel," he says unapologetically.

Who is this guy?

I slowly sit up and rub my eyes with my hands, needing the bathroom immediately from all the water I drank last night. I throw the blankets off me and start to get off my high bed when Knox grabs my arm and helps me. I'm about to tell him I'm not a ninety-year-old, but when my feet hit the ground and I wobble, I'm grateful for the assist.

"Bathroom?"

"Yeah, but I can do that myself." I laugh and pat his hand.

I quickly pee, brush my teeth, and give myself a brief once-over in my mirror. Silk pajama set, no bra, and bedhead . . . could be worse. *No. He's already seen worse.* I tame my hair a little, pinch some color into my cheeks, and then walk into my bedroom where Knox is sitting on my mattress, hands behind him, propping him up. His eyes burn a trail up my body and stop directly at my chest.

My nipples are hard, I know they are, I can feel them pointing against the silk fabric of my camisole, but with zero shame, I walk toward him.

He licks his lips and sits up as I reach him, his eyes lazy, his hands falling to my hips.

I reach out and caress his cheek, his stubble rough against the palm of my hand, a delicious feeling I completely forgot about up until now.

How is that possible, to forget the feeling of a man's coarse cheek under my touch? It should be something I crave, something I long for, but then again, Neil changed that. He changed everything about our relationship as we grew older. He took the simple things away from me like my right to touch him intimately. I tried, but toward the end he always pushed me away when I tried to hug him, or his kisses were barely a peck on my cheek if I was lucky.

I miss this, being intimate with another human without being overtly sexual.

"I'm sorry I ruined your plans last night."

He wastes no time in pulling me between his legs, keeping me in place with his hands. He's such a big man and since my bed is higher than normal to fit storage underneath, he's looking down at me.

"You didn't ruin everything. Plus, I can see perfectly down your shirt right now, which is a pleasant morning surprise."

I roll my eyes and attempt to push away from him but instead he hops off the bed, picks me up, and carefully places me on the bed where he joins me, his large body eating up the entire mattress.

"Next time we spend the night together, it'll be at my place because your bed is tiny."

"You think there's going to be another time?"

Lying on his side next to me, his upper half hovers over my body, deliciously trapping me in place.

His fingers trail up the side of my arm, a shiver spreading over my skin.

"There will be another time."

"You're so sure of yourself."

"Babe, your nipples are so goddamn hard, so if that's any indication, there will be a second time."

My face flushes but I don't let it deter me. "That's just how my nipples are in the morning, excited for sunshine."

He laughs. "Yeah, they're not excited for anything else?" His fingers glide over my collarbone and I swear, my nipples grow even harder. Is that even possible?

"Nope," I answer, even though it's a weak *nope* from me having to catch my breath.

He lowers his head to mine, inches apart as his hand travels down my arm to the hem of my shirt. Not waiting for a go-ahead, his hand slips under my shirt, and his fingers spread over my stomach.

I suck in a sharp breath, and for some reason, my legs fall open. He's nowhere near that area, but that doesn't stop my body from reacting. A deep, needy throb starts to ache between my legs as his hand travels higher to my ribcage. I shift underneath him, realizing how much I want him to touch me, kiss me, do wicked things to my body, not even caring that my two best friends are a wall away.

"Do you want me to kiss you, Em?"

I should have guessed he'd come out and ask. He's yet to be subtle since I've known him.

And yes, badly. I badly want him to kiss me, even though starting something with someone right now is not what I was planning on. I'm a woman, after all, and saying no to Knox is practically impossible, especially with his hand up my shirt and my body yearning for his touch.

"Kiss me?" I ask, my chest rising and falling at a faster rate. "Is that what friends do?"

I'm nervous.

I know I should say yes, I should pull his head down to mine and lock our lips, but this is the first guy I'm going to kiss other than Neil, and that's huge. Am I ready for that big step? Am I ready to start something with someone who has taken over my thoughts this semester?

"You're calling me your friend now?" His brows rise.

"Well, since you have your hand up my shirt, I'd say we're at least friendly."

He chuckles. "I like being known as your friend, Em."

"Yeah?"

He nods. "You're cool, one of the coolest chicks I know. It's why I can't seem to tear myself away."

His confession makes my heart rate pick up. If I were honest, I like him as a friend too. I've found such ease in being around him, like we were meant to be in each other's lives this entire time.

I bring my finger to his chest where I slowly draw circles. "I like being around you, Knox. Even though it pains me to admit it."

A deep laugh rumbles through his chest. "I wish I had that admission on camera."

"No cameras in the bedroom."

"Ever?" he asks, brows drawing high.

"Ever," I answer sternly.

"Damn." He brushes a stray hair off my forehead while his other hand holds firmly around my ribs.

Growing serious, I say, "Can we promise each other something?"

"Multiple orgasms? I don't have to promise that, babe, it's just going to happen."

I roll my eyes. "No, not that." Even though just looking at his large, strong hands, I know he can deliver.

"Then what?" He shifts so his body is completely flush against mine, his nose rubbing closely against mine.

How does he expect me to intelligently answer him when we're this close? When I can practically taste him on my lips, when I can feel just how hard his entire body is from the countless hours he's spent turning his physique into a well-oiled baseball machine?

"Um, I . . . uh."

He laughs. "Spit it out, Ealson."

"It's hard when you're all up in my business."

"Well, get used to it, because this isn't going to change."

I can see that being very much true if the last few weeks have been any indication. He's determined. When he has his sights set on something—in this case me—it seems like he's all in. It amazes me.

Gathering myself and trying not to get lost in his soulful eyes, I say, "Can we promise that . . . uh, no matter what happens to us, we'll always friends?"

"Putting a gravestone on our relationship before it even starts? That's very morbid of you." His voice is joking, but I can see the hurt in his eyes.

"I'm not putting a gravestone on it, I just . . . hell," I sigh. "I like you a lot, Knox, more than I want to make known, and I like the fun friendship we have. I don't want to lose that. And I know we've only known each other for a little while now, but I still want to keep hanging out with you."

"Ah, I see. I've won you over and you're finally admitting it."

"Are you really going to rub it in?" I ask, playing my fingers over his lips.

He nips at them and says, "Yeah, because you're stubborn as fuck."

I laugh. It's so true. I'm very stubborn.

"I might be. Is that something you think you can handle?"

"I always enjoy a challenge." He moves in closer. "And to answer your question, yes, we will always be friends."

"Even if we go out and then have a nasty breakup?"

"Not going to happen, the nasty breakup part. The going out part *is* inevitable."

"Friends first?"

He sighs. "Friends first, fuck buddies second."

He goes in for a kiss, but I stop his face with my palm. "Fuck buddies?"

He laughs. "Or passionate lovers."

"Oh my God, don't say lovers."

He swipes the tip of his thumb across the underside of my breast and in seconds, all joking is gone. My veins ignite, sending my body into an inferno. He makes another swipe and I suck in a large breath, the growing ache between my thighs intensifying. It's hard to believe that twelve hours ago I could barely open my eyes or lift my head, because right now I'm on fire, and it's only because of this man beside me. It's terrifying. *It's amazing. Like him.*

One more swipe and I grip the back of his neck, threading my fingers through his hair.

"Are you going to kiss me?" I ask, my chest arching off the mattress, seeking more.

"Fuck, yes," he says, his lips descending just as a large wail of a siren blasts in my room.

Beep! Beep! Beep!

"Holy fuck," he says, leaping up and out of bed while covering his ears. "What is that?"

I do the same, trying to stop the piercing sound from rupturing my eardrums. "Fire alarm," I shout. *Worst. Timing. Ever.* "We have to evacuate or else we'll get in trouble. The RA checks."

"Of course." We're both shouting at each other as we move around the room.

I slip on my hard-bottom slippers, throw a sweatshirt over my head, and follow him out the door where we find Lindsay and Dottie. As a group, we make our way down the staircase, which is lit up by the alarm, and out the door, finally gaining reprieve from the blistering sound.

"Holy fuck, that's loud," Knox says, his backpack slung over his shoulders. It looks miniature compared to his large body. "How often does that happen?"

"Once a month," Lindsay says while taking a bite of a Pop-Tart she carried out with her.

Next to her, Dottie sips from her "Get a Life" mug and says, "You get used to it after a while." She eyes us, and the way I'm standing awkwardly far away from Knox, hands in my sweatshirt pocket, looking anywhere but my friends in the eyes. "So, what's going on between you two?"

"Nothing," I say just as Knox says, "Fuck buddies."

"Seriously?" Lindsay gapes.

"Shut up." I playfully swat Knox in the stomach. "We are not fuck buddies, we haven't even kissed." He did touch the underside of my boob and stare at my nipples for a good five minutes, but I choose to leave that part out.

"No kiss?" Dottie asks, hand on her hip with a look of disgust on her face. "What the hell is the matter with you? The boy left a party last night to tend to you, the least you could have done is offer him a blowie this morning."

With a huge smile on his face, hands stuffed in his pockets, and those thick eyebrows wiggling at me, Knox says, "Yeah, the least you could have done was offer me a blowie."

"Ha." I shake my head. "Yeah, that's never going to happen."

"Uhh . . . it sure as shit better, because I have plans of nestling my cheeks between your legs."

"Jesus," I whisper, looking around. "Can you not say that so loud, or around my friends?"

Lindsay waves her hand over her face. "God, that's so hot. He straight-up claimed your vagina in front of our whole dorm."

I press my hand to my forehead, willing this moment to go away. "Can we please talk about something else?"

"Did you know no one has ever gone down on her before?" Dottie says, stealing the breath right out of my lungs as I drop my mouth wide and turn to my friend in shock. In what crazy world would she think that was okay to say?

"I gathered that," Knox says with a pinch in his brow.

"You know what?" I hold up my keycard to everyone. "I'm going to get some coffee."

I take off, making a promise to myself to have a firm conversation with Dottie about boundaries. I would expect Lindsay to say something like that, but Dottie? She's usually tight-lipped, so

Lindsay is starting to get to her. *I'm mortified. Completely and utterly mortified. Why say that?*

"Hold up," Knox says, catching up to me. He moves to block my progress to the coffee kiosk in the dining hall, cutting off my path. "Where do you think you're going?"

"Removing myself from that awkward conversation."

"It's not awkward unless you make it that way. So what, no one has ever gone down on you? We have ways of fixing that." He moves in closer, taking me in by my hand.

"Can we not talk about that right here? If you haven't noticed, all eyes are on you right now, which means our conversation isn't exactly private."

"Who cares?"

"I do." I point to my chest. "I care. You might be this overtly confident man when it comes to the bedroom, but I'm more reserved, okay? I don't like the term fuck buddies, and I don't want to be referred to as that. I find it demeaning. I know we're just having fun, but—"

"Wait, hold up. We're not just having fun, Em. I know I joke around a lot, but this is serious to me. I want to date you."

"Yeah, casually, I get it."

"Fuck, no. Not casually." He grows stern. "If we're dating, then we are full-on dating and that means exclusively."

I bite my bottom lip and look away. Exclusivity is more important to me than anything, for obvious reasons, but serious dating, am I ready for that?

"Do you not want to be exclusive?" he asks, looking hurt as I look back at him.

I press my hand to his chest and look him in the eyes. "I would need things to be exclusive, but I don't know about everything being so serious. I just got out of a six-year relationship. That's going to take some time for me to recover from." He doesn't know. No one really does. I became such a shell of my former self that for all intents and purposes, my friends probably thought I was fine. But I wasn't, and I'm still not. Someone I thought I could trust with my heart and body threw that away. *Viciously.* It may have been incredibly naïve to believe that Neil and I were forever, I know that now, but it didn't negate the years I thought we were. There's a crack in my heart I'm still trying to heal. I'm much happier now. More assertive. More decisive. I'm finding out who I am away from coupledom, and I like the girl I'm seeing. But, I'm still recovering. I'm still a little raw. A little timid to give my heart away again. And as much as Dottie and Lindsay know I'm cautious, they don't understand the depth of pummeling my heart took. *They didn't see me the days after I found Neil and the other girl. They didn't see the texts.*

"Then let's take it slow." He clamps his hand around mine. "We can keep things casual as you like to say, but exclusively casual."

"Exclusively casual." I smile, liking the sound of that. "Okay, what does that entail?"

"Do we need to write down rules? Is that what you're asking?"

"I mean . . . maybe."

He shakes his head then pulls me into his side. "You're going to be the death of me, Ealson."

He guides us toward the dining hall and I ask him, "What are you doing?"

"We're about to lay down the foundation of the best thing that's ever happened to us while we eat breakfast, because damn it, I'm starving. But I have thirty minutes, so we have to make it quick. I have morning study hall to run."

"Morning study hall after a Saturday night? That's brutal."

"Tell me about it. Every one of my teammates wanted to punch me in the nuts." He kisses the side of my head. "Breakfast is on you, Ealson. I hope you're ready to light up your dining hall card."

CHAPTER FIFTEEN

EMORY

I'm gobsmacked.

Utterly gobsmacked.

Sitting across from me is a man who can take down a breakfast burrito the size of his head full of eggs, potatoes, refried beans, bacon, and fajita veggies in five minutes. I'm pretty sure he unhinged his jaw and slid the whole thing in, chewing occasionally.

He reaches across the table and starts picking at my fruit. "Okay, do you want to get down to business?" he asks, casually popping a piece of pineapple in his mouth.

I blink a few times.

"Now that you swallowed that burrito whole, you're ready?"

He licks pineapple juice off his finger. "Did I impress you with my eating abilities, because there's more where that came from."

"You horrified me," I say, still in a state of shock.

He chuckles and pulls out a pen and notebook. "You learn to eat fast when you have little time in between practices and classes."

"Still . . . that thing was huge."

"If you're impressed with that, just wait until you see what else

I can do with my mouth." He winks, sending a wave of heat up the nape of my neck. I can only imagine.

Just what I need, to be turned on in the middle of the dining hall. Hello, fellow students, this is me, Emory Ealson, wet and ready for the man who can swallow a five-foot burrito whole.

I take a sip of my water, ignoring his innuendo, which only makes the cocky and confident man laugh to himself.

"Okay, let's get these rules laid out so we can get to the good stuff." He lifts his gaze to me. "You know, like kissing and all that shit."

"How romantic."

He points his pen at me. "Exactly. Very romantic." Like an idiot, he clicks the pen, dots the tip on his tongue as if wetting the ink, and makes a dramatic wave of his arm to get to the paper. Seriously, what am I getting myself into? "Okay, rule number one." He lifts a brow at me, looking super sexy as he says, "Friends forever and always."

Shit, that look, his soft voice as he said those words . . . it strikes me hard in the chest, a feeling I wasn't expecting right away. Yes, he might be very outgoing and personable like Neil, but there's a softer side to him, one I can't wait to explore more.

"Yes, friends forever." I take a bite of my eggs and lean back in my chair, enjoying the view of Knox's sly smile.

"Good." He writes it down and then starts scribbling the second rule as he talks out loud. "Rule number two: lots and lots of oral. Pantloads, no boatloads of oral. More oral than anyone can ever imagine." He actually writes that down. "Oral all the time. If there is a tongue and a pussy in the same room, they're connecting."

Jesus.

I shush him, moving my hand up and down to lower his voice. "Seriously, can you be a little less . . . proud?"

"No," he answers, while finishing his sentence, and then he looks up at me. "I want everyone to know that the only person who'll be between your legs is me." He perks his head up and speaks louder. "Did you hear that, everyone? I'm the only one—"

I'm out of my seat in seconds and clasping my hand over his mouth before he can continue. "Oh my God, Knox, please, control yourself."

He takes me by the wrist and spins me so I'm sitting on his lap, and of course . . . all eyes are on us. My back is to his chest and his arm is wrapped around my stomach, keeping me in place.

"You're too much fucking fun." He kisses the side of my neck and then goes back to writing. "Rule number three . . ." He pauses and then shakes me. "Go ahead, rule number three."

"Keep things casual."

"Hmm . . . not sure if I like that as a set rule. Can we make an addendum to that?"

Why is he so beyond adorable? I can't take it. You'd never guess this larger-than-life, outgoing, and powerful man would be so . . . cute. And I'm not talking about the physical. His personality is cute, sweet, as if he grew up with five sisters and knows exactly how to treat women: with a smidge of teasing and a whole lot of caring.

"What kind of addendum?"

He moves his hand to under my sweatshirt and my camisole to my skin where he lightly strokes his thumb. It's innocent, almost like he just needs to make that connection while we're sitting together, but it's lighting me up inside.

"Well, let's say we're casual and all, we accomplish all the oral and then you're like, holy fuck, I can't ever let this man go because he's just so fantastic in bed. We should be allowed to make the switch from casual to more than friendship bracelets, you know?"

"Are you saying like . . . boyfriend, girlfriend?"

"Yeah, that's the term I'm looking for."

Curious, I ask, "Have you ever been in a relationship before, Knox?"

"Nope," he answers nonchalantly and starts writing an

addendum to rule number three. "But it can't be too hard. You listen, you talk, you give and take, and of course . . ."

"Lots of oral." I roll my eyes. And even though I should feel stressed by this overzealous sports hotshot, I'm smiling. He's a nut . . . but he might become my nut.

"Exactly, you got it now, babe." He squeezes me and I chuckle, loving how he can make me happy in a matter of seconds. "Okay, I think we have one rule left."

"Only going with four?"

"Why not? We don't want to make things too difficult right off the bat. Let's keep it at four. And the last one is, no matter how casual we are, we are always exclusive. That means my penis is the only penis you're fondling. Got it?"

I roll my eyes even though he can't see my face. "I know what being exclusive means and trust me, you don't have to worry about that with me." My voice comes out more snide than I meant.

"Hey." He turns me on his lap so he can see me, and I can see how he's switched to serious Knox. "Are you worried about me cheating or something?"

"No," I say, hanging my head and playing with the drawstring of my hoodie. "You're a good guy, and I don't think you have that in you. But it will probably be something that's in the back of my mind."

"Because of your ex-boyfriend?"

"Yeah, because of him."

He moves his hand around my back, and the heat of his palm warms me. "You'll never have to worry about that with me, Em. I promise. I may not have been in a boyfriend-girlfriend relationship before, but that doesn't mean I don't believe in monogamy. My word is my word."

"Thank you," I say, cupping his face.

I lean forward, staring at his lips. I'm about to press my mouth against his when he says, "Are we really going to have our first kiss in the dining hall with all these onlookers?"

I smile. "I'm game if you are."

MEGHAN QUINN

A wicked gleam lights up his eyes. "You know I am." One of his hands slides up my thigh while the other cups the back of my head and lowers me to his lips.

Nervous—because Knox is only the second guy I've kissed—I try to be as loose as possible when his lips touch mine.

Soft with the perfect amount of pressure, our lips fuse together. The sounds of clanking silverware against plates and students chattering fade away, leaving only the thrumming of my rapidly beating heart to fill my ears.

Our lips part at the same time, wanting more, exploring. My tongue slips into his mouth while my fingers thread through his hair. A low groan rumbles from his chest as his grip on my thigh tightens. Our tongues work in tandem together, seeking more, reaching for more but never sloppy. Little flicks, tiny kisses, our mouths never extending too far. Gentle but new, the tension in our hands is a contradiction to the soft movements of our mouths. *I've missed this. This softness. Intimacy. Honesty.*

I could kiss this man all day. That's how good he is. How patient and relaxed he is, almost like he's letting me take charge, but I know deep down he's not. He's guiding me with his movements, slightly tilting my head, flicking his tongue over my lips, leaning into me. He uses his entire body when he kisses, and I can feel the power move from his spine to the tips of his fingers, letting me know just how much he wants me.

It's perfect.

It's—

"Yeah, Gentry. Get it, man," some douche cheers off to the side.

On a deep breath, I pull away and tuck my head into his shoulder, embarrassed that I lost control in the dining hall.

Keeping my head tucked, I ask, "How many people are staring?"

He soothingly rubs my back and says, "Pretty much everybody."

"Perfect." I laugh.

"I'm not even mad about it, because now every dickhead in this building knows you're mine."

"And I just became enemy number one with all the girls here."

"Nah, they'll just talk behind your back," he jokes.

"Great." I lift away and keep my eyes trained on him. I draw my finger across his bottom lip and say, "You're a really good kisser."

"I practice on my hand every day."

"Shut up." I push his shoulder, causing him to laugh even more.

When his laughter dies down, he says, "You're a damn good kisser too, Em. Too good." He sneaks one more kiss in. "Fuck, I hate that I have to get going now." With a sexy smile, he pats my backside and says, "Walk me out?"

"Of course. There's no way I'm staying here with all the ravenous beasts waiting to spring on me."

We gather his things, stuff them in his bag but not before signing the "rules"—so ridiculous—and then take off down the stairs and out the doors.

Once outside, he brings me to the side where he reaches into his pocket and hands me his phone. "It's time I get that number, don't you think?"

I glance at his phone but don't take it. "I don't know. If we're keeping it casual, we can still just talk through student chat."

"Over my dead body. Phone number, Ealson. Now."

I cross my arms over my chest and jut out my hip. "Do you really think you're going to get what you want by talking to me like that?"

He pulls on the back of his neck, clearly frustrated. "How are we going to do all the oral if I don't have your phone number?"

"It's called the element of surprise." I lift up on my toes and press a quick kiss to his jaw and then pat him on the cheek. "Have fun at study hall."

"You're really not going to give me your number?"

I shake my head and start to walk away. "You have to earn that."

"Uh . . . pretty sure I did over the last few weeks."

"No, you just earned my affection. My number is an entirely different hurdle." I twiddle my fingers and then turn toward my dorm, but not before I hear him groan.

I smile to myself the entire way back. Thankfully the fire drill is over, so I hit the shower right away, letting the hot water ease my tense muscles. I spend extra time shaving, making sure I reach every last inch of my body, and then I spend a decent amount of time lotioning. By the time I make my way into my room and check my phone, I have a text message from a strange number.

Brow furrowed, I open it up.

It's Knox. Have I told you how much I like your friend Dottie? She's a winner in my book. I'll catch you later, Ealson. P.S. Can't wait to play with your nipples. XOXO.

Shaking my head, I clutch my phone to my chest and then let out a low chuckle. I can't be mad about it, because frankly, I'm happy.

CHAPTER SIXTEEN

KNOX

"How's my baby?"

I scoot down on the leather couch of the locker room and prop my feet up on the coffee table while sports highlights play in the background. We have an hour and a half before practice and since I was already on campus, I decided to chill in the locker room until then.

Carson sits next to me, trolling on his phone and eating grapes, chomping away with no awareness of the sounds he's making.

Disgusting.

"Hey Mom," I say into the phone, grabbing Carson's attention. He glances at me with a knowing smile.

My mom is very well known on the team. Not because she calls me all the time to check in, but because she's *THAT* mom at the baseball games. You know, the one who shows up in ALL the college gear one can buy with a cooler, chair, foam finger, and pompoms. She's the one who gets the fans in the stands to start cheers and leads the wave. She's the first to yell at an umpire for a missed call, and she's the first one to slip orange slices into the dugout when she arrives. Yes, she still hands out orange slices. It was absolutely humiliating my freshman year, but now she's like an unofficial team mascot.

The players love her.

Coach Disik tolerates her, which is surprising since he barely tolerates anyone.

And the other parents rely on her to check on their sons when they're unable to make a game.

She's also the unofficial photographer and even started a social media group for parents of the players so everyone can keep up on what's going on with the team.

To say she's involved is an understatement.

"How's my big guy?" She also still acts like I'm ten, but I let it slide since she's truly the best mom ever and one of my best friends.

Mama's boy? Possibly, but guess what? This mama's boy gets a cooler full of baked treats every time she visits the loft or comes to a game. So, no complaints.

"Good, I'm between classes and practice right now so I'm hanging with Carson in the locker room."

"Oh, put me on speaker phone, I want to say hi."

This wouldn't be the first time. It's rare I have a conversation with just my mom. Holt or Carson are usually popped into the conversation as well. I switch the phone to speaker and say, "Say hi, Mom."

"Carson, hi, honey, how are you?"

Carson lights up like he always does when he talks to my mom. He lost his mom when he was young. It's been him and his dad for most of his life, so he's taken to my mom very easily.

"Hey Mama G." It's what everyone calls her. "I'm doing good, how are you?"

"Oh, I'm great, honey. Painstakingly bedazzling my spring hat. You know I like to make a new one every year."

"Right on, I love your hats. Your fall one was as epic as usual."

"Thank you. I spent a good month arranging all those jewels.

But come springtime, this little devil will be ready." She chuckles to herself. "So, are you two being good? Staying out of trouble."

"Always, Mom," I answer.

But Carson steps in and says, "Well, I've been staying out of trouble, but your son might be dabbling in a little trouble where the heart is concerned."

Jesus fucking Christ.

I glare at him and mouth, "What the fuck?" just as my mom emits an excited squeal.

"Oh, is that true? Are you seeing someone, Knox?"

I sigh heavily and then punch Carson dead in the arm.

Like I said, I love my mom dearly, but the last thing I need right now is the Texas inquisition from her when I can barely call Emory mine.

"Fuck, man," he whispers, rubbing where I hit him.

I drag my hand over my face and say, "I might be seeing someone."

"Might be, or are?"

"It's complicated," Carson butts in. "They're keeping it casual."

"Oh, Knox." There's disappointment in her voice. "I thought I taught you better than that. Please don't tell me she's your sex friend."

"It's called a fuck buddy, Mom, and no. We've barely kissed."

Well, kissed once. Barely might not be the right term because when we kissed, we fucking *kissed,* and it was one of the best kisses of my life. Her full lips had no problem running over mine, and her hands seemed to enjoy threading through my hair . . . in front of all the morning diners.

"But you have kissed?" My mom's voice is far too excited.

"Yes."

"But he's been after her for a while, Mama G. Ever since the first day of classes, but she's been tentative."

"Why? You don't have a bad reputation, do you?"

"No," I answer, hating that Carson is here right now. "She had a really bad breakup before she moved out here. She's a transfer

137

from California, and she's hesitant to jump into another relationship. Carson's right. She's been reluctant to spend time with me, so it's been difficult. But this weekend I made some strides, and we're casually exclusively seeing each other."

"That sounds like an oxymoron," my mom says. "Casually exclusive? What does that even mean?"

"It means we're giving each other some breathing room, but we aren't fooling around with other people."

"Breathing room?" She pauses. "Carson, what do you think of this girl? Is she messing with my son?"

He doesn't even bother to look at my pleading eyes when he says, "No. She's a good girl. I like her. She's in one of our classes, and you can tell she likes Knox. It's in her eyes. But I do think the ex-boyfriend did a number on her. Knox is playing it out right, not jumping in head first and possibly scaring her away."

Well, there are fucking miracles. Everything Carson said was perfect. Maybe I won't cut off his nuts when I'm done talking to my mom.

"Oh, the poor dear. I'm so sorry to hear that. You better take good care of her, Knox." And just like that, she switches from being skeptical to loving Emory in seconds without even meeting her. "What's her name? What does she look like?"

"Emory, and she's—"

"Oh, what a gorgeous name," Mom gushes. "How beautiful?"

"Yeah, and she's beautiful inside and out," I say, even though I feel like a dickhead. This should have been a conversation between my mom and me alone.

"She is," Carson says as he leans in, adding his two cents. "She's funny too, and gives your son a run for his money. I already told him he better not fuck things up with her."

There is clapping on the other end of the phone. "Oh goodness, when do I get to meet her?"

"Uh, not for a while. Remember what I said about things being casual? Meeting a mom doesn't necessarily scream casual."

"I would have to agree with him, Mama G. I'd wait until the

new semester. Let them figure out what they really want from each other."

"That's so far though. Can I write her a card? Let her know what a wonderful son you are?"

"Keep the stationery in the closet. No cards, Mom."

"But I just bought this new beautiful set with butterflies on it. I really think she'd consider it a classy piece of stationery. Might help you out in the long run."

"Or scare her away."

"Yeah, it might scare her away," Carson adds. "But I would love a card, Mama G. That butterfly stationery sounds magical."

Fucking kiss-ass.

"Don't let him fool you, Mom. He just wants some of your Oreo brownies."

"You kept the last batch all to yourself like a selfish prick," Carson spouts off. "I got one measly square."

"Because they're my favorite. They have Oreos and marshmallows in them, moron."

"I know what's in them and don't need the play-by-play. It's why I wanted more."

"Boys, boys," my mom says. She's used to our theatrics. Although, she must know it's Carson who's being a dick right now. "How about I make each of you your own batch? Would that settle things?"

"That would be much appreciated, Mama G. And don't forget the butterfly stationery."

"I wouldn't dream of it." Carson is all too happy with himself. "Well, boys, I should be going, skee ball is going to start soon. I'll talk to you two handsome boys later."

"Bye, Mom."

"Bye, Mama G."

I hang up and toss my phone to the side and drag both my hands down my face. "Thanks for that, asshole. Now she's going to be on me about Emory."

"You're more than welcome. That's exactly what I was hoping for," Carson answers with a giant grin.

Why am I his friend?

I look through the crack of Emory's door and spot her at her desk—head turned toward her book, hand pressed against her forehead, and her headphones on. Cross-legged on her chair in a pair of sweats, she looks adorably sweet with her nose stuck in a book.

Freshly showered and tired as fuck from a long, drawn-out practice, I make my way into her room and set my backpack on the ground before flopping on her bed. Coach drilled us today. He was on a warpath and made sure we suffered.

Up, down, up, down. I can still hear his voice chanting as we dropped to do burpees with him hovering over us. When one of the freshmen threw up, I swear I saw a smile cross the old bastard's face.

From the corner of her eyes, she catches me approaching her bed and smiles while taking off her headphones.

"What are you listening to?" I ask, sticking my hands behind my head and making myself comfortable on her comforter.

She unfolds her legs from her chair, snaps her book shut, and hops up on her bed to sit next to me.

"The Harry Potter soundtrack. Gets me all amped up to learn."

I move my hand over her thigh. "I don't think I've ever met anyone who was amped up to learn."

She picks up my hand and threads her fingers with mine. "Well, now you do." She squeezes. "How was practice? I didn't know you were coming over."

"Practice was good. I didn't think I'd make it back to the loft with how exhausted I am. And I wasn't about to let another night go by when I didn't see you. We made an agreement, I saw you in class on Monday, you denied me lunch—again—and now it's

Thursday, and I was wondering why I haven't tasted your lips since the dining hall. Are you avoiding me, Ealson?"

She smiles and shakes her head. "Never. I'm glad you're here."

"Yeah? Even though I wasn't invited to come over?"

"Yes. Gives me an excuse to stop studying." She reaches up and lets her hair out of a clip. The long, brown strands fall past her shoulders, framing her beautiful face.

"Are you trying to make me hard?" I ask, taking in her full, pouty lips while tracing my finger over her thigh.

"Seriously? I undid my hair."

"And it was sexy." I pull on her hand and shift her back on the mattress beneath me. I look toward the ceiling and say, "The fire alarm isn't going to go off again, right?"

"No, but if you're thinking of sticking your hand down my pants, you're going to have to wait."

"Why's that?"

"I have my period." She shrugs as if sharing this information is no big deal. It's not, but since we just started "seeing" each other, I'm really happy with her level of comfort she has with me.

"Shit, that sucks." I move my hand over her stomach. "Do you need anything? I can run out and get you candy or something."

She smiles sincerely and moves her hand over my cheek. "I have a stash of Pretzel M&M's I keep around for this joyous occasion. Want to break into them and watch a movie?"

Fuck, she's cute. What I said to my mom was right: she's beautiful inside and out. *And I'm the lucky fuck who gets to be with her.* Mom will seriously love this girl.

"Do you have popcorn too?"

"I think Lindsay does."

I hop off the bed. "Then it's a date."

CHAPTER SEVENTEEN

EMORY

K*nox: Dining hall, 7 p.m. Don't be late.*
I stare at the text and then look at the time. He's two minutes late. How dare he? I smile. He's so busy, and there's no doubt in my mind he's working his hardest to get here.

I lean against the brick wall, thinking back to our movie night the other night where Knox took down my entire stash of Pretzel M&M's—plus a bag of popcorn—in one sitting. The man can eat.

He also really likes snuggling, but only if he can have his hand up my shirt. He made that an "honorary" rule the other night when he slipped his hand under my shirt and pressed his palm to my stomach. According to him, he wasn't getting frisky, he just likes the feel of my skin when he holds me.

How can a girl say no to that?

She can't.

He was right when he told me his schedule was really tight. Mix that with mine, and there aren't many options for us to meet up during the week, but that's okay, because we're keeping it casual. It also makes me want him more, because the moments I do have with him fulfill a need in my soul I didn't know I had. Which only makes our time together that much sweeter.

From over the hill, I spot Knox briskly walking with Carson and Holt toward me. I know the minute Knox sees me, because a gorgeous and happy smile crosses his face. Carson taps him on the stomach and then points directly at me while saying something I can't hear, but whatever it is, Knox seems to issue him a warning.

It's a warm fall day, which means I'm wearing a cute, short black flowy skirt with knee-high knitted socks and a long-sleeved button-up blouse, and I left the first few buttons undone to show off a little cleavage for my man.

By the way he's dragging his hand over his face, he likes what he sees.

Instead of meeting him halfway, I wait for him to close the distance and when he does, he loops his arm around my neck and brings his lips to mine where he slowly works his mouth over mine. Small, closed kisses at first that build and build until my mouth parts and our tongues connect.

"Dude, I'm starving, and you're paying, so can you remove your mouth from Em's so we can get some food?"

Sighing, Knox pulls away and squeezes my side. His forehead connects with mine as he says, "You look fucking hot, babe."

"Good, because I chose this for you."

"It's appreciated." He moves his hand to mine and presses our palms together as our hands link. "Come on, dinner is on me. I owe these two, and I'm paying for my girl."

He doesn't give me time to protest as we walk up the stairs to the dining hall. There are five dining halls on campus, including one in the student union, but Lakeview is the best not only because it's where my dorm is located, but because it's on the second story and looks over Lake Michigan. It also has a make-your-own salad station I've become addicted to.

When we reach the top, Carson and Holt split up as I turn to Knox and ask, "What are you in the mood for?"

He scans the different stations and says, "I think lasagna and a side salad. And a cookie."

I chuckle. "Of course. You can't go without your sweets, can you?"

"Hell no." He kisses my cheek and says, "Meet you at the register."

Everyone splits up as we gather our dinners on the black trays. Knox pays, which in all honesty isn't a lot, because dining hall food is cheap plus he has an unlimited dining card, and we pick a table that's lined up against the large windows where we have the perfect view of Lake Michigan. Knox sits next to me while Carson and Holt sit across from us.

Before I can grab my fork, all three guys are shoveling food into their mouths. Holt has a salad and chicken with a side of fries. Carson went with a burger, roasted veggies, and a side of fries. And all three of them have Gatorades and giant cookies.

Despite the mouthful of food, Carson asks, "Did Knox tell you about his mom and how she's just dying to meet you?"

He told his mom about me? When was this? And here I thought we were keeping things casual.

I turn to Knox, who has already made an impressive dent in his lasagna. "No, he didn't. You told your mom about me?"

"Carson did," Knox says, sounding annoyed.

"And why is that a problem?"

"You don't know my mom."

"Please," Holt interrupts while wiping his mouth. He turns to me and says, "There's something you need to know about little Knox Gentry. He's a complete and total mama's boy."

What? I never would have pegged him as one.

"Really?" I ask, a smile spreading over my face. "Is that true?"

He stares at his lasagna and shrugs. "My mom might be a good friend of mine."

"He once said best friend," Carson adds.

"Seriously?" I ask, feeling frustrated. As if I needed another reason to swoon over this man, he says his mom is his best friend? What is that about?

"We're close. I mean . . . not so close she's giving me tips on how to please my girl, but we share things."

"And she makes the best brownies ever," Carson adds. "You two would get along really well."

"Which is why you two need to stay as far away as possible. I don't need them ganging up on me and talking about how I style my hair or any of that bullshit."

"I like your hair. I'd never pick on that. Now the baseball hoodie you like to wear a lot . . ." I glance at all three of them, because it's like their off-the-field uniform.

"I think she's mocking our clothing," Holt says.

"I think she is," Carson adds. "What are you going to do about it, man?"

Knox sits back in his chair and sets his fork down, already done with his meal. Only the cookie is left. Seriously, he unhinges his jaw and shoves it down his throat, there is no other explanation. "Well, boys, I guess the only thing we can do is go home, wash these hoodies, and make sure we wear them every Monday just to drive her crazy."

They laugh, and I roll my eyes. "Looks like 'all the oral' you want isn't going to happen as soon as you thought." I pop a cherry tomato in my mouth and smile while I chew. Both Holt and Carson "ooo" from my threat.

"Please, I'll have that skirt up and around your nipples before you can moan 'oh, Knox.' Don't threaten me, Ealson."

"Trust me, I can hold out. You're the one who's itching to pull my thong off."

"It's hot that she said thong," Holt says with a point of his fork.

"I agree with Em. There's no way you'll be able to hold out longer than her."

"Fuck you. I'm not a horny dickhead. I can hold out. I've *been* holding out." I can hear the competitiveness in his voice from a mile away.

Carson and Holt scoff, which only fires Knox up more.

"You don't think I can, do you?" He laughs and breaks off a piece of his cookie, a cocky attitude igniting his eyes. "Fine, it's on." He turns to me and says, "The first to break and beg for sexual relations loses."

"Oh yeah?" I say, finding this all too entertaining. He has no clue how long I've gone without sex, and to be honest, because the sex I've had has been mediocre at best, I have plenty of patience. "And what do we lose?"

"Oh, a wager." Carson rubs his hands together. "I want in."

Knox crosses his arms over his broad chest and says, "Fine, if Em cracks first, I get to pick out your walk-out songs. And I'm really digging some early Britney Spears." He turns to me and says, "And as for you, missy, if you crack first, you have to go out to lunch with me after our Monday class, finally."

I can't help the smile that passes over my lips. "Okay, fine, but if you crack, you're going to pay for a nice steak dinner for all four of us, and you have to speak in a French accent the whole time while wearing one of my skirts."

Carson and Holt both bark out in laughter. I'm so intent on watching Knox try not to show any sense of humor I don't catch who claps.

"Deal." He holds his hand out to me and I take it, but before he lets go, he says, "But you have to be honest, since it's three against one. No skewing the results."

"Do you really believe I would do that?" I ask, shocked.

"Yes," he deadpans. "Yes, I do."

I chuckle. "You're right, I would. Okay, I agree to being totally honest."

"Good." He leans in, and pinches my chin between his thumb and forefinger and presses his lips softly against mine before pulling away and says, "Game on, babe."

"Why are you two sitting out here with me?" Dottie asks. We're in the common room, on the most uncomfortable couch known to man. I'm sitting on Knox's lap as he slowly makes circles on my back with his finger, driving me crazy. We're one week in on the no-sex competition, and I'm actually shocked at his self-control. Then again, the only reason he is where he is today in his sport is because of self-control and self-discipline.

I refuse to be in a closed room with him right now, not when he smells like fresh soap and his hair is still a little wet from his shower after practice. I haven't seen the man in two days, and when he came into my dorm room, his lips immediately found mine, and all I could do to save myself was push him out into the common room.

When I shoved him and pointed at him to stay away, he laughed and made himself at home on the couch, only to pull me down on his lap and torture me with his fingers on my back. *It's bliss. And torture. Totally unfair.*

"She doesn't want to lose the bet," Knox answers, eyes trained on the baseball game in front of us that he turned on. None of us complained because frankly, we couldn't care less.

"What bet?" Dottie asks, crossing her legs under her and getting comfortable.

"You didn't tell them?" Knox's brows rise in surprise.

I push my hair behind my ear. "It's none of their business."

"What's none of our business?" Lindsay asks, walking into the room eating a popsicle.

Jumping right in, Knox fills them in on the bet, including how Carson and Holt got in on it, professing their doubt in Knox.

Laughing, Lindsay says, "You really think you can outlast Knox?" She shakes her head. "No way. You've never had good sex, and your orgasms were few and far between. Your itch needs to be scratched badly."

I really do need new friends. What ever happened to girl code around here?

"You haven't had many orgasms?" Knox asks. "Why the hell did you stay with your ex for so long?"

Ignoring Knox, I say, "Hey Lindsay, remember how we talked about censoring what you say? That would have been the time."

"Please, Knox needs to know the sexual background you're coming from." She leans toward him. "It wasn't much. Yeah, Neil was nice at first, but after they did it for the first time and then the tenth time, she didn't have anything wonderful to say. I think her exact comment was, 'I'll grow to like it.'"

"Lindsay," I snap. "Shut it."

"Grow to *like* it?" Knox drags his hand over his face as if he's in pain. "Oh hell, I wish I didn't know that."

"Because you want to fuck her even more now, right?" Lindsay asks, looking smug.

"Precisely." His finger stills and his hand slides down to my ass. He presses his forehead against my shoulder and then lets out a long breath of air. "I'm going to take off."

"Why?" I ask, disappointed.

"Because there is no way I'm losing this bet and if I stay here, with that new knowledge, I'm going to lose . . . badly." He shifts me off his lap and heads to get his backpack. When he returns, he presses a soft kiss across my lips and lingers for a few seconds before whispering bye.

After he's gone, I turn to Lindsay and sarcastically say, "Thanks a lot."

She chuckles and says unapologetically, "You're never going to win." And even though I can see the humor in this situation, because I really can, part of me is annoyed. Lindsay just shut down my time with Knox. We don't get much time together, so when time is stolen like it just was, I don't feel great. Do I love that Knox wants me so much that he left? Yes, I think so. But, who knows when we'll get to hang out again? This moment isn't about the bet, because right now, we're both losing. *And that sucks.*

CHAPTER EIGHTEEN

EMORY

E mory: *This bet was stupid.*
    Knox: *Are you saying you want to give up? If so, I'll be to your place in ten minutes. I expect you naked, legs spread.*

Emory: *It's been over a month, Knox. Over a month, and you haven't budged.*

Knox: *That's because I have a good hand and a strong imagination of how you look completely bare. It's the sexiest thing I've ever seen, in case you were wondering.*

Emory: *I have a good hand too, you know . . .*

Knox: *I see what you're trying to do. Get me all hot and bothered from the shock of hearing that you masturbate. Sorry to inform you, babe, but in my imagination, you masturbate to me anyway. Nice try.*

Emory: *Damn it. Are you really not going to budge?*

Knox: *On the first day I met you, I asked you out to lunch and you said no. My pride took a hit that day. I'm just stubborn enough to hold on to that nugget and power through. The question is, are you really that stubborn not to go out to lunch with me?*

Emory: *It's the principle of the thing.*

Knox: *Your loss.*

Emory: *You're an ass.*

Knox: *Whoa, say that again. Turned me on.*

Emory: *I hate you.*

~

"Psst, babe, over here." I look through the books on the bookshelf and spot a black backward hat, followed by a pair of blue eyes—my favorite pair.

It's December.

December. And Knox hasn't cracked, not even a little.

We've had some pretty heavy make-out sessions and the minute it starts to turn over to something more, he pulls away and turns on a movie, or starts reading a book, or looks at sports highlights. His resistance is platinum level. It's driving me crazy.

So crazy I'm just going to say it: I'm horny.

I'm the horniest girl on campus—with my competition for the title nowhere near me—because every time I'm with Knox, I'm not only faced with the hottest guy I know, but I'm left with metaphorical blue balls whenever we part.

Anytime I see him, all I want to do is tear his clothes off then let him do the same to me. I want to roll around naked, our sweaty bodies clapping together—yeah, clapping. I want to make so many noises with him, that's how freaking insane I am. It's come to the embarrassing point that whenever I see any marketing material of him around campus, I get a dull ache between my legs.

Sports brochures are turning me on.

This is so stupid.

Over a lunch bet.

A simple lunch bet. It's ridiculous, something I should have given in to, but I swear on my left nipple that's constantly hard, anytime I think about losing the bet, Holt or Carson text me with words of encouragement.

This isn't just about me.

It's about them and walking up to bat to a Britney Spears song.

So I'm holding strong. At least I think I am.

"Knox, what are you—?"

"Come over here, Em." He motions with his fingers. Fingers I have yet to experience. Fingers I want deep inside me, twiddling, flicking, massaging.

Maybe I could become acquainted with those fingers right now . . .

Wait, no. No, I can't.

Not only would I lose the bet, but if Mrs. Flower caught me with my skirt up around my waist, that would be the end of my internship and everything I've worked hard for this semester. Being under her reins hasn't been easy.

Speaking of which, I look to the left where Mrs. Flower is talking to a student, well, more like berating, and when I see that the coast is clear, I set down the stack of books I was putting away on the cart and make my way around the shelf where Knox pulls me by the hand and into his chest.

His lips find mine immediately and then his hand falls to my backside where he grips my skirt, bunching it up in his hand and lifting it to an inappropriate level. I swat at his hand, but it does nothing but intensify both his kiss and his hold on me.

We've gone through a fair amount of Chapstick over the last few months, our mouths inseparable when we're together, but our make-out sessions are nothing like this, nothing this carnal, this needy. When I pull away, I stare at his crazed eyes.

"Knox, what's going on?"

He pins my hands above my head and kisses the side of my neck. "I want you, Em. I want you so fucking bad."

Jesus. Here? *Now?*

Couldn't he have said that the other night when his hand was dancing with the smooth waistband of my silk shorts?

"What are you doing here?"

"Trying to study with the team. We're in the red room, which has given me the perfect view of your tiny ass in this short skirt, prancing around the library. It's driving me so goddamn crazy."

"You're here? With the team? Since when?"

"An hour ago," he says, his lips moving up to my jaw.

"And you didn't come to say hi?"

"Not when you're dressed like this."

I sigh as his teeth graze my skin. "I'm always dressed like this."

"Yeah, which reminds me, can you start wearing pants please? It's fucking winter."

"I have leggings. It works."

"In too many tortuous ways." His lips still, and he lets out a long breath as his head drops near my shoulder. "Damn it, Em, you're killing me."

"You think this is easy on me? This is the stupidest bet I've ever taken part in. Do you know how many times we could have had sex by now?"

"I can't even think about it or else my dick will cry."

No one likes a crying dick.

"What's going on over here?" Both Knox and I jump from the shrill voice of Mrs. Flower. We turn side by side and I swear my stomach hits the floor when I see the disapproving look on Mrs. Flower's face.

Of all people to spot us rubbing our bodies together.

"I . . . I—" *I'm so fucked.*

Oh God, I don't think I could have committed a bigger offense in the library. Considering the rules, I think Mrs. Flower would rather see me in non-fiction with a panini press than making out with my boyfriend.

I might cry.

How did I let this happen? If I lose this internship . . . *Fuck.* Only last week I felt bad for a couple who Mrs. Flowers found making out. Her fury is something I swore I'd never cause. And here I am. *Shit. Shit. Shit.*

I can't deal with this. My eyes burn, my throat gets choked, and for the life of me, I can't find any voice to deny what we were doing.

"Mrs. Flower, I'm so sorry," Knox says, using his best southern charm. I glance in his direction, watching as he slowly pleads with the frail gargoyle in front of us. "I was having a bad day. I don't get much time with my girl, and I was seeking her comfort in a place I shouldn't have. This is not on Emory." The way he uses my full name sends my pulse racing, so does his defense, and how he gently links our hands together like a united front. "She told me to go, to meet up with her when she'd finished her shift, but I was irresponsible and impatient. Please, don't take this out on her."

If I already didn't want to jump this man and hump his face off, I sure as hell do now.

Mrs. Flower gives Knox a slow once-over as she folds one bony arm over the other, a purse to her chapped lips, and a questioning look in her eyes.

"Mr. Gentry," she spits out in her perfect disciplinarian voice. "I'm surprised to find you like this. Your team has always been very respectful of these walls."

"I know, Mrs. Flower. We pride ourselves on taking our studies seriously. I was having a crappy day, lost my judgement, and made a mistake. I'm sorry."

The stick arms unfold.

Her face cracks into a smile.

And light resurfaces to her normally dead eyes.

I think I'm looking at a completely different woman as Mrs. Flower walks to Knox and pats him on the arm . . . nicely. "You're forgiven, just make sure you tell Coach Disik I said hi."

Errr . . . what?

"Not a problem." Knox winks at her, and she returns the gesture.

What the . . . what?

I'm still in shock when she faces me. Her smile turns into a thin line of distaste as if Knox is the prized meat, and I'm the onion garnish. "Emory, I suggest you get back to work."

"Yes, of course. So sorry." I curtsy and bow my head like a moron, because I have no idea how to react to the situation. Knox follows closely behind.

Once the old witch is out of earshot, he says, "Sorry about that." He grabs for my waist again but I swat him away.

"Are you insane? Do not touch me right now."

He chuckles and says, "Come on. That was fun."

"That was not fun." I glance toward her departing frame. "I'm pretty sure she has a closetful of dead intern skulls from past semesters. I am not one to tempt fate again."

He chuckles again. I'm so glad he finds this so funny. My palms are still sweating from being caught . . . and for doing a curtsey. "Fine, no more kissing in the library, but I need to talk to you, so when does your shift end?"

"Eight."

"Okay, meet me outside when you're done, and we can go for dinner at the Bear Den."

"Fine." He gives me a chaste kiss and then takes off. I want to be mad at him for putting me in a terrible position with Mrs. Flower, but from the looks of it, Mrs. Flower might be a big baseball fan, dating Knox might work in my favor.

But I would never tell him that, of course. The man's ego is already inflated enough as it is. I shouldn't forgive his non-apology, because what if I lost my role here? But I do. Because he came through for me when I needed him to. Despite our bet, and the stupidity of denying ourselves what we really want, he's committed. Damn the man, but I like that. I like that a lot.

CHAPTER NINETEEN

KNOX

The waitress places a pepperoni pizza in front of us, gives me a little wink and then takes off.

"Did she just wink at you?" Em asks, handing me a plate.

"I think she did," I say, giving her a napkin.

"Does she think I'm your sister?"

"I sure as hell hope not because that means I've been eye fucking my sister ever since we sat down. Not to mention the dirty dreams I have of you all the time."

With the large spatula, she picks up a piece of pizza, the mozzarella stretches across the table as she places it on her plate, and she says, "Dirty dreams, huh? Am I naked?"

Is she naked . . . pssh.

She's naked in a whole bunch of compromising ways.

"What kind of question is that? Of course you're naked." I grab a piece of pizza, but being more barbaric, I skip the spatula. "You're always naked. Naked upside down, naked with legs spread wide, naked on hands and knees, naked jumping up and down— one of my favorites—because dreaming of those tits jiggling is pure perfection." I kiss my fingers and flick them in the air. She snorts and shakes her head. "What about me? Do you picture me naked? Do I have a cannon of a cock?"

She side-eyes me as she bites into her pizza. "No, you have a micro penis in my dreams, and I spend about ten minutes trying to find it while it's erect."

Pizza half lifted to my mouth, I stare her down. "That's not fucking funny."

She smiles. "I thought it was." She chews. "Men are so predictable." In a fake, man voice she says, "Look at my penis, it's so big. It's the biggest thing any woman has ever seen. My massive man cock . . . eeer, look at me. Penis."

I must say, her man impression is lacking finesse.

"When it's true, it's true."

"Please. Every guy thinks their penis is the biggest."

"I don't think my penis is the biggest." I pause and then say, "I *know* it's the biggest."

She's not impressed, not one bit as she shakes her head at me, as if she's truly disappointed. "Oh, Knox, I thought you were better than that."

"I'm a dude, babe. Sorry to disappoint, but we will always think our dicks are magical and the best on the planet."

"Glad to know you're a douche like the rest; you were seeming too good to be true."

Fucking funny, this girl. It's why I can't get her out of my mind. She has this sweet and innocent air about her, but when she opens her mouth, she kills me with her witty tongue.

I wonder what else that tongue could do? Crazy sexy things, given the way she eats ice cream. *Fuck.* She's got to be an under-the-cock flicker. I'd bet my left nut on it. Christ, the thought of her flicking the underside of my cock has me harder than a flagpole right now.

A comfortable silence—well uncomfortable in my pants— stretches between us as we eat our pizza, and it isn't until we both finish our first slice that I bring up why I wanted to talk to her.

"So, about what I said in the library."

She wipes her hands on her napkin, the greasy pizza leaving its mark. "Yes, you said you wanted to talk? Was that your way of telling me this is over before it began?" She smiles, letting me know she's only joking, because that little comment nearly gave me a heart attack.

Over before it began? Yeah, fucking right. There is no way I'm ending this, not when I've barely skimmed the surface with this girl.

"Never." I smile. "I actually wanted to discuss our little bet."

"I'm not giving in, if that's what you're wondering."

Heaven forbid she does. It's fucking lunch. Who cares about Holt and Carson and their walk-out song?

Knowing her though, she's nowhere close to giving in. But I have some new thoughts on the subject.

"Nah, I know you're stubborn, babe, but I thought we should take advantage of the situation."

"What do you mean?" she asks, genuinely curious.

"Well, since we're both holding out on the physical, thanks to you—"

"How is it thanks to me?"

"Because I refuse to take blame for my celibacy."

#Fact. No horny college boy would ever take blame for his own celibacy.

She huffs. "Of course you won't own up to it."

"Should I pull out the court record?" I pretend to scroll through my phone and then point at the screen. "Ah, right here it says you bet you could hold out longer than I could." I look at her and smile. "I don't forget things like that, Ealson. This is on you."

She takes a sip of her drink and leans back in her chair. "Fine." She motions with her hand, "Proceed."

At least she knows when she's wrong.

I pick up another slice of pizza and offer it to her before I take one for myself. It's weird having a conversation like this in a busy school restaurant, but then again, our first kiss was in the dining hall next to her dorm. It's easy to ignore the raucous behavior and loud music, especially since we chose a two-person booth in the back corner.

"Since we're holding out on the physical, maybe we can focus on the other things, you know, like taking this exclusive casual relationship to exclusively serious."

"Serious?" she asks, worry in her eyes. I knew it would be a big step for her, but I need to do more with this girl than only make out with her. I want to know more. There are so many layers to Emory, so many facets that make her the way she is, and I want to dive into those. I want to learn the good and the bad about her. I want her to open up to me about everything. My mom was right when she gave me shit, thinking Em was my fuck buddy. She taught me better than that.

"We'll take it slow," I say, reaching out to hold her hand. "But I want to date you, Em. I want to take you out, call you my girlfriend, makes things official. We've been casual for a while now, so don't you think we should take things to the next level?"

Her fingers lace with mine . . . a good sign. She's not pulling away, at least not yet.

"We barely have time with each other now, how do you expect us to date?"

Valid concern, but where there's a will, there's a way.

"We'll make time. My schedule is slowing down, Christmas break is around the corner—"

"Which means I'll be going to California while you head to Texas. The timing isn't right, Knox."

"Fuck timing. I'm all in with you, Em," I admit, feeling slightly desperate. "And I want more." You would think a girl would be happy hearing that, but it only seems to make her more nervous, so I slow down a bit. "I'm not saying that sex is more. But I need you to know that my eyes are closed. You're all I see. It's you and you only. Before you freak out though, let's start with a real date. You dress up, I put on a tie, I take you out."

"You don't have to wear a tie, but maybe something other than a backward baseball hat and baseball hoodie."

I glance down at my hoodie and back up at her. "But you love this thing so much."

"Love to trash it."

"You act as if it's ratty and gross. It's Under Armour, babe, new this year. And I have five of them."

"Yes, I know. I've seen them all," she says with a sarcastic tone.

"Well . . . then, I expect you to wear a dress, not a skirt."

"You don't like my skirts?" Her brows crash together.

"No, I love them, I'm trying to punish you like you punished me."

She chuckles. "You're such a punk. Fine. I'll put on a dress for you."

"Then you agree? You'll seriously date me? Like full-on boyfriend and girlfriend type stuff?"

She swirls her straw around her drink a few times before looking back at me. "Isn't the girl supposed to ask things like that?"

"I'm an equal opportunist, babe."

She rolls her eyes and then sits up, leaning forward. She brings the back of my hand to her lips and she places a soft kiss across my knuckles. It's intimate, unexpected, and I fucking like it. "It's a date then."

"Sit." Coach Disik points to the chair in front of him.

I was called into his office this morning. His text was simple: *My office. Ten.*

Translation—when Coach beckons, you arrive when you're told. I have no idea what this is about but from the furrowed brow, I'm going to guess it isn't good.

I scroll through my rolodex of stupid shit I've done over the last two weeks, but nothing comes to mind. I'm going into this meeting completely blind.

Hands folded and resting on his stomach, he stares at me from under the intimidating brim of his hat.

"I never took you for a moron, Gentry."

Well, that's one way to start a meeting. Only causes me to shift in my seat while a bead of sweat rolls down my back.

"But what the hell are you doing?"

Err . . .

I shift in my chair again. "Would you be able to elaborate?"

"The girl."

"Emory?" I ask, trying to clarify why the hell I'm here.

"Sure." He runs his finger under his nose. "The girl in the library. Dora Flower told me about your run-in with the intern."

"Oh." I chuckle and let out a breath of relief. "It wasn't anything bad, Coach. We didn't take it any further than a kiss."

"You're not seeing this girl?"

"Wait, what?" I ask confused. "No. I am. She's my girlfriend."

"You're a dumbass. Perfect." He leans forward, lifts his hat, and runs his hand across his forehead. "You realize where you are in your life right now, right?" He holds up his finger. "One semester away from being drafted, and you get involved with a girl? That is the dumbest thing you could do. You need to focus on your future."

"Isn't a girl the future as well?" I don't know why I say it, apart from maybe I really am the dumbass Coach makes me out to be.

"So your life-long dream has been to be a boyfriend?"

Well, when he says it that way . . .

"No," I answer, feeling stupid.

"You're damn right it's not. It's to be a goddamn professional baseball player. This girl could be in it for all the wrong reasons."

"That's not how Emory is," I say. "She's different."

"They always are," Coach huffs. "Let's say she's different like you claim. What happens when she complains to you during the season that she never gets to see you? What happens when you have a fight, are you mentally prepared to push that to the side and do your job on the field?"

"I mean . . ." I've never even considered that. "I've never had a problem blocking things out before."

"You never had a girl before either, but you chose now to do so." Coach shakes his head and mutters, "Fucking moron." He blows out a harsh breath and turns to his computer where he starts typing away. "I can't force you to break things off with her, but there are plenty of other players ready to take your place if your performance suffers. Make the right choice for you and the team, Gentry."

"And what would that right decision be?" This is so fucked. He can't be serious that I have to choose between Em and baseball . . .

He tears his eyes from the computer screen and looks me up and down. "I think you know the answer to your own question." He nods toward the door. "Now get the hell out of here. I have shit to do."

I leave his office and head toward the locker room. I don't have class for an hour, so I have time to spare. When I walk in, I spot Holt lounging on one of the leather chairs, head dipped toward his phone, his thumbs beating rapidly over the screen.

I take a seat across from him, feeling defeated. He glances up and asks, "How'd your meeting go?"

Carson and Holt know everything when it comes to my life.

"Not great."

He pulls his head away from his phone. "What happened?"

"Coach found out about Emory, wants me to break things off with her." Even saying the words twist my stomach into knots.

"What? Why?"

"Thinks she'll be a distraction." I point to his phone. "Kind of like whoever you talk to day in and day out."

"You've been seeing Ealson for a while, and your game hasn't changed, why the concern now?"

"Because I'm a semester away from being drafted. I know he's looking out for me, but the way he went about it sucked ass. He doesn't even know her."

"What he doesn't realize is that some of us need the escape.

Not an escape like drugs or whatever. But a place to . . . retreat to. There's more to me than being an athlete, and I don't want to lose that."

I have no idea how long Holt has been seeing this girl of his or how serious it is, but what I do know is that he's been on top of his game ever since his nose has been buried in his phone. I asked him about her once and he said nothing, so I took that as him not feeling ready to talk about her. I wonder if he ever will be.

"Is that what this girl is to you? An escape?"

"Yeah . . . and more." He looks to the side, toward the showers and says, "She's locker room material, man."

Holy shit.

Even though I don't believe in the whole *locker room blessing* bullshit, my teammates do, and when someone says a girl is locker room material, that means a whole lot.

"Seriously?"

"Yeah. She makes me happy. When life's shit, and even when it's not, she gives me more . . . perspective I guess. Like she helps me shift my focus off myself. And fuck is she gorgeous." I've never heard Holt open up like this, so his honesty is welcome. Surprising, but welcome. "I can understand why Coach worries we'll be distracted, but what he doesn't understand is that some of us need that escape. We eat and breathe baseball. Sometimes we need to shut off that part of our brain and enjoy something other than the sport we were born to play." He shrugs, as if what he said wasn't just some heavy shit. "Em makes you happy, so don't fuck with that."

"I don't want to."

"Then don't." Holt picks up his phone again. "You know what's best for you, man. If that's Em, go for it."

"I will," I answer with determination. Coach isn't right on this one. Carson didn't shut up about Em to my mom, so I know he thinks she's cool. And now Holt. Baseball's my future, but I'm with Holt on this one. I want the girl, the one who's already my place of retreat. God, she certainly puts me in my place, and if that isn't a broader perspective, what is? No. Emory Ealson is staying.

I pick up my phone as well and start searching places to take my girl on a date. I also understand where Coach is coming from, but I've always been able to compartmentalize on the field. Being with Emory isn't going to change that.

CHAPTER TWENTY

EMORY

K *nox: What's your schedule?*
  Emory: *Friday, Saturday, and Sunday I have off . . . all perfect date nights.*
  Knox: *Do I hear a sense of excitement in your . . . typing?*
  Emory: *Maybe.*
  Knox: *That's cute, babe.*
  Emory: *What did you expect, for me to be dragging my feet?*
  Knox: *Yes, I love forcing my women to go out with me.*
  Emory: *How many women?*
  Knox: *Ten a month. I can't handle any more than that. You're number nine.*
  Emory: *Only ten, pish, child's play. Try fifteen. Ever wonder why I don't see you as much, it's because you're number twelve on my list.*
  Knox: *If I didn't know we were casually exclusive switching to seriously exclusive, I'd be worried. Those skirts attract men like flies to shit.*
  Emory: *Flies to shit? How pleasant.*
  Knox: *Texas, babe. I grew up with lots of horse shit and flies.*
  Emory: *What a beautiful childhood you must have had.*
  Knox: *Nothing beats scooping shit into wheelbarrows for cash.*

Emory: *I bet you looked hot doing it.*

Knox: *A skinny twelve-year-old me. Super hot.*

Emory: *Eh, no thank you. I only like you because of your muscles.*

Knox: *My dick will eclipse that thought once you get to know him.*

Emory: *Which will be never at this rate.*

Knox: *Mentally we've fucked at least two hundred times by now in my head.*

Emory: *Yeah? Tell me some of the things we've done.*

Knox: *Nice try, Satan's mistress. Fuck that. I'm not getting hard over text messages. No fucking thank you.*

Emory: *It will be fun, come on.*

Knox: *Nope. Not happening. I have a date to plan.*

Emory: *You're not like the average guy. Anyone else would have jumped on the invitation to sext with me.*

Knox: *I'm not average, babe. In any way. Plan to be wooed Friday night, think you can handle it?*

Emory: *Easy. I'm just wondering if you'll be able to handle the dress I'm planning to wear.*

Knox: *Bring it, Ealson.*

Emory: *Get ready to take a trip to Boner Town.*

Knox: *Erection City, here I come, I just booked a one-way trip.*

∼

"Oh my God, he's going to die."

I glance in the mirror, twirling so I can look at my backside. "You think so? The dress isn't too much?"

"Not at all," Dottie says, sitting on my bed. "And your hair, the honey highlights you added are gorgeous. They highlight your eyes."

I sift my fingers through the soft waves. I took a chance and got my hair done today, adding some honey coloring and more layers. It's not much of a change, just enough to make an impact. I spent the afternoon after classes primping for my date. I shaved all over, lotioned every last inch of my body with my best bergamot lotions, spent at least an hour on my makeup, and thankfully my hairdresser did my hair.

And the dress? Yellow with a razorback and deep V in the front. The fabric clings to every piece of my body and the hem hits at mid-thigh. I paired the dress with white heels and a white peacoat. It is winter, after all.

Knock. Knock.

"Ah, he's here," Lindsay screams while running in place.

"Settle down." I laugh. "We've seen him before."

"But this is different. You guys are taking things to the next level. What if he proposes tonight?"

"Oh my God." I roll my eyes. "We hardly see each other, but he's proposing? Get your shit together, Lindsay."

She tamps down her excitement. "Sorry, I got a little overzealous there. Want me to get the door?"

"Sure. I'm going to apply my lipstick one more time." I chose a subtle pink, but it gives my lips one solid color.

Lindsay takes off toward the door while I reapply and then fluff my hair. Dottie comes up next to me and says, "You look perfect, Emory. Enjoy tonight and let down your shield. He's a good guy, better than Neil ever was." She gives me a side hug and then takes off toward the common room where Lindsay is gushing over Knox.

"Oh my God, could that shirt be any tighter. Look at your biceps." His deep laugh floats into my room.

"I shrunk it on purpose. Did it do the trick?" I can imagine him flexing his biceps for Lindsay.

"Oh yes, is that a six-pack or an eight-pack? Can I feel?"

I take that moment to step out of my bedroom. "There will be no feeling of Knox's abs."

Knox spins around and the look on his face when he sees me is entirely too satisfying and something I'll remember for a *very* long time. His eyes peruse my body slowly as his hand drags over his mouth.

"Holy . . . shit," he says under his breath, taking a step forward. "Babe, you look . . . fuck, you look good."

"Thank you." He snags his hand around my waist and pulls me in close. He sifts his fingers through my hair, examining my new locks.

"This is sexy. I liked your hair before, but I like this even more." He glances down. "And your tits, fuck you're going to kill me with those things. Our bet was only about sex, right? I can suck on these tonight?"

Dottie snorts from behind.

"It's any kind of sex acts." I pat his cheek and then slide my hands over his black tight-fitting button-up shirt. Lindsay was right; you can see every curve of his strength through this fabric. His biceps are bulging, threatening to tear through the material. His pecs test the sturdiness of the buttons, and the taper of the shirt clings to his narrow hips, where he's tucked the hem into a pair of dark-wash jeans with a belt that sits low. Super sexy. "You look really good." I want him to know I just don't bust his balls, but I can appreciate everything about him. *Why the hell did we make this bet? I want to climb him.*

"Thank you." He lifts his hands to my cheeks where he lightly presses a kiss against my lips.

"Oh my God, they're sickeningly cute, aren't they?" Lindsay asks.

"Unfairly made for each other," Dottie answers.

Even though I want to keep my heart out of this as much as possible, because I'm still trying to put it back together, it's hard not to agree with them.

"I'm obsessed with this," I say, taking in the carts moving around the dining space. "Am I dressed too fancy for this place?" I scan the other patrons and take in their simple street clothing.

"You're dressed perfectly . . . for me. Who cares what everyone else thinks?"

After Lindsay and Dottie gushed for five more minutes, we left in Knox's truck and drove along the lake parkway until we came to Sauce and Dumplings, a beautiful dim sum restaurant right on the water. I've heard a lot of students talk about it but haven't been before. The surroundings are beautiful with the panoramic views of the lake, but since we're in a college town, the attire isn't as fancy as the candlelit restaurant.

But that's okay, because Knox is right: it's only about us.

We started out with tea that Knox didn't touch but instead ordered a Coke. Then some wanton soup, and now we're on to the main course that will be delivered on the carts. We've ordered a few different dumplings that I can't wait to sink my teeth into.

Knox picks up the first one with his chopsticks, his large hand expertly working the sticks like a pro and for some reason, it's a huge turn-on for me. Since I'm inept at using chopsticks, I default to my fork, feeling a little foolish.

"Are you ready to dive into being seriously exclusive?" he asks, taking a mouthful of what looks like a beef and broccoli dumpling.

"I am."

"Good." He holds up his next dumpling and says, "Tell me about your ex."

I should have known that was coming, but to ask so early in the evening? Risky.

"Going right for it, aren't you?"

"Yeah, because I want to get it out of the way. Get it off your chest, then we can move on. Tell me the kind of dickhead he was."

He has a point. I knew the question was going to be asked tonight. It's part of getting serious with him, we dig deeper, find out more personal things about each other. I would rather get this over with too than let it hang over our date.

"I met Neil when I was a freshman in high school and was immediately enamored. He was the first boy to ever look at me like I was pretty, the first boy to kiss me, the first to . . . have sex with me." Knox's jaw grows tight, but he doesn't say anything. "I quickly fell in love. I let him consume me. Everything Neil did was perfect, and I wanted to be a part of it, even if it meant ditching my friends on several occasions or setting my dreams aside so he could follow his. At first, he was sweet and supportive; he had an addictive personality. Fun and outgoing, obnoxious at times, but always knew how to rein it back in. I became very attached."

"That's why you stayed in California to go to school, because of him?"

I nod. "I applied to schools he was applying to and when he chose Cal State, I went with him, even though they didn't have the program I wanted to major in. But I wanted to be near him. I needed to be near him. It came to a point where he felt like my safety blanket. I'd been with him that long. But once we got to college, things started to get tense between us."

"How so?" Knox asks. I can see he's agitated in the high set of his shoulders, but his voice is soothing, even . . . interested. Neil never had the kind of self-control Knox shows. It's one of the many differences about them.

"He wanted to do things I didn't. He started to get into drugs, saying it was college and we won't have any other time to experiment. That wasn't for me though, so he'd go to parties without me while I stayed at home studying. He took advantage of that, how I take longer to learn something. Whenever I said I needed to study, he'd be out. And then one night, when I finished studying early and wanted to surprise him, I found him in bed with another girl."

Knox shakes his head. "What a stupid fuck."

"I didn't think so at first. I thought that maybe it was me, that I wasn't giving him the attention he needed, but I quickly realized that wasn't the case. He was a selfish prick, and I deserved better. I deserved more."

"You do, you deserve so much more than him."

"Yes. I know that now. After breaking up, I finished out the semester and applied to Brentwood. I got in, called up my girls asking if I could room with them, and then I slapped you in the face with a campus map. The rest is history."

"Do you miss him?"

"Neil?" I shake my head. "No. I don't miss him. There's a part of me that misses his friendship though, because in high school, he was my best friend. Losing that was really painful."

"And that's why rule number one exists, right?"

I take a bite of my dumpling. "Yeah, it is. Once I started to get to know you and realized how much I actually liked being around you, it reminded me of what happened with Neil. It's why I was so hesitant, Knox, why I don't ever want to lose our friendship. I don't just think you're hot or the sweetest guy I've ever met, I actually like you as a friend and want to hang out with you." I shrug, feeling really vulnerable. "I feel good when I'm with you, and I don't want to lose that."

"You won't. I'm not going anywhere."

"You better not." I finish off my dumpling. Chew. Swallow. Then, I ask, "So, no exes in your life I need to worry about?"

"Nope. You might have to fight off some groupies, but there are no exes in my life."

"Groupies? Really?"

"Come springtime, things get crazy. The locker room hussies, looking for that golden ticket. It's ridiculous."

"Ah, the locker room." I take a sip of my tea. "Ever consider taking me there?" I wiggle my eyebrows at him.

"Do you want to go there?" he asks, surprised.

"Have sex in a stinky, sweat-soaked room? I'll pass."

"It's a lot nicer than that. It's like a major league clubhouse. They treat us well because we bring in good money to the school." He cuts open another dumpling. "So, no comments on the no exes thing?"

"Not really, should I have some?"

"Don't girls freak out about being the first girl a guy's been in a relationship with?"

"Not me." And that's the truth. "If you were a douchebag, maybe, but you're sweet. You've been nothing but a gentleman to me, so why do I need to worry?"

He pauses, fork midway to his mouth when he cocks his head to the side, studying me. "You're so fucking cool, Ealson."

That makes me smile. I always appreciate being complimented on my looks, every girl likes to know the guy they're with thinks they're beautiful, but to be called cool by him? That spikes a wave of emotion inside of me. We really are friends, and I couldn't appreciate that more.

I give him a pointed stare and say, "Just don't cheat on me or I might have to cut your dick off in pure, blind rage."

He winces. "Deal." When things fall silent between us, he offers, "I hate what he did to you, but for what it's worth, I'm kind of glad Neil was a dickhead and therefore lost you. Because that means I get you now."

"Oh, you get me? Am I prized possession?" I joke.

Not even flinching, he smiles broadly and says, "Yup. And you're all mine."

Hot chocolates in my hands, I hold them up while Knox drapes a blanket over both of our laps. We're sitting outside a late-night coffeehouse on a deck that hangs over the lake, scattered with lounge chairs. Heat lamps warm the space while the water laps below us. We were able to secure a secluded lounge chair, away from the booming noise inside, and Knox takes no time at all snuggling in close and pulling me to his side.

The sky is completely dark. Faint stars dot the black abyss, and a few wispy clouds attempt to hide the moon. It's chilly, but the heat lamps, blanket, and Knox's warm body make everything comfortable.

I hand him his hot chocolate as he wraps his arm around my shoulders and presses a kiss to the side of my head.

"This place is so cool," I say as gentle acoustic covers play in the background.

"I came here my freshman year with a girl. We didn't hang out up here, but we grabbed coffee. I remember thinking if I was ever into a girl, I'd bring her to the deck."

"And you saved it for me?"

"Nah, brought three other girls up here before you."

"What?" I laugh and pinch his side. He yelps but chuckles as well.

"I'm just kidding . . . it was five."

"You're obnoxious."

He cups my face and turns me so I'm facing his cheeky grin. "But you like it." He lowers his lips to mine and places a soft, unhurried kiss across my mouth. He's not looking to deepen it, just enjoying the moment of our lips locking. I swipe my tongue across his lips, and he surrenders a low moan before pulling away.

He leans back against the lounger and says, "What does Christmas look like in your house?"

I rest my head on his shoulder and stare at the water. "Probably like every other household: matching pajamas with my parents and sister; big Christmas tree with crazy ornaments; cookies made to be consumed throughout the day; an adequate amount of presents under the tree. We're lazy all day, snacking and watching *A Christmas Story* on TBS."

"Really?" he asks, getting excited. "You do the non-stop marathon?"

"Of course. It's tradition."

"So do we," he says with excitement. "But we make cookies while watching it."

"Your cookies aren't already made?"

"Nope. Mom likes to make them that day as a family after presents are opened. We decorate them and watch *A Christmas Story*. I swear that poor mom in the movie was mine when I was growing up. I have two older brothers, and we were constantly asking for seconds. My mom never got a warm dinner."

"Two older brothers?" I ask. "Oh, how hot are they? I might need to trade up."

"One is married and the other is engaged. Nice try, Ealson. Plus, I'm the hottest out of the three, easily."

I hold out my hand. "Let me be the judge of that. Show me a picture."

He reaches into his pocket and pulls out his phone. He takes a second to find a picture, but once he does, he shows me the screen. Standing at least four inches taller in the middle, Knox has his arms around two guys who look identical. Instead of Knox's meticulously styled hair, theirs is scruffy and out of place. And instead of broad chests with thick thighs, they have the shape of a runner. They're cute, they are Knox's brothers, after all, but they're nothing compared to the hottie next to me.

"You have twin brothers?"

"Yup, and telling them apart is a real bitch. At twenty-seven, they wear the same shit and have the same hairstyle. They fuck with me all the time."

Oh, I can see it; a frustrated Knox trying to figure out which brother he's talking to.

"And the worst part is, their girls get in on it. It's a game they like to play with me. I once dotted Jack on the neck with a Sharpie while he was sleeping so I could tell who was who. That didn't last long."

"I think I'd like your brothers a lot."

"You would get along too well, it's scary. What about your sister? Do you get along with her?"

I twirl my hot chocolate. "We're okay. She's ten years older than I am so we're not super close, kind of in different phases of our lives. She didn't like Neil though, she made that quite clear when we were dating. I think it was one of the things that pushed us further apart. We've talked a little over the last couple of months, trying to build that relationship back up. My mom is adamant we do."

"Did you tell her about me?"

"No. I haven't told anyone about you."

"Ouch," he says on a chuckle. "And just last week I sent out a family newsletter with your face on the front and your name on the bottom, letting everyone know you're my girl."

"I hope it was a flattering picture."

"Nope, sent a real woof bag picture to everyone."

"That's fair, you know, since I haven't told my family about you."

"And why's that again?" He crosses his legs at the ankles, getting more comfortable.

"Self-preservation. I'm not ready for the invasion of my privacy. Don't worry, they'll find out at Christmas when I'm constantly hanging by my phone, waiting for a text from you."

And here's the truth I'm part terrified to share. He's probably thought me indifferent at times, a girl with a tough exterior. But I'm not really. This is offering him something that makes me vulnerable. He's awesome to joke around with, and I definitely love putting him in his place, but I can trust him with this.

"Are you saying you're going to miss me over winter break?"

"Yeah, I am. Terribly." I turn into him and run my finger over his jaw, the thick scruff of his five o'clock shadow pulling under my freshly painted fingernail. "I really like you, Knox, and I've become quite addicted to your random pop-ins and flirtatious texts. You make me feel special, something I'm not sure Neil ever made me feel."

"Damn, Ealson. I wasn't expecting you to say that." He scratches the side of his head. "You kind of made my stomach do flips."

"In a good way?"

He nods and brings his lips to mine, where he presses the softest of kisses across my mouth. "In a very good way. I like you a lot too. So even though we're breaking rule number two and not doing all the oral"—he winks—"I'm fucking happy just getting to know you."

"I think you're the first guy to ever say that."

"I'm pretty sure you're right." He laughs and presses another kiss to my lips. "But you're worth it."

～

L indsay looks past my shoulder and into my dorm room, then furrows her brow. "Where's Knox?"

"What do you mean?" I ask, rubbing my eye with my palm. "He dropped me off last night and went back to his place."

"What?" Lindsay's eyes nearly bug out of her head. "You mean he didn't make a move to peel that dress off you?"

"Nope." I sink into one of the armchairs in the common area. "We made out a little in his truck, but then he walked me to my dorm and kissed me good night. When he got back to the loft, he sent me a sweet text, and then I went to bed."

"How on earth did you two not do it last night? I'm honestly becoming sexually frustrated from you two not fucking."

I shrug and lean my head against the back of the chair in a dreamlike state. "It's more than just sexual attraction between us. We like each other past everything physical. I truly like being around him and getting to know him."

"Still, how do you keep your hands to yourself?"

"It's hard." I think back to being in the truck last night when I was on top of his lap, the hem of my dress almost around my waist as I straddled him. His hands roamed my back, mine ran over his thick chest. We kept things to our mouths only, but God, was I tempted to beg for more. Just from the strength and command in his hands, I know he's going to be amazing in bed, but now I feel determined to keep working on our friendship. The man I'm getting to know is one of the nicest—and often cockiest—I've ever known. I actually think our sexual relationship will be better the more we know about each other. Am I horny? Yes. So much. But, friends first. Always.

"Well, props to you for being so strong-willed. I would have sat on his face the first time he noticed me."

"Aren't you classy," I joke. "How are things with the freshman?"

"Ugh"—she flops to the side—"he's so immature."

"Well, he is fresh from high school, after all," I point out. "I'm sure it takes them at least a year to mature. What's he doing?"

"I can't tell you." She drapes her arm over her eyes.

"Well, now you're going to have to tell me."

"Tell you what?" Dottie asks, coming into the room, coffee in hand, her hair looking like she stuck her finger in a light socket overnight. She pushes Lindsay's legs up, sits, and then drapes Lindsay's legs over hers.

"Apparently Lindsay's freshman fling is immature," I provide.

"You haven't told her about the whole boob thing?" Dottie asks in disbelief. "Oh my God, Lindsay, you need to tell her."

"What happened?" I shift in my seat, ready for a story, because with Lindsay, the stories are always good.

"I just can't. You tell it."

"My pleasure." With a huge smile, Dottie says, "The guy likes boobs."

"Okay, so . . . he's a breathing male, makes sense."

"No." Dottie holds out her hand. "Like really likes boobs."

"Ohh-kay," I drag out, not sure where this is going.

"Two weeks ago, Lindsay invited him back to the dorm after class, when we were both gone. They started to get handsy, and he asked if he could see her boobs. Naturally, our very provocative friend said yes and whipped her shirt off along with her bra."

"Nothing new there," I tease.

"But then our good old freshman friend sat there, staring . . . for five minutes."

What the what? "No touching?"

"No," she groans past her arm.

"None," Dottie continues. "And when she tried to move things along, he stopped her and slowly circled his finger around her areola but never actually touched it."

"Like he was using some weird spiritual force," Lindsay adds.

"But no actual touching."

"No." Lindsay shoots up from the couch. "And he had the biggest boner I'd ever seen while doing it."

"Tell her the best part," Dottie urges.

She groans again. "After staring for five minutes, he left, and then the next day"—she takes a deep breath—"he gave me a pencil sketch of my boobs. It was so realistic, I even got turned on by the gesture."

"And she ended up having sex with him three times that day."

"I'm so ashamed," she groans.

"What?" I laugh, louder and harder than expected. "But you think he's immature?"

"Yes," she shouts. "Because now every time I see him, he gives me a boob sketch. I think it's hotter and hotter, and I end up fucking him again. Who has time to sketch boobs? That's so immature. And let's not even talk about what's wrong with me and why I like it."

"You like it because he's worshipping your body. Any girl would like that, even if it's in a weird sort of way."

"You don't think it's immature?"

"It's different," I say. "But different can be good. Look at me and Knox, our relationship is all kinds of weird, but it works for us. You do you, boo."

"This is annoying," Dottie says, looking between the two of us. "I need to find someone to be weird with." *Oh, Dottie. Our sweet, diabolical, and charismatic friend.* Her someone weird will eclipse Lindsay's and my men in weirdness. He'll have to be a man of steel to welcome her strength and passion.

"It will happen, just give it time."

CHAPTER TWENTY-ONE

KNOX

"Look at those sweatpants. How can you even deny yourself?" Carson asks, looking Emory up and down. "Holes, dude, there are holes. That shit is sexy."

"So sexy," Emory says, trailing her finger up her leg, around said holes, and then to my chin where she tilts my head and presses a sloppy kiss across my lips.

We're lounging in the loft, skipping a party this weekend, even though we're leaving for Christmas break next week. Finals are wrapping up. I have one left and so does Emory, but when I asked her if she wanted to study, she said she was good, as she feels confident in the material she's studied. Probably because after our date last Friday, we've really only talked on the phone, rather than seen each other. Oddly, I'm okay with that, because every night, I talked with her for over an hour.

"Stop trying to get me to break the bet," I say in between kisses.

"You're an idiot." Carson chucks a throw pillow at me. "If I was dating Emory, I would have given in to that bet after the first day."

"Because you have zero self-control."

He pops an Oreo from my stash in his mouth. "That's true."

Changing the subject, Em says, "So, Garrett, your freshman, he likes to draw boobs."

Carson laughs out loud, tipping his head back. So does Holt, who sets his phone down momentarily. "Fucking Garrett. The dude loves tits."

"Yeah, my roommate's."

"Those are your roommate's tits he's been drawing?" Carson sits up, looking shocked. "Damn, Ealson, how come you never introduced me?"

"Because she's with Garrett." Em rolls her eyes.

"Are they exclusive?"

Holt smacks Carson in the stomach. "Don't be a douche and steal a girl from your tit-drawing teammate. He earned the right to draw those things."

"How? He's a goddamn freshman with fumbling hands. You should see him behind the plate. I swear he's Coach's charity case. I don't know how he got on the team."

"Probably slipped Coach a tit drawing," I say, making my two friends laugh.

"Coach probably has a drawerful of Garrett's drawings. That dude is lonely as fuck."

"Aw, really?" Emory asks. "What about Mrs. Flower? There seems to be something between them. Her husband passed away, so maybe it could be a new love connection."

I shake my head. "Coach will never make a move. He's old and set in his ways. He lives and breathes baseball, so there's no way he'd make room for a woman in his life when he spends all his time harping on us."

"It's what makes him the best though," Holt says, checking his phone. "Hey, I have to go. My girl just got done with her shift."

"Are we ever going to meet this girl of yours?" I ask.

"Not any time soon." Without another word, Holt hops off the couch and makes his way to the front door where he leaves the loft. That was quick.

"What's that all about?" Carson asks, his eyes trained down the hallway. "I don't like him keeping shit from us."

"No idea, but he'll come to us when he's ready." I squeeze Emory and say, "Want to head to my room?"

"Please do," Carson says, not letting Emory answer. "Entice him, Em. Get him to break."

Standing up, she says, "I'll try my best."

We waste no time. I lock my bedroom door, making sure no dickheads can come in, and turn to my girl who's getting comfortable in my bed. I lean against the yellow of the door and say, "What do you think you're doing?"

"Getting comfortable." She reaches into her shirt and does some fancy fooling around until she sticks her arms back out of the sleeves along with her bra. She tosses it to the side and then takes down her hair as well, the long locks floating over her shoulders. The thin, white fabric of her shirt leaves nothing to the imagination as her pebbled nipples press against the fabric.

Jesus.

She's going in for the kill, and I feel my will slipping.

"Are you trying to kill me?"

She shakes her head. "No, just getting comfortable."

"You getting comfortable has given me a goddamn boner."

Her eyes focus on my sweatpants that are now bulging at the crotch.

She sits on her knees and wiggles her finger. "Then come here and let me take care of that for you."

"You're going to break the bet?" I ask, my brows shooting up to my hairline, my excitement peaking at an all-time high.

"No."

My hopes come to a crashing halt. And it must be written all over my face, because she chuckles and lends out her hand. "Come here, hot stuff."

Like a depressed puppy, I head to my girl, boner leading the way. She pulls me onto the bed and pushes me against the headboard so I'm sitting against it.

She straddles my lap and takes a seat . . . directly on my boner. I hiss through my teeth and clamp my hands around her hips.

"What the hell are you doing?"

"Talking to you." She smiles and shifts. "Mmm, you feel good."

"Stop it," I scold. "I know what you're trying to do, and unless you want my penis to fall off, I'd stop right fucking now."

"You're that determined to win you'd let your penis fall off?"

"Yes," I answer, glancing at her tits. Fuck, they're so perfect, and from the sight of them, she's just as turned on as me. *God, I want her*.

I have no clue how I'm not ripping her top off her right now, closing my mouth around her fucking gorgeous tits. My skin is heating, and all I can think about is her. On her back. On my cock. Fisting that hair while I fuck her from behind. *I can feel her heat on my cock through our clothing. Shit.* And I bet she knows how close I am to pulling down those sexy-as-hell torn sweats and sucking her pussy until she screams. *Shit. Why do I have this stupid bet with the sexiest girl in the world?*

I've got to get it together. Think of stats. Think of stupid baseball stats. *Anything.*

I lean over to my nightstand and desperately try to ignore the heat of her as I move. *Hell.* I take out a small box wrapped in red Christmas paper and hold it up to her. Finally finding my voice, I say, "Merry Christmas, babe." And somehow, *somehow*, I find self-control to simply watch her expression rather than look at her tits.

And it's worth it.

Her eyes fall to the box and then back at me. "You got me a present?"

"Of course." I squeeze her backside. "You're my girl, and I want to make sure you're my girl when I get back from Christmas break."

"Trust me, I'll be counting down the days." She takes the box and asks, "Can I open it?"

"Yeah."

With a huge smile on her face, she has no shame in ripping the paper off and opening the little velvet box. Her mouth drops open and her eyes turn soft. "Oh my God, Knox, it's beautiful."

I take the box from her and lift the very delicate necklace from the casing. White gold chain with a delicate heart strung through it. I knew the minute I saw it, I had to get it for her. It's subtle, almost too hard to see, but it's a gentle reminder that this girl has my heart.

"Can I put it on?"

"Please do." She lifts her hair, so I bring the small clasp around her neck, and as she leans forward so I can see what I'm doing, I clasp the two sides together. The necklace falls over her collar-bone, the heart so small, it blends perfectly with her beautiful skin. It's not ostentatious or lavish. *I need her to know that even though miles will separate us, she won't be far from my thoughts. I want to be close to her heart.* But do I tell her that? Would she feel pressure from that?

Her fingers go to the necklace where she feels it along her skin. "Thank you so much, Knox, I love it."

I bring her chin close and place a small kiss on her lips. "Just a reminder of who you belong to."

"Like I need reminding," she replies, wrapping her arms around my neck. She bites her bottom lip and says, "So, this bet . . ."

Fuck, yes, please break it.

"It's physical sex, right? Does that include dry-humping?"

I swallow hard and shake my head. "I don't think there's anything in the rules about dry-humping."

"So if I were to . . . say"—she slides off my body and pulls down my sweats. I lift off the bed to help her—"take these sweats off, would that be breaking the rules?"

I shake my head vigorously. "Nope. Not at all. That's a great idea actually."

Her thumbs loop through the waistband of her sweats. "And if I were to take these off, that would be okay?"

"Totally. Yup, take those right off."

With a devilish smile, she slowly works her pants off until she's only in a black G-string, the thin triangle of fabric between her legs barely concealing anything.

Fuck.

Me.

She pushes her hand through her hair and dips her head to the side. "What about my shirt? If I were to take that off, what are the rules on that?"

My mouth goes dry and my voice cracks when I answer her. "That's . . . yeah . . . that's totally okay."

"I thought so." She sits up on her knees and moves her hands slowly to the hem of her shirt but pauses. My dick pulses in my boxer briefs, begging for any sort of relief. In one smooth motion, she lifts her shirt over her head and tosses it to the side, leaving her completely bare-chested and beautiful.

Jesus. Christ.

Her tits.

Not huge, but perky as shit with little nipples that are hard like stone. And when she moves, they bounce slightly, letting me know there's some weight to them. Fuck, I need my hands on them, now.

"Your turn." She points to my shirt.

I want to be a savage beast and rip my shirt off from the collar to move this along, but I know what I have hiding under here, and I want to make sure I catch her appreciation. From behind my head, I pull my shirt over, then pull my arms through the sleeves and drop my shirt to the side. I sit up straight and watch as Emory's eyes rake over my chest, a sigh falling past her lips.

"Why are you so hot?"

I chuckle. "No clue, babe, but I don't want to dive into it. Come here."

She shakes her head. "Lie down flat, I want to ride your cock."

"Shit, Em."

I lie down and she straddles my lap, the tip of my cock moving past the waistband of my briefs. She reaches behind her and shifts her G-string to the side so her warm . . . wet . . . pussy is right on top of my throbbing—yet-covered—erection.

Greedy and wanting to feel her, I slide my hands up her sides to her breasts where I take both in my hands. So fucking perfect, like heaven in my hands as I squeeze and rub my thumbs over her nipples. She breathes heavily and shifts along my length, spreading her arousal as I work her tits.

"God, Knox, this is all I think about when I'm around you, feeling your cock between my legs."

Talk about a way to make a guy come on demand.

She sits back and slowly starts to move her hips. "I picture you above me, gliding your long cock in and out of me." Her eyes are closed, her hair dances down her back, and my hands now rest on her thighs as she takes control.

Slow.

I want inside her, so fucking bad.

She starts slowly, feeling me out and testing how long I can last.

Answer: not very long at all.

I've wanted Em from the minute I laid eyes on her. I've been patient. I've become her friend, earned her trust, and even though I'm desperate to bury my dick so deep inside of her, this is good enough if it's what she's willing to give me.

One step at a time. It's been my motto with her. *And she deserves that and more.*

The only protection between us is the thin fabric of my boxer briefs, which are already soaked from how turned on we both are, but she doesn't seem to mind, as she encourages me with her hips.

Hands glide along the divots of my abs as her mouth falls open and her head falls to the side, pure lust in her expression. It's sexy as shit, seeing her let go, watching her pleasure take over and seeing her give in to it. I want to see how much I can make her lose control. I want to know exactly what it looks like when her pussy clenches and I see nothing but pure euphoria unleashed.

Sucking in a sharp breath, I roll my teeth over my bottom lip and begin to move my hips to match her greedy movements, building the friction between us.

"Yes," she quietly murmurs, slipping her hands to my sides, her thumbs pressing into my skin as she tightens her grip. "Knox . . . yes."

Up and down. *Up and down.* She rubs her clit over my thick and hammering cock. Her beautiful tits shift with her rhythm, bouncing together, making my mouth water. I reach up and lift my torso as I bring one into my mouth and suck hard. She hisses as one of her hands grips the other boob and pinches her nipple. So goddamn hot. I knock her hand away and take over, sending her hips into a frenzy as a long, sexy moan falls from her lips.

She tastes so sweet. There's a hint of vanilla and something I can't place. Whatever it is, it's all Emory. *Amazing. Hot. Delicious.*

I'm quickly becoming addicted to everything about this woman.

"More," she says, bringing my head closer to her boob. I accept the invitation and suck even harder, adding a nibble that shoots her pelvis into a full-blown attack on my cock. Shit, in a matter of seconds my legs tingle and my stomach tightens.

God, my orgasm's building, and she's only been on top of me for five seconds.

"Fuck, you're so big," she says, "I love how thick you are beneath me. Love how your muscles tense and ripple with every roll of your hips."

Can't hear that enough.

I pick up my pace, shooting my hips into hers, watching as her mouth falls open with every thrust. When her fingers connect with my nipples, I let out a long, aroused moan. Fuck . . . yes. She scrapes her nails across them, causing me to jolt my hips up even harder.

"Oh God," she cries out. "Don't do that. I want to last longer."

"Don't play with my nipples then," I groan as the devil woman herself takes one between her fingers and thumb. "Fuck, Emory.

Don't." My hands fall to her thighs, where I intentionally move her faster.

She pinches again.

"God damnit," I groan. My eyes squeeze shut as my cock grows even harder with need. And when she does it one more time, I let out a guttural growl and attempt to flip her to her back, but she stops me.

"No. I want to ride you."

"And I want to fuck you," I admit, my will snapping.

"No fucking," she states, breathless.

"Emory."

"No. This or nothing. I'm not winning this bet in the heat of passion."

"Fucking hell," I say in agony. I desperately pull on the short strands of my hair, trying to gather myself.

She takes that moment to lean back and rest her hands behind her, so she's propping herself up on my thighs. My gaze falls to our connection where I catch a glimpse of her aroused and wet pussy.

Shit.

Fuck.

I want that pussy so damn bad.

I lick my lips, my eyes jumping to hers for a brief second before they fall back to our connection. *So damn sexy.* I sit up on my elbows as she leans back farther and feverishly rocks her hips, creating a scorching angle for the both of us. *She's so wet. Hot. Fuck.*

"Yes," she moans, her head falling back. "Oh God, yes. Right there," she says, moving her hips even faster.

Shit, hearing her, feeling her . . . my balls tighten.

"Knox, oh God, right there." I thrust my hips up, her tits jiggle, her mouth parts as an indistinct sound flies out of her mouth. She flings forward, her hands falling to my chest as she rides my cock harder than before, and that's all it takes. My entire body ignites and then goes numb as the first wave of my orgasm hits me like a Mack truck to the chest.

Sparks ricochet through my body the minute she groans my

name, the sound so desperate. *Fucking hell.* My hips fly up against hers, my control snaps, and we both orgasm, grinding out every last ripple of pleasure until our hips finally slow.

She slinks forward and presses her chest against mine, her sweaty and slick body sliding against mine as her hard nipples graze my skin.

So fucking sexy.

Her fingers lazily stroke over my arm as I run my hand over her backside and under the thin black string to grip her whole ass.

"You're so goddamn hot," I say, not letting up on my grasp as my other hand runs circles along her back.

She sits up a few inches and looks down at me. *Stunning.* The smile on her face. Her eyes, half-lidded with lust. *I put that there. I gave* that *look to my girl.* "I can't wait to feel you fully between my legs, Knox," she whispers.

"Neither can I, beautiful." *How about right now? I'll be ready in about thirty seconds.* "When?"

And then I see Miss Sassy reappear, and I know what's coming.

"When you break the bet."

I look at our practically naked bodies and then back at her. "Uh, I'm pretty sure your wild ways just did that."

"Oh, hell no." She shakes her head. "That was not what we bet on."

"I think we bet on oral, right?"

She nods. "Exactly." She pauses and looks to the ceiling in question. "Wait, I can't remember what we bet on now. Was it sex in general or just oral?"

"I can't remember either which means if it was just oral, I could strip this tiny scrap of fabric off you, and bury my dick between your legs, it wouldn't be breaking the bet, right?"

"Ye—" She pauses again and thinks about it. "Well, I guess not if it was just oral. But is that what we bet? Should we call Carson?"

"No. We are not calling Carson. Let's just pretend it was only oral." I flip her to her back and hover above her but before I can move in for a kiss, she palms my face to stop me.

"Don't even think about it. If you're going to put that dick inside me, you're going to go down on me first."

A shiver runs up my spine from her exception. "You know, it's really fucking hot when you talk like that." I lift her hands above her head, pinning them under my force. "But you need to know one thing: when it comes to fucking, I'm always in charge."

CHAPTER TWENTY-TWO

EMORY

I f dry-humping were a sport, Knox and I would be Olympic gold medalists.

The last three nights, we've shamelessly been grinding on each other like randy teenagers, huffing and puffing, rubbing and smashing our pelvises together until we both come with such sheer force that we pass out after. Twice at the loft, once in the dorm.

I want to say I'm embarrassed from having zero inhibition while boisterously voicing my pleasure while humping my boyfriend's lap, but I'm not.

I'm loud, it's true, but oh my GOD, Knox's penis is the best thing I've ever slid along my clit. So thick, so hard, so long.

Just . . . flawless.

The last time, I was completely naked, the only thing between us was Knox's Under Armour boxer briefs. They're made of a slick fabric, so there's no chafing, just pure, hard cock beneath me.

I shot off so fast, I twisted our rules a little and gave Knox a hand job to get him off. I don't think he minded, given the way his hands dug into the blankets below us.

I was so tempted to put my mouth on his cock, to bring it deep into my throat, but I held strong despite the burning need inside me to make his eyes roll in the back of his head with a light flick of my tongue along the underside of his length. I honestly don't know how I'm holding off, waiting, because every time I see him, a burning wave of need rips through my bones, practically bringing me to my knees.

Finals are over for me. I leave for California today, and I have about two hours until I have to be to the airport, and that's pushing it.

I glance at my phone, checking the time. Where the hell is he?

Suitcase stuffed to the side, I shift on my feet and try to ease the nerves fluttering in my stomach. He wanted to take me to the airport, and I wasn't going to fight about that, because I wanted him to take me too. Lindsay and Dottie left on Monday but since I had one more exam to take, I couldn't take the same flight as them, which means, I have the dorm to myself.

The door to our dorm opens—I gave him Dottie's key so he could get into the building—and I pose at the edge of my bed.

"Babe, you here?" his deep voice calls out.

"In my room."

I hear the sound of his backpack hitting the couch and then the door pops open. He walks in looking like a GQ model in his dark-wash jeans and light-blue sweater with the sleeves pushed up to his elbows. His hair is styled, and his eyes are popping against the blue fabric spanning across his chest.

He looks so freaking good. *I'm going to miss this. Him. Us.*

And when his eyes connect with my outfit, and I see the way his face shifts into pure lust, I can't help but get excited for what's to come next.

Decked out in a yellow lace demi bra and matching thong, I don't move while he slowly rakes over me with a heated gaze. His perusal sends tingles up my spine, especially when he kicks off his shoes, tears his sweater over his head, and makes his way toward me, his eyes never leaving mine.

His beefy arm wraps around my waist first before he runs the er up the back of my neck and brings my mouth mere inches from his.

"What's this?" he asks, his hand falling to my bare ass.

"Merry Christmas," I say, looping my arms behind me and undoing my bra.

He growls when the fabric hits the floor and my already hard nipples skim across his bare chest.

Knox's chest is thick. It's the only way I can think to describe it, as if three chests were stacked on top of each other. His shoulders and arms are carved like stone, every indentation and perfectly sculpted muscle visible. And then his stomach. Despite the intake of food I've watched him consume in one meal, his abs are tight and chiseled, and the V at his waist is deep. I'm tempted to run my tongue over the rooted divots.

"Are you my Christmas present?" he asks, sliding his hand lower down my backside, dragging my thong with him until it falls down my legs. His lips taste my neck, slowly, methodically igniting goosebumps over my skin.

"I am."

"What does this Christmas present entail? Breaking a bet?" he asks, his voice sounding almost desperate and strained. *It's exactly how I feel.*

"No, of course not."

He breathes out heavily and laughs. "You're going to fucking kill me, Em."

"I'm holding out. I really want that steak dinner."

"I'll get you a steak dinner anytime you want." His lips move up my neck to my jaw. "Just name when and where."

"It's not the same. It wouldn't be a steak dinner won from my sheer ability to resist you."

"You're not resisting me now," he says as he lowers me to my bed. Staring at my bare body, he undoes his jeans and takes them off along with his socks. Standing in his briefs, his erection pressing against the fabric, he positions himself between my legs and my heart skips a beat.

191

Oh my God, is he going to go down on me?

He licks his lips, a heady look in his eyes as he lifts one of my legs to his mouth. Starting at my ankle, he presses long, languid kisses up my calf to my knee—*my breath catches*—to my inner thigh —*my heart hammers*—to my bikini line when I gasp out loud when he parts his lips from my skin.

A wave of arousal pools at my center as he picks up my other leg and continues his tortuous, yet consuming kisses up my limb, repeating the little pecks he gave to my right leg, pausing at the inside of my knee, scraping his jawline along my inner thigh until he hits my bikini line.

Shamelessly, my legs fall open. His eyes darken and narrow, his focus on my clit. I know he can see how aroused I am; it's hard not to when I'm already so incredibly wet. I want his finger inside me. I want him to taste me like that, but we know better. One taste. That would be all it would take . . . for either of us. *One. Taste.*

Pressing forward, he kisses above my pubic bone, up my stomach to my breasts where he greedily sucks one of my nipples into his mouth while the hand not pinning mine down rolls my other nipple between his fingers. When he sucks my boob into his mouth, it's everything I've ever dreamed off. Soft slow sucks followed by hard, gasping bites.

"Oh God," I moan loudly, my hips thrusting toward his. I pull at my hands, but he doesn't budge. "Let me touch you."

"No," he mutters against my breast before he moves to the next one, taking my nipple in one suck. He nibbles, laps, sucks, and kisses, until I'm a writhing mess beneath him.

I'm about to burst. I've never experienced anything like this— the teasing touches, the lazy kisses, the appreciation of my body. *This* is what I missed out on. Thank God I left . . .

Knox makes me feel beautiful, like a desirable woman, some-thing I've never felt before. The look in his eyes when he gave me my gorgeous heart necklace floored me. And his words, *"Just a reminder of who you belong to." Everything he does and says . . . Yeah, it turns me on, but it also makes me feel precious. Worshipped. His.*

"Knox, please . . ."

"Please what?" He smiles against my breast.

Yeah . . . *please what?* I don't know what I'm begging for, all I know is that I'm begging for something.

"I can't . . . ah, God, yes, bite me again." He nibbles on the side of my breast, sucking hard and then scraping his teeth. No doubt he's leaving his mark. He works his way to my collarbone, to my neck, then my lips where he swipes his tongue across my mouth. When I open for him, he leaves me hanging and trails his lips back down my neck, lighting up my heated skin with every pass of his mouth.

He kisses my collarbone.

Between my breasts.

To my ribs.

I suck in a deep breath.

To my stomach.

Above my pubic bone.

My legs spread.

To my left thigh.

My right.

I groan.

And then he hovers, right above the juncture between my thighs. The air stills around us, my pulse hammers in my throat, my aching clit begging for release as it thrums desperately with need.

One gust of air and I'll go off, and when he lowers even closer, I almost explode. Then he kisses the spot right above my slit.

"Jesus, yes," I say. But instead of him moving down one more inch, his lips progress north. And I groan out in frustration, tears billowing at my eyes. "No, oh my God, Knox. Please."

"Please what?"

"Please lick me."

His tongue swirls around my belly button as he looks up at me. "Like that?"

"No, you ass," I say, unable to control myself. His chuckle only turns me on even more. "Lick my pussy."

"Hot damn," he mutters as he continues to move his mouth over my body. "Even though hearing you say that almost made me come in my pants, there is no way." He moves up my body, releases my hands, and scoots his briefs down so his cock juts out. A serious look in his eyes takes over as he says, "I'm clean. Just got tested a few months ago, and I haven't been with anyone since."

I swallow hard. Is this really happening?

"Me too."

On a primal grunt, he lowers his hips to mine where his cock connects with my clit. A low hiss escapes our lips as he stills my pelvis with his hand.

"Just rubbing, Em, do you hear me?" He stares at me, completely serious. "Nothing else."

"Okay." I nod, knowing what a huge step this is.

Wet-humping, I'm good with that. *So good with that.*

Still pressing my hips into the mattress, he starts to move his length up and down my slit. Slick and ready, he glides easily over me, the feeling so raw, so carnal with nothing between us that my orgasm already starts to spike deep in the pit of my stomach.

"God, Knox, you feel so damn good. I love your cock. So big."

"Can't hear . . . that enough," he grunts, eyes squeezed shut as his pace picks up. "Fuck, baby, this feels—"

"Amazing, so freaking amazing." I raise my hands above my head and grip the comforter beneath me. "Faster, Knox, oh God, faster. Yes," I breathe out when he picks up the pace.

He groans before his mouth falls to mine. I open to him, and his tongue dives down, tangling, pulling every last ounce of self-control I have left. I clamp my legs around his waist and thrust my hips into his cock when he slides up and down, creating the most beautifully exquisite friction I've ever felt.

One stroke.

Two.

Oh fuck, every nerve ending is on fire as my throbbing clit spasms along his length.

"Fuck, oh my God, yes, Knox, yes," I yell, my orgasm hitting me so damn hard that my mouth falls open, but no words escape me.

It goes on forever, sending wave after wave of pleasure up my spine.

"Christ," Knox groans and then stills as wet, hot spurts hit my stomach. His orgasm is sexy, the way his voice rumbles deep in his chest and his body shakes above mine. *So freaking sexy.* Chest filled with air, he expels it and then collapses on top of me. The weight of his body comforting, like a heated blanket on a cold, wintery day.

My hand travels up and down his back as his lips press gently into my neck. He takes in a deep breath and sighs.

"Fuck, babe, I don't want you to leave."

"I know." His head lifts, and he pushes a stray lock of hair behind my ear. I hate that we won't see each other for a month. "What happens if you run into an old fling in Texas?" *I hate how insecure I sound right now, but I can't help it.* I'm close to tears. I don't want to leave him. *I don't want to lose him.*

"Clearly I'm going to fuck her." His joking smile does nothing to ease my worry. "Come on." He squeezes my side. "You know I'm kidding."

"I hate to be that girl, but I don't find that crap funny. You know what happened with—"

"Shit, Em, I didn't mean it like that." Immediately his face softens with understanding. "I'm sorry." He leans down and runs his lips over mine before pressing his palm above my heart. "This right here, this belongs to me." He takes my hand and presses it above his heart. "And this, this right here belongs to you. There is nothing you need to worry about, okay?"

I know he's right. He's done nothing but show me true commitment. Through our make-out phase. He's been patient, willing to wait, even now when he showed incredible restraint.

Respect. He wants to know me, not just my body, and I truly love that about him.

"Okay." Tears start to well in my eyes. This is so stupid. I was never supposed to get involved with someone right after Neil, but somehow, Knox Gentry wiggled his way into my world, and I can't seem to shake him . . . not that I want to. The darkness that clouded my heart after Neil and I broke up has gone, and my soul is beginning to feel again.

Knox is everything I've hoped for in a man. He makes me laugh, he challenges me, keeps me on my toes, and . . . he cares about me. In the last few months, he's shown me the type of man he is: genuine.

"Hey, don't get upset." One tear falls down my cheek and I blink rapidly to hold back the others.

"I'm sorry." I wipe my eyes, chastising myself for showing emotion like this. "This is stupid, I don't know why I'm getting so upset."

"Because you like me . . . a lot, and you're going to miss me." When I don't answer him, he says, "You don't have to say it, Em. I can see it. I can feel it. And guess what, I'm going to miss you so fucking bad too."

With both hands, I cup his cheeks and bring his mouth to mine where I seal our lips together, wanting to capture as much of him as possible before I leave.

One month without Knox.

One month without his smile, his laugh, his teasing.

One month without his caring caresses and insane surprises.

One month without his hands, his mouth, his cock.

One month without . . . *us.*

I'm not sure how I'm going to make it.

I just hope after one month apart he still wants to be with me, because even though I wasn't looking for this, he's stolen my heart. *And I don't want him to let go.*

Maybe ever.

CHAPTER TWENTY-THREE

KNOX

"Tell me all about her," my mom says, taking a seat across from me, tea in hand and a plate of toffee from Grandma Sue between us.

"Where do I start?" I ask, looking at the ceiling of our humble ranch on our three acres of property. It's small compared to most properties in our ranching town, but we've lived here for nearly twenty years, have two horses and some chickens, doesn't take a huge amount of maintenance, so it works for our family.

"Do you have a picture?" Ever since I got back home, my mom has been grilling me to talk about Emory, but I keep putting her off, wanting to get some much-needed sleep from the grueling semester. When I woke up this morning, I told her I'd tell her everything she wants to know after I worked out, took some swings in the cages, and did some chores around the house.

Once I was out of the shower and dressed, she was waiting outside my bedroom, tin of toffee in hand, and a giddy look on her face. All she said was, "It's time."

Reaching into my pocket, I pull out my phone and hold up the screen to her. A few weeks ago, I changed my lock screen and wallpaper to a picture of Emory smiling at me. Her honey-colored hair falls past her shoulders in waves, she's wearing one of those sexy skirts of hers, and her thick lips are painted in pink. Sometimes, I just stare at it because that's how infatuated I am.

Gushing, my mom says, "Oh Knox, she's beautiful. How cute are you for having her on your phone?" She studies the picture a little harder. "Are those her real lips?"

"Yes." I hold back the sigh. They're very much real; if only I knew how they felt around my cock.

"Well, she's stunning, but does her personality match her looks?"

"Easily," I answer, taking the phone back. "She's really sweet, timid at times, and I don't think she realizes how beautiful she really is. And fuck, Mom, she's funny. Loves giving me shit."

"Now that's my kind of girl." She sips from her tea. "Are you in love?"

I shrug, truly unsure. "I'm obsessed, not sure about love. I've never been in love before, so I don't really know. But, I will tell you this, I fucking miss her hard right now."

There's a twinkle in my mom's eye, and I think she knows something I don't—something I might be a little afraid to admit at this point in our relationship—so I let her have her suspicions.

"Did you get her a Christmas present?"

"Yeah." I pick up a piece of toffee and pop it in my mouth, letting the flavors melt on my tongue before chewing. Grandma Sue knows her way around a toffee recipe. "Got her a little heart necklace, just something to let her know I'm always with her."

My mom clasps her hands to her heart. "Oh, that's so sweet. I raised such a lovely boy."

"Yeah, you did some things right," I tease.

"Some things? I did a lot of things right with you boys. All so sensitive and polite, I couldn't be prouder." Her lips hover the edge of her mug before she says, "Now, are you using protection?"

I roll my eyes, knowing that was coming. "Don't worry, Mom,

we haven't had sex." Dry-humping, yes. Dry-humping with no clothes, yes, but actual sex . . . that's a big fat nope.

And I'm surprisingly not mad about it.

Do I want to get inside her? Truly connect with my girl? Hell, yeah, but I almost like this crazy foreplay we have going on, the buildup is intense, and I know the minute we finally snap, it's going to be explosive.

Stunned, my mom sits across from me, mouth agape. I don't hide shit from my mom, so she knows I've had sex, multiple times, with multiple women. I don't go into detail, because I'm not a sick fuck like that, but she knows, and I don't try to hide it. It's what I love about my mom, she really is a best friend.

"You haven't had sex with her?"

"Nope." I pop another piece of toffee in my mouth. "I mean, we've done some things, but sex, not yet."

"That's . . . wow, I wasn't expecting you to say that."

"Are you calling me a manwhore, Mom?"

"No." She chuckles. "I'm just surprised, given your track record with women. You must really care about her."

"I do. A lot." I sit back in my chair, slouching against the Windsor back. "She was hurt badly by her ex of six years. She was really skittish at first, really wanted nothing to do with me, but I knew she was special. I took things slow and we've gradually been building a foundation . . . a friendship."

"Oh, be still my heart, I don't think I can take this. My baby is all grown up and finding the perfect girl."

"Yeah, she is pretty perfect, that's for damn sure."

"Do I get to meet her this spring?"

"I hope so. I haven't given her my schedule yet, but our first exhibition game is shortly after we get back from break. I'm kind of hoping she goes. She hasn't seen me play yet."

Brentwood is the only college baseball team with an indoor/outdoor stadium thanks to the heavy tuition and dedicated sponsors—aka, professional baseball players—making our fields the destination during the early semester months. We host many exhibitions before we head south for outdoor tournaments right before our season begins. It also makes training year around easy since we're not hindered by the weather. It's what takes our teams to the next level and why we're a force to be reckoned with.

"Well, isn't she in for a treat then? You're so wonderful to watch play."

"Thanks, Mom." And I know she means that. She's been my number-one fan for as long as I can remember, my brothers second to her. Their support is one of the reasons I've been able to succeed in my sport.

She pats the table. "You know what, I need to start bedazzling a hat for her. We can't have her looking foolish with nothing to support the team with."

Because a bedazzled hat isn't foolish . . .

But I would never say that. My mom loves her hats. She takes them very seriously and I would never ruin that for her.

"I think that's a great idea, Mom. She'll love it."

"Oh dear, I really like this girl already and I haven't met her. I can tell, Knox, we're going to be wonderful friends."

I sure as hell hope so. The girl who owns my heart will own my mom's too. It's inevitable. I've watched her welcome two sisters into our family through her genuine and heartfelt kindness, and I want that for my girl too. It's what my mom deserves. It's what my girl will deserve too.

"**M**erry Christmas, baby," I say while leaning back against my headboard and holding my phone out in front of me.

Emory's smiling face takes up the screen, a Santa hat on her head, and bright red lipstick on those delicious lips.

"Merry Christmas, Knox." I think she's in her bedroom, but I can't really tell because she seems to be sitting in a chair.

"Get anything good?"

She runs her fingers along her necklace I gave her and then

says, "Some clothes and gift cards. I also got this picture frame with a really hot, shirtless guy in it."

I wiggle my eyebrows. "Dottie slipped the present under the tree for me."

"Yeah, and opening it in front of my parents, grandparents, and Uncle Zeke was really enjoyable, especially when Uncle Zeke asked why there was a naked guy on the front."

"Oh shit." I laugh. "I didn't think about that. I wasn't naked."

"Well, the glove covering your junk isn't necessarily clothing either."

"You would be surprised how long it took me to take that picture."

"Dottie took a picture of it and uses it as her lock screen on her phone."

Of course. I drop my head back and laugh. "I wouldn't expect anything else from her. But you like it?"

"I stare at it way too much, but you could have done something about your pasty white legs."

"I thought about self-tanner but nixed that idea. I wanted you to see me au naturel."

"Slightly blinding but still sexy."

"Damn right it's sexy. I told my mom about the photo and she chastised me for a second before she started laughing. When I showed it to her, she shielded her eyes but then took a look. She appreciated the glove . . . cupping my balls."

She shakes her head in humor. "There is something seriously wrong with you, but thank you, it's my favorite present I got today. Did you get the little package from me? It's nothing like what you gave me, but it's something."

"I did. I love the cookies, fucking good. I was kind of hoping you were going to slip a pair of panties in there for me, something I could hold on to when I fall asleep at night."

"I would never do that."

"Not even a little thong?"

"No."

"Come on." I smile at her. "Loosen up, babe."

"There is no way in hell I will ever send you panties in the mail. What if the package gets lost, then some creep is going to have my underwear hanging on his wall where he stares at it every night while gripping his crooked penis. No, thank you."

"There are so many things wrong with that sentence, too many to ask about, but I do need to know one thing."

"What's that?" Her smile is so damn contagious.

"The panties, how are they hung up on the wall? Duct tape? Push pins? Nail?"

She doesn't answer right away, just blinks a few times. Finally she asks, "What is wrong with you?"

"I'm going to take that as duct tape."

∾

Knox: *BAAAAAAAAABE!!!!!!*

Emory: *Let me guess, you got my package?*

Knox: *Panties!! I'm wearing them right now.*

Emory: *Stop it. No, you're not.*

Knox: *Nah, I couldn't get them past my quad-zillas.*

Emory: *You're obnoxious. Your thighs aren't that big.*

Knox: *You haven't seen me in two weeks. They're massive, babe.*

Emory: *They're probably still the pasty chicken thighs I know very well.*

Knox: *Hey, watch yourself. They're not chicken thighs. They're beefy man legs.*

Emory: *Sure . . .*

Knox: *Keep doubting me, when I see you next, I'm going to choke hold you with them.*

Emory: *How romantic.*

Knox: *Want to know what romantic is?*

Knox: *[Picture]*

Emory: *What the hell is wrong with you? Why did you hang my panties up with duct tape?*

Knox: *Seemed like the thing to do. At least the guy gripping his dick while looking at them doesn't have a crooked member.*

Emory: *Or so you think.*

∾

E **mory:** *What is this?*
Emory: *[Picture]*

Knox: *What do you think it is?*

Emory: *It looks like a jockstrap, but I couldn't fathom why you'd send them to me with some of Grandma Sue's toffee.*

Knox: *It is in FACT my jockstrap.*

Emory: *Why on earth would you think I want this? (P.S. thank you for putting it in a Ziplock bag so it didn't taint the toffee)*

Knox: *You send me panties, I send you my jockstrap. Don't worry, babe, I washed it but did press it against my naked penis right before I sent it, in case you wanted to feel close to me.*

Emory: *You realize this is worse than texting me a dick pic, right?*

Knox: *No way, it's so much better. Consider it your new pillow.*

Emory: *Wow, we really aren't going to make it a month. I never knew we were going to breakup over a jockstrap.*

Knox: *Babe, don't hate on the crotch protector. That right there is romance.*

Emory: *Sorry to be the bearer of bad news, but this is not romance.*

Knox: *A little.*

Emory: *The opposite of romance.*

Knox: *A tiny bit of romance.*

Emory: *I almost puked in my mouth when I opened it.*

Knox: *Now you're just being dramatic.*

Emory: *Excuse me, I need the toilet again.*

∾

K *nox:* WHAT??? IS?? THIS???

Knox: *[picture]*

Emory: *Take a wild guess.*

Knox: *Why did you send me an insert to your bra?*

Emory: *Since we're sending each other things . . .*

Knox: *Babe, this is . . . please tell me this touched your tit.*

Emory: *Multiple times.*

Knox: *I could cry right now. I'm going to wear it as a face mask.*

Emory: *If you do, I'm going to need a picture of that.*

Knox: *Orrrrr, I can duct tape it next to the panties. Have a little shrine of you on my wall that I can stare at before I go to bed. Damn, I'm so undecided.*

Emory: *The possibilities are endless.*

Knox: *Or, I can have my crafty mom sew me a pillow using both panties and tit insert. Now there's an idea I can get on board with.*

Emory: *DO NOT DO THAT!*

Knox: *Already done.*

Emory: *I am not kidding, Knox.*

Knox: *She likes the color of your panties, very flattering to your skin color she says. I've been showing her pictures of you.*

Emory: *If you're not kidding right now, I'm going to murder you.*

Knox: *She also complimented your cup size and wants to know if you sleep with my jockstrap.*

Emory: *No, I wear it over my head, using it as an eye patch so my parents think I've truly lost it.*

Knox: *Aye, matey.*

Emory: *Did you really show your mom?*

Knox: *Nah, your pussy and tits are private, only for me.*

Emory: *Good answer, which means you get topless FaceTime tonight.*

Knox: *Jackpot!*

∽

E **mory:** *I'm afraid to open this package.*

    Emory: *[Picture]*

    Emory: *You sent me a jockstrap last time, who knows what this could be?*

    Knox: *Good, you got it! The person at the post office confused the shit out of me, and I had no clue what postage I was paying for.*

    Emory: *If I open this, is something going to jump out at me?*

    Knox: *Nah, babe. It's a good one. No jockstrap. No peanut snakes.*

The phone rings in my hand and I answer it immediately, letting the phone open to FaceTime so I get to see my beautiful girlfriend.

"Hey you," I say, leaning back on my headboard. I just finished a vigorous weightlifting session so my muscles feel like mush. But when Emory looks at the phone, tears streaming down her eyes, I nearly bolt out of bed. "Em, what's wrong?"

She holds up my shirt I sent her and brings it close to her nose. I was trying to think of something else to send her, something a little more meaningful and then it hit me the other day. I grabbed one of my Brentwood baseball T-shirts, sprayed some cologne on it—because why the hell not—and then packaged it up for my girl with a sleeve of Oreos. You can never have enough of those.

The tension in my shoulders eases as I realize she's crying happy tears, not sad ones. "You okay?" I ask, just wanting to make sure. When she shakes her head, that tension reappears. "What's wrong?"

She wipes a tear away, one I wish I could wipe away myself. "I miss you."

Don't smile; she won't appreciate that.

I know she likes me, but I've wondered if my feelings for her eclipse what she feels for me. Maybe that's true, but right now, it almost feels like it's equal. Hell, her admission makes me want to puff out my chest like a proud goddamn peacock. Understandably, Em was reticent and careful, but now she's opening up to me.

"I miss you too, Em."

"Ugh, this is stupid. I shouldn't be crying." She wipes under her eyes again and holds my T-shirt close to her. "But this means a lot to me, Knox. Thank you."

"You're welcome. If I knew I'd get this kind of reaction, I would have sent you a shirt way earlier. Only one and a half more weeks, babe."

"I know. I've been counting down the days. I've enjoyed time with family, but spending New Year's without you is going to suck. My mom's excited to play games and have appetizers, and all I want to do is be in your arms and make out with you all night."

"Hell." I pull on the back of my neck. "That would have been nice. Think I could have gotten some boob action too?"

"Most definitely. I probably would have hand-fed you Oreos too."

I point at the phone. "Don't you dare fucking tease me. That's a fantasy of mine."

"What is?" She laughs, that beautiful curve of her lips returning.

"You topless, wearing that black G-string, hair curled and falling over your shoulders, a sleeve of Oreos in your hand, waiting to pop one in my mouth."

"You have really strange fantasies."

"How is that strange? I think that's pretty average. If I said I wanted you to wear an alien mask while wielding a sword and putting Oreos in my mouth, now that would be strange."

"I guess so." She sighs and leans into her pillow, rolling on her side and propping the phone up. I do the same so it's as if we're lying next to each other in bed.

"Do you have any fantasies?" I wiggle my eyebrows.

A sly smile crosses over her face. "Doing it in the locker room."

"Really?" My nose crinkles and brow furrows. No way. She's showed her distaste for the locker room ever since I've known her. "You're a liar."

"I am. Plus, if we did it in there, doesn't that mean we'd have to be attached at the hip for life?"

"That's the general rule. Do it in the locker room, get married."

She shakes her head. "I don't think I can make that kind of commitment. Not when I'm second best to Oreos."

That makes me laugh. "Sorry, babe, but facts are facts. Oreos will always be my number-one girl."

CHAPTER TWENTY-FOUR

EMORY

"I can't thank you enough," I say to Dottie while glancing in the mirror one last time. "Seriously, I owe you big time."

She waves me off. "You owe me nothing. This is what friends are for."

I flew back to Brentwood a couple days early. I told my parents it's because my internship required my assistance before the student population came back, but when they both looked at each other with that knowing gleam in their eyes, I knew I was caught. I wanted to see my boyfriend, and I couldn't wait any longer.

But since I'm flying out early, the dorms aren't open, meaning Dottie got us a hotel room thanks to her dad. She was more than happy to help when I called her, and we flew back together as well, giving us some girl time.

"Are you finally going to do it?" Dottie asks, rubbing her hands together while sitting cross-legged on the king-sized bed we shared last night.

"No. I mean . . . I don't think so, unless he cracks and breaks the bet."

"Ugh." She flops backward onto the plush, white pillows. "You and that stupid bet. Seriously, get over it."

"It's not just about the bet. It's almost become the craziest form of foreplay. I've done things with Knox I've never done before. We've gotten each other off in ways I didn't think were possible."

"Like what?" Dottie asks, doubtful.

My face heats up thinking about the things we did over the phone, the things he said to me in his deep, low voice so his mom didn't hear. Or what we did before we parted for Christmas break. God, just thinking about how he felt sliding up and down my clit has me shifting in place with a distant ache.

"Just . . . things."

"Like . . . hand jobs? You've done that before."

"I don't want to get into detail, Dottie. It's embarrassing to talk about." I lean forward and reapply my lip gloss.

"Why, because you two have been at it like two horny teenagers scared to get pregnant?"

"Pretty much." I pop my lips and then fluff my hair one more time. "Do you think he'll be excited?"

"Uh, are you kidding me?" She motions to me. "I think the minute he sees you he's going to come in his pants. Especially after the conversation I overheard last night. He has a dirty mouth."

"I know." I smile, feeling incredibly lucky. "Okay, I'm off."

"And he has no idea you're here?"

I secure my purse with a package of Oreos inside over my shoulder. "Nope, he thinks I'm still in California."

"He is seriously going to lose it. I wish I was a fly on the wall when he sees you."

"I'm glad you're not, because you would probably see some naked body parts." I blow her a kiss goodbye and then meet up with my Uber driver at the entrance of the hotel. I'm only a few blocks away but given the frigid temperatures, I wasn't about to walk to the loft. Carson met up with me last night and gave me a key to the loft. The boys reported back to school a few days early, so they're at batting practice right now, giving me the perfect opportunity to surprise him.

I check the time on my phone. I'll have just enough time to get into his room and get ready before he shows up.

Carson has been sending me text updates, and they're done with showers and on their way home with pizza.

I could eat some pizza right about now, after I maul my guy first.

In minutes, I'm dropped off at the loft and make my way to the third floor. The door sticks a little when I try to open it—it's one of those giant slide doors—but I get myself in and go straight to the room with the yellow door.

For a second, I pause, a wave of anxiety hitting as memories of when I walked in on Neil with another girl. Him pounding into her from behind, on the bed we'd shared. My stomach churns and instead of pushing through the door, I lean my ear toward the wood, trying to listen in, see if I hear anything.

What am I doing?

To think of such a thing is shameful.

That was Neil. *Bastard.* This is Knox. *Devoted.* He's different in every way possible. He's attentive, caring, thoughtful, and committed. *To me.*

He would never cheat on me.

Taking a deep breath, I open his door and am immediately hit with a wave of comfort. Bed unmade, clothes on the floor, an empty cereal bowl on his desk, and his signature scent permeates the decent-sized room. I can't hold back the smile on my lips. This is my man. *God, I've missed him.*

Because I'm a nice girlfriend, I toss his clothes in the hamper—why he couldn't do that, I have no idea—I straighten out the sheets of his bed, and I carry the empty bowl to the kitchen sink just as I hear the voices of the guys coming up the stairs.

Eep!

I quickly make my way to his room, shut the door, and strip down to his fantasy.

Hair curled, check.

Topless, check.

Black G-string, check.

Package of Oreos . . . *weirdly* check.

Laughter approaches the door and I steel myself. Kneeling tall on his bed, I hold the Oreos in one hand and put the other hand on my hip while I stick out my chest.

I hope to God Knox is the only one who comes through that door.

"I'll just throw my backpack in my room," Knox says as he opens the door.

Butterflies flutter in my stomach, my nerves getting to me so much I almost feel like throwing up. That's until I see him walk through the threshold of his room. Head tilted down at first, I get to take him in from his black sweatpants, to his tight-fitting long-sleeved shirt and backward baseball hat.

I've missed him so freaking much.

He sets his backpack down and goes to leave the room, which gives me panic, so I clear my throat, causing him to snap his head up quickly. For a second, he blinks a few times as if he doesn't believe what he sees.

"Holy. Shit."

I'm about to say *surprise* when a female voice comes up behind Knox. "Knox, baby, I'm going to put my stuff in your room too."

In slow motion, the door pushes open more and a very attractive woman steps into his room. Long blonde hair, petite frame . . .

Fuck. No. No.

I quickly throw my arm over my breasts and sink into the mattress just as Knox says, "Mom, get out."

Mom?

Oh.

My.

God.

And then, as clear as day, I see the same eyes I've loved staring into over the last month over FaceTime.

"Huh?" she says, looking at me. Shocked, she stumbles back, hitting the wall and then covers her eyes. "Oh goodness, my apologies. Excuse me." She shuffles out of the room and shuts the door, leaving me so humiliated.

On the verge of tears from the emotional rollercoaster my heart just took, I flip over on the bed and bury my head in the pillow, barely able to comprehend what just happened.

Knox's mom, his apparent best friend, just saw me topless and in a G-string on her son's bed . . . holding out a package of fucking Oreo cookies.

Oh.

My.

God.

Kill me now.

My face burns in embarrassment, and tears sting my eyes as I try to erase that entire scene out of my head.

And the worst part? I thought he was cheating on me . . . For that *split second*, my heart sank to the wood floor, leaving me breathless with a crack in my barely healed heart.

Tears fall and I hold back a sob that wants to escape. *He wasn't cheating on me, he wasn't* . . .

But her voice, God, that was the worst few seconds of my life. *Knox, baby* . . .

The mattress dips and Knox's hand slides up my thigh to my bare backside. He leaves his palm on my ass as he leans down and presses a kiss where his hand is rubbing. From there, his lips press a hot and seductively wet trail up my back, to my shoulders, and then to my neck where he pushes my hair to the side for better access.

"Babe." He rolls me over, revealing my naked upper half and my fallen tears. His eyes soften as he wipes at my cheeks. "Em, it's okay."

"I'm so humiliated." I drape my arm over my eyes as my tears flow, unable to stop myself from crying now. *This is not . . . this is so horribly not what I wanted.*

His warm body lies next to mine as his arm falls across me, pulling me into his chest. He removes my arm from my face and turns my chin so I'm forced to look him in his beautiful eyes. It only makes me cry more.

"Baby." He chuckles, pressing kisses across my eyes and cheeks. "Don't cry, it's okay. My mom doesn't care."

"It isn't just that." I take a deep breath. "For a second, when I heard your mom's voice, I thought you were bringing someone back to your room with you."

"Em." He sighs and pulls me in tighter. "You know you're all I want."

"I know, and it was a split second, but that second hit me harder than I was expecting. It was as if everything that was right in my world was just stolen from me."

"I can see how that would be upsetting, but Em, you're all I want . . . ever." He kisses my forehead then my eyes again and travels his lips down to mine, where he's soft and sweet, inaudibly communicating how much he truly likes me.

With every press of his lips against mine, the dark cloud that started to steal my happiness begins to disappear until my head feels clear again, and my hand snakes up past the hem of his shirt. Muscle contracts under my touch as he groans against my mouth.

"Babe," he whispers. "You can't touch me like that, not with my mom on the other side of that door."

"I missed you, Knox."

"Fuck, I missed you too." His tongue brushes against mine before he pulls away and cups my cheek. "I missed you so goddamn much, and I seriously can't believe you're here . . . in that. You're so fucking hot."

I glance down, still slightly embarrassed. "I wanted to surprise you."

"Mission accomplished. I fucking got hard as stone seeing you when I walked in. Shit, babe, I had a boner in front of my mom."

I stifle a laugh against his shoulder. "Why didn't you tell me she was here with you?"

"She surprised me last minute, coming back with me. She's here for two weeks. Rented an Airbnb in the building across from ours. She loves watching the exhibitions."

"Looks like you're the guy to surprise."

"I loved your surprise way more." His hand falls between our bodies where he cups my breast in his hand, his thumb passing over my nipple, hardening it to a tight peak from the callouses on his rough hands.

"God, Knox." My head floats back. "I want you so bad right now it's ridiculous."

"And you choose to tell me that with all my boys and my mom in the living room, waiting to have pizza together?"

"I know, I'm sorry." I prop my body up and his eyes immediately fixate on my breasts.

"Shit," he mutters right before pushing me back down on the bed where he spreads my legs and lowers his hand down past my G-string to find me already wet. "Christ, babe. You're so wet."

"Want you, Knox." Encouraged to return the favor, I reach my hand into his waistband and grip the base of his cock. He hisses harshly between his teeth as his head drops forward. He sits back and pushes his pants and briefs down over his ass, giving me better access and then returns his hand to my clit where his thumb circles the little nub.

"You have to be quiet, Em. I love when you moan my name, but you have to be really fucking quiet."

I nod. "I can do . . . oh God."

"Emory," he chastises, his hand stilling. "I'm dead fucking serious. Quiet."

I seal my lips together and nod again. But Jesus, what he's doing feels so good and when he moves two fingers inside me, I nearly gasp loud enough for his neighbors to hear.

"Damn it, Em. I'm going to stop."

I shake my head and smooth my hand over his cock and up to the head where my thumb passes over the top. "No, please," I whisper. "I'll be good. I promise."

"Oh-kay," he chokes out when my thumb rubs the underside of the head of his cock. "Oh fuck," he groans quietly into my ear. "Shit, babe, I'm not going to last long."

"Me neither," I gasp as he makes small circles over my clit. "Oh, right there. Yes, Knox." I can barely hear my own voice, I'm hoping from being so quiet, and not from the pounding of my heart.

"I'm there, Em," he says on a grunt, his release lethal to my ears, shooting off my own.

My back arches, my clit pulses against his thumb, and my hips rotate against the pressure of his hand.

"Fuck," I whisper, pulling on the back of his neck while riding out my pleasure, floating down slowly until I'm completely spent.

Breathing heavily, we both look at each other, casually touch one another, running a finger over a cheek, a thumb down the back. Our smiles stretch across our faces as a silent exchange passes between us; we're together again.

"I'm so goddamn happy you're back." He places a kiss on my nose. "Thank you for the best surprise ever."

"You're welcome. Now if you can help me out of your bedroom window so I don't have to face your mom, that would be great."

"Stop, she's going to love you. Get dressed, it's time you meet her."

"I hope she didn't see any of my girly bits."

"Nah, you covered up fast." With one last kiss, he hops off the bed and we both clean up and get dressed. Looks like I'm about to take the next step in this relationship: meeting the mom.

CHAPTER TWENTY-FIVE

KNOX

H oly shit, my girl is here. Walking in and seeing her on my bed in . . . well, virtually wearing nothing, there are no words to adequately describe that feeling. *Apart from undeniably hot. Stunning. Horny.* But it was seeing the necklace around her neck, the one I gave her, hanging close to her heart . . . my girl. She said she hadn't taken it off, and maybe I'm a proud ass, but I liked it. Topless except for the gift of my heart.

And as we walk out to the living room with fingers laced together, I still can't believe she did this. Took an opportunity to be here waiting for me. I loaned Emory some of my clothes, a pair of sweatpants and a T-shirt that is entirely too big on her, but it's better than just a G-string. Which I would have been fine with, but given that she's going to be eating pizza with my mom and teammates, I'd prefer her covered up, despite how perfect her ass is.

When we enter the living room, all eyes are on us and I can feel Emory cower behind me. Keeping a strong hold on her hand, I say, "Any pizza left?"

"Tons," Carson says, pushing a box toward us. "You must be ravenous."

Fuck, I knew Emory was too loud.

Slightly cringing, I turn toward my mom, who's enjoying a piece of pizza while sitting cross-legged on the couch. She looks . . . happy.

"Uh, Mom."

"Oh yes, honey, come sit down." She pats the chair next to her and motions for us to take a seat.

I do as she says and pull Emory onto my lap.

"This must be Emory." My mom wipes her hand on a napkin and holds it out.

Still shy and blushing, Emory says, "Mrs. Gentry, it's so nice to meet you. I'm so sorry about that back there. I'm completely humiliated that you saw me like that."

My mom waves her hand in dismissal. "Oh, nothing to be humiliated about. You should actually be proud. You have quite the beautiful bosom."

I choke on my own saliva as the room erupts in a fit of laughter, all the guys on my team intent on hearing our conversation.

"Mom." I attempt a scold through a fit of coughs while Emory's hands cover her face in sheer embarrassment.

Unsure of what she said wrong, my mom looks around. "What? It's true. So perky with wonderful nipples. I wish I had such a set on me."

Jesus.

Christ.

I mean . . . yeah, Emory has some mouth-watering tits, the best I think I've ever fucking seen, but I don't need my mom appreciating them, or getting me hard as she describes them in detail to the entire living room.

I catch some of the eyes of my teammates falling to Emory's covered-up chest.

"Hey." I motion around the room. "Eyes up here, dickheads."

They laugh and go back to their pizzas.

Still unapologetic, my mom continues. "And your physique is quite beautiful, but I will tell you two things."

"Mom, maybe we just drop it."

She shakes her head while chewing on a piece of pizza. Swallows. "This has to be said." We quiet down, and I grip Emory a little tighter, trying to convey to her just how sorry I am about what my mom is about to say. "Oreos in bed, sweetie, is not a good idea. Think of all the crumbs."

Emory nods. "You're right, Mrs. Gentry. That was careless." There's a note of humor in her voice, and I see the small smirk that curves the left side of my mom's lip upwards. Fuck, it sends a beam of joy right up my spine.

My girl is so damn cool.

"And although quite attractive, the undergarment you chose isn't very sensible. It barely covered your nether regions."

This time, she blanches. And I don't blame her.

"What kind of undergarments?" Carson asks.

"I believe your generation calls it a Z-string."

"A what?"

"G-string, Mom." Why did I just correct her?

She nods, realizing her mistake. "Yes, G-string. Oh, it was quite lovely on Miss Ealson, but very insensible. You don't wear those all the time, do you?"

Almost every goddamn day, but I don't say that.

"No." Emory shakes her head. "Just while holding Oreos in bed . . . topless."

Her answer shocks my mom, but before I can cover for her, everyone in the room, including the woman who raised me, busts out into a fit of laughter. It's then I look around and notice something important: Emory fits into my entire world. *And* my mom just approved my girlfriend's tits and met her match in sass . . . sounds like this girl belongs here, forever.

~

My teammates have retired to their respective rooms, giving Emory, my mom, and me some alone time together in the small common space near the bedrooms. We have multiple common room areas in the loft and since the big one is taken up by five of my teammates, including Carson and Holt playing baseball on the team PlayStation, we sectioned ourselves off.

I thought about bringing my mom into my room, but my bed is unmade and given the mind-blowing hand job Emory gave me an hour ago, I thought it would be weird to have my mom sitting on my bed. I can only imagine what she would say if she saw evidence of our coupling earlier.

With Emory on my lap, because I refuse to let her sit anywhere else, I keep my arm firmly wrapped around her waist and my hand resting on her hip. She leans into me, thankfully feeling a little more comfortable.

My mom crosses her legs and brings a cup of tea to her mouth. She carries teabags in her purse so wherever she goes, she can enjoy a cup of her favorite hot beverage. She even has a specific tea wallet where she holds three different types of tea at all times. An English breakfast, a green tea, and a peppermint. They are for specific times of the day or mood.

Right now, she's drinking peppermint. I can smell the fresh and minty flavor from here.

She tilts her head to the side after taking a sip of her tea, studying us. "You know, I can't get over how beautiful you two are together. One of those couples you love to follow on Instagram, you know, the really cute ones that are so sickening in love that you can't get enough of them."

Way to drop the love bomb, Mom.

Jesus.

Thankfully Emory doesn't show any kind of hatred for the term but instead says, "Like Jennifer Lopez and A-Rod?"

"Yes," my mom answers with excitement. "Oh my gosh, I'm obsessed with watching their stories. The little videos they do together, I just can't get enough of them. J-Rod," my mom says dreamily. "Oh gosh, what would your couple name be?" She thinks about it for a second. "Emox . . . or Knemory. Oh I love Knemory. Sounds so poetic."

"Knemory does have a nice ring to it," I add.

"I don't know, what about Emorox?"

"Ohhh, that sounds like a name that belongs in The Game of Thrones." Taking on a more masculine voice, my mom says, "Look out, Jon, Emorox is coming over the hill, with her fire-spitting dragons, Knemory and George."

"George?" Emory laughs out loud, covering her mouth. "Why George?"

"Well, look at the names they have in that show? They're all exotic names you've never heard before—Cersei, Gregor, Arya—and then in waltzes good old Jon Snow. It's only fair that the dragons have a lemon in the bunch as well."

"Uh, Jon is anything but a lemon, Mom," I defend. "He was raised from the dead."

My mom's mouth drops, pure and utter shock in her face. "Jon Snow dies?"

Shit.

Emory elbows my stomach. "Where the hell is your GOT etiquette? You never talk about the facts of the show until the air is cleared about how far someone is in watching. You are one of those people who spoils everything for someone just catching up to the trend."

Ahem

"I mean . . . uh . . . he doesn't die."

"You just said he is raised from the dead," my mom says.

Feeling guilty, I reply, "Well, at least he's still alive, right?"

She slumps against the cushion of the couch and mutters, "Unbelievable."

"I'm sorry, Mrs. Gentry, that your son is a barbarian and broke your GOT trust."

Pressing her hand against her forehead, my mom says, "You

know, I blame myself. I thought I taught him a shred of decorum, I guess not."

"Don't blame yourself," Emory coos. "You did everything right. It comes down to the hooligans he hangs out with. There's only so much you can control after they leave the nest."

"You're absolutely right," my mom agrees and leans across the couch to smack me in the back of the head.

"Hey," I complain while rubbing the sore spot. I look between the two women in my life and I say, "I don't like this ganging up on me shit."

"You wanted us to get along, right?" Emory asks. "Well, I happen to like your mom, especially since she complimented my bosom."

"Ah, I see." I continue to look between the two of them. "You're okay with my mom catching you with your shirt off now, moved past the embarrassment?"

Emory's eyes narrow. "With that kind of attitude, it might be the very last time you see me topless."

My mom raises her fist to the air, as if to say, "Girl Power." And then she says, "You tell him, Emory. Don't let him push you around."

"I wasn't pushing her around—"

"You keep that beautiful bosom under lock and key, and if you have a temptation to show anyone, just flash me."

"Mom, do you realize how wrong that is?"

"Want to go to the bathroom right now, Mrs. Gentry?"

"I would be delighted to."

They both stand but before they can make a move, I pull on Emory's hand, bringing her back down to my lap. "No way in hell is that happening. Jesus, what is wrong with you?"

They both laugh, getting too much joy out of their newfound connection. I can't be mad, because it isn't very often you find a girl your mom accepts, and from the twinkle in my mom's eye, she really likes Emory. *Makes me feel fucking awesome.*

CHAPTER TWENTY-SIX

EMORY

"What should I expect tomorrow?" Curled into Knox's chest, I rest my hand against his bare skin, drawing small circles with my finger as he calmly threads his hands through my long locks.

"Since it's an exhibition, nothing too special when it comes to pageantry, as they save that for our first home game of the season, but you do need to prepare yourself for my mom."

"What do you mean? I've spent the last two weeks getting to know her, she's fantastic."

"She's insane when it comes to baseball, especially my baseball games. She said she had to go home early because she was tired, but that was a lie. I know exactly what she's doing."

"And what's that?" I can't imagine Mama G—yes, I get to call her that now—doing anything out of the ordinary. She's a little outspoken, which I love, and she's a really good time, so I envision that kind of personality carrying over to the game. Unless she turns into someone completely different.

"Prepping. She is her own personal caravan at games. I'm talking flags, foam fingers, snacks for the crowd and the team. She has multiple outfits she tries on the night before, giving her time to decide what she wants to wear to the game, and I'm not talking fancy getups. She bedazzles her own baseball wear. She was once asked to take off her Brentwood denim vest because the sparkles were distracting the players, reflecting off the lights."

"You're lying."

"I wish I was. She's the real deal, babe." Mama G is the real deal, and it's easy to see where Knox gets his fun, lighthearted personality from. Seeing the two of them interact together makes my heart happy.

"If that's the case, I hope she has a foam finger for me, because I'm excited to cheer you on."

"Yeah?" He presses a light kiss to my forehead, his lips lingering. "I'm excited to show you my skills."

"You think you can impress me?"

"Oh, I know it, babe. You've never seen anyone like me out on the field. I wear tight pants, so it's not just my sheer talent on display. I'm a total smoke-show too."

I chuckle. "And so modest."

"I'm just preparing you. You might get really turned on. I don't want you having an orgasm in the stands tomorrow, especially next to my mom. She saw your boobs, but seeing your O face, that's crossing a line."

"I'll try to contain myself," I deadpan.

Changing the subject, he asks, "What do you plan on wearing tomorrow?"

"Uh . . . clothes."

"You better be wearing clothes, but are you planning on wearing any Brentwood stuff?"

"The only thing I have is a simple T-shirt with the college logo. I don't think that will be warm enough. You said it's chilly in the stadium?"

"During the winter, yeah. The school doesn't want to pay to heat the whole thing for exhibition games. Here's an idea, why don't you wear one of my sweatshirts."

"The things I hate?"

"Yeah, it would be hot."

"It would be huge on me. You wear an extra-large, Knox."

He twirls my hair around his finger. "Do one of those twisty things off to the side that girls do all the time."

"With a bulky sweatshirt?"

He sighs against my head, wisps of hair floating from the exhale. "Please."

It's one word that breaks every single wall erected. The tone of his voice, the way he asks, I can't possibly deny this man.

Sitting up, hand on his chest, I stare at him. His eyes search mine for a few short breaths before I say, "I would be honored to wear your sweatshirt."

"Really?" His eyes light up with hope. *My man really is easy to please.*

"Really. You're my best friend, after all."

The corner of his mouth tilts up. "I like the sound of that."

"And my man," I add before closing the space between us and pressing my lips against his.

He hums against my mouth and flips me to my back. "I like the sound of that even better."

H*oly.* *Hell.*

Knox was not kidding when he said Mama G was her own caravan. I'm sitting on a Brentwood University portable cushion wearing a bedazzled baseball hat with a Brentwood baseball blanket over my lap while eating a B-shaped peanut butter and jelly sandwich.

I can't go into her outfit with all the razzamatazz happening, nor can I describe the excitement this woman is brimming with. It's as if she's never had a Christmas before and today is her first one. That doesn't do it justice.

She's beaming.

"Look at our boy out there." She loops her arm through mine, holding me close. "So tall, so handsome."

And those pants.

Yowza, Knox wasn't kidding. He is a total smoke-show out there.

Tight white pants, perfectly tailored shirt that molds to his broad frame, a baseball cap that shadows his eyes, and a black sweatband on the same hand he holds his glove. It's hot.

Really hot.

So hot that I'm thinking about all kinds of naughty things I shouldn't be thinking about while sitting next to his mom.

And I'm not the only girl who notices just how sexy Knox is in his uniform. In the student section of the stadium, there are multiple signs and desperate women vying for his attention.

Knox, I want your baby.

Come home with me, Knox.

Party, my house, you and me, Knox.

It's shameful, embarrassing, and frankly, pathetic. I could never imagine being one of those girls, flaunting themselves for a mere look. Well guess what, desperadoes, the only thing Knox is paying attention to is the game on the field.

And that's the honest truth; his concentration is impeccable as the first inning is underway. He blocks out the rest of the stadium and focuses on the game, constantly moving around at shortstop, calling out the outs, delivering signs to his outfielders. He's commanding, and it's another reason why I can't wait to get him back to the loft and see what other kinds of situations he can command.

"Don't worry about those girls," Mama G says. She must have caught my gaze. "They're at every game, throwing themselves at the players, but Knox never gives them a second look. I raised him well enough to decipher between quality"—she eyes me up and down—"and trash." She glances at the student section.

"Thank you, Mama G. I appreciate that."

She gives me a side hug and says, "I adore you. You're the first girlfriend he's ever had, did he tell you that?"

I nod, as the crack of the bat sounds off. A ball is hit up the middle and before it gets past the infield, Knox makes a diving play, springs to his feet, and throws the guy out at first. The play lasts no longer than a few seconds, he's so fast. Both Mama G and I clap vigorously, cheering for our boy.

He stands and holds up two fingers to his teammates as they pass the ball around the infield and finally throw it back to the pitcher. I watch Knox carefully, the way he carries himself on the field with an abundance of confidence, almost as if he's daring batters to try to get the ball past him.

I've never been a huge baseball fan, but I think that play and the way Knox's butt looks in those pants, just made me a fan for life.

"That was amazing," I say, still astounded. "He's so quick."

Mama G holds a hand to her chest. "He just keeps getting better and better, it's really impressive to watch. Being under Coach Disik's training has vastly improved his skills from when he was in high school. It's been hard, having him so far away, but coming to Brentwood was worth every mile between us."

It's endearing to see just how much Knox's mom loves him, a pure, genuine, unconditional love. I consider my own feelings as I watch him get into position for every pitch.

Do *I* love him?

I think about him every moment I get a chance. I crave his touch, his voice, his hands dancing through my hair. I crave his warmth and his charm, his teasing and his sweet kisses. There are moments when he walks into my dorm and my breath catches in my throat from the mere sight of him, and when we part, it feels like a piece of me is leaving with him.

Is this what I felt for Neil? That I hated his absence, but loved every minute with him? No. This feeling is very different than what I felt with Neil.

I wear the necklace Knox gave me every day, and I remember

what he said when he gave it to me every day too. *I know I'm his.* So, that begs the question, *do I love Knox Gentry?*

I think I might be too scared to admit it to him, but, yeah . . . I think—

"This season is going to be so much fun with you coming to the games. The parents are nice and all, but I enjoy some younger company." Mama G nudges my shoulder, pulling me from my thoughts. "You don't talk about things like hip replacements and hemorrhoids."

"Hemorrhoids?" I quiver. "Have some of the parents really talked about that?"

"Oh yeah, it's retched." She shivers. "But now I have a girl-friend I can watch the games with."

Hannigan strikes out the batter, gathering a big cheer from the fans, while the boys jog off the field. Knox ducks into the dugout and then quickly reappears with his bat, batting gloves, and helmet. With every pull of his batting gloves on his hands, his fore-arms ripple, and his jersey emphasizes his strong shoulder blades, and pulls on the front revealing his prominent pecs.

Yup, a huge fan of baseball.

"Let's go, Knox," Mama G yells, startling me in my chair. She chuckles and clutches my hand with hers. "Sorry about that, dear, I have a bit of a megaphone mouth. You'll get used to it."

"It's okay, I'm ready for everything now."

The catcher throws the ball down to second as Knox steps up to the batter's box. He stares at his bat for a few beats, then looks over at Coach Disik who does some fancy signaling with his hands, finishing it off with a clap. Large paw to the top of his helmet, Knox takes one step into the batter's box, swings his bat around, and then sets up for the pitch.

"Does he always bat first?" I ask.

"Yes. In high school, he dabbled as the second hitter, but because he's a contact hitter and has incredible speed, he's usually number one."

The first pitch is thrown and it's high. Knox holds back.

"That's it, Knox, let him pitch to you. Don't hit that crap."

I hold back the chuckle that wants to pop out. She's so serious, I love it.

Knox resets and waits for the next pitch. I'm holding Mama G's hand. It's a game that doesn't matter, but as Knox said, to Mama G it means everything.

The pitcher winds up his arm, delivers the pitch, and Knox swings, connecting with the ball and sending it into right center. Like a bolt of lightning, he's out of the box and rounding first. Mama G is bouncing up and down and cheering as the rest of the crowd erupts as well. He hits second but doesn't stop, instead, he flies to third as the ball is being thrown into the infield. I hold my breath, the play close as Knox slides into third and the third baseman delivers the tag.

Bent into position, the umpire waves his arms out to the side, calling safe. I jump out of my seat, screaming and clapping with Mama G.

"That's my boy," she calls out.

"Good job, Knox," I say, feeling slightly out of place, but wanting to cheer him on. Either he doesn't hear me or he's really good at staying focused, because he doesn't acknowledge my cheer. It doesn't matter. Watching him in his element, seeing how intensely inserted into the game he is amazes me.

Holt steps up to the plate and instead of patting his helmet while he gets into the batter's box, he holds it up to the umpire while slowly bringing his bat up to his shoulder after Coach Disik does his dance of hands.

"Oh, I think they're going to squeeze."

"Squeeze? What does that mean?"

Whispering, Mama G says, "That's when Knox runs on the pitch and Holt bunt's the ball, squeezing Knox in across the plate."

"What if he doesn't bunt the ball? Whatever that means?"

"Then Knox will be caught at home. That's why it's imperative Holt gets the bunt down."

Sitting taller in her chair and a little more forward, she watches on bated breath as the pitcher winds up and just when he starts to release the ball, Knox takes off from third and sprints toward home.

"Ah, he's going for it."

The opposing team screams "squeeze" just as Holt lays down the bunt and knocks the ball toward the first baseman. The other team has no chance at getting an out as both Holt and Knox are lightning fast. Knox dives head first into home only to pop up and jog toward the dugout . . . but not before looking up at me in the stands and giving me a wink.

I swear to the Lord Himself, I nearly faint.

Feeling wobbly, I take a seat, unable to believe just how sexy this entire sport is. Diving men, rippling muscles, the element of surprise. How have I never spent any time watching baseball before?

Maybe because I wasn't personally invested in it until recently. Now that my boyfriend plays, I'm already starting to work out ways to clear my schedule so I'm at every home game.

"Oh bless my romantic heart," Mama G coos. "He winked at you."

"He did, didn't he?"

"He really did." Mama G snuggles in closer, and I feel a sense of euphoria wash over me. I love everything about this: the feeling I get seeing my man play, Mama G at my side, the tight pants . . . it's perfect. "I can feel it, this is going to be the best season, yet. The perfect way to end his college career and go on to the big leagues."

Errr . . . what?

End his college career? As in . . . not this year, right?

"You mean, next year," I say. I'm surprised she's confused. My mind's in overdrive right now too.

"No, this year."

What? Not wanting to put Mama G on the spot, but needing some clarification, I say, "Oh yeah, this year . . ." What has Knox *not* told me?

"You know, when Knox told me he was entering the draft after his junior year, I was a little apprehensive because I really want him to finish his degree. But after his talk with Coach Disik, I can see this is the best move for him."

What is she talking about?

I've just been sucker-punched in the stomach by Mama G—like a hit and run—but the culprit sits in the dugout twenty feet away.

Knox is entering the draft after this semester? Was he planning on telling me that at any point in time? *What does the draft even entail?* Does that mean any team could pick him up? What does that mean for us? I have at least three more years at Brentwood until I earn my master's in library science, so there's no way I can move around to wherever he'll be.

Not wanting to make Mama G feel bad for completely dropping a bomb on me, I play it cool, needing a little more information. "Yeah, it's such a huge opportunity for him. Do you know who might be interested in him right now?"

"Well, Coach Disik was saying Arizona, Miami, and the Bobcats, of course, but that last one is a long shot."

Arizona?

Miami?

Those are so far away. A plane-ride away. Too far to comprehend at this moment.

"Wow, that's amazing." I swallow hard, my throat growing tight on me. *He's leaving? He's pursued me . . . but he's leaving?* Surely, I must have this wrong, but Mama G just knocked all the air and hope right out of my lungs, leaving me with a sickening stomach ache and a bruised heart.

What the hell am I supposed to do with this? *The man I think I love is leaving . . .*

CHAPTER TWENTY-SEVEN

KNOX

"Not bad boys, not bad," I say, towel wrapped around my waist as I quickly dry off with another and slip on some boxer briefs. "That's a great start to the pre-season."

We ended up annihilating Riverbend eleven to one. After the sixth inning, Coach pulled all the starters and gave the second-string some playing time. Sitting in the dugout, watching the underclassmen perform just as well as us gave me a sense of excitement for the season. We have a solid group of guys with real talent. Even Farkle stopped prancing across the diamond. Riverbend isn't an easy team, so I couldn't be more excited about our victory, despite it meaning nothing.

Carson sits next to me, pulling on pants as he says, "I have plans tonight and they consist of me lounging in my bed, a plate of your mom's brownies on my chest, and watching Downton Abbey."

I stare at him blankly.

"What?" He shrugs. "I don't have a girl to go home to after the game like you and Holt, so I'm shacking up with brownies, unless"—he wiggles his eyebrows—"your mom is looking for a young stallion to keep her warm tonight."

It's not the first time Carson has joked about wanting to hook up with my mom, it's been an ongoing joke since freshman year, but with every year that passes, it's almost like he grows more and more serious about it.

I know he'd never make a move, but if he ever did, I would murder his penis. I would stick that thing so far in a meat grinder, he wouldn't know I was serving up his own dick in a sausage casing until it was shoved halfway down his throat by me.

"Stay the fuck away from my mom."

He laughs, knowing that shit pisses me off.

"Are you meeting up with Em?" Holt asks, tying up his shoes.

"Yeah, I think we're going out to The Hot Spot with my mom."

"Hey." Carson slaps my leg. "Want to turn that third wheel into a double date?"

"Fuck off, man."

"Come on." He stands and pulls his shirt from the hanger in his locker. "I would be a really good daddy to you."

Holt mutters, "I would pay good money to see that."

"So would I," Turbo, our centerfielder, chimes in.

"Me too," Brock says from his locker.

I motion to the room, pointing to all of them. "Fuck off, all of you."

They laugh in unison, and I can't be too mad if it brings the team together . . . me being uncomfortable.

"Hey cap," Brock calls out, letting the room die down before he asks his question.

"What's up?" Pants now on, I do quick work of my shirt and shoes.

"About the locker room rules, as freshmen, are we allowed to bring someone back here?"

Oh Jesus, this bullshit again.

"No," Carson answers for me. "Only upperclassmen. You're a fucking baby, how do you even know what a vagina is?"

"I know better than you this year."

"Ooo," the team laughs and chants.

"Because I have standards, you motherfucker. I'm not about to fuck any willing pussy that throws itself at me. And the locker room isn't a place for hookups. It's sacred." Carson steps on his "soapbox" and gives a warning to all the guys in the room. "There are only two upperclassmen on this team with serious relationships: Holt and Knox. They're the only two permitted to bring girls back here."

"Not interested," I say, while slipping my jacket on.

"What?" Brock calls out. "I thought you and Ealson are serious."

"We are," I answer as the entire team listens in. "But I don't need some stupid legend to confirm what I already know: she's the girl for me."

I pocket my loose items and give Holt and Carson knuckles before taking off. I told my mom and Emory to meet me outside the locker room so we can go to dinner. Normally I stay completely focused during the game, but for the life of me, knowing Emory was in the stands with my mom, I couldn't refrain from glancing over in their direction on occasion during the beginning of the game. Loved finding the most beautiful smile I've ever seen shining back at me.

I had one of my best games of my career, going three for three with two RBIs, a stolen base, and a stellar glove at shortstop. Having Emory there felt right, exactly how it's supposed to be. Her confidence in me. Her cheers. It wasn't a distraction but something that gave me strength.

When I push through the doors of the locker room, I quickly scan the hallway—thankfully only athletes and family members are allowed in this part of the stadium—and spot my mom in all her shiny glory, but no Emory. Huh, that's strange.

Maybe she's in the bathroom.

"There he is, Mr. Triple." My mom pulls me into a hug and squeezes me tightly. "You were amazing out there today."

"Thanks, Mom." I pull her away and look around. "Where's Em, is she in the bathroom?"

"Oh no, she left in the fourth inning."

"What? Really?" How didn't I notice? Maybe because at that point I chastised myself for looking in the stands too much and stopped, refocusing on the game. "Why?"

"She felt a migraine coming on. She told me she gets them on occasion."

"She does." I start to worry, remembering how bad her migraine was last time. "Was she sick? Do you know if she got home okay?"

My mom nods. "Yes, her friend Dottie came to pick her up. Lovely girl."

"Okay." I chew on the side of my cheek, wondering what I should do.

My mom presses her hand against my arm, pulling my attention back to her. "It's okay if you want to go check on her, Knox."

"But we had dinner plans," I say as I start moving toward the parking lot.

"We can reschedule. It's fine. I'm quite tired from all the cheering anyway. Go check on Emory."

I lean down and kiss my mom on the forehead. "Thanks, Mom. I appreciate it and hey, thanks for sitting next to Em, it was great seeing you two in the stands together."

"I adore her." She holds her hands to her heart and then something flashes over her eyes, changing her expression from content to slightly concerned. "Before you go, I think you should know we talked about you entering the draft today, she seemed to have some—"

"You what?" My stomach falls to the floor.

"I mentioned this being your last year."

"Mom," I groan, pressing my hands to my head. "Fuck, why did you say that?"

"Well, I don't know. I thought it was public knowledge since

there are articles written up everywhere speculating about who's
going to draft you. You didn't tell her?"

"No. I didn't. I was, shit, Mom. I was trying to find the right
time to tell her. It's been a slow process, getting her to date me, to
trust me, and I was going to tell her this week, after you left."

She cringes. "I'm sorry, honey. I really thought she knew."

"What did she say? Was she mad? Is that why she left in the
fourth?"

She shakes her head. "No, she said she had a migraine coming.
Would she lie about that?"

"I don't know," I say sarcastically. "Maybe, if your boyfriend's
mom tells you he's leaving after this semester to God knows where.
Jesus, Mom."

"Oh dear. I really feel like a boob. I didn't mean to let the cat
out of the bag."

I sigh, hating that I'm making my mom feel bad. Letting out
my frustration, I pull my mom into a hug and say, "I know, and I'm
sorry for getting angry, but I've worried that Em's had one foot out
the door, ready to bolt at any time. I told you a bit about her past
relationship, but he cheated on her, and it took a while to convince
her that I wasn't him. That she deserved much, much more than
that. That I'd never be anything but honest with her. And this . . ."
Fuck. Em. I have no idea how she's going to respond to this. I drag my
hand through my still-damp hair. "You don't mind if I take off, to
make sure she's okay?"

"No, I insist, please, go to her."

"Thanks, Mom." I give her one more parting hug and take off
toward my truck where I quickly make my way to Emory's dorm.
Thanks to Dottie being friends with the resident director, she
scored me a key to the dorms, so I make my way to their suite. Not
wanting to barge in, just in case any of the girls are indecent, I
knock on the door and stick my hands in my pockets, willing my
nerves to settle.

Everything is going to be okay. I'm going to first make sure
Emory is not in too much pain, and then I'm going to talk this out

with her. Help her understand that this is my last semester at Brentwood, but I'm committed to her, and even if I move across the country, she'll always be mine. *I'll always be hers.*

As I wait for someone to answer the door, I try to work out what to say to Em. I've tried so hard to convince her that we're solid, and I hope to fuck she's only hiding while she processes what Mom told her. That's got to be it. She's a thinker, needs time, and I'll be there by her side so we can see this hiccup through.

CHAPTER TWENTY-EIGHT

EMORY

"Okay, talk," Dottie says, taking a seat on my bed next to me as Lindsay pulls up a chair along with a tray of Lofthouse cookies.

They both take one, but my stomach is too twisted and tied up to even consider anything at this point.

"We let you sulk for over an hour, and now it's time you talk and tell us what happened." Lindsay breaks off a piece of her cookie and plops it in her mouth. "Was it his mom? Did she say something mean to you?"

"No." I shake my head. "His mom is amazing, and I don't think she could ever say anything to hurt someone's feelings."

"Okay," Dottie says. "So why did I have to pick you up from the stadium and listen to you cry all the way back to our dorm?"

"And how come you're not eating our sacred cookies?"

"Yes, how come?"

Both my friends bear down on me. I should have known better than to call Dottie, but I had no choice with every out that passed by, my heart grew heavier and heavier. By the fourth inning, I was on the verge of tears, faked a migraine, and begging Dottie to pick me up ASAP.

The minute I shut the door to her car, I broke down, and I've been crying ever since, not as heavily, but tears are still falling.

Looking out my window, I say just above a whisper, "He's leaving."

"Knox is leaving?" Dottie asks.

"Yes, after this semester, he's entering the draft." I wipe a tear. "I had no idea, and his mom let it slip today."

"Oh shit," Lindsay says, cookie half-crumbled in her mouth.

"Like, he's not coming back to school?"

"No." I turn toward them. "I looked it up on my phone. You either enter the draft after you graduate from high school or you wait until after your junior or senior year in college. He's throwing his name in after this semester and guess what, a million teams are scouting him from all over the country. I researched it. He's considered one of the top prospects."

"And you're only realizing this now?" *Ouch. That stings.*

"I know it's stupid, but honestly, we never really talked about anything like that. He's talked to me about practice and the guys on the team, but we've never spoken about the future because we've been taking baby steps. Small steps that have led to one of the best things in my life . . . and that's going to be taken away from me."

"How do you know—?"

Knock. Knock.

We all turn our heads toward the hallway that leads to our door.

"Who's that?" I ask, wiping away my tears as best as possible.

"I told Julianne across the hall she can borrow my straightener." Lindsay gets up and heads down the hallway where we hear her open the door. "Let me . . . oh, hi."

There isn't a return hello, but instead heavy footsteps sound off down the hallway. *Crap.* I'd know those footsteps anywhere, and before I can direct Dottie to get out of my room, Knox appears at the doorway, looking distressed and with damp hair that looks like his hand has been running rapidly through it.

"Knox." I sit up, trying to hide the emotion bubbling up inside me, but he can see it all over my face.

Keeping his eyes trained on me, he says, "Dottie, would you mind giving us some privacy?"

"Yeah, that might be a good idea."

She hops down from my bed and pats Knox on the shoulder before closing the door behind her. Still staring me down, he says, "You don't have a migraine."

There's no use lying to him, so I shake my head and say, "No, I don't."

"So you lied to leave the game. Why?"

"It just became . . . too overwhelming."

"What did?" He takes a step forward, closing the distance between us until he's sitting on my bed.

Hands on my lap, I twist them together, wondering how I should go about this. Ever since I've known Knox, he's always been upfront about everything—well, besides this being his last semester—so I decide to be the same.

"When were you going to tell me this was your last semester here?"

Visible regret washes over his face as he turns toward me on the bed and takes my hands in his. Just from the sorrowful look, I can't find it within me to be mad at him, especially since the reason he's leaving is to pursue his dreams, something he's been working toward for so long.

"I was going to tell you this week. Been waiting to gain the courage."

Our fingers twine together. "So, tell me then."

He pushes his hand through his hair then pulls on the back of his neck before tilting his head in my direction. His beautiful blue eyes connect with mine, eyes that have pulled me into some of the happiest moments I've had. But now, I look into those eyes as a blow is about to be delivered that I'm not sure I can come back from.

"At the beginning of the school year, I thought I'd enter the draft after I graduated, but I spoke with Coach, and he said I'd be killing my career before it started if I didn't enter the draft after this year. There are teams ready to make an offer, and they're just waiting." *He's known since the beginning of the school year?*

This should be exciting for him, to talk about his career right before it booms into something amazing, but instead his voice is somber. I hate that.

I lift his chin and smile at him. "Knox, that is so freaking amazing. You should be proud of yourself."

"I am," he sighs. "But I know it will put a strain on what we have going on."

I press my hand to his cheek. "You don't have to worry about me, Knox. Focus on your season and what's to come."

And I mean that wholeheartedly. There's no doubt in my mind that I love this man; he's resurrected my heart from the ruins Neil left behind, and because of that, I want him to be happy, to do what he's meant to do—play baseball.

Even if that means I'm out of the picture.

"But I am worried about you, Em. This . . . Christ." He stands from the bed and starts pacing. His steps are almost frantic, unsure which way to go. "I wasn't planning on this, getting involved with someone. Coach Disik thought I was a dumbass for starting something up with you, but I couldn't stop myself." He looks up, his eyes connecting with mine like an arrow straight to my heart. "That first day, Em, when I caught your map with my face and peeled it back, revealing your stunning features, my heart hitched in my chest." Tears begin to well in my eyes. "And then you opened your mouth. Your wit knocked me on my ass, and I knew I had to be around you, to make you a part of my life. It was stupid to pursue you, knowing I was leaving after the end of this semester, but I wouldn't change a thing about it. Not one damn thing."

"I wouldn't either," I admit, even though my heart is slowly crumbling in my chest, the dread of what's to come hovering above us.

"So, then let's make this work, Em." Excitement brews inside him as he comes back to the bed. "I know it's going to be hard but—"

"I think you should focus on your future, Knox."

His face falls. "Em, that includes you."

I shake my head, a tear falling down my cheek that he quickly wipes away. "You and I both know how hard that would be. I have at least three more years here until I finish my master's. Who knows where you're going to end up. The season is long with not much break between."

"But you have the summer off. You can come visit."

"I have to work during the summer, Knox. And I don't have the money to fly around wherever you are."

"I'll pay for it."

I give him a *get real* look. "If you think you're going to be flying your girlfriend around the country on a minor league player's income, you're delusional."

He grips the back of his head angrily and stands again, both elbows pointed out, his shirt riding high on his waistband. "Then what the hell are you saying, Emory?"

Pained and frustrated, my name doesn't sound beautiful falling off his tongue, not this time. It feels like he used it as a punishment rather than a term of endearment.

Knowing this is going to be one of the most heartbreaking things I ever do, I swallow hard and pour my heart out, ready for it to be sliced. "I'm saying this is going to be too hard. You're going to be working your ass off on and off the field, preparing for the next chapter in your life. Moments spent together will become few and far between and then you're going to leave. We don't even know where."

"It could be Chicago."

"It *could* be, but their farm teams are scattered around in different states, so that still doesn't work. I want nothing more than to be with you, Knox, to come home to your arms every night, but in reality, that's not what's going to happen. We're both on two different paths in our lives, and I don't want to try to make this work when we both know deep down, it won't."

"You don't know that." His voice rises. "Why am I the only one here committed to us?"

"I'm committed," I answer, feeling like I was just slapped in the face.

"You're not committed, Em. You're throwing in the towel at the first sign of things getting difficult. Does Christmas break not mean anything to you? We were separated for a month and we made that work. How is this any different?"

"Because there was an end date. I knew I was going to see you again in January, when school came back. And I'm sorry if you thought Christmas break was a walk in the park, but it wasn't for me. I missed you. Terribly. To the point that I would cry at night, wishing I was in your arms rather than a cold, lonely bed." His face softens. "It wasn't easy for me. None of this has been easy for me. You're . . . you. Amazing, obnoxious, consuming you. I get lost in you, Knox. You've become one of my best friends, and I love sharing the good and bad days with you. I love giving you shit, because you give it right back. When I'm around you . . ." *All I want to do is bury my head in your chest and let you hold me for hours on end.* "When I'm with you, I know who I am. I like who I am."

"Then why the fuck are you trying to end this?" he yells, arms out to the side. "Stay committed to me, Em." His hand raps his chest. "Make this work."

"I am committed to you." I wipe away another tear, my breath starting to become heavier and heavier as my throat closes. "I'm committed to seeing you happy."

"You want me to be happy? Well guess what, Em, you are what makes me happy. You. And you're taking that away."

Oh God. I suck in a breath and will my shaky limbs to hold strong. I want nothing more than to erase this day and go back to how things were—without the knowledge that Knox will be leaving—but I can't do that, nor can I hold him back either.

"Is this because you don't trust me to be out on the road? You don't trust that I won't hook up with someone else? I told you, I'm not your fucking ex-boyfriend. I would never treat you the way he did. Ever."

"That's not it. I trust you, how can you question that?"

"I don't know," he answers angrily, still pacing. "Fuck, I don't know why we're having this conversation. We should be out to dinner with my mom, celebrating the win, but instead, my fucking girlfriend is breaking up with me." He sinks into the chair of my desk and rests his forearms on his knees, completely deflated.

I don't know what to do. How to fix this, how to make him see what I see. After watching him play today, his future is going to be incredible, and I refuse to be the reason he doesn't give it his all. This is all for him. Yes, I'm shattering my own heart. Yes, I feel like I'm breaking into a million pieces. I'm barely strong enough to lose him now, so I know I'll never recover if I grow closer through experiencing even more amazing moments with this incredible man. I just can't. And I don't want him feeling torn and undecided because of me. That's not fair to him.

"How can this be any different, Knox? If this were a perfect world, how would you play out this relationship? Do you see a future with me beyond dating?"

His head lifts, but he stays hunched over.

"You're fucking kidding me, right?" The muscles in his jaw pulse as he stares me down. "I see more than a future, Em. Fuck, I . . . I . . ."

"Don't say it. Please don't say those words, not right now." I shake my head, tears in a constant flow now. "Not in this moment."

He must sense the kind of impact those three words would have, how they'd be coated in negativity rather than a positive, joyful moment they should be cherished in, because he shuts his mouth and folds his hands together.

His teeth roll over his bottom lip before he says, "If I had a choice, this is how it would play out. We'd move past this moment, you'd come back to the loft, and you'd sleep in my arms. We'd stay together the rest of the semester growing our bond stronger until the moment I have to leave. From there, we'd promise to make the effort to see each other. Talk every night, send each other gifts, just like over winter break. Only an extended period this time. It will be hard, we'll get in fights, but in the long run, we'd always come back to each other, because"—he motions between us —"we're meant to be together."

I curl my knees to my chest and rest my face in my hands, trying to envision how that would work. He makes it seem so simple, and yet, three years is a really long time, three of the most important years of his career, where he needs to work his way up through the farm system. He can't be worrying about me and where my head is at. He needs to worry about himself, and that's something I won't budge on. This is his dream, and I'll be damned if I distract him from giving it his all.

"I care about you, Knox, and I want nothing more than to follow through on what you just laid out, but we need to be real about this. You're going to be consumed with baseball, and I want you to be consumed by it, I want it to be your life, your obsession. And that can't happen if you're worrying about me and how I'm doing, what my mental state for that week is because I'll be honest, it will be erratic with you gone. That's not fair." I slide off the bed and walk to him, his large sweatshirt hitting me mid-thigh. I push him back on the chair and take a seat on his lap. His arms immediately wrap around me as I lift his chin so he has to look me in the eyes. "Rule number one." I lightly press a kiss across his lips, taking in the softness one last time. When I pull away, I say, "Friends forever and always."

"Shit," he mutters, his chest rising and falling faster than normal. "Baby, please don't do this, we can make it work."

"We could struggle to make it work and then, a year in, we break up because we can't handle the distance, the unpredictability, and then we'd be worse off than if we end things now. You know I'm right."

He presses his head against my shoulder.

"But we'll always be there for each other; we signed on it. Friends first, Knox."

"I don't want to be your friend. I want to be your boyfriend, your goddamn forever." His hands drive up my sides, holding my ribs, holding on to me tightly. "I want you forever, Em."

When he pulls away, tears falls from his eyes and in that moment, every nerve ending in my body goes numb as I watch the man I love cry—cry over what we had and what we're losing. It's the last thing I want to do, to inflict this kind of pain on Knox, but I don't have a choice. He needs to be free, to focus, to be the man, *the exceptional ball player* he deserves to be.

Mustering every ounce of courage I have left in my bones, I wipe his tears away and say, "I want you forever too, but I know when forever has to change." I cup both his cheeks and stare him in the eyes. "You are bound for wonderfully epic things, and I can't wait to see you accomplish everything you deserve. And I will be there, Knox. I will be the girl cheering for you on the sidelines, but in a different capacity, as your friend. The way we started."

"I want more. I want you."

I press a light kiss across his lips one last time, unable to stop myself. "I want you too, but I know what it's like to get lost in someone else and forget about everything you worked for. I won't let that happen to you. I refuse." Tears run down both of our faces. "You're going to be amazing, Knox Gentry, absolutely amazing. And later on, down the road, when we're thirty and unable to handle a hangover anymore, I hope we're still friends, still cheering one another on, still in each other's lives, because you mean so much to me." *I love you. I love you. I love you.*

Friends forever.

That's what we promised each other.

But sometimes promises are made to be broken . . .

CHAPTER TWENTY-NINE

KNOX

"Gentry, my office, now," Coach Disik shouts into the locker room and then quickly disappears.

I groan and throw a shirt on over my head, my hair still wet from my shower, my muscles aching from the one-hundred-plus pushups we were forced to do at practice . . . because of me.

My head is not in the fucking game, because it's back at Emory's dorm room, along with my heart. Two days ago, she tore my world apart. I understand what she was saying, her reasoning, but what I don't get was why she wouldn't at least fucking try to keep us. *I just want her to try.*

She doesn't want me to get lost in her, well, too fucking late for that. I'm pretty sure I got lost in her the minute I drunkenly held her boob in my hand and passed out.

"Coach is going to rip you a new one," Carson points out. "It looked like he wanted to shove his bat up your ass during practice."

"Give him a break," Holt says from the side. "He's hurting."

"Because of a girl, and that's why Coach is going to kill him."

I came home that night, without Emory, and went straight to my room. Thanks to Carson being a nosey motherfucker . . . and because my mom asked him to check on me, I ended up having a heart-to-heart with him and Holt about what happened. Carson, the dickhead, agreed with Emory, saying she had made really good points, but Holt felt for me, saying if his girl did that he wouldn't know what to do with his life, especially since he took her to the locker room after the game and sealed the goddamn deal.

Maybe I should have done that, even though I don't believe in the legend. Maybe I should have given it a shot. If I did, Emory and I might still be together.

What the hell am I thinking? No locker room bullshit is going to change Emory's way of thinking. The minute she made up her mind, there was nothing I could say or do to change it.

And she wants to be fucking friends.

Yeah, that sounds like a whole bunch of fucking fun. I want to be friends with the girl I love rather than be the man who gets to kiss her when she's sad, or hug her when she's happy. Sure, friends, what a great idea, so much fucking better than being able to take her naked beneath me and watch as I make her come over and over again.

Yup, friends is way better.

I stand and slip my hat over my head. "Mom is making everyone dinner before she leaves tomorrow. She's serving at seven, prepare to eat."

I take off toward Coach's office, knowing I'm about to be roasted like I deserve. The boys will head back to the loft for my mom's going-away party. When I spoke with her last night and told her what happened, she blamed herself. I told her no matter how Emory found out, she still would have had the same reaction. Emory thinks she's *saving* me, *helping* me, but in the long run, she's *hurting* me, because I need her. She takes all the stress away. She wants baseball to be my obsession, I get that, but baseball has been my obsession ever since I can remember. But I now truly understand what Holt meant about his girl. Emory's been *my* retreat, my place where I can step back and recharge. I know my game was more on point because I *wasn't* eating, sleeping, and drinking baseball. *She gave me a broader perspective.* She gave me a chance to breathe, but now she's let me go and that's been taken away.

I don't bother knocking on the partially open door of Coach's office, but walk through and take a seat in front of him, knowing exactly what he's going to say.

"It's the girl, isn't it?" he asks, not sugarcoating anything.

"Yup." I stick my hands in my hoodie pocket and slouch in the chair.

"Do I want to know?"

"You don't need to worry about anything, because she broke things off with me so I can focus on baseball."

"Smart girl." He leans back, holding a pen in his hand, occasionally clicking it, the sound grating on my nerves. "You need to focus, Gentry. You've come too far to throw it all away now."

"I'm not throwing it away," I say, being assertive for the first time in front of Coach.

He stays calm. "No? Then tell me what happened at practice today, because you couldn't catch a goddamn grounder or throw a guy out if your life depended on it."

"Everyone has an off day."

"Not you." He shakes his head. "You're impenetrable. It's why I recruited you. It's why you'll be drafted as one of the first prospects this summer. You've never let an outside factor encroach on your play, which is also why I made you captain and put you in charge of those asshats." He gestures toward the locker room. "You're one of the greats, so don't lose that edge right before your big goddamn moment."

I look down at my sweats, hating that I'm about to say this, but Coach needs to know. "I loved her. The first girl that ever made me feel something. She gave me air outside of baseball. She improved my game, not impeded it."

"She is now."

"Because she broke up with me. Fuck." I sit up, growing irritated. "I'm allowed to be a human with feelings."

Coach Disik studies me for a few beats before tossing his pen on his desk and folding his hands over his stomach. "You're right, you're allowed to be human, and that's why I'm going to give you the day off tomorrow. Figure your shit out, and don't have another day on the field like you did today, do you hear me?"

"What? You want me to take the day off?" I ask, thoroughly confused.

"Yes. Wallow, eat shit food, do whatever you need to do to refresh and get back here. And I'm only doing this because since I've known you, you've never missed a practice and you've never denied staying late or coming early. I need your head in the game, Gentry. Find it tomorrow and then return to the man I know you are." He nods toward the door. "Now get out of here before you start bawling like a baby. That shit makes me uncomfortable."

"I'm not going to bawl," I say, standing from my seat. "Thanks, Coach."

"Yeah, well, I once lost someone I cared about deeply, so I know how it is." A rare confession from the relentlessly driven, uncompromising man.

"Sorry to hear that." I bite my bottom lip and try to add a joke to ease the tension that's built up in the room. "Don't worry though, Coach, she wants to be friends."

That grants me a straight-up guffaw from the old man. Head tilted back, a shake in his shoulders. "Fuck, they always want to be friends. Don't women know that's impossible?"

"Well, she's bound and determined."

"Good luck with that. Don't let her give you false hope."

"I won't." Because even though the last thing I want to be is friends with the woman I love, I would never break a promise I made her.

Friends always.

At least that's what I thought, but promises fade, and eventually . . . so do friendships.

$\sim$

My bedroom door flies open, and Holt and Carson stand on the other side, determined looks in their eyes as they take me in.

I've had better days.

I don't need to look in the mirror to know there's Oreo crumbs and milk paste ringing my lips, nor do I need to lift my armpit to know things are a bit ripe at the moment.

"I tried to stop him," Holt says before Carson hops on my bed and whacks an empty package of Oreos off my stomach.

"You need to take her to the locker room."

"Jesus Christ," I mutter, dragging my hands over my face. "I don't believe in that shit."

"Start believing, because it will fix everything."

I sit up and press my back against my headboard. "A fictional belief that magical powers are hidden in the walls of our locker room is not going to fix anything. Emory's mind is made up, she doesn't want to be with me."

"Bullshit, she does. We all know she does. But you need to sprinkle some of the magic on her to convince her. I have a whole plan."

"I told him to leave you alone," Holt says, arms crossed and leaning against the opening of my door. "Clearly, he didn't listen to me."

Not paying Holt any attention, Carson continues, "Believe the legend or not, but every girl that's been taken into the locker room has ended up with a ring on their finger from the respective player who gave her an invite. If you can get Emory to give you one more shot, meet up with you, we can get her in there and let the walls do their magic."

I stare blankly at Carson. *What the fuck is he thinking?*

"You've lost your goddamn mind. You told me you agreed with Emory, approved of her *sacrifice* for me. I'm not fucking taking her to the locker room hoping she'll want to be my girlfriend again.

That's just fucked, man." *Christ, we didn't have sex when we were together, so there's no way ...*

"You never know until you try. I have a plan, we can find her on campus, tell her you're hurt—girls love rescuing guys in pain—lead her to the locker room, and that's where you flip her skirt up and diddle her right there against the shower walls. She'll have the best orgasm of her life—"

"For fuck's sake, Carson, shut up. Stop this. Stop disrespecting Emory." I shake my head. *I hate this.* "She gave up on us. It's done. Period."

Silence falls. *I've never spoken like this to Carson.* I can see he's just as surprised as I am.

"Let's go, man," Holt says, eyes on me. *He gets me.*

"You're not even going to consider my idea?"

"No."

Frustrated, Carson hops off my bed while shaking his head. "You know, you think it's a joke, but that locker room has powers, mark my words. You're going to regret this."

I lift my arm and point to the door. "Go. Now." I'm so pissed off. What was Carson thinking?

They both exit the room and I slump back into bed.

The only thing I'm going to regret is pursuing Emory Ealson in the first place. I should have left her alone that first day on campus. I should have let her find her own way.

But with the way her innocent and timid eyes looked at me, fuck, I couldn't have walked away. I wanted to know more about her, and I didn't relent until I did.

A lot of good that did me.

Now, I'm left with a broken heart, an idiotic plan to get the girl to fall for me again—so not using it—and a stomach full of Oreos that didn't even taste good going down.

Great, she ruined fucking Oreos for me.

CHAPTER THIRTY

One Month Post Breakup

Emory: Good luck in Texas. Tell your mom I said hi.

Knox: Thanks, we're at the airport right now. I hate traveling with the team. Everyone stares at us, because we have to wear the same warmup gear.

Emory: You hate people staring at you? That's hard to believe.

Knox: I'm so shy, can I bury my head in your tits?

Emory: You know there isn't enough room to accommodate your massively sized head . . . and ego.

Knox: From what I remember—drunk, passed out with tit in my hand—you have enough weight in those tits to handle me.

Emory: No flirting.

Knox: Wow, you consider that flirting? Where the hell was I going wrong telling you instead how beautiful you are? Note to self, talk about Emory's boob weight.

Emory: Stahhhhhhp.

Knox: If you want to talk about my dick weight, feel free.

Emory: I don't want to embarrass you.

Knox: Oh, I see what you did there, implying my dick is small. Well, I think you know that's not the truth.

Emory: Wouldn't know, never had it in any of my holes.

Knox: I literally just spit my drink all over Carson. Now he's pulling at my pants, trying to trade. Thanks a lot.

Emory: You're welcome. Safe flight.

∼

Two Months Post Breakup

Knox: Carson said he saw you in the library today.

Emory: Wow, cool story, bro.

Knox: I wasn't done typing.

Emory: . . . I'm waiting.

Knox: He said you were talking to some girl who was trying to date me, telling her I have a small, un-weighted penis. What's that shit about, buddy?

Emory: Was he drunk? Because that never happened.

Knox: Pretty sure it did.

Emory: No, it didn't. It was in the quad, not the library.

Knox: Why do you have to ruin my jokes? You take things too far.

Emory: Let me guess . . . you're going to need to cry in my bosom again?

Knox: It's only fucking fair. I'm so distraught, so please bring your tits to me.

Emory: There's more to my body than my boobs, Knox.

Knox: What's that? Sorry, I was staring at a picture of you in a bikini top you posted on social media.

Emory: What did I tell you about flirting?

Knox: Hey, friends flirt. I flirt with Carson constantly. I think we're one dick pic away from making out on Saturday, which reminds me, are you coming to the party?

Emory: No. Lindsay, Dottie, and I are going to a show in Chicago, courtesy of Dottie's dad.

Knox: And how come I wasn't invited?

Emory: Because last time I saw you in person, you "accidentally" kissed me at a party.

Knox: I tripped, thank God your lips were there to catch me.

Emory: *You pulled me into a corner and made out with me . . . for an hour.*

Knox: *Uh, it takes two people to make out, so point that accusatory finger right back at yourself, ma'am. And you were the one who had their hand up my shirt.*

Emory: *It was a weak moment for me.*

Knox: *Want to have another one tonight?*

Emory: *No.*

Knox: *Come on, like old times, let's grind it out and hey, if my dick accidentally slides into you, then so be it.*

Emory: *It's nice to see how delusional you are.*

Knox: *Apparently only where you're concerned.*

∾

Five Months Post Breakup

Knox: *You left your bra here last night.*

Emory: *Throw it out. I'm never coming to another party again.*

Knox: *Why? I had one hell of a time catching up with my friend.*

Emory: *Because, we can't do that anymore.*

Knox: *What? Make out, feel each other up, and then watch you sprint out of my room, leaving me with blue balls? I agree, let's get naked next time.*

Emory: *You sucked on my nipples.*

Knox: *And fuck have I missed those nipples.*

Emory: *Seriously, no more parties. You're lethal at those. We are just friends.*

Knox: *Yeah, well aware. You tell me every time I see you.*

Emory: *Well, I just want to make sure you remember. It seems like you tend to forget whenever we're near each other.*

Knox: *It's because I've never in my life wanted anyone more than I want you.*

Emory: *Knox . . . please don't say things like that.*

Knox: *You can ask me to stop, but I never will. I'll never stop wanting you.*

~

Six Months Post Breakup

Emory: *Are you nervous?*

Knox: *No, but I wish you were here.*

Emory: *I flew home early.*

Knox: *I know, without saying bye.*

Emory: *Please don't be mad. I don't think I could have said bye in person.*

Knox: *You owed me a proper goodbye, Emory, but instead you snuck away.*

Emory: *I didn't sneak away, I . . . hell, I didn't trust myself. The distance is good.*

Knox: *The distance is bullshit.*

Emory: *Knox, don't. This is a huge day for you, and I want to celebrate it.*

Knox: *If that's how you truly feel, you'd be here.*

Emory: *Don't start a fight, please.*

Knox: *What the fuck, Emory? Two weeks ago, you were in my bed, letting me hold you all night and then you just up and leave without even a goddamn goodbye? And then text me out of the blue as if everything is okay? It's not fucking okay. You're fucking with my head.*

Emory: *I'm fucking with your head? You're the one who keeps tempting me, stroking my arm, leaning in to me to whisper in my ear. I can only be so strong, Knox. This isn't fucking easy on me either.*

Knox: *And yet, here we are, acting as "friends." Great plan.*

Emory: *Don't be an asshole. You promised friends first.*

Knox: *Because I wanted in your pants, not because I wanted to be friends.*

One hour later.

Knox: *Emory, I didn't mean that.*

Knox: *Please, don't shut me out. I'm sorry. I'm just so goddamn frustrated with this entire situation. I miss you. You didn't say bye. Fuck, I want you here.*

Knox: *Answer your phone.*

Knox: *Em, please . . .*

Emory: *Congratulations on being drafted. The Bobcats are lucky to have you. Good luck.*

Knox: *Emory, please answer your goddamn phone.*

Knox: *Em, please. You promised friends forever.*

❧

One Year Post Breakup

Knox: *Trained with Coach Disik over winter break. Heard he asked Mrs. Flower out on a date. Did you know that?*

Emory: *He's been coming into the library to "check out" baseball books. I had to direct him on where to find them. He wanted nothing to do with those books and everything to do with Mrs. Flower.*

Knox: *He said he's never seen anyone more beautiful in his life.*

Emory: *Why does that make me want to throw up a little in my mouth?*

Knox: *Because you always thought she looked like a praying mantis.*

Emory: *Yup, that's it.*

Knox: *Sorry I missed seeing you.*

Emory: *Yeah.*

❧

Two Years Post Breakup

Knox: *Coach and Mrs. Flower eloped? What?*

Emory: *News of the century.*

Knox: *Were you invited?*

Emory: *No, my internship has been over for a bit.*

Knox: *Oh . . . what are you doing now?*

Emory: *Working at a local school library, getting my hours in.*

Knox: *Cool, just like you wanted.*

Emory: *Yeah. Seems like you're doing good at spring training.*

Knox: *Fingers crossed I get called up.*

Emory: *You will.*

~

Three Years Post Breakup
Emory: *Congrats on starting. Are you nervous?*
Knox: *Nah, feels like I belong here.*
Emory: *You do.*

~

Four Years Post Breakup
Emory: *Mia Franco? Wow, is she as nice as she seems in person?*
Knox: *She's pretty cool. Keeping tabs on me?*
Emory: *It's hard to miss your picture on the gossip magazines with the most famous actress of our generation.*
Knox: *I hate those things.*
Emory: *Well, you're bound to be on them if you're dating Mia Franco.*

~

Five Years Post Breakup
Knox: *I ate an entire package of Oreos for dinner. Thought you would appreciate that.*
Emory: *Still addicted?*
Knox: *Yeah, and now I have Mia addicted too.*
Emory: *She needs to eat some. #TooSkinny*
Knox: *Don't hate.*

~

Six Years Post Breakup
Knox: *I'm drunk.*
Emory: *And I'm waiting for Harvey to get home.*
Knox: *Who the fuck is Harvey?*
Emory: *My boyfriend. Didn't you read my Christmas card?*
Knox: *Too painful.*

Emory: Well, he's my boyfriend. Hey, sorry to hear about you and Mia.

Knox: Sure you are.

~

S even Years Post Breakup
    Knox: Happy Birthday.
Emory: Thanks.

CHAPTER THIRTY-ONE

EMORY

Eight Years Later
"I'm not reading that book again." Cora flops on the desk chair next to me and tosses *Mother Bruce*, this week's story-time book on the desk. "I love Bruce, I really do, that bear owns my heart. But I can't stomach telling it again, especially when the kids don't appreciate the effort I put into telling the story. The boys constantly try to pinch each other and the girls are always doing each other's hair. This isn't a free-for-all, it's story time."

I chuckle, pushing my paperwork to the side and turning toward my good friend. Cora started working at Cedar Pine Elementary a year after me, once Mrs. Gunderson retired after thirty years of service. She taught me everything I know, and somehow the stars aligned and I became head librarian while Cora is secondary. Together, we are an unstoppable duo. We delight students with fun and interesting stories, we teach them problem-solving techniques in conjunction with their in-classroom lessons, and most importantly, we make reading fun.

We've dedicated ourselves to making this the best library in the state of Illinois. Our library is quaint with bruised and battered books, but we go above and beyond, using our own salaries to decorate the library and turn it into something magical.

I live quite modestly in a studio apartment just outside of the city. I'm doing what I've always wanted to do—educate children through literature, so I'm happy.

"They've ruined *Mother Bruce* for me," Cora continues.

"Aren't you being a little dramatic?"

"Maybe, it's that time of the month. Can we please have a girls' night out tonight? I want all the tortilla chips and tons of margaritas."

"I can arrange that. Let me see if Lindsay and Dottie are free."

I shoot a text to my two best friends, who both still live in area. After we graduated, we swore to stay close together. Lindsay teaches third grade at Cedar Pine—she applied so we could be at the same school—and Dottie is a bigwig at her dad's company, living the single life to her fullest. I swear it's a new guy every week with her, but she's too afraid to become attached, because she's been used by guys . . . far too many times. Everyone seems to know who she is and how much she has in her bank account, so she keeps everything casual with men. It works for her.

Lindsay is the first to text back.

Lindsay: *YESSSSS! Girls' night. I love my baby, but I could use a night without him kicking me in the crotch as I wrestle him to the ground to put on his pajamas.*

Emory: *Perfect. Cora wants chips and margaritas.*

Dottie: *Come to my place. I'll have my chef make homemade chips and extra-strength margaritas. It's Friday, so you ladies can sleep over if need be.*

Excited, I look up at Cora. "Dottie said she can have her chef make us homemade tortilla chips."

She perks up. "And guac?"

I type back.

Emory: *And guac?*

Dottie: *It will be a fiesta. Just bring your yoga pants and oversized shirts. We're dining fine tonight, ladies.*

Lindsay: *I think I just orgasmed . . . while my kids are playing Thumbs Up, Seven Up.*

Emory: *Seriously, you can't say shit like that.*

Lindsay: *Whatever, none of you have kids. You don't know what it's like to be a single mom. I already talked to Nana Grace. She's in for the night. I'm passing out at Dottie's.*

Dottie: *Not in my bed.*

Lindsay: *Fuck that. I want the big pillows. I have a date with your bed whether you like it or not.*

I set my phone down as a student walks up to me. "Miss Ealson, could you help me find a Judy Blume book?"

"Of course, sweetie." I stand and make my way around the desk, but not before flicking Cora in the arm to look alive. She resumes her position as the perfect librarian and starts helping out again. Sometimes we need five minutes to let it out, and then we're back in the game. I don't how I got so lucky with my friends, but I'm grateful. Years ago, I thought the sun would never shine again, but here I am happy, healthy, and with three incredible women as my best friends. Life is good.

～

"I s your chef single?" Cora asks, popping another chip in her mouth. "Because I would marry him just for these."

"He's gay," Dottie informs. "And his partner is a baker."

"What?" Cora's eyes widen. "How on earth did you score that perfect combination?"

"Drunk at a gay bar, came across Yan and George, and got to talking. Best decision of my life going to that bar that night."

Curled up on Dottie's enormous couch that overlooks the skyline of Chicago, I sink into the plush cushions and say, "This was exactly what I needed. I've felt so stressed lately with the budget cuts I have to make." I take a long pull from my straw, the lime of the margarita puckering my lips. "I knew getting into education would be rewarding and infuriating at the same time, but when they ask me to make so many cuts from an already minimal budget, it seems impossible."

"How much do you need? I'll write a check right now," Dottie says so casually. Did I mention she's loaded?

"I'm not taking your money, Dottie. It's bad enough you bought the library all new computers. You're done donating."

"Gah," Cora gasps while grabbing my hand. "I can't believe I forgot to tell you." She sits up taller. "I think I was so consumed with the kids making me hate *Mother Bruce*, but I got the best email today, one that will help out your budget problem."

"Oh yeah?" I chuckle. "Do you have a sugar daddy who's going to give us a couple thousand dollars for new books?"

"Not a sugar daddy, but the Bobcats."

All our heads snap to Cora as our postures stiffen, straws dropping from our mouths.

"Did you just say the Bobcats?" Dottie asks, on the edge of her seat.

"Yeah."

"As in . . . the baseball team?" Lindsay pries.

"Yes, the baseball team." Confused, she looks between us. "Are you huge fans?"

Taking the lead, Dottie says, "We're going to need the details, right now. Don't skip out on anything."

Looking uncomfortable, Cora shifts, clutching her margarita to her chest like if she says the wrong thing we're going to snatch it out of her hand.

"Um . . . well, I saw they were doing community outreach with a bunch of schools. I have a friend who works over there and asked her how to get Cedar Pine's library in the mix. She gave me the name of someone to talk to. I emailed them and applied to their program. I got the email this morning that we were chosen as one of the facilities to receive a grant from the team. I didn't want to say anything to you because I didn't want to get your hopes up. It's twenty thousand dollars."

I momentarily forget who it's from as I blink rapidly at Cora.

"Twenty thousand dollars? Holy Crap, Cora, we could do so much with that."

"I know. We can actually get those plaster trees and new media center we've dreamed of."

"Exactly." She looks between us and then asks, "So why does everyone look like they're about to throw up from the news? This is good, we should be happy."

Dottie sets her now empty margarita glass on the coffee table and folds her hands together. "Is there any media behind accepting the check?"

"Yes." Cora lights up. "That's also really exciting. We get to take pictures with some of the players."

My stomach drops and nausea quickly rolls my fresh margarita around.

"Oh shit," Lindsay says before gulping down the rest of her drink as her voice cracks. "Yan, we're going to need a refill."

"What players?" I ask frantically, my margarita instantly wanting to make a return.

"Uh, I don't know. They didn't say. Why?" Poor Cora, she looks so confused and I feel bad.

Dottie exchanges a look with me, silently asking for permission. I nod and scoot deeper into the couch, pulling a blanket over my legs.

"The reason we ask is because we know one of the players."

"Seriously?" Cora apparently doesn't read the room well, because she's nearly bouncing in place. "Who is it? Wait, let me guess." She taps her chin. "Uh, ooo, is it Walker? No, it's Lincoln. Wait, no, he didn't go to school here like you guys did." And then her eyes light up even more. "Oh my God, if you say it's Knox Gentry I might fall over and die. Is it him? Is it Knox?"

"Yes."

Dottie barely gets out the one syllable before Cora starts freaking out. "Holy shit, you guys know Knox Gentry? Like know him, know him, or just you know . . . *we went to school with him, saw him at a party* kind of thing."

Dottie goes to answer, but I stop her, needing to say this myself. "Knox and I were a thing."

"You were more than a thing," Lindsay says. The sad look on her face digs up the many unresolved, unsown memories I have of him

"Wait"—Cora spreads her arms out to the side—"you and Knox Gentry went out?"

"They were boyfriend and girlfriend. He was obsessed with her," Lindsay says. "Like, obsessed."

Bringing my knuckles to my chin, I try to vanish into the couch, hating this is coming up when I'm trying to enjoy an evening of drinks with the girls. If I'm honest, I've never gotten over him. How could I? He was . . . God, he meant everything to me. He was the man who showed me there were great men out there. Men with honor, patience, strength, and faithful hearts. He showed me what true love could be, even though we never said those words to each other. And God, he was the man who picked me up and pieced me back together after Neil tore me apart. That seems so long ago now, but it's another thing I am thankful to Knox Gentry for.

And setting him free was the hardest thing I've ever done. I hadn't been strong enough to fully break it off, which was why I found myself with his lips over mine months later. On and off we hooked up, never going past anything but kissing and feeling each other up, but still, I'd craved his comfort.

One night before graduation, before he was drafted by the Bobcats, Neil kept texting me, over and over, wanting to talk to me. He was drunk and decided to poke the hurt he'd inflicted. Before I knew what I was doing, I was at Knox's loft, bawling my eyes out. I'd broken up with him, but he still took me into his arms and offered his love and comfort. We didn't do anything that night but hold each other, and it broke me all over again, knowing I was saying goodbye forever to my heart. That was the last time I saw him in person.

Even though we live in the same city, our wavelengths have been on completely different tracks.

He doesn't know I live here. But at this point, would he really care? It's been eight years, he dated Mia Freaking Franco, and has had many supermodels draped over his arm at events. To be fair, they've often been friends rather than lovers, so I've heard, but the bar has certainly been set high for any woman vying for his attention.

We barely speak to each other, only really texting on birthdays now. The friendship we promised each other completely fizzled out and now . . . we're mere acquaintances. *Friends who once meant more.*

At this point, I'd be surprised if he recognized me with my shoulder-length, wavy bob, and the few pounds I've put on since college.

"Oh my God, how come you never told me this?" Cora asks, smacking my leg.

"We didn't part on the best of terms."

"Did he break up with you? Was he a dick?"

"No." I shake my head, thinking back to that awful night when I broke things off, the tears in his eyes, the pleading to reconsider. My throat closes tight as I hold back the crushing pain threatening to spill over. Eight years later, and I'm still a mess about our breakup. "He was going to be drafted, and I didn't want to hold him back. I wanted him to focus on making his dreams come true. Baseball needed to be his number one, and I knew if I was still with him, that wouldn't be the case."

"So you sacrificed your love for him?" Cora holds her heart. "Oh, that gives me too many feels."

At that moment, Yan appears with a new batch of margaritas. Thank. God.

"He wasn't happy. Actually, he was really angry with me, but we vowed to be friends. That slowly dwindled over the years and now we barely talk. Really just on each other's birthdays. We're cordial toward each other, but I doubt he'd want to see me. I didn't really give him a proper goodbye before he left school after being drafted. It was just too hard to see him again." I tug on a few strands of my hair. "And I don't think I can see him, even now. I barely made it through school after he left, constantly being reminded of what we had. It's why I don't watch the games."

"Wow." Cora practically drains her margarita. "When I called for a girls' night, I wasn't expecting you to say you once dated *the* Knox Gentry. I have so many questions, but out of respect, I'm keeping my lips sealed."

Good, because I think she'd be horrified to learn that despite being together for many months, Knox and I never actually had sex. And I can say to this day, that is one of the biggest mistakes of my life.

That stupid freaking bet.

The most we ever did was . . . wet-hump? If that's what you want to call it and to date—this is going to sound really pathetic—that's the best orgasm I've ever had.

So, so pathetic.

But it was with Knox, and that's what made it different. Everything with him was different, and it's the exact reason I can't see him, why I can't be in his presence. Not now, not when I'm still not over the man eight years later. I tried. I tried to move on, and for a while, I was happy with Harvey, I guess. But Knox was simply too good and had ticked every single box of what I wanted in a man. He'd loved me. I know that. But at times, it's been hard to believe when I've seen who he's dated over the years.

"He's not going to be there, is he?"

"No clue. They usually send relief pitchers to these things, you know? Doubtful."

I sure hope she's right.

~

"Where are you right now?" Dottie asks over the phone.

"In the bathroom," I whisper. "I can't do this, Dottie. I seriously feel like I'm going to throw up."

"You don't know if he's going to be there. What did the media person say?"

"She wasn't sure who was picked to join the ceremony and read to the kids."

Dottie grumbles. "See, that's just irresponsible business. She should know exactly who's going to show up and at what time. I would never hire her." She's one hell of a ruthless businesswoman, which is why she's one of the wealthiest women in Chicago. Her fortune stems from the countless hours she's put into the business since she graduated, not because of her dad. "Just remember what Cora said; they send the lemons to these events while the starters prep for the games. They have a home game tonight, so there's no way he'll be at your school."

"What about Carson?" I ask, knowing fully well the dynamic duo who once played together in college now share the middle positions on a major league field.

"Same thing. He's a starter, he won't be there."

"And what about the pictures that will be taken? What if Knox sees them when they're blasted all over the place?"

"Hmm . . ." Dottie pauses. "Well, maybe you substitute Cora for the pictures. She has a great smile, and she was the one who applied."

"True. Which means, I don't have to be here. I can go home, right?"

"You know that's not an option. You already asked the principal."

I did. I'm not ashamed of it.

"I know. Ugh." I shake my whole body, loosening my limbs that seem to be tensing tighter and tighter by the second. "Okay, I can do this. He's not going to show up, Cora will be in the pictures, everything is going to be okay."

"Exactly, everything will be fine."

With that, I exit the stall I hid myself in and take one last look at myself in the mirror. I was hoping and praying all morning I wouldn't see him, but just in the off chance he does show up, I've decked out in my slimmest black wrap dress, red heels, and matching red lipstick. It's only natural to want to look good for an ex.

I make it out to the library in time for everyone to show up. It's right before lunchtime, Lindsay's class was the lucky class to be chosen—hmm, how did that happen?—and the team's social media specialists come flooding in, along with some very tall, very built players.

Standing next to Cora, my breath heavy in my chest, I scan the faces of the guys walking in as the kids cheer. Lindsay walks up next to me and gently nudges my shoulder, letting me know she's here for me.

Three guys, and they're men I don't know.

Thank. Fuck.

From the side of her mouth, Lindsay says, "See, relief pitchers and second-string, so you have nothing to worry about."

She's right, I have nothing to worry about. I relax and put on a smile rather than the tense crazy look I'm sure I was holding. We watch as the kids clap and cheer, some reaching out for high fives. The guys are great with the kids, looking larger than life in their jerseys and finely tailored jeans.

"Miss Ealson, we want to formally thank you for showing interest in our program," one of the ladies says, and for the life of me I can't remember her name.

"Oh, please, don't thank me. This was all Cora. She applied and made this happen." I pull Cora next to me just as a flash of white comes trotting through the door.

And my heart stops beating.

Pushing his hand through his hair, looking like he just ran from the parking lot to the library, Knox saddles up next to his team-mates and mutters, "Sorry, I got held up."

The kids scream in excitement, calling out to Knox who plasters on his charming smile and waves to all of them.

Frozen in place, unable to breathe, my heart pounding in my throat, I stare and watch as his eyes scan the library slowly, taking it all in until he makes eye contact with me.

And that's when every ounce of composure and strength shatters.

From one shocked look.

Fuck.

CHAPTER THIRTY-TWO

KNOX

"What's up, Roark?" I say into my phone. My agent has the worst timing ever. "I have a library event to get to."

"Yeah, I know, but I wanted to quickly discuss your upcoming contract. They want eight years for two hundred sixty million."

"You know I don't care about this shit." I drag my hand through my hair. "I seriously hate all of this. Can't you just figure it out and let me know when all is said and done?"

He chuckles before saying, "I think you're the first player to ever say that."

"I want to play ball in Chicago, that's all. I want the Bobcats to be the only team I play for, so can you make that happen?"

"Aye," he says in his Irish lilt. "It's why you hired me. I'll hit you up when we have the final offer."

"Thanks."

I hang up, pocket my phone, and quickly exit my car. I'm late, I know I am, but I also didn't want to have that conversation in public, nor could I ignore it.

I jog to the front office and am quickly waved in by the staff and directed to the library. The education initiative the team has taken on became a program I really wanted to get involved in. Over the last few years, during our off-season, I finished my degree and earned my master's in education. It's been a long time coming, but what it means is if anything happens to me on the field, I have a backup plan.

Because of my education background, I told the front office I wanted to be involved in this program as much as possible. And giving back to libraries, that involves a more personal desire.

The school is a little rundown, but full of colorful paintings and decorations made from paper, strung and hung on the walls. There's a bulletin board dedicated to the Bobcats that's super cool. Baseballs made by the students out of construction paper and red-colored macaroni hang in the dedicated space along with a giant thank you.

I find Cameron and step up next to him. "Sorry, I got held up."

"No problem, they're just starting," he says as the children start to cheer and go slightly crazy. Some of them bouncing on their butts in excitement.

I bend slightly and start waving at them, loving their joyful faces. When I get a chance to finally focus on a family, I want a big one. I'm still relatively young in my major league career, so I have some time before I settle down.

Scanning the room, I take in the meek surroundings, noticing the tear in the carpets and the worn-out furniture. The walls are colorful with decorations, and fake plants are scattered about, but you can tell the money we're donating today will really help out.

My eyes roll over the school staff and I swear, I'm seeing things. I blink a few times before focusing my eyes again, but they're still showing me the same blast from the past.

Emory?

Is that really her?

No fucking way.

Her hair is much blonder, shorter, but those eyes, those goddamn fuckable lips, and those luscious tits . . . it's her.

And from the shocked look on her face, she wasn't expecting to see me here.

That makes two of us.

Emory Ealson. In Chicago? For how fucking long? *Is that still her name? Is she married?*

A glance at her left ring finger tells me there isn't a change of last name, at least not yet.

A gauntlet of emotions passes through me in a matter of seconds. Shock, anger . . . desire.

Fuck, she looks so damn good, even better than I remember.

After she left without saying goodbye, I tried to keep my distance. I turned off all notifications from following her on social media, not wanting to see what she was doing, or who she was doing. I tried to make that solid break. It took some time, but after a few years, I was able to move past what we had, at least that's what I tried to convince myself. From the way my heart is about to beat out of my chest, I'm going to guess I didn't sever those feelings. I buried them.

Vanessa, who's in charge of the education initiative, starts her speech, something about the Bobcats stepping in to promote education and sports, but nothing registers as I continue to stare at Emory. Her eyes flicker away, her face burning red, her avoidance obvious.

But I don't let up. I keep my eyes on her the entire time. When we're handing over the check, when the principal makes a speech about where the funds will be going, my eyes stay directly on her.

She doesn't pay me the same regard though. She's doing everything in her power to avoid looking at me, even staring at those red heels of hers that make her legs look incredibly long.

"Can we get a picture with everyone?"

Vanessa motions with her hands for the staff and players to gather together behind the big check, but instead of joining, Emory takes a step back, pushing her way behind the desks where she pretends to look at some paperwork.

"Miss Ealson," Vanessa calls out. Emory's last name plunges a sword into my chest. All the times I called her Ealson. The way I teased her, made her laugh, threatened her with kisses while using her last name. Fuck. "Please, come join us."

Emory looks up, but waves her hand in dismissal, not saying a word, but trying to put on a good show. When Vanessa probes again, Emory shakes her off once more. It isn't until the principal asks her to join that Emory gives in and stands next to . . . *what the fuck is Lindsay doing here?*

When I catch her eyes, she looks guilty and . . . excited at the same time. Does Dottie still live in Chicago too? *What the hell is going on?*

Anger boils at the base of my spine. Have they been here since college? And they never once reached out? It's not like playing for the Bobcats is a goddamn secret. My face is plastered all over Chicago.

What the fuck happened to friends always?

Trying not to lose my goddamn cool, I put on a smile for the camera, read a story to the children, shake some hands, and spend a little time with the kids before they head to lunch. Vanessa dismisses us, but instead of leaving like my teammates, I stand in place, waiting to see if she'll approach me, if she'll come up and say hi, if she'll look at me one more goddamn time. When she doesn't, I have no other choice but to call her out on this bullshit.

CHAPTER THIRTY-THREE

EMORY

Never in my life have I had a panic attack, but I'm almost positive I'm about to have one. I can barely breathe—only short intakes of air are piercing my lungs. My throat is so emotionally tight I can barely speak, and every single inch of my body is shaking with nerves.

He wasn't supposed to be here. I wasn't ever supposed to see him again. I've made it a priority to avoid him at all costs, but here he is, in the flesh, never taking his eyes off me.

After the event is over, I turn to Cora and whisper in her ear, my voice barely audible over my pounding heart. "I . . . I need"—I choke on my words, tears starting to flood my eyes—"I need to get out of here."

"Go." She touches my arm. "I'll take care of this."

"Thank you," I mouth, because my voice has stopped working.

Without looking back, I bolt to the tiny office Cora and I share—mainly used to get away for a few seconds and have a bite to eat.

I shut the office door and lean against the wall. The moment I squeeze my eyes shut, tears stream down my cheeks and a sob slips past my lips. I slide down the wall, my hand covering my mouth to muffle my cries.

This is exactly why I avoided seeing him, because despite the time apart, everything is too raw.

Seeing him, standing there in his jersey, looking sexier than ever, it took everything inside me not to break down and cry for the loss of what we had, what our future could have been if circumstances were different. I might have ended things with Knox, trying to ensure he gave his future his all, but my heart never broke up with him. My heart never let go of him.

Squatting against the wall, I try to regain my composure, taking deep breaths and willing myself to pull it together, and then the door opens. I glance up, expecting Cora, but in place of my good friend is the man I'm still very much in love with.

I spring up to stand and quickly wipe away my tears as he shuts the door behind him.

His cologne, fresh and clean, fills the small space, followed by his ripped and sculpted body. He's bigger than he was in college, thicker, more of a man, which is saying something since Knox was already physically in top form.

"Wh-what are you doing in here?" I ask as he stares me down, his eyes stealing any strength I have left, which is pretty much none.

His jaw works to the side before he says, "I see old habits don't die hard, huh?"

"What are you talking about?" I ask, taking a step back, needing some space from the powerful presence in front of me.

"Leaving without saying goodbye." It's a well-deserved jab, but it doesn't mean it doesn't hurt . . . bad.

"I . . . didn't think—"

"How long have you lived here?" He folds his arms across his brawny chest, his pecs thick and defined beneath his jersey.

No *hi*. No *how are you*. No, *wow, I haven't seen you in a while*. He's skipped past all pleasantries, strapped on a load of anger, and he's going right for it.

Nerves bounce around in my stomach, twisting and churning. I've dreamt of those eyes, but instead of sharp brows hanging over them, they were full of love. I've dreamt of those lips, but instead of a thin line of irritation, they were pressed against mine. And I've dreamt of those arms, but instead of folded and closed off, they were wrapped around my body, holding me tightly against him.

I can't seem to breathe around him, or find my words for that matter. It's too much—the memories, the way he smells, the hard look in his eyes. There's so much anger, so much unsaid between us. The wound I created never truly healed. That's evident right now.

"Are you going to answer me?" he growls. "How long have you lived here?"

I swallow hard, my hands twisting together in front of me, palms sweaty, nerves shot. "I . . . uh." Tears fall down my cheek. "Since college."

"Since—" He sucks in a sharp breath and spins around, pushing his hand through his hair as if he can't possibly believe it. Finally, when he faces me again, he speaks through gritted teeth. "You've lived here since fucking college and you didn't tell me?"

"You had your own life. I didn't want to mess that up."

"You *were* my life, Emory. Fuck!" He pulls on the back of his neck with both hands and looks to the ceiling. More tears stream down my face. "I can't believe you've been here all along, knowing I'm a goddamn phone call away, and never connected with me. What happened to friends forever? What happened to staying in touch?"

"It goes both ways," I say on a sob.

"Yeah, it sure fucking does. Which means the minute you knew I was called up to the majors you should have let me know where you were."

"You were with Mia."

"Fuck Mia. She was nothing compared to you. Goddamn, Emory, don't you realize how you fucking destroyed me in college?

How breaking us up . . . don't you know how much that killed me? You were the girl I wanted, the person I wanted by my side, for life. And you took that away and then hid it from me. You've been under my fucking nose this entire time and never said a goddamn word. Is it because you really want nothing to do with me? Did you mean more to me, than I did to you?"

I suck in a sob and try to steady my breathing, but my voice comes out choppy and hoarse. "If that were the case, do you think I'd be this upset?"

"I don't know." He throws his hands out to the side. "Maybe you're embarrassed you got caught."

"If that's what you really think, you don't know me at all."

"Yeah, apparently I don't," he whispers-shouts, probably realizing we're only a door away from a bunch of people. "The girl I knew would never have hidden herself away from me. She was feisty, strong, sure of what we had together. I don't know who I'm looking at right now."

How can he possibly see anything but love and desire for him? How can he see me shiver with emotion under his stare and think it's anything but the all-consuming love I still have for him?

Mustering enough courage to speak my mind, I say, "The girl you're staring at right now isn't embarrassed she got *caught*, nor is she as lifeless as you're depicting." I point to my chest, my shirt wet from the tears that won't stop. "This girl is full of life, full of hurt . . . full of regret. A day hasn't gone by that I haven't thought about the decision I made in college." A sob escapes me. "Not a day goes by that I don't think about what we used to have, the bond we shared. And although it was my decision to end things, I wouldn't have changed what I did because you're exactly where you're supposed to be." I wipe away a tear. "Starting shortstop for the Chicago Bobcats."

"I could have done that with you, Em."

"Don't fool yourself, Knox. You couldn't have, and I'm not rehashing my decision with you. What I did was right for both of us."

"It was right for you," he snaps. "It was what you wanted, and you didn't give me a goddamn chance to discuss it with you. You made your decision and then we both had to abide by it. It wasn't fucking fair."

"You wouldn't have made the right decision."

"And who decided what the right decision was? You?" I don't know how to answer that, but he doesn't give me a chance. "Color me stupid, but when you're in a committed relationship, you usually make decisions together, not one-sided conclusions. But then again, that's what our entire relationship was, wasn't it? You making demands, and me fucking bending so I could get a moment of your time."

"That's not how it was," I shoot back. How did we get in this moment? So angry at each other? "I was protecting my heart."

"Because another shithead hurt you. You punished me for his past behaviors the minute we started dating. You never gave me a goddamn chance."

"That's not true," I say, my voice rising, hating that he still can't see the reasons behind everything I did. "I was protecting my heart because the minute I met you, I knew you'd ruin me in the best way possible. Everything about you—from your personality, to your commanding eyes, to your sweet, yet teasing voice—I knew any man who came after you would never compare."

"And yet, you still broke us up."

"I protected you." I push my hand against his chest, moving forward into his space. "I protected you from my weak heart. Do you really think I wanted to break up with you? I fucking loved you, Knox. You were the man who pieced me back together and showed me my worth."

His eyes narrow, his chest heaves, and his hands pulse in and out at his sides, anger rolling off him in waves.

"I thought we weren't allowed to say those words in anger," he says, his jaw so tight his mouth barely moves when he talks. "We've never said them to each other and you choose now to say them, eight years later, when it doesn't matter?"

"If it doesn't matter, then why do you care? If none of this matters to you, why are you in here? Are you just trying to hurt me? Because if you are, job well done."

"I'm hurting you?" He points to his chest. "Do you realize what I had to do to try to get over you? I almost lost my starting position. Coach often threatened to bench me because I couldn't get my head out of my ass. My entire first year in the minors consisted of me struggling mentally, because I was hung up on you. You think you helped me? That you protected me? No, you took away the one thing that kept me sane. And I'm still damaged from it. I *still* think about you and dream about you." He takes a step forward, closing the space between us, the air around us shrinking. "I still wonder about what it would be like to have your lips all over my body, to eat your pussy until you scream, to be buried so deep inside you I'd never want to leave."

Hands shaking, I keep them firmly linked together, the temptation to reach for him too strong.

"But you don't have those same feelings, the same thoughts, do you, Em? Because this relationship we had, I was always all in when you had one foot out."

I grind my teeth together. "Stop insulting me." I push my fingers against his chest. "Stop treating my feelings as meaningless." I poke him again, but this time he clamps his hand over my fingers, sending a bolt of lust straight up my arm as he drags me closer to him. "Stop—" I suck in a deep breath when his other hand wraps around my waist.

"Stop what? Pushing you to admit the truth, that breaking up with me was the worst decision of your life?"

Because he stands at least a foot taller than I am, I glance up into his smoldering eyes as they search mine. The usual light pools of blue I memorized in my head are a dark, stormier color, casting a sense of warning over me. His face is sharper, his grip stronger, his voice deeper as he demands answers from me.

"Just admit it, Em."

"Why? So you can tell yourself you were right?"

"Yes."

"No," I say while pushing him away, but he snags my wrist and spins me around so I'm pressed against the wall of the tiny office. His hand presses into my hips as his gaze roams my body, the heat between us crackling like fire embers, ready to ignite into something bigger.

"If you won't admit to it, then tell me this . . . do you still have feelings for me?"

He moves his head closer, stilling the air around us as his heavenly scent spins and twists my stomach into knots. After eight years of barely any contact, of trying to avoid seeing this man, it's as if his presence has unlocked a flood of emotions, and I'm slowly drowning in them, one breath at a time.

His question hangs between us as I try to comprehend what to say. Do I still have feelings for him? The truth is, I never lost them. Always in the back of my mind, in the back of my heart, I carried a gauntlet of feelings for this man. And no matter who I dated or how hard I tried to forget, he was always a part of my life, a piece of who I am.

"If I did . . . what would you do? Laugh in my face, tell me I told you so, and storm out of this room?"

If I didn't think his eyes could narrow more, I was wrong.

"If you really think this is a trap to prove you wrong, you're widely off base." His grip tightens. "This isn't a trap. This is a test."

"A test?" I ask as his hips press against mine. I suck in a sharp breath as my body instantly melts into his, my wobbly legs barely holding me up. "What kind of test?"

His hands move up my arms, over my shoulders, to my neck where his calloused and rough fingers grip my jaw. Eyes intent on mine, electricity bouncing between us. The old flame that burned bright in college reigniting.

"This kind of test," he says right before angling my mouth up and pressing his lips against mine. It's a soft peck at first, as if he's making sure I'm not about to run, but when I hold still, he deepens the kiss and the hold he has on me.

Soft, yet different, with a sense of desperation I've never felt from him before, his lips carefully move across mine before his tongue parts my lips and dives forward. My hands slink around his neck. My body presses into his. Flashbacks of our time together hit me square in the chest.

When I first truly met him on the quad. That smile when he peeled the map off his face.

That first kiss, in the dining hall when everyone around us faded away.

The night he held me when I had a migraine.

The parties.

The joking.

The lust-filled glances.

It's like a memory reel on fast forward, spinning through my mind as I sink into the most delicious pair of lips I've ever tasted.

I've missed this. How could I not when I never stopped loving him? He wasn't a college fling, or a steppingstone to the next man in life, because Knox will always be *the* man.

His mouth slows, his tongue gradually dragging over mine before he pulls out and takes a step away, leaving me pinned against the wall, chest heaving, nipples aching for his touch.

In disbelief of what he did, he takes one more step back, as if he doesn't trust himself.

"Fuck," he says under his breath while turning around. "Fuck," he says a little louder.

"Knox—"

"I swear to God, Em, if the next words out of your mouth are we shouldn't have done that, I'm going to lose my motherfucking shit." His back is tense, his shoulders practically kissing his ears from the tension in them.

"I wasn't going to say that."

"Then what were you going to say?" He turns to face me, stress written all over his gorgeous face.

He's struggling. He doesn't want to want me, but he does. I can see the indecision in his eyes with a small hint of need.

I have a decision to make, another big one. I can either walk away from this man, and try to set him free from this hold we have on each other, or I can put my heart on the line and try to make something of this serendipitous moment.

I take a deep breath and say, "I was going to say . . . will you go on a date with me tonight?"

CHAPTER THIRTY-FOUR

KNOX

Deep breath.

I stare at my bat and tune out the crowd, the beat of the music trying to pump up the fans in the ninth inning. We're down by one, and I have shit to show for today's game.

Letting out a deep breath, I step into the batter's box and get into position.

Pederson, Toronto's closer, has been lights out all season, and being that I'm two deep in the count, he might just have another K under his belt soon.

He looks over to first where Dunn is leading off, cautious not to get picked, because we're in the bottom of the ninth and getting picked off at first with no outs while down by one is a cardinal sin.

Pederson winds up then delivers his side-arm throw right into the zone. I swing and hit air, the sound of the ball clapping against the catcher's mitt ringing through my ear.

Motherfucker.

I rip off my helmet and yell into it as I make my way into the dugout. When I reach the stairs, I trot down them quickly, ignoring the glare of my coach, tossing my bat, helmet, and gloves near the helmet cubbies, and make my way toward the end of the dugout where I grab a drink.

What a fucking shit game. I can't remember the last time I played this shitty. And it's all because my past came back to haunt me.

I still can't fucking believe Emory has lived in Chicago this whole time.

This whole fucking time.

I'd like to say I wasn't still pining for a small moment with the girl of my dreams, but that would be a lie.

"Dude, what the fuck is going on with you today?" Carson asks, coming up to me. "You're acting like this is your first time hitting in the big leagues."

I drag a towel over my face, keeping my voice low around the cameras. "My head's not in the game."

"No shit."

The crowd erupts, and we look to the field where Flores just hit a single, advancing the runner. At least someone's contributing to the team today.

"What's going on?" he asks, looking gravely concerned.

He should know. He knows the only thing that has ever thrown off my game, the one thing that can pull me out of my game mind-set: Emory.

"At that check ceremony today, I ran into Emory."

"Em—" He shakes his head. "Wait, what?"

"Yeah, she's a fucking librarian at one of the elementary schools we donated to."

"She lives in Chicago?"

"Yeah, she never fucking left."

Carson lifts his hat and scratches the top of his head. "Holy fucking shit."

"Yeah. Let's just say, everything around me turned red when I saw her, and before I knew it, I charged into her office where I found her sobbing. I went from angry to furious. She drove the stake between us."

"Shit." The crowd cheers again and Kennedy takes first, drawing a walk from Pederson. Hell, one out, bases loaded; we might actually win this game. "What did you do?"

"What every other heartbroken fool would have done. I yelled at her, blamed her for everything, and then pressed her against the wall and fucked her mouth with my tongue."

"Oh fuck." He chuckles. "Dude, you made out with her?"

"Yes, and I'm not kidding when I say it was the best fucking kiss of my life, better than our first. It was like I'd been holding my breath for eight years, and I finally let it out. I was so caught off guard by how much she shook me, that I pulled away and swore up a storm."

"Sounds about right."

"What happened after that?"

Like two gossiping hens in the corner, I take a sip of my drink and say, "She asked me out on a date."

"What? Are you fucking kidding me? She asked you out? After everything you two have been through?"

"Yeah." I pick up a towel and drape it over my shoulders only to wipe my face with it.

"What did you say?" The crack of the bat pulls our attention to the field. The ball flies into the outfield, deep. Dunn tags up at third and barrels down the third baseline once the ball is caught. He slides into home, tying up the score.

The team congratulates him with fist bumps and high fives when he reaches the dugout. We join in on the celebration but once it dies down, I say, "I told her I'd think about it, and then I left. She texted me the address to her apartment and said if I felt like coming over after the game, I know where to find her now."

"Damn, dude. Are you going to go?"

"I have no fucking clue, but my game tonight is a clear indication that I need to do something, I need to figure this out."

"Do you want to see her again?"

"Fuck . . . yeah, I do. But I'm still so goddamn mad."

"Understandable. I had to almost beat your sorry ass for taking so long to get your head in the fucking game when we were drafted. Then, and clearly now. But she's the one girl you've never been able to get over."

"What are you saying?" Out of nowhere, the crowd erupts and our teammates hop out of the dugout in celebration.

We won, I have no idea how, but we did. Carson and I follow closely behind as he shouts to me over the cheering fans. "You need to see what she wants. You owe it to yourself to do that much."

As the team cheers and coolers of water are tossed around, I don't feel anything but a dull thump beneath my chest, a pulse that's trying to resurrect itself.

Seeing her will either be the best, or worst, decision of my life.

Fuck if I know what to do.

Truck parked, I glance up at the deli sign that reads Joe's Meats.

What the hell is she doing living above a deli shop?

The streets are barely lit, there was a group of guys a few streets down partaking in what I can only imagine is some drug dealing, and there are bars on every single window on the road she lives on.

What the actual fuck?

I pocket my keys and head to the side door where Emory directed me in text and take the stairs two at a time, my feet falling heavily on the worn-out, rickety staircase.

After the game, I took my time showering and dressing. I didn't text her to let her know I was coming, unsure if I could actually drive to her. I didn't want to make a promise I wasn't sure I'd keep, but somehow, my truck found her apartment.

There's only one door at the top of the staircase, the wood painted so many times that the door actually looks goopy rather than smooth.

Before I can convince myself to walk away, I rap on the door and stuff my hands in my pockets. There's some rustling, followed by the creak of a floorboard, and locks being shifted.

The door opens, and on the other side stands a surprised, tear-filled Emory.

Fuck, she probably thought I wasn't coming.

Wearing white joggers and a grey tank top, she wipes her face quickly and clears her throat. "Knox," she squeaks out, "I . . . I didn't think you were coming."

"Can I come in?"

"Yeah, of course." She opens the door wider, revealing a very small but homey studio apartment. Her bedroom is separated by a small partition, and she's made enough room to have a small loveseat across from an even smaller flat-screen TV. Incredibly modest, her apartment is the size of my bedroom, but it's her.

I take a step in as she shuts the door behind me.

Still unsure what to do, I stand in her tiny entryway, hands stuffed in my pockets.

She's the first to talk. "I watched the game." She glances at the ground. "Congrats on the win."

"Thanks. I did nothing to contribute."

"You got hit by a pitch, that's something."

Shit, I hate that she makes me chuckle. "My grandma could stand there and do that."

"Bet she wouldn't have been able to walk it off though. Probably would have ended up with a cracked rib and a concussion, out for two weeks."

I shake my head. "Don't be fucking witty right now."

Her lips thin out. "Why are you here, Knox?"

"Because you invited me."

"But if you're going to be mad at me, if you're going to be mean, I'd rather you leave."

My brows shoot to my hairline. "What the hell were you expecting? For me to flip a switch and be okay with everything between us? I don't work that way, Emory."

"Then maybe this wasn't a good idea."

"Are you kidding me? Throwing in the towel already?"

"If I was throwing in the towel, I never would have invited you over. And if I knew you were going to be a complete and utter ass, I would never have let you into my little world."

"Yeah, little is right." I scan the space.

Her voice grows angrier as she says, "Do not come into my home and insult it. I don't have a multi-million-dollar salary like you. Mine is meager, and I often spend it on new things for the library when I save enough. And I'm fine with that, because I love those kids. I don't have to smile for a camera and leave. I'm actually in the thick of things."

Packing the punches: two can play at this game.

"Get off your soapbox, Emory. Just because you're at the ground floor, doesn't mean you're Joan of Fucking Arc. I do what I can, given my schedule. And I show up to events like today because I want to, not because I'm forced."

"You sure looked forced today," she mutters while turning away.

"I was off my game because my ex-girlfriend came out of nowhere. So excuse me if I was a little stiff."

"You're so quick to blame me for everything."

"Because you're to blame. Why can't you see that? Do you not remember that night? Faking a migraine, going back to your place, punching me in the gut as you delivered your decision. You are one hundred percent to blame."

"I don't see it that way," she argues. "And it's astonishing that you're so blinded by rage that you can't put yourself in my shoes for once—"

"Put yourself in my shoes," I shout, pounding my chest. "Put your fucking self in my shoes, Emory. See if you're able to hold your cool and act like nothing happened."

"I was in your shoes," she shouts back. "I felt the same pain, the same heartache, even worse because I was the one who had to be a grown-up and make the decision."

"You think you were hurting just as much as me? Unbelievable."

She puts her hands over her face and shakes her head. "This was pointless. I don't know why I invited you here. You're never going to see it my way."

"Yeah, this was pointless." I take a step back, my heart sinking in my chest as I do.

"Just leave, Knox. I don't have any fight left in me."

"That was clear in college, giving up before we had a chance to fight for what we wanted."

Her eyes snap at mine, defeat quickly replaced by rage. She walks to the door, opens it wide, and says, "Before I met you, I was emotionally abused by a man I thought was supposed to love and protect me. When I arrived at Brentwood, I was barely held together by sticky tape. Remembering to take deep breaths was a labored task for me. And then I met you. You wanted something right away, but I was still broken. Knowing how special you were, I took my time, making sure I could slowly build myself back up and be the type of woman you deserved, someone as selfless and kind as you. I grew and I built and I slowly started to feel worthy . . . of you." A stray tear falls down her cheek, and my heart wants me to reach out and wipe it away, but my head refuses to show any weakness. "After Christmas break, I knew I could be everything you needed, the strength, the rock, and then I found out you were being drafted. *And* that you had made that decision before we got together. I was whole. I knew I was still being held together by tape, stronger tape, but tape nonetheless. I knew I'd cause more damage to you than you needed. I knew my neediness would distract you, our distance would irritate you, our lack of communication would affect your game, and I couldn't have that. You deserved more. That's why I ended it, because *you* deserved more. And you got your *more*, Knox. You achieved *your* dreams. And as you've pointed out, my life is much, much smaller and insignificant in your eyes." She takes a deep breath and then points out the door. "And right now, even though seeing you again has drilled a crack in my barely dried concrete self, I know I deserve more than your insults and misunderstandings. Leave . . . please."

I chew on the side of my cheek, contemplating my next move, but when nothing comes from my mouth, I know what to do.

Turning my back on her, I take one step toward the door, then another, then another until I'm out of her apartment, and once again, out of her life.

CHAPTER THIRTY-FIVE

EMORY

The door slams, I fall to my knees, and I sob into my hands. I put my heart out there and he stomped all over it.

But honestly, do I have the right to be mad at him? Not really, because although I didn't admit to it, I have thought about putting myself in his shoes and how I would've reacted if he had done what I did to him. The rational part of me says, *oh, I understand*, he was trying to help me, to serve me in the best way he could.

But the passionate side of me, the side my heart dictates, would be just as angry as he is, because what we had was special. What we had was unlike any relationship I've ever experienced. I've never been so consumed by another human, nor have I ever felt more worshipped.

We were the perfect match.

And yet, sometimes the perfect match has to be separated.

Trying to lift myself from the ground, I take a deep breath, calm the ragged sobs escaping past my lips, and start to peel myself off the ground.

I steady myself and head to the kitchen for a napkin to blow my nose when there's a slight knock on my door. I whip around to stare at the entryway, wishing at this moment I had X-ray vision.

Is he back? Does he want to fight more? Is it one of my fellow neighbors from the connecting building? We do have paper-thin walls.

Feeling slightly embarrassed from the shouting match and who possibly heard it, I walk to the door and open it to find not a concerned neighbor but . . . Knox once again standing on the other side. Both of his hands are gripping the molding of the door and his head is hung low in defeat.

Pulse picking up, my hands shaking uncontrollably, I try to find the words to say something, but nothing comes out. Broken with a tiny ounce of hope, my mind questions why he's standing there, why he's back at my apartment after such a bitter shouting match. Instead of finding the words to greet him, I wait for him to speak.

After a few painstakingly long moments, he lifts his head slowly, his blue, stormy eyes connecting with mine. His arms pulse at his side, his knuckles white from holding the molding so tight. Intense and impassioned, his body vibrates with mixed emotions passing through his eyes and for the life of me, I can't read him.

Finally, his lips part and in a tortured voice, he says, "I fucking love you, Emory." Every sound, every flash of light, every beat of my heart stops as he reaches out, grabbing me by the back of the neck, and hauling me toward him. Stunned, my hands fall to his chest finding my balance. He angles my head so I'm forced to look him in the eyes. "I love you so goddamn much that I can't seem to let my heart stop bleeding until I have you in my arms. I need you in my fucking arms."

"I . . . I . . ." Air is barely reaching my lungs.

"Tell me you don't feel the same way. Tell me right now, and I'll walk out this door and never bother you again, but if you have an ounce of love for me, you'll invite me back into your apartment. What's it going to be, Em?"

There's confidence in his voice, a command I remember hearing many years ago, but it's contradicted by the shake in his hand at the nape of my neck and the rapid beat of his heart beneath my palm.

I never stopped.

"Answer me," he demands, his patience falling short.

"I . . ." My voice shutters. "I love you, Knox. I never stopped, and I don't think I ever will."

Lips tight, jaw flexing, I worry for a moment he's about to push me away, but when he steps into my apartment and slams the door, he hauls me into his arms and walks us over to my bed where he lays me down gently and stands over me. Reaching over his head, he yanks on his shirt and pulls it off, revealing the sexiest chest I have *ever* seen.

Holy.

Shit.

Knox had already been fit with defined pecs and sculpted abs, but college Knox is nothing compared to grown-up Knox. He's added on weight, but not fat, just pure muscle. He's broader, has more meat on his bones. Above his hips, there are muscles that twitch and move with his breath. His abs are perfectly chiseled and sculpted. His arms and shoulders are sharp in their angles, bulky in all the right places, and between his pecs, there's a definitive line where one begins and the other ends. An Adonis that takes my breath away.

And also makes me self-conscious.

I look to the side and bite my bottom lip, not really wanting to strip down in front of this athletic powerhouse.

"Lose the shirt, Em."

I clench it tighter. When he sees my apprehension, he squats in front of me and lifts my chin. "Lose the shirt."

"I'm different, Knox. I'm not the same girl."

"Yeah, you're right. You're even more beautiful than I remember, so lose the shirt." His hands go to the hem and he slowly pulls it over revealing my black cotton bra. My boobs are bigger because of the weight I've gained, and there's more to my ass than there used to be. Not to mention, my stomach isn't as flat, nor do I have as much confidence as I did in college. I never had a problem stripping in front of Knox before, but now, it feels like a spotlight is highlighting every insecurity.

I wrap my arms around my waist and look away. "I've put on some weight."

Once again, he tips my chin with two fingers so I'm forced to look him in the eyes. "Trust me when I say this, Em. You are by far, the most gorgeous woman I've ever seen." He reaches behind me and with one hand, unclasps my bra, letting the weight of my breasts push the fabric down.

"Fuck," he mutters, laying me back and hovering above me. "Em, your tits . . ." His voice cuts off as he takes one in his hand and squeezes. His hand works over the round globe, exploring its new size, my increased sensitivity. My nipples peak, and he takes that moment to lower his mouth to the rosy nub. With his head bent forward and his body over mine, I glide my hands across his back, every muscle twitching beneath my palm.

Sucking hard, he squeezes one breast while pulling on the other nipple, shooting waves of pleasure through my veins. The ache I have for him grows exponentially when he lifts up, smiles at me, and then grabs the waist of my pants and pulls them down along with my thong.

"Shit, Em." He stares at me. "You wax?"

"Yeah," I answer, my face burning red as he lowers himself between my legs.

We talked about this, we joked about it for months, we even bet on who would break first, so for it to finally be happening almost seems unbelievable.

"I've been dying to know what you taste like." Without hesitation, he spreads my legs, pushing my knees out. He then licks his lips and looks up at me. "I'm not going another minute without finding out."

His head dives between my legs as his fingers part me and his tongue reaches out and barely flicks my clit.

"Oh God," I moan, my back sinking into the mattress as my hands fall to my sides, gripping the comforter.

"Are you still a virgin when it comes to your pussy being licked?"

I want to tell him yes, I want to tell him this will be the first time for me, but unfortunately, I wasn't a saint over the last eight years, and I doubt he was either. Hell, I know he wasn't. So I choose honesty.

"No."

His jaw pulses as he studies me through lust-filled eyes. "Well then, I'm going to have to erase the memory of anyone else's tongue stroking your clit."

Instead of diving in like I thought he would, he takes his time, blazing kisses along my inner thighs. Unhurried, he savors every single kiss, his tongue peeking out for a few as he works his way to my apex, pressing his mouth above my pubic bone, then lower, and then on my slit, stealing a gasp from my lips.

He works his way to the other leg, repeating the same delicious torture along my skin. His lips cause goosebumps to spread over my legs, his hands hold me in place, not letting me take charge, and his mouth does sinful things I've never felt before.

Nips.

Sucks.

Licks.

I'm writhing beneath him, and he's still avoiding the spot where I'm aching the most.

Wet and turned on, I groan when his mouth travels north up my stomach rather than south.

"Knox, please, God, I need your tongue."

"Have you forgotten about the other men?"

"Oh my God, yes. Please, I want you. Only you." Against my stomach, I feel his lips curve into a smile before he lowers his mouth slowly until he reaches my center. He pauses, spreads my lips with his fingers, and then lightly flicks his tongue across my clit so I can almost barely feel the stroke. Like a whisper, grazing over my most sensitive spot, the pleasure pooling at the base of my spine strikes up with every featherlight touch.

"Knox," I breathe. I try to twist, to lift my hips for more pressure but he holds me still, lightly flicking over and over until I can feel the smallest of orgasms start to spasm through my center. It's so small, so not what I want that I try to hold back. I try to think of something else, to will it to stop. It's almost as if he can hear my thoughts, because his tongue stops and he lifts his head up, leaving me hanging, my clit throbbing, my need for release causing me to cry out.

"Wh-what are you doing?"

"Watching you. You're on the edge, aren't you?"

"Y-yes," I answer my voice incredibly shaky.

"Good, then tell me again, tell me how you feel about me."

I fling my arm over my eyes, in disbelief that he stopped. "I love you, Knox."

"Look at me and say it."

I lean up on my elbows and stare down at him, his chiseled face so handsome, his brows perched over his heady eyes. "I love you, Knox."

He licks his upper lip and then buries his face between my legs and presses his tongue thickly against my clit. The pressure is almost unbearable before he lets up and lightly flicks, then long, hard strokes.

He repeats that pattern. Light, hard, light, hard. Thick, thin, thick, thin.

My body seizes on me, and his name is falling off my tongue in a wave of unadulterated passion. My body convulses, my hips ride his tongue, and my orgasm is unlike anything I've ever experienced, consuming every last inch of me.

He doesn't let up; he doesn't stop moving his tongue until I'm a heaping mess on the mattress.

I can barely hear him above me, undressing until he's scooting me farther up the bed and his cock is strapped with a condom, hard as stone, poised between my legs.

Straddling me, he leans down to press a kiss against my lips. His tongue swirls over mine and his hand finds my breast where he kneads, rolling my nipple with his finger and grinding his length against my leg.

It's hot.

It reminds me of every time we were intimate without going all the way.

His panting, his heavy body above mine, the slickness of my arousal all over his cock.

God, I want this. I want him . . . forever.

"I've waited so goddamn long for this moment," he says, connecting our foreheads. "I've waited to look you in the eyes while I enter you. I've waited to see how snug your pussy is around my cock. I've waited to come inside you. I've been waiting way too damn long." His limbs shake and I reach out, cupping his face.

"I've waited too, Knox. This is all I've ever wanted. You are all I ever wanted." Sitting up, I push him back on his knees and grip the back of his neck, dragging his mouth across mine. The heat between us turns up to unprecedented levels as his cock dances near my entrance. His hands run down my back, to my ass where he grips me tightly and groans.

"Fuck, Em, your body, it's so goddamn hot."

"Knox, don't—"

He flips us quickly so I'm sitting on his lap, and his back is against the bed, the tops of his thighs supporting me.

"Ride me. I want to watch you. I want to see your tits bounce, your hips rotate. I want to feel that ass against my legs. I want all of you."

If it were any other guy, I'd think he was just saying things to please me, but when I take a second to study Knox, he's completely and utterly sincere, which makes me feel sexier than ever before.

Pushing my hair to the side, letting it float over my shoulder, I press my hands against his rock-hard abdomen and lift my hips up. He reaches between us and positions his cock at my entrance. On a deep breath, I take him in, one slow inch at a time.

"Ah . . . fuck," he blows out, the veins in his neck becoming more prominent. "Em, Jesus Christ, you're so tight. How long has it been?"

"Two years," I say, not fully seated yet, allowing my body to adjust to him. "Too long."

"Shit," he groans, hands falling to the tops of my thighs.

A few more inches. Every time I lower down farther onto him my insides clench around him involuntarily.

"Em, you have to stop that. I won't last."

"I . . . I can't control it," I say, leaning over and lifting up only to fully sit again.

"Fuck," he shouts, every muscle in his chest on fire. "Don't move, give me a goddamn second."

I rock my hips back because if I don't move, I'll lose my mind.

"Em, stop."

I shake my head and grind down on him.

"Babe . . . ah shit." He thrusts upward, impaling me so hard that I can feel my orgasm already building.

"This position, it's . . . it's too much. I'm going to come too fast," I say.

Apparently not wanting that, he flips me to my back and hovers above me, pulsing his hips in and out of me.

"Oh God, this is too much as well." My hand snakes up to my breast where I give it a squeeze, pulling on my nipple. Knox's eyes darken to completely black as he watches my hand intently, the way it plucks and pulls at the hard nub.

From the sight of me, he rocks in and out, picking up the pace, his force driving me up the bed until he's gripping the headboard with one hand and pushing my leg wider with the other. The tension in his chest . . . it's unbelievable. The ripple in his abdomen is mesmerizing. And the guttural sound popping past his lips is such a turn-on that my core's contracting, and a numbing sensation falls over my entire body, pooling at the juncture between my thighs.

My back arches and my cries fall onto Knox's lips as he takes my mouth with his, pulling my orgasm from me. White-hot pleasure sears me in half as he pounds into me, hitting me in exactly the right spot. I continue to come as he grunts at the same time, falling victim to his orgasm as well. He rides us through the wave of ecstasy until he starts to slowly come back to earth.

Head bent toward my shoulder, hips barely rocking in and out of me, he says, "Holy fuck." He lifts his head, sweat caressing his hairline, shock crossing his handsome features. "Holy fuck," he repeats. "Em, that was . . ."

"That was eight years overdue."

"That was more than eight years overdue. That was the best fucking experience of my life." He lowers to his elbows, pressing some of his weight onto me, which I don't mind. It's comforting. It's what I need. "Jesus Christ, I don't think I can feel my legs." He chuckles and places a light kiss across my lips.

Lovingly, I run my finger over his back, my stomach twisting in knots of what's to come, of where we go from here. Everything about this moment with Knox exceeds my wildest imagination, but a part of my brain is still struggling to accept his anger. His refusal to see things from my perspective.

The question is on the tip of my tongue, but I hold back, not wanting to ruin the moment. *I can't lose him again.* Instead, I snuggle into the man who's held my heart ever since I met him. I wore his necklace for so many years after we separated, until it broke from being so thin and delicate. At the time I believed it was symbolic, that something so precious couldn't survive the test of time. *I grieved that loss too.*

There are so many words we need to say. So many corners of our hearts we need to open again. But not yet.

Knox demanded I tell him I love him as if he's been starved of true love for years. I've always thought it was just me who felt starved. Empty. *Alone.*

But now he's here.

His scent surrounds me. *Intoxicating.*

His heart beats alongside me. *Solid.*

His love holds me. *Relentless.*

I fall asleep in his arms. *Peace.*

When I wake up the next morning, I'm sore in all the best ways, until that pain shifts in the worst way.

He fucked me . . . and he left.

CHAPTER THIRTY-SIX

*MORY

I slam the door behind me, the power of the swing shaking the walls.

"Holy shit," Lindsay says, spinning at her desk. "Can you warn a girl before you come flying in here like a . . . hey, what's wrong?" She glances up and down, taking in my disheveled appearance and barely done hair. "Oh no . . . did something happen with Knox?"

That's all it takes.

The waterworks spring a leak and tears start cascading down my face as I take a seat in one of the small desks made for third graders. Lindsay rushes over to me and sits on the desk, facing me.

"Start from the beginning."

"We don't have that much time. The kids are going to be back from gym any minute."

"Then give me the CliffsNotes."

She hands me a box of tissues and I quickly dab at my eyes, not wanting my makeup to smear any more than it already has.

Getting ready this morning was next to impossible, because I couldn't stop crying. After I first woke up and couldn't see Knox, I thought maybe he went out to get us breakfast; you know, people do that. But when he didn't come back, or text, I completely lost it. Did he really come to my apartment, take what he wanted, and leave? Was all that talk about loving me just a way to get into my pants?

Was he punishing me for what I put us through?

Every single possible question ran through my head, going unanswered. I sent him a text, asking if he was okay, but when I didn't get a response in return, I took that as his brush-off.

Everything he said to me last night, the look in his eyes, the way he touched me, I thought it was all genuine, that he truly loved me.

I guess I got played.

By the last person I ever thought would do that to me.

"You know how I asked him out," I say, in between hiccups.

"Yeah, ballsy, I love it."

"Well, he finally showed up at my apartment, still raging. We fought, I asked him to leave, and after a few minutes, he came back and told me he loved me."

"Oh my God, really?" Lindsay asks, excitement brimming in the corners of her lips.

"Yeah, I told him the same, because I do, Lindsay. I love him so much, I never stopped."

"I could have told you that. What happened after that? Why are you crying now? Shouldn't we be planning to have drinks to celebrate?"

I dab at my eyes again as I try to choke out the next part of the story. "We uh . . . we had sex."

"Gah, for the first time. Was it everything you imagined? How was his body? God, I bet it was amazing."

"Read the room," I say, causing her to zip her lips. "We had sex and it was . . . it was more than I could have ever asked for. We fell asleep and this morning when I woke up, he was gone."

"Wait, what? Did he leave a note or anything?"

I shake my head. "No, I sent him a text, but nothing."

"Are you fucking kidding me?" Lindsay grows angry. "He

THE LOCKER ROOM

fucked you and left?" I nod, unable to confirm the worst part of this story. "I'm going to kill him. That's it. I'm buying a ticket to the game tonight, I'm going to somehow make my way to the locker room, and I'm going to murder him. What the hell was he thinking?"

Steadying my voice, I say, "I think he was trying to teach me a lesson, almost like, he got what he wanted from eight years ago, and now he can finally move on. I feel so cheap." *So small.* How did he become that man? The arrogant son of a bitch who not only belittled me about where I live, but used me for sex with the intention to hurt me. He earns millions of dollars every year, and although I thought it would never go to his head, clearly it did. Did *not* see that coming.

Lindsay starts to pace, anger rolling off her. "I can't imagine him being a dick. He's always been so freaking nice, but then again, being an adult hardens you. And the way he was looking at you yesterday when he finally spotted you, he did not look like a happy man." She spins around. "Good God, if this was all for revenge I'm literally going to lose it. Have you told Dottie? She knows people, she can make him disappear."

Although my heart is shattered to pieces, I let out a little laugh. I love my friends so much.

"You're the only one I could stomach telling right now." I hear kids starting to filter in from their gym class, so I stand and wince from how sore I am. I lean forward and say, "And do you know what is awful? I swear I can still feel him between my legs with every move I make. I'm so sore. It's just a constant reminder of what happened."

The kids' voices get louder, so Lindsay presses her hand to my shoulder and whispers so no eager children hear her. "Don't worry, after work, we're having an emergency meeting with Dottie. He's going down."

I chuckle and nod, one more stray tear falling. I quickly wipe it away, as the kids come scampering in.

"Hi, Miss Ealson," all the kids call out. I give them masked smiles and head back to the library where I'll try to hold it together for far too many more endless hours.

~

"Are you really not going to tell me?" Cora asks, as we clean up the library, shuffling through all the returned books.

"Unless I want to break down again, I'm going to keep my lips sealed until after school lets out. Which is three more hours."

"Do you want to grab something from the corner for lunch with me?"

I press my hand to my stomach and shake my head. "No, I'm not very hungry."

"Which means you probably don't want me to bring you anything back either."

"No, it would just be wasting money. Thank you, though. I really appreciate it."

"Okay." She lets out a long sigh. "I feel bad leaving you here. Maybe you want some fresh air?"

"I'm really going to be a Debbie Downer here, Cora. I want to hide in a hole right now." Plus walking anywhere, even if just down to the corner deli, seems like a nightmare. I'm so sore, and I'd rather not be reminded with every step what I did last night, what happened. *How he treated me. Rejected me.*

"Fair enough. I know the feeling. Well, I have my phone, so if you need anything, let me know."

"I will, thank you."

When Cora leaves, I head to the office and check my phone for the fiftieth time since this morning. There are three text messages, but none from Knox.

Leaning back in my chair, I open up the text messages.

Dottie: Lindsay sent me a text, told me in brief terms what went down. Emergency meeting tonight.

Dottie: Come to my place. I'll have Yan make us those delicious crab cakes.

Dottie: *I have a private investigator. We're going to bring this moth-erfucker down.*

I laugh at the last text before more tears stream down my face. It's like there's no cure to stop them, no matter how hard I try.

Not in the mood to text her back, I set my phone down and rest my arms on the desk and my head on my arms. I take that moment to soak in the overwhelming sorrow. The heartache that seems to be walking over me like a dark cloud, never letting up.

I thought . . . God, I thought that after he confessed his love, he'd want me. I was so wrong. It's just unfathomable that he would be so mean. He's never hurt me like this, then again, he made it quite clear how badly I hurt him.

But to seek vengeance, it doesn't—

Knock. Knock.

I prop my head up just as the door opens, Cora's head popping through the crack.

"Hey, are you okay?"

"Yup." I give her a fake smile and wipe at my eyes. "Fine. Was there something you need?"

She bites on her bottom lip just as the door swings open wider and Knox stands on the other side.

My heart seizes in my chest from the mere sight of him—*again*—and when he excuses himself past Cora, thanking her and closing the door, I lose all ability to breathe. From behind his back, he holds out a bouquet of flowers and then studies my face, confusion in his expression.

"Hey, what's wrong?" he asks, his voice soft.

What's wrong? He can't be serious.

What is happening right now?

Is he really here, standing in front of me, holding a bouquet?

"Wh-why are you . . . here?" I swallow hard, my voice cracking with emotion.

"Why are you crying?" He rounds the desk and kneels in front of me, forcing me to look him in the eyes. "Babe, what's wrong?"

Babe?

Am I missing something?

"You . . . you left. This morning, when I woke up, you were gone, and when I texted you, you didn't respond."

"I told you I had morning weights, and I would see you for lunch." His brow knits together. "Em, I left you a note."

"What?" My mouth quivers. "Where? I didn't see it."

"On your nightstand, next to your phone. Jesus, did you think I left you without saying a damn thing?"

Shamefully, I nod. "I thought you got what you wanted after eight years and left."

"Fuck . . . no. Christ, Em, I told you I loved you last night. Does that not mean anything to you?"

"I'm sorry." I bury my head in my hands, relief starting to ease up my spine. "I didn't know what to think. Everything has happened so fast, seeing you again, falling for you all over again, spending the night with you. I'm honestly a mess." He wraps his arm around my waist and pulls me close, hugging me. "I love you, Knox, and after last night, when I woke up without you in my bed, I couldn't fathom what happened. Maybe I wasn't as good as you thought, maybe I wasn't the same girl, maybe I wasn't—"

"Maybe you need to stop thinking so low about yourself and see the woman I see." He pushes a stray hair behind my ear and traces his fingers down my neck. "You're beautiful, inside and out. You're so fucking kind and sweet. You're passionate, and even though it will still take me time to accept what happened between us, I know, deep in my fucking bones, that you're the most selfless person I know."

A sob escapes me.

"I love you, babe, and nothing is ever going to change that."

"But . . . you didn't answer my text message."

"Phone died last night. Didn't charge it. I was kind of too busy fucking you to remember. I came straight from training to here, because I have an important question to ask you."

"You do?"

He nods, the corner of his lips peeking up in the sexiest of ways. He hands me the flowers that I clutch to my chest, letting the floral fragrance ease my nervous heart.

"Emory Ealson"—he takes my hand in his—"after over eight years of knowing your beautiful self, I'm going to ask you one more time, and I really hope you don't say no." He takes a deep breath, connects his beautiful eyes with mine, and asks, "Will you go to lunch with me?"

The most unladylike snort shoots out of me right before I cover my mouth. This is really happening. He's kneeling in front of me, confessing his love, bringing our entire relationship full circle, and I couldn't love him more for it.

I reach out and caress his face, still in shock that he's here, wanting me again. "But, Knox, you lost the bet last night. Which means . . . you owe me a steak dinner in one hell of a revealing outfit."

His smiles grows wider. "How about this? You go to lunch with me right now, and this weekend, after our afternoon game, I take you out for steak, and then for dessert I eat that delicious pussy of yours."

Can't argue with that.

I lean forward and press a chaste kiss across his lips. "Deal."

I pace my living room unable to stand still. The girls left an hour ago after I filled them in on everything, and I mean everything. Their questions were very specific, and I had no problem answering them because after this morning, I wanted them to fully be on Team Knox.

And they are.

They couldn't be happier for us.

I called my mom when I got out of work and told her every-thing. She screamed for a good five minutes and then broke down into sobs, thanking the good Lord for bringing us back together.

She was always a huge Knox fan, especially after seeing what he did to pull me out of my Neil funk.

Now, I wait.

The Bobcats won. Four to two, and Knox was incredible, making a few diving plays, one into the stands, and hitting three singles across the field. It was amazing watching him again. I always felt like he was an art form on the diamond, a perfect example of what a baseball player should look like and play like. Seeing him execute his moves so simply, after all the hard work he put in, it was a huge turn-on.

Its why I'm thrumming with excitement, pacing back and forth, waiting for him to come to my apartment.

From outside, a car beeps, stilling my pacing. I run to the window where I catch a glimpse of Knox walking to the back door.

He's here.

I scan my clothing one last time, a simple nighttime romper with nothing underneath it. Check my hair, cute and styled—I might have taken a shower and made myself more presentable after work. And pop my lips, making sure my Chapstick is still fresh.

Pleased with how I look, I run over to the door and fling it open, just in time for Knox to be at the front. His smile consumes me, and I can't help myself as I leap into his arms and wrap my legs around his waist. He holds me with ease and works his hands up my back, a chuckle on his tongue.

Hands gripping my ass, he walks into the apartment and slams the door with his foot, only to spin me around and plaster me against the wood. His lips find mine with greedy hunger, and his fingers dig into the flesh of my butt, sliding beneath the shorts of my romper. Although I'm not comfortable with the weight I've put on, his love of my body—his desire *for* my body —is helping. Just as he helped my broken heart all those years ago.

Groaning, he pulls away and observes my outfit. My nipples are puckered and poking against the fabric of my romper. There is no disguising how turned on I am. "Are you wearing anything under this?"

I shake my head. "No. Thought you'd want easy access."

"Fuck, babe, you know me so well."

I reach in for another kiss but when he pulls me away and sets me on my feet, I'm thoroughly confused.

"We need to talk."

And just like that, my heart plummets to the floor. Those four words are a death sentence to every relationship. Nothing good comes from "we need to talk."

"About what?" I ask, feeling almost stupid for being so excited that he was here.

He takes my hands and leads me to the couch where we sit. Still holding my hand, he links his fingers with mine and when he stares at me, I see unmistakable adoration. I realize I'm not about to experience heartache, but I'm about to embark on a journey.

"I love you, Em, more than anything, but we have some hurt feelings between us. Some things were said, some misunderstandings, years of neglect to our friendship."

"Yeah, I know." I lower my head but he tilts my chin up high.

"We could rehash it," he continues. "We could pivot around in circles until we're blue in the face, but I don't want to do that. I want to build off what we have and make this into something more. I know what you did in college was selfless, wanting me to focus on baseball, I get that completely now, and it's one of the many reasons why I love you so much. But I want you to listen to me when I say, my life is a thousand times better with you in it. However I can take you. Over the last few years when our communication started to dwindle, something deep within me was missing, and when I saw you for the first time in the library, that something resurfaced. Anger overshadowed it for a second, but once that blew away, I realized, it's you I want, you I need."

Beyond the point of an emotional basket case, I attempt to blink back the tears, but it's no use. They fall, but he catches them on his thumbs.

"I want to move past the hurt and the pain, and I want to focus on the good with you. The fun, the jokes, the teasing . . . the passion. I want all of it." He swipes another tear. "Do you want that, Em?"

I nod, not giving a second to consider. "I want nothing more."

The corner of his lips curve as he reaches into his pocket. "Perfect, I was hoping you were going to say that because I have something for you." From his pocket, he pulls out a flashy, silver object and hands it over.

I take it out of his palm and look at the medallion. "What's this? A keychain?"

He chuckles and rubs his thumb over my furrowed brow. "Sort of. It's a key to my apartment. I want you to move in with me."

"Wait?" I look at the circular object. "How is this a key?"

"It's magnetic, fancy shit." He takes my hand in his. "Did you hear me? I want you to move in."

Yeah, I heard him, and I'm trying not to jump out of my skin in excitement. But just to be sure, I say, "You don't think it's too early?"

"No."

He's so confident, so sure in this decision that I want to test him a little bit more, because my answer is on the tip of my tongue, but I want to make sure this is what he truly wants.

"We just got back together like twenty-four hours ago, and you want me to move in?"

"Yeah, because it feels like we've been together forever. You're the one I want everything from, Em. I'm giving you my heart and soul and . . . my apartment." He glances around my tiny studio. "I can't have you living here, not with the hooligans outside and the lock that barely works on your door. I was fucking worried sick, knowing this is where you live. It's not safe, and I need you safe for my own peace of mind."

I hold up the keychain thing. "And I'm guessing your place is safe?"

"Very." He winks. "Plus, it has amenities."

"This place has amenities." I point to the floor. "Did you not see the easily accessible deli below?"

"Uh yeah, I can smell the meat, babe."

I shrug. "You get used to it."

"Come on, move in with me, give me the gift of waking up next to you every morning."

Well, how on earth can I say no to that?

"You're not going to change your mind in a few months, realize there's someone better out there for you?"

"No, because I'm looking at her. You're the girl I've been looking for that's better than anything I could dream up. You're it for me, Em. You're it." He leans in, his lips inches from mine. "What do you say, be my roommate?"

I twist my lips to the side, pretending to mull it over.

"What kind of roommate are we talking about here? Do we share a bed? Do you cook? Clean?"

Moving in closer, he whispers, "I clean, can't cook for shit, but I know how to fuck my girl, and that will make up for it, I promise."

"So that's a yes on the bed sharing?"

"That's a hell yes." He presses his lips to mine and pulls me onto his lap, his hands reaching up the back of my romper where he starts to unzip it. The sleeves fall down my arms and instantly my boobs are exposed and his hands are all over them.

"You know I didn't say yes, yet."

His head lowers and his mouth is in my nipple, and between sucks, he says, "I'm making the decision for you."

I chuckle and then gasp when he bites down.

This man is going to be the death of me.

I pull away and scoot down his body until I'm sitting between his knees. "If that's the case, I think I'm going to make a decision for the both of us. It's about time you see what else these lips can do."

His eyes narrow. "Jesus Christ, I think I just came in my pants."

I begin undoing his jeans while saying, "I sure hope not,

because in your pants wasn't where I was planning for you to come."

He leans back on the couch and spreads his legs, pure joy pulling at his lips. "Goddamn, Emory. I'm so fucking in love with you."

I don't know how this happened, how I possibly reconnected with Knox Gentry, but I know one thing for sure: I'm going to be one selfish girl, because there's no way in hell I'm ever letting him go again. This decision to stay is the perfect one.

EPILOGUE

KNOX

"Thank you, again. This means so much to me."

"Well deserved," Coach Disik says, shaking my hand one more time. I remember the first time I met him, how intimidating he was, but now, I don't get a small quiver when I see him. But then again, since I'm no longer on his roster, he's eased up.

I squeeze Emory's hand and ask, "Are you ready?"

She nods and waves to Mrs. Flower. "It was great seeing you again."

"You too," she replies coldly. I don't know if the old coot has ever been able to lighten up.

"Take care, Gentry. And I'm counting on those tickets."

"I got you, Coach."

I give him a quick pat on the back and hop off the stage where my mom gathers me and Emory into her arms. To say my mom was over-the-moon excited about me reconnecting with Emory is an understatement. We FaceTimed her together and I swear, she nearly had a heart attack. It was the best thing I've ever witnessed. After she screamed for what seemed like ten minutes, we told her we just rekindled our old flame—Emory's words, not mine—and

313

we're now living together. My mom was on the next flight out. She spent a week fawning over Emory, taking her out to do girly shit, and bonding with my girl. It felt good knowing how much she's still accepted in my life.

Carson and Holt were just as shocked as Lindsay and Dottie. We had everyone over for one big party to celebrate. Got fucking wasted and ended up having a giant sleepover. Emory kept saying it was like her dorm days, while Carson was on the verge of tears about the loft years. What a fucking douche.

"I am so proud of you," my mom says. "My baby is in his college's hall of fame, and I can't believe it." Taking a deep breath, she continues, "I knew you were meant for great things, Knox, but honestly, the greatest thing you ever accomplished was landing this girl right here. You gave her your heart and soul. No one will ever mean more to him, Em." My mom takes Emory's other hand and holds tight. "I could not be happier to call you the mother of my grandchild."

I glance at Emory's small but growing belly.

Yeah, I couldn't be happier either.

When Emory first found out she was pregnant—drunk sleep-over night, yeah, someone forgot a condom—she was so nervous to tell me, but fuck, I cried. I cried so damn hard that I felt like my mother. We're having a baby. We made a living thing, and the girl I'm madly in love with is the mother. Yeah, I'm fucking pumped.

"Thank you, Mama G. But this day really is about Knox."

She waves her hand in the air. "He's had his moment. Let's talk about you now."

"Or, I can show Emory something and we can meet you at The Hot Spot in thirty minutes. Grab us a table?"

My mom concedes, gives us both a kiss, and then takes off.

"You want to show me something?"

"Yeah, they hung a picture of me. It's hot, and I want you to get all kinds of turned on."

"There's something seriously wrong with you."

Not caring that she thinks I'm weird, I tug her hand and lead her away from the event center space and down into the narrow hallways of the stadium, straight to the locker room. Thanks to Coach, I have a workable key, but he told me to keep it in my pants. I just laughed him off.

When I open the door, I go to pull Emory in, but she plants her feet.

"You have got to be kidding me. Are you really taking me into the locker room?"

"Come on, babe, just go with it."

"I'm not having sex with you in here." I tug her into the space, ignoring her statement.

"How else am I supposed to guarantee you'll be mine for life?" I say as I pull her into my chest, right in the middle of the room where I hold some great memories.

She gives me a side-eye and then points to her protruding stomach. "I'm pretty sure here's your answer. Plus"—she looks around—"I thought you didn't believe in all that locker room crap."

"I don't, but at this point, I'll do anything it takes to make sure you never walk out of my life again."

"Never going to happen." She rubs her thumb across my cheek. "You're stuck with me, Gentry."

"In that case." I reach to my back pocket and pull out a piece of paper, handing it to her.

Brows knitted together, she takes it and glances down. "Why are you giving me a campus map?"

"Open it up." I nod.

Skeptical, she opens it, revealing what I wrote inside. Her gasp carries through the room as she looks up at me, but she has to look down, because I'm bent on one knee, holding a ring box to her. On the inside of the map, I wrote, "Spend your life with me."

"Oh my God," she whispers.

"Em, from the moment that map hit me—yes, I stole it from you—I knew you were something special. I also think I knew it when I passed out with your tit in my hand, because honestly, I never forget a good pair of tits. And, baby, you have the best tits around." She rolls her eyes but tears fall as well. "You are everything I need in my life and more. You're the mother of my child, the love of my life, and my best fucking friend. Please make me the happiest man on this planet and be my wife."

She nods, words unable to fall past the tears.

I scoop her into my arms and twirl her around, elated . . . no, fucking overjoyed that this girl will forever be mine.

I place the ring on her finger and we both marvel at it. She tells me it's too much, I tell her I wish it was bigger. She kisses me all over my face. I let her.

When she pulls away, I wiggle my eyebrows and nod toward the showers. "Want to get naked?"

"We are not doing it in here."

I think about it for a second. "Then bend over and let me finger you. We have to do something, babe. We need to seal the deal."

"Holt has gotten to your head."

"It worked for him."

She sighs heavily and looks to the side. "Fine, one fingering and we're done."

I laugh. "Come on, babe, you know I always use at least two."

THE END

Made in the USA
Las Vegas, NV
17 March 2025

19712323R00177